Praise for
Trail of the Spellmans

"Private investigator Isabel 'Izzy' Spellman is not your typical gumshoe . . . irreverent . . . amusing . . . [*Trail of the Spellmans* is] a wise (and wise-cracking) choice for mystery readers seeking a break from the genre's bloodier fare."

—*Booklist*

"Engaging. . . . Lutz's dry, biting humor is in full force."

—*Publishers Weekly*

"Enormously humorous. . . . Lisa Lutz has a distinct flair for comedy. She does an outstanding job introducing fresh and unforgettable characters while painting laugh-out-loud scenes."

—*Advocate Weekly*

"Twisted, fun. . . . You can't help but grin."

—*St. Louis Dispatch*

"[Lutz's] fifth entry in the series, *Trail of the Spellmans*, is the best yet as both the professional interests of the investigators and the personal relationships amongst the Spellmans collide in spectacular fashion."

—*Alfred Hitchcock's Mystery Magazine*

"[Lutz] does an outstanding job introducing fresh and unforgettable characters while painting laugh-out-loud scenes. . . . Fresh, lively and consistently humorous."

—Bookreporter.com

"Lisa Lutz's Spellman books are always hilarious, but *Trail of the Spellmans* reminded me how serious funny books can be. As precocious as the Spellman kids have always been, they're only now really coming of age and the result is, yes, hilarious, but also tender and melancholy and full of hard-won wisdom. This one's going to stay with readers for a long time."

—Laura Lippman, award-winning author of more than 15 books, including the recent novel *I'd Know You Anywhere* and *the Tess Monaghan series*

Praise for *The Spellmans Strike Again*

"Lie back and enjoy this tale of intergenerational gumshoe mayhem."

—*Kirkus Reviews*

"[Lutz] delivers another engaging blend of wisecracks and crime-solving."

—*Booklist*

"Fans of comic mystery who haven't already discovered the Spellman family series are going to want to read this book and then rush out for the other three. . . . If you like Janet Evanovich, you are going to love the Spellmans."

—*The Globe and Mail*

Praise for *Revenge of the Spellmans*

"Izzy is off for another wild ride in Lisa Lutz's third madcap private-investigator novel. . . . Izzy's life . . . is so well documented—and she is such an endearing mess—that we want to find the evidence supporting her."

—*San Francisco Chronicle*

"Amazingly, it all makes sense in the end, and Isabel and her quirky family are such good company that you won't mind even when it doesn't."

—*People* (three stars out of four)

"San Francisco PI Isabel 'Izzy' Spellman endures court-ordered therapy sessions as well as blackmail in Lutz's wacky crime novel, the third entry in a series that keeps getting better and better."

—*Publishers Weekly* (starred review)

Praise for *Curse of the Spellmans*

"This is one of the best comic novels I've ever read, and that includes Carl Hiaasen and Janet Evanovich. The Spellmans—a collection of misfits whose family business is a private detective agency—are hilarious, smart and irresistible."

—*The Globe and Mail*

"Fans of *The Spellman Files* will laugh just as loudly at the comic antics chronicled in this sparkling sequel."

—*Publishers Weekly* (starred review)

"The snappy, honest narration by *Get Smart*–obsessed Izzy keeps things popping, with its mix of trade talk and brutal honesty."

—*Kirkus Reviews*

Praise for *The Spellman Files*

"Move over, Carl Hiaasen. . . . *The Spellman Files* starts out funny and does not let up. . . . Simply put, this tale of the Spellman family is irresistible, and you hate to see the romp end."

—*St. Louis Post-Dispatch*

"[Isabel Spellman is] the love child of Dirty Harry and Harriet the Spy. . . . It's not the mystery of how these cases ultimately resolve that will pull readers through, but the whip-smart sass of the story's heroine, ace detective of her own heart."

—*People*

"Hilarious. My enjoyment of *The Spellman Files* was only slightly undercut by my irritation that I hadn't written it myself. The funniest book I've read in years!"

—Lauren Weisberger, author of *The Devil Wears Prada* and *Chasing Harry Winston*

TRAIL OF THE
SPELLMANS

Document #5

Lisa Lutz

SIMON & SCHUSTER PAPERBACKS
New York • London • Toronto • Sydney • New Delhi

Simon & Schuster Paperbacks
A Division of Simon & Schuster, Inc.
1230 Avenue of the Americas
New York, NY 10020

First Simon & Schuster trade paperback edition May 2013

SIMON & SCHUSTER PAPERBACKS and colophon are registered trademarks of Simon & Schuster, Inc.

For information about special discounts for bulk purchases, please contact Simon & Schuster Special Sales at 1-866-506-1949 or business@simonandschuster.com.

The Simon & Schuster Speakers Bureau can bring authors to your live event. For more information or to book an event, contact the Simon & Schuster Speakers Bureau at 1-866-248-3049 or visit our website at www.simonspeakers.com.

Designed by Davina Mock-Maniscalco

10 9 8 7 6 5 4 3 2

The Library of Congress has cataloged the hardcover edition as follows:

Lutz, Lisa.
Trail of the Spellmans : document #5 / Lisa Lutz.—1st Simon & Schuster hardcover ed.
p. cm.
1. Women private investigators—Fiction. I. Title.
PS3612.U897T73 2012
813'.6—dc23
2011032509
ISBN: 978-1-4516-0812-0
ISBN: 978-1-4516-0813-7 (pbk)
ISBN: 978-1-4516-0814-4 (ebook)

To my two favorite Morgans,
Morgan Dox and Morgan Freeman

TRAIL OF THE
SPELLMANS

SURVEILLANCE REPORT: VIVIEN BLAKE

I do my job. I watch. I take notes. I snap pictures and record video. I document subjects' activities through a filter of twenty years of disassociation. I don't judge. I don't manipulate the evidence. I simply report my findings to the client. The client can use the information however they see fit. At least that's the line I feed them. But the truth is always a murkier business.

November 2

2330 hrs

Female subject, 5'5", 125 lbs, dark brown hair, wearing blue jeans and a gray hooded sweatshirt over a dark green military jacket, exits a San Francisco apartment building at Twenty-sixth and Noe. She walks east down the street, scanning the parked cars. She presses a remote key and looks for a flash of headlights. A BMW winks in the distance. Female subject spins in a circle, checking her perimeter; approaches car; gets inside; and starts the engine. She drives east down to South Van Ness Avenue and makes a left turn, stopping on the corner of Seventeenth and South Van Ness at the establishment of Oscar's Auto. Subject drives vehicle into covered garage. Unable to establish a visual on subject for fifteen minutes.

1

2345 hrs

Subject and an unknown male (midforties, heavyset, wearing blue mechanic's jumpsuit with the Oscar's Auto logo embroidered on the breast pocket) exit the office of establishment. They approach a tow truck with the same logo painted on the side. Subject slips an unidentifiable object into her pocket and jumps into a truck with unknown male. Investigator follows subject vehicle to a liquor store. Unknown male enters the store and leaves three minutes later with a large brown bag (about the size of a six-pack of beer).[1]

The tow truck returns subject to the residence on Twenty-sixth Street where she was previously seen exiting. Subject rings the buzzer. (Could not establish unit number.) Female subject then enters the building and all visual contact is lost.

The preceding events would appear innocent enough to the naked eye, but let me enlighten you as to what the naked eye missed just a few hours earlier that evening: Female Subject met the owner of the BMW in a bar; Female Subject was not of legal drinking age; Female Subject was not the owner of the vehicle taken to Oscar's repair shop. Finally—and how could you know this?—Oscar's Auto is a well-known chop shop, doing an arthritic limbo under the radar of the law. Subject, based on my three weeks of surveillance, was a regular menace to society, masquerading as a high-achieving coed.

My phone rang just as I was about to end the surveillance and head home. The caller ID said "The Tortoise." Someone had been tampering with my phone.

"Hello," I said.

_____
[1] I have an eye for this sort of thing.

"Where is everyone?"

"I don't know, Dad." For the record, I wasn't withholding information. I really didn't know.

"I'm tired of always being alone in the house."

"You're not alone."

"Other than You Know Who."

"Why doesn't You Know Who have a nickname yet?" I asked.

"I think we're going with 'You Know Who' as a nickname."

"Kind of messes with our animal theme, don't you think?"

"Sometimes you got to break protocol."

"True," I said. I couldn't have agreed more.

"I'm lonely."

"Sorry to hear that, Mr. Tortoise."

"And I hate my nickname. I should be able to come up with my own."

"Did you call for a chat?"

"Dinner did not go over very well."

"The roast?" I asked.

"Inedible."

"And that's something coming from you. Did Mom blame me?"

"No, she took full responsibility."

"Where is she?"

"Origami or pie making, I don't remember."

"Those are two very different things, Dad."

"Any action tonight?"

Silence.

"Are you there?" Dad said. I could hear him tapping his finger on the phone, like it was an old transistor radio.

"I thought we were no longer sharing information."

"Only on cases we're working separately. So, any action?" Dad repeated.

"Not unless you consider studying or watching TV—or both—action."

"Good. Can you drop by the house on your way back? I need the surveillance camera for tomorrow."

"What's tomorrow?"

"You know better than to ask questions like that."

I waited outside the Noe Valley apartment for another five minutes, gathering my thoughts. Female subject peered out of the window, checking the empty street, and then defenestrated herself, hanging from the window frame and dropping four feet to the ground. She then sauntered down the street in the direction of her apartment, just over a mile away.

After my conversation with the Tortoise, I made a quick U-turn and watched female subject through my rearview mirror. I had to ask myself whether I was doing my job or if I was an accessory after the fact.

At home, I found my father staring at a stack of paperwork that had to be filed. Filing always made him sad, borderline depressed, and since he thought he'd seen the end of those days, to have them return only stoked his sadness. He pressed the intercom button when he saw me.

"The Gopher has landed," he said.

"I really wish you'd stop that," I said.

"I can't," he helplessly replied.

"Where's Mom?" I asked.

"The Eagle[2] is on the tarmac."

"It's just pathetic," I muttered as I left the room.

The Eagle was indeed on the tarmac (or the couch, as it is commonly known), watching the evening news.

On the drive to Spellman headquarters I debated, as I have over the last three months, how much information I should divulge. I'm a spectacular liar ("magician of the truth" is the new phrase I'm working with). I've studied deception enough to know the universal tells, and I can embody

---

[2] I'll explain all this animal crap shortly.

honesty to virtually anyone, except a member of my family. With them I have to turn my behavior inside-out, assume a liarlike demeanor at all times—toss in sarcasm with the truth. A salad of honesty and deception is the only way I can get away with an untruth. My point is that I was planning on lying to my parents about the evening's events and there is a particular way to go about it.

"Did the Sparrow flee the nest at all this evening?" my mother asked, staring at the evening news.

The Sparrow did indeed flee the nest, and another nest, and then she stole a car. With the right delivery, I could both manage a lie and have it read like the truth.

"Not unless you count a study break of grand theft auto," I sarcastically replied.

"Write it up," said Mom. "I think it might be time to tell the Blakes that this surveillance is merely a drain on their bank account."[3]

"Maybe we wait just a little bit longer," I replied.

"Why?" my mother asked suspiciously. "That doesn't sound like you."

"It's finals week. She could be distracted."

I fetched a beer from the fridge and sat down on the couch next to my mom.

"Don't forget to write the report," Mom said. "It's always better to do it when it's fresh in your mind."

"'Subject remained in her apartment for five hours studying.'" I spoke as if into a tape recorder. "It shouldn't take very long to type that up."

Silence finally set in.

Television is the perfect anecdote for unwanted conversation. I don't know how humans ever survived without it.

After a few bars of the grating evening-news theme song, an earnest middle-aged man related a story about a brutal triple-murder-followed-by-

---

[3] Shockingly, my mother shows occasional bursts of fiscal integrity.

suicide in Vallejo. He looked appropriately grave for two full seconds and then turned to his female counterpart.

She nodded, furrowed her brow, and said, "A tragedy . . . And now, I believe we have some breaking news about the tree sitters in Berkeley."

The camera shifted to the image of a khaki-and-windbreaker-clad newscaster in front of the oak grove on the UC Berkeley campus. Over the hum of protesters and bullhorns, the newscaster shouted into the microphone.

"For a week now, tree sitters working in shifts have lived on the three-hundred-year-old oak tree in protest of a campus development project that would require the trees' removal. Negotiations began last week but have stalled . . . University officials are once again at odds with the environmental activists who have proven to be worthy adversaries in the past . . ."

Just then my father entered the room and planted himself next to me on the couch. "You have to admire their dedication," he said.

"I want to know when they use the restroom," my mother said.

"That's what the bucket is for," I said.

The newscaster continued his report.

". . . The tree sitters have managed to maintain a constant vigil by working in shifts. In the middle of the night there was a changing of the guards, when the police were called away by a disturbance in the sculpture garden . . ."

The camera panned over to one of the grand old oaks and closed in on the tree sitter du jour. The reporter continued. "Currently the police are trying to find a safe and peaceful way to end the standoff. We will keep you posted on the latest developments."

The news cut to an Ivory Soap commercial. My mother picked up her cell phone, pressed number three on her speed dial, and waited until the voice mail kicked in.

"Rae. This is your mother calling. Get the hell out of that tree right now!"

Part 1

SURVEILLANCE

(September)

THE MAN IN THE LIBRARY

For reasons that will forever remain a mystery, my sister scheduled the client meeting at the main branch of the San Francisco Public Library—specifically, the government section, which is low traffic, offering privacy for a new client intake. The file was left on my desk with all the relevant details, including the time and place of the meeting and a brief description of the client: male, five feet eleven, brown hair, brown eyes, fortyish, average in every way (apparently his own description). The only other detail in the newly minted file was the client's contact information and his name: Adam Cooper.

I arrived early, sat down at one of the glass-encased study desks, and read the same page of a chess theory book that I had been reading over and over again. When I heard footsteps approach, I immediately stuffed the book in my bag. The last thing I needed was to get ensnared in a long-winded discussion on chess strategy when I don't know any.

Adam Cooper was indeed average in every way—the kind of guy who could confound a police lineup by virtually blending into the wall. That's not to say that Mr. Cooper's face was entirely void of character, but the character surfaced at unsuspected times. The only other thing worth mentioning was that he wore a navy-blue sweater vest. Any time someone under the age of sixty wears a sweater vest it's worthy of comment.

"Are you the Gopher?" he asked me with an ironic grin.

"Excuse me?"

"The woman who confirmed the appointment said that I should ask you that question to be sure I was meeting the right individual."

"You are meeting the right person," I said.

I'd never been asked that specific question before—"Are you the Gopher?"—but I had a feeling where it originated from. And I can assure you that the originator was going to suffer the consequences.

"Why do they call you the Gopher?" he asked, smiling. And here, a spark of character surfaced, teeth short and crooked in a way that made him seem friendlier. Maybe it was the sweater vest he wore, or the goofy boat shoes, or the way his bangs hung a little too low on his face. If pressed at the time, the one word I would have used to describe Adam was "harmless."

"Call me Isabel," I replied.

"Is that your real name?"

"No. It's 'the Gopher.' But I use 'Isabel' professionally," I said.

"That makes sense," Adam replied, taking a seat.

"So, Mr. Cooper."

"Call me Adam."

"Adam, how can I help you?"

"I want you to follow my sister."

THE WOMAN IN THE
NAVY-BLUE RAINCOAT

Ascrap of paper rested on the floor next to the trash bin. Sloppy script sliced between the ragged edges. I was about to toss it in the trash when I caught a glimpse of a flurry of borderline-illegible words, followed by a phone number.

Margrt S. (sounds like alligator)
Husband
Not suspicious
Maybe nothing
September 33rd—high noon
415-***-****

I found my mother and Demetrius[1] in the kitchen reviewing a list of baking classes at the CIA (Culinary Institute of America; there certainly is an unusual cross-section of organizations that also use that acronym—see appendix).

"I'm thinking about taking a pastry-making class. What do you think?" Mom said.

---

[1] You could either go straight to the appendix or show some patience and know that I'll get to him shortly.

"I'd rather you didn't," I replied.

"Show your mama some respect," D said.

"Respectfully, I wish you wouldn't. Now I am changing the subject.[2]

"I found this scrap of paper on the floor," I said, tossing it on the table. "I want to make sure it's okay to chuck it."

Mom pushed her reading glasses down to the bridge of her nose and studied the note. "Rae phoned the client to verify. I think she left the file on your desk."

"What is it?" I asked.

"I took a call after my root canal. Clearly I was on more drugs than I thought. It's under the name Slayter."

"That's a weak rhyme with 'alligator,'" I said. "And I can't remember the last time September had thirty-three days."

"Since most of the call was a blur, I can't comment," Mom replied.

"Maybe you shouldn't answer calls when you're on narcotics," I suggested.

"Sounds like an excellent company policy," Mom replied.

"You know what else might be an excellent company policy? Getting some work done," I said. I had noticed in recent weeks my mother growing increasingly slack on the job.

"I'll get to it later," Mom said. "Now, if you could excuse me, I have to decide between taking a master class on pies and one on cupcakes."

"Do they offer Toast-Making 101?" I asked, heading back into the office.

There was indeed a Slayter file on my desk, generated by our seasonal employee, and my sister, Rae. While her notes were more organized, they were almost as baffling as my mother's.

---

[2] I've discovered that formally announcing a subject change holds far more sway than just simply changing the subject. Try it yourself sometime.

Client: Mrs. Margaret Slayter
Contact Info: [redacted]
Meeting Time: September 3, noon.
Location: Botanical Gardens, GG Park
Description: White female, midforties, navy-blue suit
Slayter: The rhododendrons are nice this time of year.
Reply: So are the azaleas.
Notes: Client will sketch out details in person. Most likely a
    domestic case.

I promptly picked up the phone and dialed.

"What?"

" 'The rhododendrons are nice this time of year'?"

"That's what she says," Rae replied. "You say the other thing."

I read off the sheet: " 'So are the azaleas'?"

"Bingo."

"I don't get it."

"Rhododendrons and azaleas are the same flower."

"I don't care if they're man-eating plants."

"Those are a myth."

"Does the case relate to horticulture?"

"You know that word?" Rae replied with mock enthusiasm.

I opened the middle drawer of Rae's desk, extracted a two-pound bag of M&M's, and poured the contents of said bag out the window.[3]

"Why are we taking client meetings with lunatics?"

"I spoke to her for fifteen minutes. She's completely sane."

"Then why are we having a summit in the botanical garden and talking about flowers?"

"I thought you could use the fresh air and the code phrase is so you know you're meeting the correct individual."

---

[3] When my sister was little, I told her if she buried the M&M's she could grow an M&M tree and have a lifetime supply. She watered them with Kool-Aid for two weeks until my mother disabused her of that notion.

"How about names and a handshake?" I suggested. "Why the cloak and dagger?"

"Dad's running an experiment."

"What kind of experiment?"

"He thinks if we add a layer of cinematic intrigue to our client meetings—code phrases, exotic locales—we could charge more."

"Are you serious?"

"Yes. And he might be onto something; it already worked on the Bloomsfield case."

"This is ridiculous," I said.

"Maybe," Rae replied. "But if it works, who cares? Plus, Dad said I can come up with the code phrases, so I'm totally in."

"I'm totally out," I replied.

"Take it up with Dad," Rae said.

"You can count on it."

"Oh, and I almost forgot. Wear a trench coat and sunglasses to the meeting. Clients go crazy for that crap," Rae said, and then disconnected the call.

I wish I could tell you that I promptly phoned the client and rescheduled the meeting under more professional circumstances, but after consulting with my father, he insisted that we continue with the experiment. Only so much can be expected from a case that was born under a cloud of anesthesia.

"The rhododendrons are nice this time of year," said the woman in the navy-blue suit.

"So are the azaleas," I replied.

The woman in the navy-blue suit swept a nearby bench with a newspaper and took a seat. She was in her midforties, but the preserved kind, like she spent her spare time with her head in a freezer. It wasn't just her face that she'd spent a small fortune on, to lock in a single expression; her

14

clothes were all designer from top to bottom. I learned to distinguish the difference between designer and knockoffs from a case a while back— otherwise, I couldn't give a shit. What I can tell you for certain is that her handbag cost more than my car. While I understand the desire to have the best (single-malt scotch is indeed better than most blends), I still have to wonder what deformity of character makes someone think that a bloated leather handbag that can be ripped off your shoulder by anyone with good leverage is an item to covet. Suffice it to say, I knew the client had money and I was happy to take some of it off her hands. I sat down next to her in my snug trench coat and undid a button for comfort.

Since her face bore no scrutable expression, I stared straight ahead. If the point was for us to blend into the scenery of the botanical gardens, we failed. Other than being Caucasian, we shared no resemblance and looked positively silly next to each other, I'm sure. I even noted that my slouch was in direct contrast to her rigid upright posture, no doubt the result of a personal trainer.

The client's name was Mrs. Margaret Slayter. That's exactly how she'd referred to herself when my sister took the call.

"Thank you for meeting me," she said, fidgeting nervously with the buckle on her purse.

"How can I help you?" I asked.

"I want you to follow my husband."

THE GIRL WITH THE
RAP SHEET

Generally when charged with a surveillance assignment, I have some historical ammunition for the job. But with the Cooper and Slayter jobs, I was provided very little information. Adam Cooper simply said that he wanted his sister followed because he was concerned about her well-being. When I asked him to be more specific, he said that he didn't want to create an investigative bias. (An interesting concept, but a first in my career.) As for Mrs. Margaret Slayter, I asked her if she thought her husband was having an affair and she replied, "I simply want to know how he spends his time. It's not important for you to know why."

The thing is, usually we do know why.

A week after we took on the Cooper and Slayter cases, I found the Vivien Blake file. Her name was scrawled on the tab of a file folder sitting open on my mother's desk. A high school photo with the requisite cloudy blue backdrop mingled with an unusual assortment of other documentation. The girl in the picture was wearing cap and gown and smiling the way you smile when it has just been demanded of you. Other than the reluctant toothy grin, the young brunette had the appeal of a young woman with a bright future ahead of her. Adolescents are not our typical investigative fare. Since we usually discuss active cases in our office, it was unusual that I hadn't even heard the name on a file that was already two inches thick.

"Tell me about the Blake case," I said when my father eventually entered the office.

"We took the meeting last week," my dad replied defensively.

"Okay."

"You were busy."

"Okay."

"I think you were at Walter's."[1]

"I'm sure I was. Tell me about Ms. Blake."

"Her parents hired us."

"To find her?" I asked.

"No. She's not missing."

"Then why did her parents hire us?"

"The Blakes want us to follow their daughter."

My father settled into his chair and made an effort to appear extraordinarily busy. Before I continued interrogating him, I decided to familiarize myself with the Blake file. It began with an e-mail she wrote after her first month as a freshman at Berkeley.

To: Ma and Pa Blake

From: Vivien Blake *(vblake99@gmail.com)*

Re: greetings

Mom and Dad,

I hope this e-mail finds you well. Despite your concerns before I left home, I have not become a drug addict, a cult member, or a hippie. Sadly San Francisco isn't what it used to be. I'll own up to eating too much pizza and soda, but you must allow me a few vices. I can honestly report that I'm attending all of my classes

---

[1] I'll get to him shortly.

except the eight a.m. world history seminar. I tried to get into the noon one, but it was overenrolled. I just buy the notes later. You can do that, you know. I think it's also worth pointing out that I got an A on the first world history exam.

As for church, I haven't made it there yet, but it's on my to-do list. I would go if it started at noon. I don't know why they haven't implemented late-riser services yet. It's a niche most religions have failed to tap into.

I do have a favor to ask, aside from more pizza money, if you think of it: If you're concerned about me, call me. Not my room-mates. Sonia found that last phone call a bit . . . how do I put it? Awkward. Most parents don't do that sort of thing. Just so you know.

Not much else to report: I'm alive, my clothes are relatively clean, I'm getting enough sleep, and all the golf carts of the world are where they should be. And if they're not, it was not my doing.

Give Prof. Fuzzy a kiss for me. Remember, that's a two-person job. If I were you, I'd wear gloves.

Love, your law-abiding daughter,
Vivien

It took me about an hour to scrutinize the Blake file. The story is simple enough. Vivien's parents were concerned about their daughter, a straight-A student and class president who'd been accepted at a number of Ivy League schools but decided on the equally impressive and yet less expensive Berkeley. She was also a bit of a rebel, with a bent for getting into the kind of trouble that occasionally resulted in mild police intervention. Her parents wanted her tailed to make sure that the trouble she was currently getting into would not interfere with her education or future prospects.

To put it bluntly, they were scared of and for their daughter. They collected her e-mails as evidence rather than keepsakes. She was a different sort than they were. Harvey Blake was a life insurance salesman, always calculating risk. His wife was a homemaker of the old-school variety, the kind that ironed her husband's shirts and had dinner on the table at six forty-five on the dot. But their daughter was someone else. For years they had shared their house with a polite, friendly, free-spirited alien.[2]

Still, as far as I was concerned, Vivien Blake was simply a strong-willed young woman figuring out her place in the world. Since I had spent decades stirring up trouble, why would I investigate someone who was no worse than I at her age and yet managing to excel at the same time?

After I'd reviewed the file and the "evidence" within it, which included letters from sleepaway camp, text-message transcripts, a month of e-mails, and a photo of Vivien wearing a homemade prom dress constructed out of tinfoil and duct tape, I took a stand. I waited until my mom and Demetrius returned from their client meeting, so I had a full audience.

I dropped the file back on my mom's desk. "I vote no."

"I wasn't aware of any vote taking place," Mom replied. "I'll need some more time to campaign."

"Mom, it's a clear invasion of privacy."

"Sweetie, if you haven't noticed, invading privacy *is* our business."

"This crosses a line," I said. "I thought the whole point of college was to get away from your parents."

"Then how come you never went?" Dad said, consulting the ceiling as if it were a grand philosophical question.

"We're talking about Vivien now."

"They're concerned parents," Mom said.

"They're paranoid parents."

"She's been in trouble in the past."

"Who hasn't?"

"In one night, she stole half a dozen golf carts from Sharp Park," Mom said.

---

[2] Much of this information I gleaned from my mother at a later date.

19

"She relocated them," I replied. "They were discovered the next day."

"In a cow pasture!" Mom replied.

"Still, they were returned, unscathed, to the golf course and no one could prove that she did it. She's a genius, if you ask me."

"Technically she has a genius IQ," Dad piped in, and quickly turned back to his work.

"Isabel, she has a rather extensive juvenile rap sheet," my mother said.

"Fifty percent of the people in this room have a juvie record," I replied, speaking for myself and Demetrius.

I looked to D for some support, but he refused to meet my gaze, sifting through papers on his desk for the sole purpose of avoiding the debate being waged around him.

"D, do you have anything to say?" I asked.

"I think the muffins are ready," he said, taking a brisk walk into the kitchen.

Dad, too, remained mum, not wanting any part of this conflict.

"Al, what's your opinion?" my mother said.

"Who cares?" I replied. "You guys only get one combined vote anyway."[3]

"That's my opinion," Dad said.

"Coward," I said.

"I have to live with her," he said.

"You tried to slip this case by me," I said. "We agreed to vote whenever there was a dissenting opinion."

And so we voted. The outcome was one-one, as expected. We needed a tiebreaker. I entered the kitchen as Demetrius was plating the muffins. He set three aside on a separate platter.

"I think he's catching on," D said.

"Then we ride this wave as long as we can."

"I don't feel good about the deception," Demetrius replied.

---

[3] A clause in the revamped bylaws that I demanded on our most recent revision. It's only fair—they always vote the same way.

"Let it go. We have other matters to discuss."

"I don't want to be the tiebreaker," D said.

"Too bad," I replied. "It's part of your job."

The deciding vote used to be Rae's until we discovered she could be bought and ousted her from any interoffice conflict resolution.

"Don't try to sway his vote," Mom said, entering the kitchen. She took one muffin off the main tray and another from the trio of outcasts. "Al's?" she asked.

Demetrius nodded his head and reentered the office. Mom and I followed on his heels, each adding a layer to our own dissenting opinion. Mom briefly switched her attention to the muffins, trying to remember which one was the contraband and which the whole-grain doorstop. She weighed them in her hands and figured it out. She passed Dad the muffin from her left hand and dug into the one in her right.

"A freshman in college should not be under surveillance," I said.

"They're concerned for her future, Isabel."

Demetrius sat behind his desk and, like my dad, tried to pretend we weren't talking to him.

"Demetrius," I said, demanding a reply. "Remember who freed you."

"Stop playing the 'I got you out of jail' card," Mom said.

"I'm Switzerland," Demetrius said, as usual.

"There's no Switzerland in Spellman Investigations. Everybody picks a side," I intoned.

Dad took a bite of his muffin and made a face. Not a good one. Then he said, sounding as dry as the muffin most likely was, "Once again, D, you've outdone yourself."

"Thanks, Al," D replied, knowing that the compliment was a bald-faced lie.

"Just break the tie so I don't have to listen to them arguing for the rest of the day," Dad said.

Demetrius was clearly in conflict over this decision. Having had no privacy of his own for fifteen years, he wanted to respect it in others, but he couldn't help but feel concern for the young coed. But one might suppose that there is a rather profound distinction between not being able to use a toilet in private and being watched from afar by a pack of harmless PIs.

"Take the case," Demetrius said. "She's legal now. If she crosses the line, she could have a record for the rest of her life."

And that is how we caught the case of Vivien Blake.

Even I'll admit that there was something bizarrely symmetrical about our recent caseload—surveilling a husband, a sister, and a daughter all at one time. I know what you're thinking. Surely all three cases will become ensnared and converge at the end. But don't get ahead of yourself. That kind of shit only happens in detective novels. How about you quit guessing and let the story unfold as it may? Even I don't know how all the pieces will fall.

FILLING IN THE BLANKS

I suppose it's time to take a crayon to this primitive drawing and color between, on, and outside the lines. If you are in the mood for a more complex portrait, you can read the previous four documents. It's up to you. Remember, I can't *make* you do anything. So don't get peeved at me because I've merely made a suggestion. To simplify matters, however, I will refer you to the appendix, where you'll find a detailed summary of all the key players in the saga. As it turns out, I am the most key player.

My name, if I haven't mentioned it already, is Isabel Spellman. I am the thirty-four-year-old middle child of Albert and Olivia Spellman. I have a history of delinquency and minor arrests, but I like to think most of that is behind me. Unfortunately, others do not concur. I have a much younger sister, Rae, who is currently a sophomore at UC Berkeley and carrying on my torch of rebellion, although her take on it is far less aimless and booze soaked. Rae lives in our brother's basement apartment and remains a part-time Spellman Investigations employee. PI work is in our blood. Rae began working for the family business at age six, trying desperately to follow in my footsteps. I started at twelve, not being quite so eager to follow the footsteps in front of me. The family business eventually became my profession because I had a knack for it and I didn't have a knack for too many other things—especially legal activities. I used to think that one day I would find my real talent and move on. Turns out, this is my real talent. It might sound as if I've reluctantly accepted my fate, but that's not it. I'm fine with my fate, but with it comes responsibility and sometimes the self-doubt eats away at me. The problem with being a private investigator is that you end up making ethical decisions every single day, and I've come to accept that I'm not always right and when I'm wrong, I can't always see it. That said, I'm right most of the time.

The only other Spellman spawn is David Spellman, my older brother. David was at once the raven-haired golden boy and the black sheep of the family—a freakishly handsome, high-achieving lawyer with a closet full of fancy suits and a jaw-dropping collection of male skin-care products. I am, however, referring to Old David. New David is now a stay-at-home dad to eighteen-month-old Sydney. The contrast between the two Davids is not quite Jekyll and Hyde, but close. Old David was a shark, the kind of handsomely perfect man whom some people find unsettling. Being his sister, I found him more obnoxious. He had an enormous capacity for vanity but managed to come off as down-to-earth. People were drawn to him because he made them feel special. He remembered their names, asked questions, recalled insignificant details of their lives like a politician. I don't tend to remember data unless I can use it against you at a later date. But I suppose there's no point in talking about Old David anymore. He's gone and I don't think he's coming back. I can't say that I miss him. He always made me feel less than, even though that rarely was his agenda. But New David has taken some getting used to. New David has lost all concern for personal vanity or ambition. All of the energy previously expended on himself is now devoted to his daughter, Sydney. He's kind of like Old David's sloppy doppelgänger, with an eighteen-month-old girl permanently attached to his hip. While my family has had trouble adjusting to this new incarnation, I can't imagine what it's been like for David's wife.

David is married to Maggie Mason, a defense attorney who once dated

Henry Stone, my Ex-boyfriend #13, although we're still together.[1] That might sound confusing. (I've always referred to boyfriends, current and former, in the past tense. It just seems easier to anticipate the worst up front.) I'm pretty good at finding fault in people, but I haven't had much success with Maggie. I suppose since she refuses to hide her flaws, you stop looking for them.

Now let me tell you about the newest member of the Spellman clan. At least the newest member who doesn't use a sippy cup. Demetrius Merriweather, employee of the month for six months running, has a history that could fill a book in itself.[2] Eighteen years ago Demetrius was wrongly convicted for the murder of his neighbor Elsie Collins. D, as I like to call him because I'm prone to laziness, spent fifteen years in jail for a crime he did not commit. Maggie[3] and I worked his case pro bono until his release six months ago. Demetrius's remaining family resides in Detroit. He was welcome home any time he wanted, but after a Christmas visit, D decided he'd grown too accustomed to the California climate, despite the fact that he experienced most of that climate for a mere one hour a day. Immediately upon his release, my parents offered him the attic apartment (where I lived for many years) and a job. D is a God-fearing man capable of profound forgiveness. His integration back into the outside world appears seamless. But nothing is as it seems. Like everyone I know, he's hiding something.

Almost two years have passed since I've found the need to document my family's activities. A lot can happen in two years, as you'll see. As much as one might like to believe that I've eased into adulthood without a fight, let there be no mistake. I'm still fighting.

---

[1] I'll get to him in a few pages.

[2] Part of a book, to be precise. (Document #4)

[3] If you've already forgotten who she is, I suggest you see a doctor or at the very least take up Sudoku.

THE DEMETRIUS EFFECT

While there have been many unwelcome changes to my work life, the presence of Demetrius Merriweather cannot be added to that list. He works harder, more efficiently, and less erratically than any other employee on the Spellman Investigations payroll—including myself. He's also a talented cook, an excellent conversationalist, and at times the only voice of reason in the household. That said, every silver lining has its cloud.

Sometime after Demetrius Merriweather moved into the Spellman household, my mother began putting on airs. I suspect the trouble began shortly after she attended church with D and found there were more than a few people in this crazy town of ours who believe in respect, forgiveness, and waking up early on a Sunday morning wearing bright colors in freshly pressed ensembles unmistakable for sleepwear. My mother also noticed that many of Demetrius's new church friends were well mannered and managed to speak in complete sentences without using four-letter words as emphatic adjectives. It was only then that my mother picked up on the fact that Demetrius himself was well mannered. This had slipped her notice even after three months of working in the same office.

Even though he lived under the same roof as my parents, D always said good morning and good-bye (only when he was leaving, of course) instead of my usual form of greeting[1] and adieu.[2] When asked a ridiculous question, Demetrius would reply diplomatically: "I'm afraid I don't know" or "I'll Google it later," or "That's certainly something to ponder."

"You know, D has never, in the entire time I've known him, asked me if I've smoked crack," my mother said to me one early morning, during the footnoted coffee, making a point that I still can't ascertain. What I can tell you is this: After thirty-some years of living with the manners equivalent of franks and beans, my mother developed a taste for champagne and caviar.

It was sometime after the Church Incident, as I would come to call it, although I know that it was no incident, that my mother changed. She quit swearing cold turkey. However, like a lifelong smoker, there was the occasional relapse, which would result in either the first syllable being halted abruptly, or a complete word or phrase followed by "pardon me." Pre-Demetrius Mom thought nothing of peppering even the most mundane phrase with an F-word. "Pass the fucking casserole," for example, was a phrase for which I'd need at least all twenty digits to count how many times I've heard it.

But those days were over now. "Please" and "thank you" replaced my mother's most colorful language. It was like watching an unnaturally polite game of Mad Libs, as my mother cut out her instinctual language and glued in a more civil version. Live and let live, I say.[3] However my mom wants to talk is her own business, but I take issue when she tries to foist her wishes on the rest of us.

My mom's first etiquette lesson went something like this:

"Mom, pass me the stapler," I said.

She replied by clearing her throat.

"You need a cough drop?"

"No."

---

[1] Grunting and demanding coffee.

[2] "I am so outta here."

[3] That's probably the first time I've said it.

"Can I have the stapler?"

"Can I have the stapler . . . *what*?"

"Huh?"

"What do we say?"

"I don't know. What do we say?"

"'Please.' 'Can I have the stapler *please*.'"

"We don't say that."

"Yes, we do."

"Fuck it. I'll get it myself."

Of course in the time it took to have that conversation, I could have amassed every stapler in the household. I made a mental note not to ask for anything within shot-putting distance in the future.

I saw my mother checking Demetrius out of the corner of her eye. He was speed-typing a surveillance report with his index fingers and not paying us any mind.

"Please watch your language in this household," Mom said to me, her volume raised to be certain that Demetrius could hear, or Mr. Snodgrass next door.

"Mom, D was in prison for fifteen years; he's heard worse. I bet he could teach you a few words."

"This is a business establishment. We should maintain professional standards."

"Since when?"

"Since a civilized human being started working here."

"D, do you care if I swear?"

"Not unless you're meeting my mama."

"See?" I said, looking at my mama. "I promise when Mrs. Merriweather visits we'll treat her like the queen of England."

One would think that a man who just got out of prison would be rough around the edges, or worse, sharpened like a blade. But none of the ex-con stereotypes suit D. Except one. He could never have his back to the door. (We had to do a lot of furniture rearranging during his first few weeks with us.) My point is, things changed when Merriweather moved into the Spellman household. He was now a member of the family, and he would come to recognize that came at a price.

Case in point: When I was in the process of investigating Demetrius's wrongful conviction, I wore a T-shirt that read:

Justice 4

Merri-Weather.

I wore it fairly often—maybe a couple times a week—so I had extras made to avoid any laundry hassles. When D was sprung, I stopped wearing the shirts and they disappeared. Then they reappeared. On Rae, who has taken to wearing them whenever she comes to visit. This D finds particularly irksome since he is currently free and believes that justice eventually won out. Rae, however, made one minor adjustment to the shirt. She added dollar signs, framing the message. Her "message" to Merriweather being that justice will only be served after he files a colossal lawsuit and has a couple million bucks stashed away for a rainy day, or a mansion in Pacific Heights.

Their conversations usually follow a similar pattern.

D: Rae, can you please stop wearing that shirt? It is a reminder of a time I wish to forget.

RAE: I would like to respect your wishes, but I can't.

D: Why not?

RAE: There is a statute of limitations on police misconduct lawsuits. I would hate to see you squander a chance to be a millionaire.

D: I don't want to be a millionaire.

RAE: That's just silly. Everyone does.

D: I don't want to have this discussion anymore.

RAE: We'll talk again next week.

While Rae is in school, her work schedule has been capped at ten hours a week; the parental unit wanted to make sure that her studies took priority. On the clock, her duties could range anywhere from client billing to surveillance. Since she has access to the main server from her laptop, sometimes I only see her on Friday afternoons for the weekly Spellman Investigations board meeting. This is when we discuss new cases, handle any in-house disputes, and allow Rae the floor for her myriad business improvement plans—Rae has always liked money, but a college business course took their relationship to the next level. In fact, my sister, once the most dedicated investigator in the family, now seems at times to be no more than a consultant. Although, an enthusiastic consultant to say the least. We used to have her stick her relentless business plans into a suggestion box, but when Rae discovered that I had been shredding its contents, my parents appeased her by giving her the floor for fifteen minutes every session. Once she's said her piece, she loses interest in the meeting and kills the rest of the time texting and staring at her watch, punctuating each remaining minute with a loud, tired sigh.

THE GOPHER, THE EAGLE, THE TORTOISE, AND THE WEASEL

Aside from the common abridgement of "Izzy" from "Isabel," I have never had an official nickname other than "That One," which I heard most often during my adolescence. And I think it's important to mention that I never wanted one. It's also important to mention that in the Spellman household what I want has never been of much interest to the relevant parties.

It was late afternoon when my dad and Rae returned home from a day-long and rather tedious surveillance. My sister's reward for eight hours of only Dad's company was a hot-fudge sundae, of which they both partook. I suspect the dessert had a pharmaceutical effect on the brain chemistry of the duo, since their spirits were enhanced in a way that usually involves spirits. When they entered the house, Rae spotted my mother napping on the living room sofa.

"The Eagle is sleeping," she whispered.

"Where is the Gopher?" Dad asked.

Unaware that I was the Gopher, I exited the kitchen and headed to the office, brushing past my kin as if they were invisible.

"The Gopher is on the move," my father said in a conspiratorial whisper.

Dad and Rae followed me into the office and explained how they

31

spent their entire eight hours together: designating a nickname for each family member. When I quizzed the relevant parties for a bit longer, I discovered that Dad had napped for two of those hours while Rae studied. Another three were killed in active pursuit, which would trim superfluous talk. So, in all fairness, they only spent three hours coming up with sobriquets. Still, an unwise use of time. The time killer, as it turns out, was not in working out my nickname or Mom's; it was duking it out over the nicknames for the two individuals in the car. Dad was baptized the Tortoise right off the bat and no matter how many times he tried to shake it off for something cooler, Rae applied another layer of Krazy Glue. Dad's first Rae moniker was "the Tasmanian Devil," but both agreed that it was ridiculous to give someone a nickname that took so much longer to say than the real thing. Finally he settled on "the Weasel," which Rae refused to accept without a second opinion, which I promptly provided.

Rae scowled and said, "Whatever. I can think of worse things."

A few lingering questions remained after their lengthy exposition.

"What about David?" I asked.

"We still can't decide whether to nickname Old David or New David, so that one is on hold."[1]

"What about Demetrius?"

"We all call him D, so we figured one nickname was enough," Dad said.

"You're the Gopher, in case you missed that part," Rae said.

"No I'm not."

"Yeah, you are. Do you want to know why you're the Gopher?"

"No, thank you."

"Because you like to dig and don't care what pretty flowers you disturb as you tunnel through the dirt."

---

[1] Old David would definitely be the Shark. I have no idea what animal New David is. Maybe the Kangaroo.

"I don't want a nickname."

"That's the thing about nicknames, you don't get to decide."

The telephone rang, ending this conversation at long last.

After a brief exchange, my father hung up the phone and turned to me.

"That was Walter," he said.

"What is it this time?"

"He thinks he left the stove on again."

I suppose there's just one more case on the Spellman docket that I haven't mentioned.

WALTER PERKINS

Walter Perkins's "case," if you can call it that, was simple enough. During his intake meeting (in those glorious pre-code-phrase days), he explained that he needed a responsible person to check on his apartment now and again, when he was out of town. I suggested a neighbor or a friend might be more appropriate for the position and he explained that sometimes he needed someone to check on his apartment even when he was in town but indisposed. I asked him how often he thought these services would be required and he explained that it could be one time a month or weekly or daily, making a stab at sounding casual, but the crack in his voice gave him away.

At the first meeting, Perkins struck my mother as nervous and edgy, and his attempt to present the job as commonplace gave him a ticlike laugh, underscoring the lie. My mother told Mr. Perkins that she would check our schedule to see whether we could take the case. This wasn't our typical investigative fare and something about the simplicity of the job didn't sit right with Mom.

She then proceeded to engage in a rather lengthy investigation of our potential client—a habit we discourage, for cost-cutting purposes. Walter Perkins is a math professor, without any criminal records or civil suits in his wake. He was recently divorced, but the settlement ap-

34

peared amicable. Still, my mother's suspicion spread like a bad rash.

Over the course of three days she made inquiries to be certain we weren't getting saddled into cat-sitting, dog-sitting, botanical gardening, or checking in on a home that was not, in fact, Walter's. When she had exhausted all of the most inconvenient possibilities, we took the case. Or, more specifically, I persuaded her to take the case. Times are rough; we can't turn down easy work just because it isn't in our usual repertoire. Walter made an unlikely request, but there wasn't anything unethical about it. After Mom agreed to my demands, her only stipulation was that I handle all direct communications with Walter, who she said had the distinct whiff of a Scharfenberger.[1] I couldn't smell it, so I phoned my new client; we negotiated an hourly rate and he handed me the keys to his apartment.

In the two months we'd worked for Walter, I'd grown quite fond of him as a client, though I'd only met him once in person. Our interactions usually followed a similar chain of events:

Walter phones. He thinks he left the stove on. Or perhaps his apartment door is unlocked. Sometimes a window is ajar (he is on the fourth floor, so I'm not exactly sure what he's worried about—flies?); sometimes the bathtub might be overflowing.[2] Or an appliance is left plugged in. Or an errant sock accidentally fell from the laundry basket. Sometimes his fears are more catastrophic.

The apartment is burning, flooding, collapsing for no good reason. These fears abate when I visit Walter's home and assure him nothing is amiss. In fact, the only time anything was ever amiss in Walter's apartment was after I checked it for a gas leak and Walter noticed my footprints on the unblemished beige carpet when he returned home from work. This dis-

---

[1] Frank Scharfenberger, d. 1996. To date the most difficult client we've ever had.
[2] Even though Walter doesn't take baths. I asked.

turbance was quickly remedied by my removing my shoes and combing the carpet upon departure, each visit.

As it turned out, Walter didn't travel, but he was close to losing his job because of his abrupt departures from the campus, which sometimes took place midlecture, even midsentence. They apparently gave him the appearance of a convict making a run for it. Now all Walter had to do was make a quick call from his office or send a text message from behind the lectern.

It was 3:42 when I reached Walter's apartment. After entering and checking the burners, I phoned him with the usual good news.

"All clear," I said.

"Thank you," Walter replied, sighing deeply, as if he had been holding his breath.

"Anything else?" I asked because there's usually something else.

"Can you check and make sure that the bathroom sink is shut off?"

It's possible to fake check when I'm speaking into a phone line and know, based on ample history, that the answer will be no, but I never humor Walter. I'm paid for the work and I do what is asked of me.

"All clear," I said, securing the faucets, even though they were already secure.

Walter sighed again, thanked me, and ended the call. As I combed the carpet, backing into the front door, I noticed that the electric cord on his toaster was still plugged in. Among Walter's plethora of fears, electrical fires rank third after sewage backups and water-line breaks. I unplugged the cord and gazed at the outlet with a surprising sense of unease. It was as if someone else were in the apartment with me. Surrounded by erratic behavior, I think I've found some comfort in Walter's religious consistency. I resolved to keep this inconsistency to myself. If Walter thought he was slipping, his condition would only worsen. Once again I combed the carpet and departed, wiping the doorknob with a handkerchief on my way out.

You might be thinking that a problem like Walter's would be better served by professional help. Believe me, I conveyed that very same sentiment after my third visit to his home. Walter assured me he had been through the gauntlet of physicians, psychiatrists, psychologists, psychics, spiritual healers, and even a life coach—whom he claimed was the biggest scam artist of the bunch.

Until Walter's wife moved out, his situation was somewhat under control. Spellman Investigations brought him back to his previous state of equilibrium. "Equilibrium" is not a word usually associated with my people.

DOMESTIC DISTURBANCES

With the Spellmans there is always a steady simmer of conflicts, oddities, and subterfuge. And I cannot deny that I've come to find all of this quite ordinary. But as with any family, these things accumulate like the imaginary slow drip of Walter's bathtub faucet. Only on occasion do I notice a sudden deluge.

It was just another Wednesday in October when a series of unusual events took a mundane morning into an evening of chaos. It began like any other day. I was in the office filing because I chose rock over scissors. I suppose that's the kind of comment that requires explanation.

Every employee of Spellman Investigations despises filing. I'd argue that I loathe it the most, but then we'd get into a who-hates-filing-more debate, which is almost as tedious as the job in question. Throughout the years, we've flipped coins, drawn straws, used a lottery system to dispense with this odious chore. When D came to work for us, he kindly took over the chore, always filing when no one else was in the room to stop him or offer to take over. But then the oft-absent Rae suggested that between D's cooking (which he enjoys) and grocery shopping (my mother never picks out the right item), we were treating D more like a personal assistant than an associate investigator. Since D is everyone's favorite, we suddenly saw the error of our ways and decided to split the job between the four full-time employees.

However, unlike sane people in a similar situation, we didn't attempt to evenly split the chore. Instead, Rae suggested we play rock-paper-scissors for it once a week to determine who does the filing. For reasons I still cannot explain,[1] we all agreed.

One would think, the game being only marginally skill based and almost entirely odds based, that approximately a fourth of the time, I would be saddled with this chore. My average was 72 percent[2] at the time.

So, there I was filing for the third week in a row and the phone was ringing and the office was empty and I noticed that my mother and D's "coffee break" had extended well past two hours. In fact, in recent weeks Mom's hobbies had made her work absences rather pronounced. I certainly enjoyed having the office to myself, but not at the expense of our work. At first I thought of Mom's extracurricular activities as a kind of dress rehearsal for retirement. But lately I'd begun to find holes in that theory; something else was at play. I noticed a stack of paperwork growing on my mother's desk and caught a series of errors in surveillance reports that were typed in the early hours of the morning. I decided to put an end to her coffee break and searched the house for Mom and D.

I found them both seated on lawn chairs in the back garden, lazing about like it was an aimless Sunday afternoon. If I haven't mentioned a garden before, that's because there wasn't one. Another one of Mom's very recent hobbies had been gardening. She'd planted some perennials and something that I swear looked like a marijuana plant. My mom, apparently reading my mind, said, "Isabel, don't try to smoke that. It's a Japanese maple leaf."[3] I took a moment to note the status of the greenery; everything was still alive, but that's not saying much—they were alive when

---

[1] A group brainwashing experiment, perhaps?
[2] Yes, I keep a spreadsheet.
[3] Sadly, it was true.

she got them and it'd only been about a month. Forget about the garden. The absent employees reclined in their chairs with the exact same book in hand and, oddly enough, almost identical baffled expressions on their faces. Between them sat a plate of D's secretly famous cranberry scones. Even though I wasn't hungry, I snagged one and dug in.

Typically, my mother crammed alone for her punitive book club meeting. I'd yet to get a proper answer for why she joined the club in the first place. The entire affair had the air of espionage about it. For most women, a book club is at worst a nuisance and at best a great way to get free food and wine (and literature, if you're into that sort of thing). But I couldn't figure what my mom was getting out of it. She rarely had anything interesting to say about the book or the other group members and was always cramming at the last minute in a comprehension-challenged state of stressed-out speed-reading. This month Mom had fallen particularly far behind, and since work was relatively slow, she solicited D's assistance as a human CliffsNotes. However, the time crunch was so severe that Mom could only tackle the first half, while D read the second half blind, offering up the mere bullet points. He was also battling a series of questions that arose out of the narrative incongruity.

"Who is Mark?" D asked.

"Her spiritual adviser."

"Got it."

"What's happening now?" my mother asked D.

"Lynette has enrolled in five courses from the Learning Depot: pottery making, molecular gastronomy, tai chi, assertiveness training, and speed-reading."

"I should take that one," my mom said.

Demetrius continued: "She decides she wants to quit the assertiveness class but comes up with a lie about a family emergency as an excuse, not recognizing the inherent irony of that behavior. Who is this Loretta lady? She keeps talking about her and not in a friendly way."

"That was her best friend whom she found in bed with her golf instructor."

"Why aren't they speaking anymore?" D asked.

"Because she was also sleeping with the golf instructor."

"Okay, that explains a *few* things," D replied.

"Just be grateful you missed the ten-page invective on golf."

"I never played," Demetrius said.

"Miniature golf is better," my mom said authoritatively.[4]

"I love miniature golf," D replied. "At least I used to."

"We should have a company miniature golf day," my mom said.

An interruption was required at this point.

"What's the name of this book?" I said, taking another bite of D's spectacular baked good.

"*This Road I Call My Heart,*" D replied, shaking his head in disbelief.

I almost choked on the scone.

"I think I might be ill," I said.

"Give it a minute, the nausea will pass," said D.

"Can I take the scones to the book club?" Mom asked D. "That might buy me another month."

D nodded his head once while continuing to skim the pages with a tinge of bafflement on his face. My best guess was that a middle-aged woman's coming-of-age memoir was not his usual literary fare.

"Remind me again why you're doing this?" I said.

"It's good to have hobbies," Mom replied with an undertone I couldn't put my finger on.

All I knew was that the book club was a cover for something more complicated. If I wanted answers, questions were not how I would get them.

---

[4] I think she's played like twice in her lifetime.

SIBLING CONFLICT #157

I t used to be my habit to keep lists of various aspects of my life. Some prefer a diary, but I like the cold, clinical nature of a spreadsheet. Most of my lists have been neglected for years. (I quit documenting my misdemeanors at least twelve years ago; that's not to say I haven't committed any. But keeping a list started to seem like keeping evidence against myself.) Anyway, some lists remain. And, as of the writing of this document, we've now reached #157 in the sibling conflict department.[1]

After work, I drove straight to my brother's house for a reconnaissance mission requested by Maggie. The fact that checking in on David kept me checked out of my own life was simply an unforeseen benefit. I couldn't remember the last time I had an evening at home. I knew Henry was growing suspicious and annoyed and probably a few other adjectives and I'd have to do something about that. But until I sorted out a few things, I would stick to the Avoidance Method™, my primary go-to plan when something is amiss in my personal life. You might start wondering what was amiss, but I don't feel like discussing it right now. We're on the subject of David, which is far more interesting. Why are other people's troubles so fun when our own are so tedious?

---

[1] This list is not exhaustive; I can't keep track of everything, you know.

Ever since David became the proud father of Sydney, his ability and desire to socialize with people over the age of five has diminished considerably. Maggie has solicited help from all of the family members, but I take particular pleasure in the task.

My parents also follow the cult of Sydney, basking in the angelic glow of their eighteen-month-old granddaughter. So far, no one has noted that, based on history, not a single Spellman woman has ever grown up to be anything remotely resembling angelic. Still, my brother's acute metamorphosis has not gone unnoticed by the unit. That said, with New David comes new Sydney and the cost-benefit ratio is definitely in their favor. Even if New David is an eyesore.

Always garbed in fuzzy slippers, sweatpants, and any of a wide variety of holiday-themed pajama tops, David's primary accessory is a cotton cloth he dangles over his shoulder, which is commonly covered in Sydney's mucous or some half-masticated food item left over from her last meal. This means a sour odor trails him around the house. Sometimes the mere sight of him makes me want to run in the opposite direction.

Maggie was pulling into the driveway when I arrived. As we converged at the front door, my sister-in-law put a hundred-dollar bill in my palm.

"What's this for?" I asked.

"Drinking money," Maggie replied.

"I'll need another fifty for David."

Maggie, oddly enough, dug back into her purse.

"I was joking," I said.

"Just make sure he comes home drunk," Maggie said as she unlocked the front door.

"That won't be very difficult," I replied.[2]

* * *

---

[2] I've seen New David get tipsy on two glasses of wine; Old David would require a fifth of scotch.

Sydney was sitting on a blanket on the living room floor with my brother, composing a tune on a primitive xylophone. David, sadly, was attempting to write lyrics to accompany the random notes. Maggie gawked for a moment, then hunched down, smacked her knees, and called to her daughter. "Sydney, come to Mommy," Maggie said.

"She's not a dog," David said, for what I guessed was not the first time.

"She needs to practice walking," Maggie replied. "You carry her around all day."

Sydney stumbled to her feet and approached her mother with the gait of most tavern patrons at closing time. The resemblance vanished with the adorably alien voice that replied.

"Mama!"

Maggie swept her daughter up in her arms and pointed at me.

"Look who I brought home," Maggie said.

Sydney performed her usual vacant stare, which on a grown-up I would translate to *You look familiar; have we met?*

"How's it going?" I said to Sydney, nodding a polite hello.

"How's it going?" David repeated in a harsh tone of mockery.

"I don't speak toddler, okay?" I replied. "One day she'll respect me for it."

"What are you doing here?" he asked.

"I invited her," Maggie replied.

"I should warn you, if you're staying for dinner, we're only having fish sticks," David said. "Can I get you a juice box?"

"Yeah. If you put some vodka in it," I replied.[3]

"No, you and Izzy are going out," said Maggie. "Now. To a sports bar. I'm sure there's a basketball or baseball or even hockey game on tonight. You will drink beer and eat chicken wings or something like that."

"I couldn't possibly go out tonight. I'm exhausted. Plus, I promised Sydney we'd finish *Lord of the Rings* before bedtime."

---

[3] Not a bad product idea, if I say so myself. I'm kind of busy, so have at it.

44

"You know she doesn't understand a word you're saying."

"She understands more than you think," David replied.

"I'll be reading to her tonight," Maggie replied, "and I think we'll stick with *Green Eggs and Ham.*"

"She doesn't like it when you patronize her."

"Are we going to a bar or not?" I said. "Because I have to start drinking right now, no matter what."

"Help yourself to the liquor cabinet," David said.

It was easy to ascertain that any persuading wasn't going to happen in the near future, so I poured a healthy glass of the good bourbon. Lately, just about anything could slip by my brother.

There was a knock at the front door. David answered it. Our sister, Rae, stood on the threshold accompanied by a motley assortment of overstuffed luggage.

"I'm packed," she said, stating the obvious. Overstating it, to be precise. Her car was parked in the driveway; the entrance to her in-law unit was just a few short steps away. Instead of loading the car en route, she'd dragged her luggage around the house, past her car, and up David and Maggie's front steps to make a point in the most dramatic way possible.

"I wish you all the best," David said formally.

My family isn't all that formal, so that was weird.

"Are you going somewhere?" I asked Rae, taking a sip of bourbon.

It's hard for me to explain the perfection of that moment, witnessing a conflict that was not my doing with a free drink in hand.

Rae ignored me and spoke only to David. "Once again, I'm sorry," she said.

"What are you sorry about?" I inquired.

"Nothing," David quickly replied. "We will not speak of it again. I take it you've found a place to stay."

"I'll be fine," Rae replied with equal formality.

It was like catching the third act of a drawing-room play.

"Good-bye then," David said.

"Good-bye," Rae replied. She turned on her heel and hauled her luggage down the stairs, grunting along the way.

"Is Rae taking a trip?" I asked no one in particular, although I wasn't asking Sydney.

Maggie just shook her head. "David is making Rae move out."

"Why?"

"I don't know."

"You don't know?"

"I tried *everything*," Maggie said. "No one is talking. I swear these two would make excellent prisoners of war."

"Can I try?"

"Knock yourself out," Maggie said, taking Sydney into the kitchen to feed her or something.

"What did Rae do?" I asked David.

"I'd rather not speak of it."

I pulled the hundred out of my pocket and waved it in front of my brother.

"Will Benjamin Franklin change your mind?"

"Isabel, let it go."

"Never."

"Don't you have places to be?"

"I do. I just don't want to be there."

"Well, you're free to stay for fish sticks."

"I was hoping to lure you to a dive bar tonight to watch the game."

"What game?"

"Oh, no. It's worse than I thought."

"One day, you'll understand," David said. I was pretty sure I wouldn't.

"One drink, David. That's all I ask. Just prove to me that you're still a man."

"One drink," David replied.

We walked to the closest bar, where David ordered a glass of red wine, sipped it for twenty minutes while recounting his entire day with Sydney, then put $20 on the bar and departed so swiftly I didn't even have a chance to protest.

I took the hundred from my pocket and handed it to the bartender. "Next round is on me."

THE AVOIDANCE METHOD™

The bar was mostly empty, so it took longer than you might expect to go through the hundred that Maggie gave me and the forty-eight bucks I had in my pocket. I could feel the buzz of my cell phone in my jacket but ignored it until I'd left the bar and was strolling up Polk Street. I didn't bother listening to my voice mail since the messages were easy to anticipate.

My cell buzzed in my pocket again. I checked the caller ID. This time it said, "Private caller." It could have been a trick from home, but I decided to pick up anyway.

"Hello?"

"Hello."

"Hello?" I repeated.

"Can I ask whom I'm speaking to?" said a female voice on the other end of the line.

"You called me," I replied.

"Actually, I believe you called me," said the voice again.

"I don't think so. Who are you?"

"I'm not comfortable giving out that kind of information to strangers."

"Me neither," I replied.

"Perhaps I've made a mistake," the woman said.

"Sounds like it," I replied, and disconnected the call.

I sent Maggie a text and told her that I'd pick up my car in the morning.[1] I caught a cab and twenty minutes later, I was home. This home is different than the last home I might have told you about. It's a single-family dwelling in the Inner Sunset. I've reduced the pros and cons to two. Pro: I can sneak through a window. Con: Somebody else could sneak through a window. Also, it's far roomier than my previous homes, but I have a roommate, which sort of offsets that particular pro.

As I've said before, I'm not as partial to doors as the next woman. A window can often work just fine as a mode of entry and exit. In this particular case it worked out better because, frankly, I didn't want the person I was cohabiting with to know I was home.

I circled my house and checked the perimeter for lights. Henry's as eco-friendly as they come, so no light remains in a room where no human is present. In fact, I've often been left in the dark when Henry departs a room. Habit, he tells me, but sometimes it just seems rude. The point being that if a room was dark, I knew the coast was clear. I climbed through the window of the downstairs office and flicked on the desk lamp. My phone vibrated in my pocket, giving me a start and causing me to smack my knee against the steel-framed desk. As I grimaced in silence I looked at the caller ID and for reasons that still escape me—thrill seeking, I suspect—I answered it.

ME: Hello?

HENRY: Where are you?

ME: Home. Where are you?

HENRY: Very funny.

---

[1] They have a set of keys, since this is not an uncommon occurrence.

ME: Actually, it *is* kind of funny.

HENRY: Seriously, where are you? She's starting to get suspicious.

ME: Of what?

HENRY: Of you.

ME: How so?

HENRY: That you don't exist.

ME: That's just silly. We have pictures, don't we?

HENRY: She'd prefer the real thing.

ME: I think her opinion will change soon enough.

HENRY: Why are you whispering?

ME: Because I don't want anyone to hear me.

HENRY: Isabel, our guest flew out here specifically to meet you.

ME: Have you taken her to Fisherman's Wharf yet? Because that's usually why people fly to San Francisco.

HENRY: Isabel, when are you coming home?

ME: Don't wait up.

HENRY: What are you doing?

ME: I'm on a surveillance right now. I'll call you when it's over.

Before you judge me, I'd like you to consider this: At no point during that conversation did I lie to Ex-boyfriend #13. I was indeed at home. And I was also on a surveillance.

San Francisco has an unnatural number of houses that include the unfortunately named in-law unit. At first, when Henry and I were house hunting, I balked at the concept, fearing that one day (God forbid) my parents would somehow take ownership of the apartment out of a sense of entitlement. It required much cajoling to convince me that such a fate would not be mine. My mother finally got me to cave, explaining, point-blank, that she would prefer a low-rent convalescent home to cohabiting with me in her final days. I was mildly offended and spectacularly relieved.

The main entrance to the house is on the right side, up an abbreviated flight of stairs. The socially acceptable in-law entrance is on the ground level on the left side of the house. In the middle is the garage, which both units have a secondary access to. I slipped out of the office, which is in the in-law unit; went through the garage entrance; and climbed the rickety stairs to the interior entry to the main house. That door opens into the kitchen; I was in excellent eavesdropping position. The voices—one male, one female—echoed crisp and clear. It was as if I were a silent participant in the conversation.

Allow me to introduce you to Gertrude Stone, Henry's mother.

GERTRUDE: Why don't you have any pictures around?

HENRY: They're still in boxes.

GERTRUDE: Surely you keep a picture of her in your wallet.

HENRY: [*sigh*] Well . . .

GERTRUDE: Why all the intrigue? She exists, right?

HENRY: For the last time, Mom. She exists. I swear. She's just working late. You'll meet her tomorrow morning.

GERTRUDE: Why wouldn't you keep a picture in your wallet?

HENRY: I did! She stole it.

GERTRUDE: Why?

HENRY: Because she saw this movie once where a woman was showing a picture of her boyfriend to some woman at a bar. The second woman was later robbed and picked the boyfriend from the wallet snapshot out in a lineup.

GERTRUDE: Well, did he do it?

HENRY: Yes, but that's not the point. Seeing his picture and then seeing him rob her made the identification easier.

GERTRUDE: What are the odds of Isabel ending up in a lineup anyway?

HENRY: Better than you'd think. Can I get you anything else, Mom?

GERTRUDE: I could use a nightcap.

HENRY: You had wine with dinner.

GERTRUDE: That was two hours ago, Henry.

HENRY: Would you like more wine? I don't think you finished the bottle.

GERTRUDE: No. I would like a proper drink.

HENRY: I think I saw some sweet vermouth in the pantry.[2]

GERTRUDE: So, how have things been going with this imaginary girlfriend of yours?

HENRY: Fine. You will meet her tomorrow.

GERTRUDE: So do you see wedding bells in your future?

HENRY: I can't imagine Izzy approving of any ceremony involving bells.

GERTRUDE: Have you talked about children?

HENRY: I would rather not have this discussion.

GERTRUDE: So you haven't talked to her?

HENRY: How's Edna?

GERTRUDE: Dead. Last spring.

HENRY: Tragic.

GERTRUDE: She was eighty-eight. Why haven't you talked about kids? It seems like it would come up eventually.

HENRY: We have peppermint schnapps.

GERTRUDE: Why on Earth do you have schnapps?[3]

A subtle intervention was required. Both the conversation and beverage offerings had to be rerouted. I slipped down the stairs and used my mobile. He picked up on the third ring.

"Hello."

"It's me," I said.

"I know."

"How's everything going?"

---

[2] Believe me, we've got more than sweet vermouth. A rich client gave me a bottle of Glenlivet after a particularly tiresome investigation. I hide the good stuff from Henry since he's always offering it to uninvited guests (Bernie Peterson) and other unsavory types (my family).

[3] Excellent question.

"Fine."

"Good."

"Do you have a new ETA?"

"Not just yet. But I thought of something. If your mom wants a drink, there's a bottle of whiskey in my closet inside a green rain boot."

"Why?"

"I like whiskey. Why?"

"Forget it."

"Feel free to offer her some."

"Okay. Anything else?"

"Yes. I'm missing the other boot. So if you see it around, let me know."

"Good-bye, Isabel."

I decided that sitting in a stairwell all night eavesdropping on a conversation in my own home was undignified, so I searched the office for a recording device that I could plant just outside the door. Then I could listen from the luxury of the office. Much more dignified.

I began searching my desk, which is essentially a receptacle for every item that I considered might someday come in useful or I didn't know how to recycle. It's also littered with an unruly number of thumbtacks, old candies, and expired electronic equipment, which might very well be emanating hazardous radio waves.

I stabbed myself a few times with an escaped pushpin and tried to recall my last tetanus shot. I tell you this only so that you understand that my guard was compromised, which gave Henry plenty of time to sneak down the stairs in his slippers and enter the in-law unit without my knowledge. Just when I spotted a listening device from circa 1992 in the nether reaches of the bottomless desk, Henry entered the office.

I shot out of the chair, spun around, and aimed the tape recorder as if it were a switchblade. As my heart rate slowed to a solid thud, I slumped back into my chair. "You scared me."

"Is that all you have to say for yourself?" Henry replied.

I searched the cluttered office and the equally cramped recesses of my mind and came up empty.

"Yep."

"I'll see you in five minutes. Please enter through the front door. Forget it, any door will do."

Complaining about potential in-laws does appear to be as solid an American pastime as, for example, baseball, and while I was prepared for all sorts of criticism to both pitch and bat away, I had almost none. Gertrude, who goes by "Gerty" and fully acknowledges that it's not much of an improvement, was quite possibly the exact opposite of what I expected. To put it bluntly, I expected an older, female version of Henry, which somehow didn't translate well in my mind.

Gerty had a lovely long mop of gray hair, loosely clipped back off her neck. She wore a pair of baggy blue jeans and an oversized men's striped shirt. Several bracelets dangled from her wrist, and she wore a collection of mismatched necklaces and large hoop earrings. When she smiled, she was usually laughing, and deep creases formed around her mouth. Starbursts of crow's-feet framed her eyes. She wasn't fighting her age, which somehow made her seem much younger than her sixty-eight years. I spotted only a hint of makeup on her face—red lipstick, faded over the day. I noted chipped nail polish and a shirt that was wrinkled from sitting in luggage, I suspect. I suddenly realized that Henry's control gene, his fetish for order, his solid intensity, did not come from this woman. Gerty was relaxed and free and blind to the bread crumbs on the table. She was also better company than most of the company I invite over of my own free will.

For the most part, she asked random questions without any pointed prying. She told bizarre and hilarious anecdotes of Henry's childhood. When he first discovered there was a number you could dial that would tell you precisely what time of day it was, he called the number every morning and set all the clocks in the house to the correct time. Even the slightly unreliable wind-up watches in their home were virtually always on the nose.

A few hours had passed and all the good booze was gone (mind you, there wasn't much left in the boot when we started). Gerty suggested a beer run. Henry suggested that we had both had enough to drink; his mother then shot eye-daggers at her son and told him it was past his bed-time (which it was). Henry was in bed by midnight and, based on anec-dotal history, asleep by 12:05. I think that's one of the benefits of having a clear conscience.

I was looking forward to a few more hours of quality time with Gerty, drinking and getting more of the inside scoop on Ex #13. I was not surprised to learn that Henry played the trombone in the marching band and tried to start a Young Republicans club when he was ten. Gerty grounded him for a week, after which he saw the error of his ways. I asked if Henry resembled his father since he clearly did not take after Gerty, and she confirmed that he was the spitting image—in both appearance and character—of William Stone. I had an army of questions on the tip of my tongue, but Gerty fired back and twisted the conversation in the direction I'd been sidestepping all night.

"Let's be serious for a moment, Isabel."

Serious is seriously not my thing, but I was being polite for the guest and didn't mention that.

"Sure. Okay."

And then Gerty asked me the questions that she had been asking Henry during my interrupted reconnaissance mission. As you might expect, I didn't have the answers. I looked at my watch and announced that it was past my bedtime.

"Next time, just tell me to mind my own business," Gerty said.

"Would that have worked?"

"Sleep tight."

Easy for her to say. My conscience hasn't been clear for thirty years.[4]

I slipped into bed as stealthily as possible. Apparently not stealthily enough. The moment I rested my head on the pillow, Henry stirred and then mumbled.

"How long are you going to play this game?" he asked.

---

[4] Age four: the year of the permanent markers.

THE WEEKLY SUMMIT

We originally called it a company meeting, but my father thought the tone wasn't quite professional enough and redubbed our Friday-afternoon powwows as the Weekly Summit in the futile hope that these hour-long gatherings would stop tumbling into low-rent group therapy sessions. During the weekly summits we discuss new cases, handle any in-house disputes (which can be quite numerous for an organization that pays only three full-time employees and one part-timer), and organize the workload for the week ahead.

I've never attended a summit in which at least one party didn't have a private agenda, and this week was no exception. Once the family nick-names were doled out (and protested) and the code-phrase clinical trial voted in,[1] I took the floor with what I believed was a valid argument that would undoubtedly be persuasive.

After a full review of the Vivien Blake case, I wanted it disappeared. I believe in privacy even though it is my job to invade it. While I have on occasion breached my own code of ethics for my work, the Vivien Blake case gave me pause more than any other. If she were to learn of her parents'

---

[1] The original vote was 2-2, but Demetrius jumped ship when he was threatened with a nickname.

betrayal—and no matter how you cloak it, a betrayal it was—that relationship could be destroyed forever. There is a sharp distinction between being under direct scrutiny by your parents and being scrutinized by an agent of your parents. One is a family matter; the other is harassment.

Since I had lost the vote when the original discussion took place, it was only at the summit that I learned that Rae was to become the primary operative on the case. Aside from the case being at odds with the whole keeping-Rae-focused-on-her-schoolwork agenda, the method of the investigation struck me as ethically dubious. This wasn't a simple surveillance job; we were planting an undercover operative in Vivien Blake's world. With Rae, the perfect collegiate mole, Vivien would never know that she was being watched. That's always the goal, of course. But usually, subjects at least have a fighting chance of figuring out they're under investigation. Vivien had been a minor only six months ago. I believe in the folly of youth. I believe in rebellion and questioning authority and I even believe it's okay to commit a few misdemeanors now and again. "Try to steer clear of felonies" is my motto.[2] But Vivien wasn't being given the chance to sow her wild oats. Speaking from a point of authority, it's best to get that shit out of the way when you're young.

I just assumed I'd have an ally in my sister on this subject. I was shocked when she studied the file and agreed to the case without even a moment of doubt.

"Rae, don't you have a problem with this?" I asked.

"No," Rae flatly replied.

"Why not?"

"Because surveillance is part of the job," Rae replied.

"She's only eighteen," I said.

"And instead of moving into a dormitory like your average freshman, she chooses to rent an apartment in San Francisco. That's a lot of responsibility for a girl that age," Mom said.

"It's still not a valid reason to take the case."

---

[2] In fact, that will be the title of my memoirs, should I ever write them.

"This isn't a time to turn down work," Dad said.

"It's not all about money," I said.

At this point Rae turned to Demetrius and said, "Ignore her. It's almost always about money."

Demetrius then made a show of looking at his watch. "Time for my lunch break," he said, escaping the final scraps of the meeting.

I turned to my sister, trying to find a way to reach her. "What would you do if Mom and Dad hired someone to follow you?"

"I'd shake him and get on with my day," she replied.

"You *really* don't have a problem with this?" I asked again.

"Nope."

It was then that I finally accepted that Vivien Blake wasn't going anywhere, or more specifically, wherever Vivien Blake was going, we were going to know about it.

In a weak retaliation against my sister's alignment with the unit, I tried to burrow down to the core of the David/Rae mystery dispute.

"Rae, why don't you tell Mom and Dad about the prostitution ring you were running out of David's house?" I said.

"They know why I was kicked out," Rae replied.

"Oh yeah? Why?" I asked.

No answer. I cleared my throat.

"Anyone planning on answering my question?" I asked.

"I thought everyone knew," Dad replied.

"No, not everyone," I said.

"She was dipping into his liquor supply," Dad replied, trying to look appropriately concerned, but since dipping into the liquor supply is the equivalent of littering in the alternate universe of Spellman crimes, his expression belied the intended sentiment. Rae was getting a tap on the wrist and it was for a crime she did not commit.

"Is that what David told you?" I asked.

"I thought the punishment was a bit harsh," Dad said. "But his home, his rules."

"Huh," I said, watching my sister aimlessly shuffle papers on her desk to avoid my gaze.

I sent my sister a quick text message.

I'm onto you.

Get a life.

In the last five minutes of the summit we split the office work and delegated the surveillance cases. Mom and Dad took the case of the Man in the Library; I took the Lady in the Navy-Blue Suit; Rae, as predetermined, studied the file of the Girl with the Rap Sheet; and per my agreement with Mom, Walter Perkins was all mine. As for Demetrius, he steered clear of all surveillance assignments. "Call me crazy," he once said, "but following white people around doesn't sound like the wisest pastime for an ex-con." I told him he didn't know what he was missing. He argued that he did, since he used to case joints when he was a TV thief. To each his own. I couldn't help but feel a tinge of excitement over the broad scope of our new casework; aside from the break in monotony, it provided me with some excellent quality time away from the office, and hence, my family.

However, other people's families were a different story. As I drove home from work, I found that I was almost looking forward to another evening with Gertrude Stone.

She was out cold (or napping as some people call it) on the living room couch but woke as soon as I arrived home (through the front door, no less). The moment she saw me, she rubbed the sleep out of her eyes, got to her feet, and said, "Let's get out of here."

"What have you got in mind?" I asked.

"A friend of yours called and invited us to the grand reopening of the Philosopher's Club."

"What friend?"

"I'm afraid I didn't catch his name."

"Did he have an Irish accent?"

"No."

"Are you sure?" I asked.

"I dated a mick once; I know what they sound like."

Automatically assuming that Milo was back in town, I couldn't help but feel a sudden shift in my personal weather. Was it possible that Ex-boyfriend #12 (Connor O'Sullivan) had skipped town and returned the bar to its rightful owner, which meant that I could become a rightful patron once again?

"Let's go," I said, calling a cab. I had a feeling that neither of us would be in any condition to drive after we knocked back a few.

"I'll leave a note for Henry," Gertrude said.

The note read: *Isabel and I are not here. Love, Mom.*

Twenty minutes later, feeling a surprisingly pleasant buzz of anticipation at the prospect of seeing my old friend Milo, Gerty and I entered the dim cave of the Philosopher's Club. The familiar scent of hops and dishrags brought back comforting memories. I looked to the end of the bar, and whatever hint of a smile had begun to surface faded quickly. The bartender, on the other hand, was all aglow when he saw me. "Ain't you a sight for sore eyes," he said.

"You're back," was my only reply.

"You betcha," he said. "Bernie's back for good."

The next thing I knew, I was trapped in a bear hug and I couldn't get out.

EDWARD SLAYTER

Monday morning at eight A.M., I began my surveillance of subject Edward Slayter. I sipped coffee and sat in my car three doors down from his home and waited for him to depart for the day. According to Mrs. Slayter, he had a board meeting at nine A.M. His driver would pick him up somewhere around eight thirty. At eight twenty-five, a black Town Car drove up to the Slayter residence in Pacific Heights. A male driver in a black suit and tie left the car double-parked, idling in the middle of the street.[1] Since the Slayters have a fat driveway, especially for San Francisco, I found this behavior particularly irksome. However, the Town Car was not left idling for long. Not quite forty-five seconds after subject's driver rang the Slayters' doorbell, Mr. Slayter strode down his driveway and got into the backseat of the car.

Edward Slayter was described by his spouse as a handsome, fifty-five-year-old male, with short-cropped salt-and-pepper hair, with an athletic but not overly muscular build. The clinical nature of her description struck me as a bit odd. Spouses usually add humanizing details—he has a scar on his chin from when he fell out of a tree as a child; there's a mole above his

---

[1] If I were a lawmaker, double-parking would be on par with aggravated assault and grand larceny.

eyebrow that he talks about having removed every now and then; he has an ever-so-slightly receding hairline, which he monitors religiously. But Mrs. Slayter added no personal flourish to the portrait of her husband. The only unnecessary detail she added was that his walk was always brisk, as though he were in a perpetual rush. Since Mr. Slayter was a busy man with many fiscal responsibilities, this detail seemed extraneous.

My instructions were simple, too simple: Monitor subject's activities. If they strayed from his reported schedule I was to promptly notify Mrs. Slayter via text message. Typically, further documentation is requested—photographs, videos, and written reports. I asked Mrs. Slayter if she was interested in any of that and after a brief, reflective pause, she said, "I don't believe that will be necessary at this time."

The driver zigzagged across side streets to South Van Ness Avenue, one of the primary veins that run through the city, and turned south. The dense morning traffic forced me to keep a close tail, which is always problematic if you're following a subject who is expecting a tail. As far as I could tell, neither the driver nor the subject took much notice of the navy-blue Buick that was never farther than two cars behind them.

As expected, the Town Car pulled up in front of 111 Market Street. Mr. Slayter did not wait for the driver to open his door. He was one of that rare breed of rich folk who still know how to open and close car doors all on their own. Subject leaned into the car again and spoke briefly to the driver. Subject closed the door and the Town Car pulled back onto Market Street and disappeared into the distance. Subject then entered the building, but not without first holding the door for a few other pedestrians.

Street parking in downtown San Francisco requires good karma or ESP, as far as I'm concerned, so I never even consider it an option. I found a ridiculously pricey garage nearby and gave the attendant an exorbitant tip to keep my car near the exit. Then I sat on a stoop outside the building and opened a book to kill time. It was a slow death. The next time I checked my watch, only an hour had passed. I returned to my reading until I felt a shadow above me.

"Do you like chess?" a middle-aged man in a shabby wool sweater that smelled of body odor and, I think, one of those pine-tree air fresheners you get at the car wash asked with a wide grin on his face. He was missing a tooth, which as far as I could tell was better off than the ones that remained.

"Excuse me?" I said, trying to breathe through my mouth.

"Do you like chess?"

"No," I flatly replied.

"That's funny," he said, smiling.

"Why is it funny?"

"Because you're reading a book on chess."

"Oh, I get it."

"See, it's funny."

"I don't find it as funny as you do," I replied.

"Would you like to play?"

"Play what?"

"Chess."

"I just told you I don't like the game. Why would I want to play?"

"If you don't like chess why are you carrying a chess book around?"

"Because my boyfriend wants me to like it."

"But you don't."

"I don't."

"Have you told him?"

"He thinks we should have some common activities."

"That makes sense. Can't you pick something else?" he asked.

"That's the problem. There really isn't anything else."

"I see," he said. "But you like him?"

"Of course."

"Did you like him right away or did it take a while?"

"It took a while," I replied, suddenly feeling awkward having such an intimate discussion with a stranger.

"Sometimes it takes a while to like chess. Also playing it is more fun than reading about it."

"That's true about almost anything."

"So, do you want to play?"

"You've got a chessboard on you?"

"Always."

"Huh."

"Just a friendly game."

"What would make it an unfriendly game?"

"I don't know; it's just a saying."

I checked my watch and the entrance to 111 Market. Twelve forty-five P.M.

Mr. Slayter had told his wife that after his noon meeting he was likely to have lunch at a downtown restaurant. The man with the unfortunate tooth decay took my silence as acquiescence and promptly pulled a board and a jangling felt pouch out of his canvas bag. He took a seat next to me and began setting up his ivory army.

"Okay," I said. "But if my friend shows up, I'll have to run, even if we're in the middle of the game."

"Charles Black," the man said. "My friends call me Charlie. But I always play white, so don't let my name confuse you."

"I should warn you, Mr. Black, I'm not very good at this."

"Call me Charlie," he said.

"Okay, Charlie."

"What should I call you?"

"Jane."

"That's easy to remember."

"I know," I said. That's why I picked it.

One hour later, Charlie had apparently broken all of his previous chess records by winning ten games in a row. In fact, one of those games,

Charlie explained,[2] was called a fool's checkmate, a rare and laugh-
ably quick win that almost never happens, even when playing the most
amateurish opponent. I congratulated Charlie for my impressive defeat and was saved from future humiliation when I saw Edward Slayter
leaving the building. Mr. Slayter stood alone on the threshold of the
skyscraper doors and scanned the area as if he were looking for a tail.
In fact, he looked right at me and then moved on. Eventually he pulled
a piece of paper from his pocket and began walking up Montgomery
Street.

"That's my friend," I said to Charlie as I got to my feet.

"That's your friend?" Charlie said with a sprinkling of concern.

"Yes. I have to go," I said, tossing my bag over my shoulder.

"But he didn't wave or anything," Charlie said, still with the concern.

"We're the kind of friends who don't wave," I said.

"Oh. I see," Charlie said politely.

"See you around," I said. And then I waved.

Charlie waved back and smiled; I hoped he didn't read too much into
that wave.

Mr. Slayter's next appointment was not lunch. If you're thinking I have a
scandalous tale to tell involving hookers, loan sharks, bookies, or even a
mistress, let me set you straight. Mr. Slayter had a doctor's appointment,
plain and simple. This was easy to verify since he entered a building that
required signing in at a security desk. I don't often mention this fact, but
terrorists have made some parts of my job quite a bit easier. I probably
won't mention that again.

Since I was to inform Mrs. Slayter if Edward deviated at all from his
plans, I sent her a text message with the information gleaned from this remarkably dull surveillance. Ten minutes later Mrs. Slayter sent me a reply,

---

[2] I hadn't yet gotten to it in any of my reading material.

thanking me for my hard work and suggesting I conclude the surveillance for the day.

I returned to Spellman Investigations headquarters and was surprised to find a vacated office. Instead of taking advantage of the peace and quiet and catching up on work, I decided to head down to the basement and catch some Zs on the cot. I'd had yet another barn burner of a night with Gerty. She seemed to have taken a shine to the Philosopher's Club. Frankly, I didn't know how much longer I could keep up with her. Even I usually stay in on a Sunday night.

TRAPPED . . . AGAIN

Some people don't learn lessons as quickly as others do. The Spellman basement has been home to a wild variety of punishments spanning close to three decades of my life. In my early youth, my parents would stage military-like interviews to find out the truth behind the finger paint on the walls or the sticky/sweet substance that now lived in the carpet. I suppose the methodology is the same whether you're interrogating a war criminal or a second grader. Remove all forms of distraction, create an uncomfortable environment (dim lighting, rickety chairs), and starve the person of natural light—for a child, even five minutes works.

My point is that I've endured many uncomfortable situations in that room.

Then again, sometimes you need a nap and the room is as dark as a high-quality hotel room and people leave you alone in there and so you sleep and then you wake up and you overhear a conversation and you can't leave the room until the relevant parties have finished the conversation and left the office, so they don't know you've heard it. And the next thing you know, four hours have passed. When you do finally escape, you have to jump through the office window and you scratch your arm on the way out and you start to wonder if you're getting too old for this sort of thing. You think one of these days the urge that you've been tussling with your whole life—the need to get to the bottom of everything—will fade out. But it hasn't yet and you wonder if maybe you need to take a more proactive approach and maybe you think it might be time to go back to the shrink. Then your train of thought is interrupted by Mr. Peabody next door, who has just witnessed your defenestration and is giving you that look he always does. You take your sleeve to the windowsill and pretend you're dusting and then you walk along the side of the house to the front door and enter.

I found my father foraging in the refrigerator. My mother was planted on the couch, which provides a direct view of all activities in the kitchen. Dad once suggested a rearrangement of living room furniture and I eventually came to realize that it was so that any couch dwellers couldn't keep up with kitchen activities. He went so far as to solicit the services of our gardener to help him move the couch. Gardener's services were solicited again when my mother returned home, insisting that things remain in their rightful place. Mom's not too obsessed with the location of household furniture (though she's rearranged the office at least ten times in the past twenty years in an effort to improve work production), so I suspect she was onto him right away. Dad pouted the rest of the day.

I watched my father watch my mother out of the corner of his eye as he used the refrigerator door to block Mom's view and grab a cookie off of a baking sheet on top of the stove. Dad slipped back into the office, where I followed him. "Not one word," Dad said as he dug into the cookie. A quizzical expression flashed across his face as he consumed the baked good. "This is excellent," Dad said. "Why is D so hit-and-miss with his baking?"

"Why don't you ask him?" I replied, knowing the answer.

"That would be rude."

"What's new?" I asked. I asked that because after overhearing Mom and Dad's conversation, I knew that something was new.

"Not much," Dad replied.

"When I say 'What's new' I'm not just referring to what might be new in your life, but more like is there something I should know?"

"I love you," Dad said, eating his cookie.

"No, that's not it," I replied.

"When somebody tells you they love you, you should say 'I love you' back."

"I love you, Dad. So, anything you want to tell me?"

"Um, I think you're doing a good job."

"Thanks, so nothing's new?" I asked again, hoping my repetition would become tiresome enough to result in an answer.

"Since the last time you asked, I finished the cookie," Dad said.

"If that's how you want to play it," I replied.

"What's new with you, Isabel?" Dad asked.

"Nothing," I replied. "Absolutely nothing."

Two hours earlier

Now might be a good time to describe that conversation I overheard, which caused me to be trapped in the basement, followed by a window escape and an extremely unsuccessful Dad interrogation.

Footsteps and fuzzy voices overhead woke me from a fitful nap. I climbed the basement stairs but stopped short at the door. I didn't want to interrupt the clearly private conversation between the unit. It went something like this.

MOM: Do you have an ETA?
DAD: Not yet. But soon.
MOM: I still think it's a bad idea.
DAD: We have no other option.

70

MOM: I understand.

DAD: We'll get through it.

MOM: We'll see.

DAD: We've been through worse.

MOM: You sure about that?

DAD: I have it under control.

MOM: Al, at some point you might have to make a choice.

DAD: I know. And I'll make the right one.

Believe me, I've tried direct questioning on many occasions; it's never been a successful route for me to take. That conversation could have been about anything—financial difficulties, an issue with a client, or even marital problems. I hid in the basement because I didn't want to tip off my parents, but I knew something was going on—something very serious indeed.

I left my father in the office to digest his illicit cookie and returned to the dining room, where I found D watching his afternoon soap (a habit that apparently started thirteen years ago in prison) and my mother indulging in her latest hobby.

"Mom, what are you doing?"

"Checking out some online dating sites," she replied.

"That's generally frowned upon when you're married," I said.

"For D," Mom said, maintaining her gaze on the computer screen.

"He'll never agree to it," I said.

"Already has," Mom smugly replied. Mom waited until she heard the blast of a commercial to directly interrupt D. "D, what's the tallest woman you'd date?"

"Surprise me," D replied, decidedly uninterested in the endeavor.

"Six-three?"

"Why not?"

Mom studied the candidate's profile and shook her head. "Forget it. She'll only date water signs."

It seemed that intrigue was popping up like spring flowers that day. There was no good reason D would allow my mother to set him up on dates. Perhaps this was one mystery I could get to the bottom of. I plopped down on the couch and gazed at the TV screen. D's soap never interested me much—there was way too much history to catch up on (and no appendix to help you out), but I feigned interest.

"So . . . um . . . did things work out between that guy with the awful tan—Blake, that was his name—and that woman with the eye patch?"

"Christina?"

"Is there more than one woman on the show with an eye patch?"

"No."

"So, how are things with Blake and Christina?"

"Why the sudden interest?"

"Why the sudden suspicion?"

"You don't care about my program," D said. "Something else is on your mind."

"Fair enough," I replied. "But you can say that about anything. I mean, don't you currently have something else on your mind besides your program?"

"Yes," D said. "How I can get you to leave me in peace for just fifteen more minutes."

"Done."

I sat in silence and watched another orange-hued male and tangerine-shaded woman conspire in a murder plot against a wealthy heiress with vertigo. Apparently, the plan was to knock her down a flight of stairs, which would be plausible under the circumstances. D shushed me when I asked how they'd benefit from the crime. When the show finally ended, he explained that the orange man was married to the old lady with vertigo.

"That's kind of gross, don't you think?"

"Love is deaf, dumb, and blind."

"And orange, apparently," I said.

"Excuse me?"

"Why does everyone have a fake tan?" I asked the universe.

But D answered: "I long ago stopped trying to figure out half of the weird shit white people do to themselves. Any other questions I can fail to answer for you?"

"Yeah. Do you need some backup with my mom?"

"Excuse me?"

"The whole Internet dating thing," I whispered. "Clearly, she's manipulating you in some capacity. I can have her taken care of, if you know what I mean."

"Is it so hard to believe I might want to go on a date after being in prison for fifteen years?"

"No, but handing over the reins to my mom is."

"It's a jungle out there. I'm just allowing her to clear away some of the brush."

"So, how's it been going?" I asked, trying to change the tenor of the conversation from interrogative to interested.

"I've met a number of nice ladies."

"So, approximately how many nice ladies have you met?"

"I've been on four dates so far."

"How many second dates?" I asked.

"None."

"Interesting."

"I haven't met anyone special yet."

"Is that code for 'they were all crazy'?" I asked. "That's what you get when you let my mother pick your dates. Now, if you gave me a shot at it . . ."

"I'm officially ending this conversation," D said.[1]

---

[1] He learned it from me.

"But I have some helpful suggestions."

"And I have a job to do," D said, returning to the office.

I followed my mother into the kitchen and was about to tackle another branch of the investigation when she gave me the slip with a question of her own.

"When were you going to tell me that Henry's mother is in town?"

"After she left," I replied.

"You weren't planning on introducing us?"

"Not really."

"Why? Are you ashamed of us?"

"Of course I am."

"Very funny, Isabel. I invited Henry and Gertrude over for Sunday dinner. Any special requests?"

"Order in."

"You can come too, if you like."

"I'll think it over," I replied.

"I have to decide between inviting David and Rae. Do you have a preference?"

"Why is it either/or?"

"David won't come if Rae is here."

"Seriously?"

"It's worse than I thought," my mother said.

"It's worse than *I* thought," I said.

"Do you know what happened?" Mom asked.

"No idea. You?"

"Well, obviously, it has nothing to do with the liquor cabinet. I'm not in the mood to play *Sophie's Choice* yet again, so you tell me who to invite."

"David," I quickly replied. "Get him sloshed and maybe he'll talk."

"I like the way you think," Mom said. "Well, I'd love to stay and explore the many angles of my children's dysfunction, but I'm late for my class,"

Mom said as she slipped her arm through the straps of a canvas bag and made her way to the door.

"What's in the bag, Mom?"

"I don't believe that's any of your concern," she said, waving a cheery good-bye.

I promptly entered the office and got to the bottom of at least one matter. Well, not quite the bottom. Somewhere in the middle, I suppose.

"Dad, I'll keep that cookie secret, even the next one, if you tell me what 'class'[2] Mom is heading to right now."

Dad pulled a calendar from his desk and said, "Let me check her schedule. What day is it?"

"Monday," D answered.

"Monday is sculpting," Dad said. "And book club once a month."

"Give me that," I said, approaching his desk.

Dad reluctantly handed me the calendar. I don't believe he was under any directive not to provide this intelligence, but he was under a directive not to eat baked goods.

I was shocked to discover a traffic jam of "leisure" activities on the calendar, all in blue ink, blanketing the page like a tidal wave. There was virtually no time unaccounted for beyond work hours. I made a photocopy of the page and returned it to my father. I provide for you now my mother's hobby schedule for the month of September.

Monday, 6–9 P.M., Beginning Pottery; 8:00 P.M., book club
    (second Monday of month)
Tuesday, 5–6 P.M., yoga; 7–10 P.M., Russian 101
Wednesday, 6:30–8 P.M., crochet[3]
Thursday, 7:30–10:30 P.M., Tarting It Up
    [fret not; it was a cooking class]

---

[2] Finger quotes were required.
[3] Her script was sloppy, so it could have been "croquet."

Friday, 7:30–9 P.M., Music Appreciation

Saturday, 9–10 A.M., yoga; 11 A.M.–1 P.M., decoupage

Sunday, 9 A.M.–12 P.M., volunteer work; 2–3 P.M., tennis;

    5–6 P.M., prep for family dinner

I had so many questions that it was impossible to unite them in any semblance of logic or order. I simply chose them at random like scraps of paper tossed in a hat.

"What the fuck is decoupage?" was the first to surface.

"Some kind of craft thing," Dad replied.

"It's the technique of decorating with cutouts from a newspaper or magazine on a flat surface and coating with a layer of finish," D explained.

"I'm confused. Why would somebody do that?"

"I did it in prison once or twice in art class. It was kind of relaxing."

"In prison, the point is to kill time. I wouldn't be surprised if you took a knitting class as well."

"Knitting would have been very popular," D replied. "And dangerous."

"Since when does Mom volunteer?" was the next question that fought through the competing interrogatives.

"She's worked at the food bank on a few occasions."

"Dad, what's going on?" I asked. "It isn't like Mom to have outside interests."

"She's been taking yoga with me for the last few years," Dad replied.

"That's to make *you* go to yoga."

"What's the harm in your mother having a hobby or two?"

"She's booked solid."

"She promised me she'd drop a few after the first couple of weeks."

"You don't think she's up to something?" I said.

"She's taking some classes to broaden her horizons."

"Russian!"

"Spanish was at a bad time," my father nonchalantly replied.

"You know more than you're saying."

76

"Maybe you should get a few extracurricular activities of your own. Then maybe you won't be so preoccupied with your mother's."

"I have extracurricular activities," I smugly replied.

"I'm sorry," Dad said. "I forgot you play the Game of Kings. How's that working out for you?"

KING, QUEEN, CASTLE, HORSE

Three months earlier

"What did you do?" Henry asked as he returned from the kitchen.

"I took your castle with my horse."

Henry sat his cup of chamomile next to my whiskey beside the chessboard. "Please call the pieces by their appropriate names."

Sigh.

"What is the horsey called?" he asked in a condescending tone.

"Um . . . knight."

"And the castle?"

"I'm drawing a blank."

"Rook."

"Oh yeah."

"What did you do?"

"I took your rook with my knight."

Henry studied the chessboard.

"First of all, if you're going to take thirty minutes to decide on your next move, the least you can do is wait for me to return to the table before you steal my rook."

"Steal? Is that the proper language for the game?"

"It is when you're cheating."

"I didn't cheat."

"This isn't poker, Isabel. You need to show some good sportsmanship."

"We've met before, right?"

"I'm going to let the rook-stealing slide just this once."

"Thanks."

"Check," Henry said, and the game was over.

The three previous times we played chess together, Henry had made me study the endgame. To ensure that this would not happen again, I slid my arm across the board and knocked the pieces back into the box.

"Once again, I'd like to remind you that the only reason we're playing chess is because your dentist overbooked one day."

This is, in fact, truer than you can imagine. An emergency root canal was to blame for my current state of forced chess study and weekly losses. Henry was trapped in the waiting room of one Daniel Castillo, DDS's office without any of his own reading material. Dr. Castillo (Ex #11) had left the magazine subscription duties to his full-time office manager, who has an unnatural fondness for trashy rags. The options were Hollywood tabloids or women's magazines. Henry read, cover to cover, an issue of a magazine geared toward women in their thirties on a nose-diving mission for marriage, called *Me*.[2] (So, if you're talking to your friend about the magazine, you'd say, "Hey, have you read the latest *Me Squared*?") One of the many articles he read (which included an astrological fashion assessment)[1] was a piece on relationship compatibility that strongly encouraged the sharing of each other's activities. Turns out Henry and I, up to that point, had not shared any activities besides watching *Doctor Who*

---

[1] Which, logically, should have crippled the magazine's credibility.
[2] This is not a footnote.

and debating the many issues on which we do not concur. I debated that the debating alone offered us plenty of shared experience, but Henry stood his ground and demanded that we each choose an activity that we could do together.

I didn't choose, thinking this phase would blow over. But when Henry bought me a book called *Chess for Imbeciles*, I realized how serious this had become. My only response was retaliation. I chose beer tasting as my hobby. This, as far as I was concerned, meant going to a dive bar and drinking beer.

Henry, however, had a more lofty approach and would often arrange tours at local microbreweries. If you ask me, listening to someone lecture you about why beer tastes the way it does kind of takes the fun out of drinking it. Plus, when they say "tasting" they're dead serious about that. You're lucky if you can get a pint in you after a three-hour tour.

But I digress. Much to my dismay, when I returned home that night, I found Gertrude and Henry in the midst of what appeared to be an intense and evenly matched game of chess.

"What's going on here?" I asked, feeling a bit betrayed by Gerty.

"Just a friendly game," Henry said.

"Why do people always have to add the word 'friendly'?" I asked.

"To remind people like you not to cheat," Henry replied, sliding his bishop across the board and taking his mother's knight.

"You can always forfeit, Gerty, and then we can go get a drink."

"This won't take long," Gerty replied, taking Henry's rook.

"He hates losing his rook," I said, taking a spectator seat.

"I especially hate it when it's taken by a pawn three rows down when I'm not looking."

"I wouldn't have pegged you for a chess player," I said to Gerty without bothering to hide my disappointment.

"I'm not."

"And yet you seem to be decent at it," I replied, judging purely by the mass of Henry's material[3] by the side of the board.

"Henry's father taught me ages ago. I got tired of losing so I began taking lessons with a grand master. I decided that one day I was going to win, no matter what it took."

"How long did that take?" I asked.

"Seven long years," Gertrude replied. "Check."

While Henry stared at the board, attempting to retrace the series of moves that derailed him, Gerty got up from the table, grabbed her coat, and said, "Izzy and I are going to grab a drink. Care to join us?"

"Again?" Henry asked. "You went out last night. I think you could use a night in, Isabel."

I couldn't risk the exposure of a night alone with Henry; he had that look he gets when he wants to have an *adult* conversation. I was going to stick with my usual—the Avoidance Method™.[4]

"I think I could go out again," I said.

"Dad phoned earlier. Did you call him back?" Henry said.

"I'll do it tomorrow," Gerty replied. "He's probably asleep by now."

"Don't stay out too late," Henry said.

"Don't wait up," Gerty replied.

---

[3] Chess term. Just a fancy word for "pieces," that's all.
[4] I know, I know: Henry's a great catch and I don't deserve him. I've heard it all before. Do me a favor and mind your own business.

THE FOURTH WALL

O ne of the many benefits of Rae's reduced workload is a reduction in the time that I must spend in her company. She surfaces only on Fridays for the summit and the occasional Sunday-night dinner, which have been less religiously enforced since the arrival of Sydney.[1] The next time Rae showed up at the office, she was once again wearing the doctored $$ JUSTICE 4 MERRI-WEATHER $$ T-shirt. D tried to ignore her by avoiding eye contact, which I've noticed is effective with some animals but not so many people, and definitely not Rae.

"Have you had time to read the material I sent you?" Rae asked D.

D, not looking up from his computer, replied, "Been busy."

"You should look it over, D. You're running out of time. The statute of limitations on a malicious prosecution case is two years. You've got six months left. But the waiting doesn't look good. You lose credibility."

"Thank you, Rae," D firmly replied. "If I wish to discuss this matter further, I will contact Maggie. Do we understand each other?"

"Is there a subtext I'm missing?" Rae asked.

D finally looked her straight in the eye. "I don't want to have this conversation with you again. If I choose to pursue this matter, which is un-

---

[1] One day, when she knows a few more words, I will formally thank her.

82

likely, I will discuss it with my attorney, not a college girl who checks her stock portfolio every hour. Now, do we understand each other?"

"What have you got against money?"

"That will be all, Rae," my mother said with a note of finality in her voice. On occasion Mom adds a certain edge to her tone and you just instinctually know not to cross it.

Rae quietly returned to her desk and got back to work.

The Sparrow got a new nickname after a week of being tailed by the Weasel.

"The Sparrow's a snore. I thought this case had some juice," Rae said, sounding like an old cop from a bad TV show. An hour after the Demetrius incident, Rae submitted her first surveillance report on Vivien Blake and was clearly nonplussed by the coed's bland freshman behavior. Apparently, Vivien went to class, the library, an occasional movie, sometimes a coffee shop, and *one* party, at which she imbibed exactly two beers.

"The least she could do is take some hallucinogens like everybody else at Berkeley," Rae said.

My father shot my mother a concerned glance, which my mother nodded away.

"Relax. She's just messing with you, Al."

My father then perused the file and furrowed his brow. Of all our current cases, one might have expected Vivien Blake's to offer at least a shred of indecency.

"How do you know she had two beers?" I asked.

"Because I was also at the party."

"You crashed a party to follow a suspect?" I asked.

"What were my options?" Rae said.

"Did you make any new friends?" Dad asked.

"I was on the job," Rae replied.

"How many drinks did you have?" I asked.

"Only two."

"Young lady, you're still underage," said one member of the unit. I can't recall which.

"I had to blend in."

"Club soda and cranberry juice looks just like a sea breeze," Mom suggested, sounding ridiculously prim.

"If you keep following her into parties, she's going to make you," I said.

"Maybe that's the way to go. I befriend her and then I can give you the inside scoop."

"*Absolutely not,*" Dad said. "This is not some undercover DEA operation. It's a simple surveillance. If you can't maintain the standards that we've imparted to you over the past . . . how many years—"

"Fourteen," Rae replied, sounding positively bored.[2]

"—then we'll take you off the case," Dad said.

"I got it," Rae said.

"Maybe we should tell the Blakes that there's nothing there. It's a lot of money to spend on a fishing expedition in a swimming pool," Mom said. I could tell the company bookkeeper and the sympathetic parent with fiscal responsibilities were in an internal war.

"Give it another week," Dad said.

"Okay," Rae replied. "Can I go now?"

"You have more important places to be?" Mom asked.

"Always."

"I remember when this job used to be your life," Mom said wistfully.

"Some people grow up," Rae said, obviously jabbing at me.

I held my tongue but gave her the finger; I know, not a grown-up thing to do.

"We were talking about work, I believe," Dad interrupted.

"Yes, give the Blake job one more week," said Mom. "But remember the fourth wall. Surveillance is like theater."

---

[2] Rae's twenty, so you can do the math.

"I get it," said Rae.

"So, you know what the fourth wall is?" Mom asked.

"We studied Diderot in high school, Mom," Rae replied snappishly.

"Who the fuck is Diderot?" I asked.

"Is it necessary to use the F-word?" asked Mom.

"Since we're pitching fancy theater references, David Mamet sure thinks so," I replied.

"You know who David Mamet is?" Rae asked.

"Why don't you shut up and eat some M&M's?"

"Excellent idea," Rae replied, opening her desk drawer to the bag of mealy carrots I had placed in their stead.

"It's really tragic that at your age a lame prank gives you so much pleasure," said Rae.

"How is that tragic? It means I potentially have a lifetime of happiness to look forward to."

"Eventually I'll strike back."

"Bring it," I replied. "You're no match for me."

"You got that right. It would be like a shark fighting a puppy."

"Well, if we're fighting on land, which we are, I think this puppy will do just fine."

"Since we're on the subject of theater," Dad said, "why don't we all pretend that there's a fourth wall between us?"

THE IDLE CEO

While Rae was on the trail of Vivien Blake, I commenced my surveillance of Edward Slayter, who was coincidentally also a snore. Slayter was the head of a major investment banking firm, on the board of numerous worldwide charitable organizations, a coveted public speaker, and an avid tennis player, and yet on three of the five days I was surveilling him, he took an extended lunch break in Golden Gate Park, sitting on an isolated bench by North Lake, feeding ducks. This particular pond (not a lake) was tucked away off of JFK Drive, so I had to plant myself in the trees with a set of binoculars to maintain a visual on the subject.

I phoned Mrs. Slayter to inquire about her husband's recent activities.

"Yes," she answered the phone.

"This is Isabel."

"I know," Mrs. Slayter curtly replied.

"Your husband is in the park again."

"And?" Mrs. Slayter asked.

Based on experience, the next obvious question a spouse would ask is "Is he alone?" She didn't ask.

"He's alone," I said.

"Does it look like he will be leaving any time soon?"

"Well, he still has half a loaf of bread left."

"He's eating *bread*?" Mrs. Slayter asked incredulously. "How odd. He never eats bread."

"No, he's feeding it to the ducks."

"Oh, that makes more sense."

"Does it?" I asked, since duck-feeding hardly seems like a common pastime for a CEO.

"Excuse me," she replied. "I am quite busy right now. Feel free to text me when he's on his way home or back to the office."

While I was aware that Mrs. Slayter was anxious to end the call, I'm quite good at pretending not to notice verbal cues. "Is your husband particularly fond of ducks?" I asked.

"Excuse me?"

"Does your husband like ducks a lot?"

"Not that I'm aware of."

"Then I wonder why he's visited the park three times this week and dropped two and a half loaves of sourdough on them."

"Ms. Spellman, I really must go."

"One more question: Is this behavior ordinary?"

"What behavior?"

"Loitering in parks, taking in nature, and whatnot."

"No, but maybe work stress has gotten to him."

"Maybe you should suggest a vacation," I suggested.

"What an extraordinarily original idea."

Then Mrs. Slayter disconnected the call. Mr. Slayter took a turn around the lake and returned to the same bench, where he sat and stared blankly into the distance.

My cell phone vibrated.

"Hello."

"There's an electrical fire at my apartment."

"Well, probably not," I replied.

"Still, just to be safe."

"I'll call you after I've investigated."

"Thanks, Isabel."

"Good-bye, Walter." I phoned my mother, who was in the midst of sur-veilling the sister of the Man from the Library and couldn't break away. I texted Rae, but she was in class. My father was at a lunch meeting and D was manning the office—which could have been left unattended for a legit-imate emergency, but an imaginary electrical fire didn't count. Still, until I phoned and confirmed that his suspicion was wrong, Walter wouldn't be able to think of anything else. I wasn't comfortable skipping out on the Slayter surveillance even though Slayter was merely duck-watching.

On a hunch, I made one more call.

"Fred Finkel.[1] How quickly can you get to Golden Gate Park?"

"What's in it for me?"

"Twenty-five an hour and a case of O'Doul's."

"Make it thirty and you can keep the fake beer."

"I'm at JFK and North Lake Drive. Make it snappy."

"You're not in a position to bark orders," Fred replied.

"Is that so? Because if I remember correctly you have a certain skel-eton in your closet that I think you'd like me to keep to myself."

"It's hardly a skeleton," Fred replied.

"Are we going to yap on the phone all day or are you going to get your ass over here?"

"Good-bye."

Twenty minutes later, I passed the binoculars to Fred, showed him the tar-get, and made sure my cell number was programmed into his speed dial. I then borrowed his bike and rode the two miles to Walter's apartment, unlocked the door, and entered a home that was clearly not engulfed in flames. I slipped off my shoes and checked the power cords in the kitchen. No appliance was plugged in—except the oven and the refrigerator. I

---

[1] Rae's charming, but odd, boyfriend. Great name, huh?

checked the bathroom faucets and they were also clamped shut. Not a drop of water could possibly escape. I phoned Walter to ease his mind. "No electrical fire."

"That's a relief."

"I double-checked the faucets and electrical cords. Everything's clear."

"One more thing. Can you make sure that the water line to the washing machine is turned off?" Walter asked.

"Of course."

I walked over to the closet that housed Walter's washer and dryer.

"It's off."

"Thank you, Isabel. I don't know what I'd do without you."

"Maybe you'd have to get better."

"Good-bye, Isabel."

As I combed the rug with a carpet rake, erasing evidence of my presence in Walter's apartment, I spotted evidence of someone else in Walter's apartment. It was a heel print made from some kind of smooth-bottomed shoe that rested at a right angle by Walter's front door. There was a single print, which could have easily been Walter's, only Walter never misses his shoe print. *Never.* It occurred to me that it was possible that Walter had a guest over and missed the print. Although Walter rarely has guests. It's also possible that Walter's excessive vigilance was being transferred to me and I was overreacting to something that I would otherwise have not given a second thought to. I raked the carpet clean of all evidence of life and departed.

When I returned to the park, I found Fred Finkel sitting next to Edward Slayter on the park bench. They were sipping cups of coffee from a café just off of Lincoln. I phoned his cell.

"Hello?" Fred answered.

"You're doing it wrong," I said.

"I see. That's an interesting proposal," Fred replied.

"What part of surveillance don't you understand?"

"I'm afraid I'm quite happy with my long-distance carrier. But should I decide to make a change, I'll keep you in mind. Good-bye."

For the next twenty minutes Fred and subject sat on the bench, drank coffee, communed with nature, and chatted about God knows what, while I crouched in the shrubbery on a wet patch of gravel, dying for a warm beverage myself. Eventually the two men stood, shook hands, and parted ways.

I walked past my incompetent operative as I followed subject to the corner of Chain of Lakes and Fulton Street, where his driver was waiting for him. Subject entered the vehicle and departed. I returned to the lakeside bench, where Fred was sipping the last of his coffee.

"Did he tell you where he was going?"

"Home," Fred replied.

"You're fired," I said.

"Final paycheck," Fred replied, extending the palm of his hand.

I relinquished whatever bills I had in my pocket and texted Mrs. Slayter that her husband was on the way home and the surveillance was over.

"You don't usually buy surveillance subjects a cup of coffee," I sharply suggested.

"He bought. Not my fault. He was wandering along Lincoln Drive, I was on his tail, then he turned around, looking lost, asked me where the closest coffee shop was. He made me. What was I going to do, follow him around while he searched for coffee and risk making him paranoid? The logical solution was to steer him in the right direction. Besides, I couldn't let him go to a Starbucks, which is where he would have gone if I didn't help him. It's important that we support our local small businesses or our entire world will be composed of strip malls with chain stores. Maybe you're a big fan of the Olive Garden, but some of us want more out of life than a bottomless soup bowl and unlimited bread sticks."

I paused a moment to make sure Fred didn't have an off-point fast-food diatribe he needed to get out of his system.

"I'll keep that in mind the next time I'm in the mood for homogenized Italian food."

"Thank you."

I pulled another forty dollars from my pocket and showed it to Fred. "All this can be yours," I said.

"What's the catch?" Fred skeptically replied.

"Tell me what Rae did to David."

"She didn't do anything to David," Fred replied.

He was telling the truth. I had no doubt about that, but sometimes you can lie behind the truth. There was more to the story, but he didn't reach for the dough. Fred was no canary. I needed to find another bird to sing.

SUNDAY-NIGHT
DINNER #48

My family's obligatory Sunday-night dinners have always had the atmosphere of a disappointing baseball game: lots of shouting, subpar and semidigestible dining options, and various individuals occasionally making a run for it. You could also say that by the end of the evening there are usually clear winners and losers. And, since baseball is not really my game, I should probably end my analogy there.

Since Gertrude was the guest of honor and famous for giving birth to one of the most polite individuals my mother has ever met, Mom was on her best behavior, which (if you ask me, and if you're reading this, you do) is also her most unpleasant. Obsequious Mom is a hovering shadow of her more lively self. In fact, this new version of Mom has cropped up quite often with the arrival of D. That's not to say that Old Mom has vanished entirely. But she can toggle between the two with the simple ease of flicking on and off a light switch.

"Mom" had purchased flowers as a centerpiece and consulted Demetrius on the entire dinner menu. I'm pretty sure the food was excellent, since D was involved, but distractions swarmed the room like killer bees. Who could concentrate on a well-executed roast?

Had Gerty been the kind of woman I'd expected Henry's mother to be, I would have provided her with a full debriefing on the family and suggested

92

various methods of coping throughout the evening: boozing, excessive use of the restroom, and, if all else failed, taking advantage of an easily navigable escape route from the den. But Gerty could take care of herself. When she arrived, I kissed her on the cheek, handed her a scotch on the rocks, and said, "They're all insane," to which she replied, "Who isn't?"

I suppose there are a few other details worth mentioning. When Sydney arrived with her parents I said to my niece, "Hey, Sydney, what's going on?" As usual, she merely stared at me.

"Can you please act normal around her?" David said.

"That's exactly what I'm doing."

"You don't talk to a toddler like that. How do you expect to bond with her?"

"I'll slip her five bucks on the way out. That always worked with Rae."

"She's eighteen months old, you can't give her money. She'll eat it."

"You just defined our problem in a nutshell," I said. "Sydney and I have nothing in common. I'll bond with her when she learns the value of a dollar."

David then held his daughter up close to my face like maybe she was nearsighted and couldn't quite place me.

"Sydney. Say hello to Aunt Izzy."

Sydney said, "Banana."

"I don't know how you expect me to bond with someone who calls me 'banana.'"

I noticed D in the kitchen with his coat on, giving my mother strict instructions on when to put the biscuits in the oven and when to take them out.

"Olivia, set the timer. It's right there; it takes two seconds. Why ruin your dinner with the smoke alarm going off again?"

"What's going on?" I asked.[1]

D looked at his watch and said, "Make sure your mama sets the timer."

[1] Please note that this was precisely the same way I'd addressed Sydney, so how could someone accuse me of abnormal behavior?

"Where are you going?" I said, worried about losing my only non-Spellman guest for backup.

"I have a date," D replied.

"Tonight?"

"Yes."

"A florist," Mom said with a note of pride. "I picked her," she then whispered.

"Text me if any questions arise," D said.

"*Horosho provesti vremya,*" Mom said to D.

"What does that mean?" I asked.

"'Have a good time,'" Mom translated.

"*Dosvedanya,*" D replied, making a beeline for the door.

I got in step with him because there was some shift in his manner when my mother mentioned the word *florist.* I smelled a lie, to put it bluntly. I've found (and you may not agree) that the best way to sniff out a lie is to call someone on it immediately.

"D, what are you up to?"

"I'm going on a date."

"With the florist?"

"With the florist."

"I don't believe you."

"I'm sorry to hear that," D replied, opening the front door.

"Why the need to keep secrets, D?"

"Have a lovely evening," D said, smugly tipping an imaginary hat.

Unlike the rest of the family, I don't have much leverage with D—he doesn't have to prove anything to me. But I knew for a fact that he was lying. Unfortunately, he was out the door before I could implement any of my backup methods.

As far as Spellman family dinners went, this one was surprisingly low on drama. My mother and Gerty got along swimmingly once I pulled my mother aside and told her that I would break a glass every time she used the word *splendid* or, *delightful*.[2] David and Maggie had a quiet bickering session over Sydney upon their arrival. My bionic ear (literally a device that amplifies sound across the room) informed me that Maggie wanted to have Sydney tested for some kind of delayed language function and David adamantly refused, ending the conversation then and there. Over dinner I had to admit that Maggie might have had a point.

My mother served Sydney sliced apples and Sydney repeatedly called them bananas. She also called the juice box and all green vegetables bananas, but when my mother finally served her a banana, Sydney said, "No apple!" After which David explained that Sydney hates bananas. My mother, thankfully, held her tongue.

Gertrude then thanked my mother for a wonderful evening, suggested they get together for lunch sometime, and called a cab, explaining that she had plans to meet an old friend for a drink.

"What friend?" Henry asked.

"Emily."

"Who is Emily?"

"A friend from college."

"Why haven't I heard of her?"

"Because we didn't go to college together, dear. Remember, you weren't born yet?"

"Were you close?"

"Mortal enemies. But time heals all wounds. At least most flesh wounds."

"It was a reasonable question," Henry said.

"Can't help myself, dear."

"Call me if you're going to be late," Henry said.

"How about you just assume I'm going to be late? In fact, maybe as late as tomorrow morning."

---

[2] Had I adopted this policy at the beginning of the evening, her entire ten-piece glassware set would have been demolished, along with half a dozen wine goblets.

"You might stay over?"

"We have a lot of catching up to do."

"Call me and let me know either way."

"Good night, Henry."

Just when my mother ordered me to roll up my sleeves and do the dishes, my cell phone rang.

"Hello?"

"My toaster is on fire."

"I'll be right there."[8]

Henry drove to my new favorite client's apartment and waited in the car as I went upstairs to "investigate." As expected, nothing was aflame. However, when I performed my usual walk-through, I found the bathtub on a slow drip, with the plug soundly in place, the water cresting toward the edge. I reached into the claw-foot tub and removed the stopper, displacing water onto the tile floor. I waited for it to drain and soon realized that this was not merely a case of Walter's forgetfulness but deliberate sabotage. I had to decide whether I should feed Walter's general paranoia and OCD or find the culprit on my own.

Back in the car, Henry and I made small talk. Or what I like to call "evasive talk," where we talk about everything but what we should be talking about.

"I think it might rain," Henry said.

"Light showers, I read."

"They really should fix the potholes in the street."

"Why don't you fix them? Just get some gravel and tar and have at it," I said.

"No. I think I'll just write another letter."

"Because that clearly works."

---

[8] Note to self: Send Walter a nice fruit basket for Christmas.

Silence.

"So, that went well," Henry said.

"What?"

"The dinner."

"Oh, yes. It did, didn't it?"

Silence.

"Maybe we should take a vacation," Henry said.

"From each other?" I asked.

"No. I meant together. Do you want to take a vacation? From me?"

"I just get confused when people say 'vacation' instead of 'disappearance.' I didn't mean anything by it."

Before I could dig myself further into a pothole, my mother called. Usually I'm more than happy to send her to voice mail, but I welcomed the distraction.

"It was a lovely evening, wasn't it?" Mom said.

"Yes," I said. "For once it was actually a good meal," I added, thinking she was fishing for a compliment.

"Thank you, sweetie. I'm quite fond of Gerty."

"Please stop talking like that."

"She's great company."

"I agree."

"I thought of something after you left."

"If you have one more drink, you might forget it," I suggested.

"You know who Gerty reminds me of?"

"I have no idea."

"You."

"Have that drink, Mom," I said, disconnecting the call.

While Gerty and I bore no physical resemblance, I had to admit that my mother had a point. Objectively (and I like to think I can be that on occasion), I found something oddly familiar about Gerty's general evasiveness, her refusal to tell Henry where she was going or where she had been, and her fondness for booze. However, no one wants to think that her boyfriend digs her because she reminds him of his mother, so I brushed that thought aside as best I could and focused on more pressing matters. Like, for instance, what was Gerty hiding? Because she was definitely hiding something.

PAPERWORK

I t is company policy to have all surveillance reports proofread by an employee other than the operative on the case. I wasn't assigned to the Blake case but I pulled my sister's second surveillance report off of my mother's desk and cleared the next few hours for Rae's grunt work. You'd be surprised how quickly a client will turn on you if you provide a sloppy report. If you think about it, documenting hours of nothing is a tricky job. If the subject is doing nothing—like sleeping—how much filler is reasonable?

6:45 A.M.   The sun rises over the horizon, casting its rosy glow upon the sleepy suburban neighborhood. Investigator believes the subject is still sleeping. Neighbor #5 exits residence, sits in her car, and carries on a ten-minute cell phone conversation. Neighbor #5's vehicle should have the muffler checked. Neighbor #3 appears to steal Neighbor #4's newspaper. Neighbor #2 puts recycling in Neighbor #3's bin.

6:55 A.M.   A light turns on in subject's kitchen.

7:05 A.M.   A garbage truck meanders down the street, picking up refuse. Neighbor #6 stands on her porch and waves at one of the sanitation workers. He waves back. They exchange a warm glance. Investigator believes that they are having an affair.

For the record, that's too much detail. The subject is the star of this one-person show and only suspicious behavior that relates to her should be described.

Now let's return to our subject, Vivien Blake. Surveillance is a pricey endeavor; even many well-off clients can't afford round-the-clock operatives. Often clients will pick windows of time to have the subject under surveillance, hoping that the chosen window will shed some light on subject's extracurricular activities. Mr. and Mrs. Blake chose a weekly stipend, which covered fifteen hours of a one-person job, which we were to use at our discretion. Since Rae was the primary investigator, the time frame of Vivien's surveillance was mostly under Rae's domain. However, it was understood that she would vary her hours to oversee a wide variety of Vivien's chosen habits.

The rest of Rae's report sufficiently covered an appropriate cross-section of time and, to her credit, was professional, typo free, and had just the right amount of detail. However, there was one detail that was missing—one that virtually no client would ever think of.

Surveillance Report: Vivien Blake

Thursday, September 15

900 hrs   Surveillance commences. Subject is believed to be inside her residence at [redacted]. Investigator waits in Dolores Park across the street.

952 hrs   Subject departs residence and walks three blocks to Muddy Waters Coffee House on Valencia Street. Subject enters establishment. Investigator also en-

	ters café and finds corner table away from subject's view. Investigator observes subject drinking coffee and studying. A large textbook sits on the table.
1115 hrs	Unknown male #1 (early twenties, light brown hair, medium build, average height) sits down at subject's table. Unknown male #1 drinks coffee and appears to be studying in silence with subject. A brief communication is observed.
1145 hrs	Unknown male #1 leaves a brown paper bag on the table and leaves café.
1200 hrs	Subject puts the paper bag into her backpack and leaves the café. Subject walks to the Sixteenth Street BART station.
1215 hrs	Subject boards the Fremont train.
1243 hrs	Subject exits at the Berkeley station and walks to the Berkeley campus.
1300 hrs	Subject enters library and sits down next to unknown male #2 (early twenties, brown hair, thin build, average height). Subject gives unknown male #2 brown paper bag.
1315 hrs	Subject leaves library and returns to BART station, taking the train back to San Francisco.
1400 hrs	Investigator ends surveillance.

Rae's report covered two more days of Vivien studying and having a few meetings that could be either suspicious or not. It also included a twenty-three-hour period in which Rae could not locate subject at her residence or any of her known haunts.

However, it wasn't the specifics about Vivien in the report that I found suspect. It was the investigator. I made the alibi call first, since I know how to play this game.

"Fred," I said into the receiver.

"Isabel," he replied.

"Have you aided my sister on any surveillance in the past week?"

"No. And I think it's unlikely that she'd ask."

"Maybe because you haven't gotten the concept down."

"Did you call me to tell me that I screwed up again? Because you made that clear the first time around."

"It was worth mentioning one more time."

"Anything else, Isabel?"

"Nope. Thanks, Fred."

Then I phoned Rae. She picked up on the fourth ring.

"What do you want?" she asked.

I hung up and sent her a text: That's not how you answer the phone.

She replied a minute later: Not how U txt

FU (how's that?)

UNTCO[1]

What?!!!

:-o zz[2]

I phoned again.

"What do you want?" she rudely answered once again.

"I want you to stop being a pain in my ass."

"Then get to the point."

"I'm reviewing your surveillance report on Blake."

"On who?"

"On Vivien Blake."

"Who?"

"On the Sparrow. Satisfied?"

"I left that report for Mom to cover."

---

[1] According to the text-message dictionary: "You need to chill out."
[2] Apparently the emoticon for "bored"; notice how it requires as many characters as "bored."

"Mom's busy. Have you seen her hobby load?"

"You're still not getting to the point."

"Did you have help on the job?"

"No."

"Did you lose visual on the subject at any time?"

"No. I made that clear in the report," Rae impatiently replied.

"So at no point did you break surveillance?"

"No. Is there anything else?"

"That will be all," I said, disconnecting the call.

There was no point in tipping my hand to Rae just yet. My sister was hard to manage when she was young, but as a citizen of legal age, with complete access to vehicles, money, and the myriad tools of the trade we had taught her, she had become a wild variable in any equation. She was that chemical in a chemistry experiment that caused an inert substance to explode.

I couldn't go to my parents with the flimsy dirt I had on my sister. She faked a surveillance report. My evidence? Rae can't go four hours without peeing. It's thin, I know. But I've worked jobs with her for fourteen years and that's a simple fact. Why she would doctor a report was my first question. And, secondly, what did she do to David?

A few hours later, I sent a follow-up text: IO2U.

Rae refused to reply, probably because my acronym hadn't entered the lexicon just yet. But I am hopeful it will one day.

I'm onto you.

BAD DETECTIVE

Four weeks had passed since we took on our collection of domestic cases and I still couldn't tell you why my sister had doctored the Vivien Blake report, or why Gerty extended her San Francisco visit for another two weeks and then virtually disappeared, or what motivated my mother to rush off to classes that she clearly did not enjoy. I still had no idea what Rae had done to my brother. Nor could I comprehend why Mrs. Slayter wanted Mr. Slayter followed. The one thing I could say for certain was that there was no reason to surveil Edward Slayter. Because Mr. Slayter did nothing at all.

I should clarify: Mr. Slayter went to meetings, he met men in suits for lunch, he met more men in suits for dinner, he went for long strolls in the park, he had tennis dates and even a few doctor's appointments. Mrs. Slayter merely wanted to know where he was and yet she didn't seem particularly interested in what he was doing when he was there.

At one point I suggested she stick a tracking device in his coat pocket when he left the house, which might have been more accurate and cost-effective than hiring a PI. She seemed to mull the idea over for a few seconds and then replied, "But sometimes he leaves his coat at the office."

I voiced my concern to Mom at one point. She asked me if Mrs. Slayter was current with her payments. I replied that she was. Our conversation ended there.

I voiced my concerns to Dad. He asked me the same question Mom did. I gave him the same answer. "Then what's the problem?" he replied.

The problem was that I didn't trust Mrs. Slayter. It's one thing if a client asks me to follow a suspicious spouse, but following an unsuspicious one is a truly uncommon request. I've been at this job long enough to know when I'm being played and I couldn't shake that feeling when it came to Mrs. Slayter.

When I was younger, I always had an excess of broke friends to hire on a moment's notice for backup on a surveillance job. In the intervening years those friends moved away, got married, had kids, became gainfully employed, or discovered that surveillance was about as interesting as bird-watching. No offense to bird-watchers.

My point: I had to call Fred again, since what I was doing was in the shady section of the PI department store.

"Now, let's go over this one more time, Fred," I said when I dropped off Finkel in front of Mr. Slayter's office building on Market Street. "All you have to do is follow him and text me his current location. You don't provide subject with directions, transportation, or medical advice, or offer to buy him lunch. Got it?"

"What if he's hit by a car?"

"Call 911."

"What if he's bleeding profusely?"

"The ambulance guys will take care of it," I said.

"They're called EMTs," Fred replied.

"Finkel, do you want to make fifty bucks in cash or not?"

"I do."

"Then shut up and do as I tell you."

Silence.

"Got it?" I asked.

Silence.

"Acknowledge you understand me."

Fred nodded his head. I drove off before he could convince me to take him off the job.

Mrs. Slayter sent me a text message while I was parked three doors down from her house, requesting her husband's coordinates. I informed her that he was at the office, which, as I far as I knew, was the truth.

Fifteen minutes later, Mrs. Slayter left her home carrying a gym bag and wearing what I presume were workout clothes. There was some writing on her ass, which I couldn't make out, so I kept staring at it. I couldn't figure why you would have something written on your butt unless you really wanted people to stare at it. For the record, the primary reason I stopped wearing my extra JUSTICE 4 MERRI-WEATHER T-shirts was because I got tired of people reading my chest. Another thing I noticed about Mrs. Slayter was that she was in full makeup, which I think is kind of gross if you're going to the gym. Turns out Mrs. Slayter wasn't going to the gym.

Mrs. Slayter pulled her Mercedes out of the driveway and turned north, making a right on Gough Street. I started my engine and was about to sneak in behind her when a black Audi cut me off. The driver didn't notice my cheap Buick on his tail. He was too focused on following the Mercedes. I hung back just a bit to keep a low profile and followed the Audi, following Mrs. Slayter to the Four Seasons hotel. Mrs. Slayter valet-parked. The driver of the Audi followed suit. Since I knew I'd miss the party if I tried to find a metered spot on the street, I valet-parked my crappy Buick. To the valet's credit he treated me like I was driving a Benz.

"Are you a guest, ma'am?"

"No, and please don't call me 'ma'am.'"[1]

---

[1] While I'm on the subject, this kind of goes for everyone. I've never met a woman under the age of fifty who likes being called "ma'am." In fact, I prefer "hey you," "lady!" "missy," "the one in the green shirt" (obviously only if I'm wearing a green shirt), and "whatsyourname" to "ma'am" any day of the week.

* * *

I rushed into the lavish lobby of the swanky hotel to catch a brief glimpse of Mrs. Slayter entering the elevator with an unknown male. The unknown male, I should mention, was approximately twenty years younger than her husband and not unattractive. While they did not show any affectionate exchange during my brief sighting of them, they were riding an elevator together to the guest-room towers of the Four Seasons.

I then scanned the expansive lobby and found a known male comfortably seated on a plush beige couch, reading a newspaper.

"Dad, what are you doing here?"

INTERSECTION

"The question is, what are *you* doing here?" my father replied, folding his newspaper in quarters.

"I was in the neighborhood."

"Would a straight answer every once in a while kill you?"

"I don't know; I've never tried it."

"You know this place is kind of above your pay grade."

"We need to do something about that. So, Dad, what case are you working on?"

"I'm on a surveillance job for the Sweater Vest."

"Who is the Sweater Vest?"

"You took the meeting."

"You mean the guy from the library?"

"We call him the Sweater Vest, because he wears sweater vests."

"Do you see now why this nickname business is idiotic?" I asked.

"Right now it's not working for you and me, but Rae and I have no problem with it."

"The client's name is Adam Cooper, right?"

"Yes. Now, would you like to tell me why you're here?" Dad asked.

"Who are you surveilling?" I replied.

"Meg Cooper, and you still haven't answered my question."

"The blonde who got into the elevator with the younger man?"

"Yes, Isabel. What's going on?"

"Meg Cooper is Margaret Slayter."

"And that is?"

"Margaret Slayter is a client. She hired me to follow her husband."

"Is her husband at this hotel?"

"No."

"Then what are you doing here?"

"I followed Mrs. Slayter here."

"Why?"

"Because something was fishy about the job."

"Isabel, you were not hired to follow the client; you were hired to follow her husband. You need to leave immediately."

"Wait, how long has Margaret/Meg been seeing this man?"

"End of discussion."

"But I need to know why she's hired us. I think it's to keep track of her husband while she—"

"Isabel, if you aren't out the door in five seconds, you're fired," my father said.

I can usually tell when my father is bluffing, and this was no bluff. In fact, his face was turning a shade of crimson that only occurs when he's either drunk or about to go into a rage.[1]

I was out the door on the count of two.

I checked my phone when I got in the car and saw a text from Finkel from just ten minutes before.

Sub on move.

Where?

1799 Clay Street.

---

[1] Which I recall only from the aftermath of crimes committed during my misspent youth.

ha ha.

No. Seriously.

UR a dead man.

ha ha.

No. Seriously.

1799 Clay Street, in case I haven't mentioned it, is the address of the Spellman compound. As I approached the front door, Fred surfaced from the small alley that divides our house from the next.

"What's he doing in there?"

"I don't know," Fred replied, appearing genuinely baffled. "You think he made me?"

"He made you the other day when you had coffee and chatted like a pair of biddies on a park bench. But that doesn't explain what he's suddenly doing at our office." I pulled sixty from my wallet and passed it to Fred. "Keep-your-mouth-shut money."

I could tell he was about to question the overpayment on a botched surveillance, but I needed him in my corner. One day I'd need a favor from Fred and I was merely laying the groundwork.

"Sorry," he said.

"Get out of here."

Just then a black limousine double-parked in front of the Spellman house and idled there for about five minutes. I paused along the side of the house until I saw my mother walk Mr. Slayter to the front door. They shook hands and my mom said she would be in touch. Mr. Slayter got into his limo.

Once the car was out of sight, I entered the house. "What did that man want?"

"The one who just left?" Mom asked.

"Yes. Did he tell you his name?"

"Mr. Slayter. Don't we have another Slayter case?"

"What did he want?"

"He had the oddest request."

"Let me guess. He wants you to follow his wife."

"No," my mother replied. "He wants us to follow him."

Part 11

THE WALL

(October)

BRICK BY BRICK

Conflicts of interest are not unusual in my line of work. San Francisco is a small city, and the PI business has taken a beating. With Harkey (our main competition for twenty years) out of the picture,[1] there are only a handful of other firms in the city, and most people would prefer a mom-and-pop shop to the corporate ice cube[2] that is our main competition. It's not unheard-of to have domestic cases intersect, but a three-way intersection was new territory.

Dad called Mom from the field after our collision. He told her to keep me in the office until he returned home. While I still had a window to gather information, I used the time to get to the bottom of Mr. Slayter's visit. Unfortunately there was no bottom to get to.

"So a guy walks into the office looking to hire someone to follow him and you don't ask why?"

My mother sighed impatiently. "Of course I asked, dear, but he wouldn't say. He merely said that he wanted an investigator to document his daily activities."

"Didn't you find that suspicious?"

---

[1] Thanks to me. If you'd like to know more, document #4 has details. That's all I'm saying.

[2] No, I'm not going to tell you their name and provide free advertising.

"I found it unusual."

"Did you ask him how he came to our agency?"

"Yes."

"And?"

"He said that he found us on the Internet."

"Interesting."

"Rae did an excellent job redesigning our website."

"Did he say anything about his wife?"

"That's all I can tell you, dear."

I stacked files and errant paperwork in an untidy pile on my desk—my typical end-of-day ritual. Then my mother explained that we were to have an emergency company meeting and I would have to wait in the office until Dad returned home. I grabbed a beer from the refrigerator and turned to a chess study website to practice my endgame, which Henry had informed me was sorely lacking. Although at other points he'd mentioned the same thing about my opening game and middle game.

"I'm still on the clock," I informed my mother.

"Then you should do some filing."

"Three out of five," I said, holding out my fist. Mom and I played rock-paper-scissors to decide who would file, and I won. Which I had been doing ever since Demetrius pointed out that I favored rock (then launched into a long-winded explanation about how my preference for rock indicates my personal preference for inertia, since when you're a rock you don't have to do anything at all). After I stopped favoring rock I had a whole lot less filing to do. And I like to think that in the not-too-distant future filing might become as obsolete as fountain pens.

My mother tried to amuse herself with idle gossip while she stuck pieces of paper inside folders inside larger folders with letters on them. See how dumb that sounds?

"So Demetrius is going on a lot of dates," my mom said. "I hope he finds someone special."

"Mom, has it occurred to you that D isn't actually going on the dates?

Because what kind of grown man lets his fifty-seven-year-old employer control his Match.com account?"

"Yes, dear, that occurred to me."

"Do you know for a fact that he is actually braving the singles world?"

"Truth be told, I had some suspicions and I followed him one night. He was having a perfectly nice dinner with a very attractive woman who I believe works at a veterinary clinic. She had no profile picture, so I can't be sure it was the same one, but I have vetted all of them. No pun intended."

"Did they go on a second date?" I asked.

"No. D said there was no rapport. He said she carried a Hello Kitty purse."

"That would be a deal-breaker for me too."

"Anyway, he's been on a few other dates, but so far, no one special."

"You understand, Mom, that if he does meet someone special, he will eventually move out."

"I do," my mother said. The tone of her voice had shifted. I had clearly touched on a dental-level nerve. I switched topics to ease the tension. "Don't you have a class tonight that you're missing?" I asked. I took a photocopy of Mom's schedule from my drawer and reviewed it. "Ah, yes, Monday you have Beginning Pottery. Curious that you have nothing to show for it."

"My pieces are still in the kiln," Mom replied.

"Likely story. Are you even going to these classes?"

"*Krasivaya bluzka*,"[3] Mom said, in Russian, I guess.

"What does that mean?"

"It means 'Of course I am.'"

Inside my desk, I turned on my digital recorder.

"How do you say, 'Where is the restroom?'" I asked.

"Where is the restroom," Mom replied.

"Hilarious. In Russian, please."

_____
[3] "I like your shirt."

"Vy ne mogli by govorit' pomedlennee."[4]

"How do say, 'What time is it?'"

"Etot mužčina platit za vsë."[5]

"How about 'My hovercraft is full of eels'?"

"Ostav'te menja v pokoeugrey."[6]

"You're up to something. I'm sure of that. Why don't you just tell me so I don't have to investigate?"

"Excuse me," Mom said. "I have some crocheting to do."

My mother then opened her desk drawer, withdrew a canvas bag, and removed a crochet hook and a misshapen mass of yarn.

"So it is crochet, not croquet. What on earth are you making?"

"A *hat*," Mom snapped. "Isn't it obvious?"

"Not in the slightest."

Just then we heard a key in the front door and an unnerving squeak of the hinge. From the end of the hall my father shouted, "Chinese wall." Then Dad swung open the far quieter office door and repeated himself more dramatically. He took off his coat and tossed it on the back of his chair, rolled up his sleeves, and said, "We're enacting a Chinese wall immediately."

Dad pulled the Adam Cooper file from the cabinet (subject: Meg Cooper [also known as Margaret Slayter]) and locked it in his desk drawer. He then passed me the Margaret Slayter file (subject: husband Edward Slayter) and said, "From now on, your mother and I will deal exclusively with Adam Cooper and you will handle only the work requested of you by Mrs. Slayter. We will each take care of billing individually and there will be absolutely no communication between either side on the cases.

"And, Isabel, your only contact with Mrs. Slayter should be as a client. You provide the information she pays for. End of story. Even if we'd never

---

[4] "Please speak more slowly."
[5] "This gentleman will pay for everything."
[6] Leave me alone. I'm going to give her that one.

discovered this conflict of interest, you should not have been surveilling the client. If that ever got out, our reputation could be sold at the five-and-dime store."

"They don't have those anymore," I replied.

"Nothing about this is funny, Isabel."

"Maybe not funny," I replied, "but it is kind of awesome, if you think about it. Also, did Mom tell you about Mr. Slayter visiting the office?"

"Briefly," Dad replied. Then he turned to my mother. "Please call him back and tell him that we cannot offer our services to him at this time."

"Something is going on here that is not your typical domestic non-bliss," I said.

"That is not our concern," my dad replied.

"What if Mrs. Slayter hired us to babysit her husband while she has an affair?"

"We have no evidence of that fact," Dad replied.

"We kind of have something resembling it. What if Mrs. Slayter is having us track her husband's moves so she can plan a hit on him?"

"That only happens in detective novels," said Dad.

"One of these days we're going to catch a murder," I said.

"We can dream," my mom replied.

"Do you want me to take you off the Slayter case?" my father sternly asked.

"Yes, and put me on the Meg Cooper case. We can swap for a week and then swap back."

"I meant," my father said, correcting me, "do you want me to take you off all cases?"

"Well, of course not."

"Chinese wall it is. There will be no further discussion. Agreed?"

"No. We're not really in agreement."

"Agree or you're on desk duty until all conflicting cases are closed."

My dad was serious; I had no other recourse.

"Agreed," I replied, and maybe I meant it at the time.

* * *

Imaginary walls are merely boundaries. As you've undoubtedly gathered by now, I'm not particularly practiced with that sort of thing. When my father calls for a Chinese wall—and it's only happened once before[7]—I take it seriously because he takes it seriously. And when I don't take seriously things that he takes seriously, my day-to-day life becomes difficult. When I say "difficult," I don't mean that my father is rude or gives me the cold shoulder or even yells at me; I mean that the simple things in life become challenging. My car won't start, my winter coat goes missing, my breath spray is replaced by vinegar, my keys don't work as well as they used to, the heel on my left shoe falls off. The sabotage is subtler than the type practiced by, say, Rae or my mom. My father's tactics avoid direct assault. He is not calling for war. His goal is to make me believe I'm experiencing some cosmic retaliation for my misdeeds.

For many years when this sort of thing happened, I actually thought that maybe something bigger than me or my dad was at work. That was until I caught him filing down one of my shoelaces. I wasn't up for the level of vigilance required to overtly defy my father. There had to be another way.

After work, I had a drink at the Hemlock to try to figure out a route around the Chinese wall. One beer down, I had no bulletproof solutions to my problem. To occupy myself, I decided to tackle less troubling and more scalable information blockades.

First I phoned Henry to tell him I would be late.

"I'm going to be late," I said.

"I see," said Henry.

"So I won't be home for dinner."

"Wasn't expecting you."

---

[7] Ten years ago. A divorced couple fighting over custody of their cat, Irving.

"Oh. I guess I've had a lot of late nights recently."

"Anything else?" Henry said. I've gotten the cold shoulder from him before, but this time he was putting his heart into it.

"I washed the dishes this morning. Did you notice?" I said. I was working on having some redeeming qualities.

"I did," Henry replied, unimpressed.

"So you don't plan on throwing me a parade or releasing a bunch of doves or something?"

"Anything else, Isabel?"

"Say hi to your mom."

"She's not here," Henry replied.

"Where is she?" I asked. Silly question.

"I don't know. She left a note that said, *I'm not here.* I think she thinks it's funny."

"I kind of think it's funny," I said.

"I don't," Henry replied.

"I'll be home as soon as I can," I said.

Henry hung up the phone without saying good-bye.

I phoned Gerty to see if I could convince her to spend some time with Henry, since they had barely seen each other in the last few weeks. Other than the notes, I couldn't be sure that Gerty was still even in the city. In fact, if she didn't date them and change them daily, I would have called the cops. I phoned her cell and left a message on her voice mail. She never did return my call.

RECREATIONAL SURVEILLANCE

From the bar, I phoned Dad to get the location of Mom's purported pottery class. He picked up on the first ring.

"Hi, Isabel."

"Hi, Dad," I said. I've grown to miss that part of the phone call where you identify yourself. Mostly I miss the part where I misidentify; caller ID has definitely cramped my style. "What's going on?"

"Nothing," Dad said, letting out a deep sigh.

"Is something wrong?"

"It's just so lonely here," Dad said. "Your mother's gone all the time and I don't know where D is. You want to come over? We could play gin rummy or just drink."

"Rain check, Dad. So, Mom's at pottery tonight?"

"Yes, pottery," Dad said.

"Where is the pottery?" I asked. "Shouldn't our house be swimming in ceramics by now?"

"She doesn't bring it home anymore."

"So you've seen it?"

"I saw one piece. I made the mistake of laughing. Your mother can be more sensitive than you might imagine."

"Uh-huh. Where is this class of hers?"

"Isabel, she really is taking a pottery class tonight."

"Why all the hobbies?"

"She's trying to keep busy, that's all."

"Have you noticed her work is suffering?"

"It's a phase. It'll pass."

"Where's the class?"

"You're wasting your time, Isabel."

"Maybe I want to take up pottery."

"She's at Sharon Art Studio, next to the carousel at Golden Gate Park."

"Bye, Dad."

I drove straight to the park and wove up the short tree-lined road to the art studio. I circled the building, peering into lit classrooms stocked with a mismatched collection of amateur artists, all paying rapt attention to their paintings or sculptures or the instructor's lecture. I found my mother in the back of the pottery class, straddling a wheel and having a physical altercation with a mass of clay. My lip-reading skills informed me that my mother's moratorium on profanity was purely for Demetrius's benefit. The female instructor, whom I could have spotted in a lineup sight unseen (there are still some patchouli-scented, flower-power retirees left in the city), approached my mother and appeared to offer her soothing words. My mother appeared to respond with less soothing words. The instructor backed away slowly, like you would from a rabid dog.

The snippets of Russian Mom had integrated into her vocabulary, the painstakingly tangled crochet yarn, and a few baked goods that were above par for her, but below par for even an amateur baker, all pointed to the fact that my mother was indeed developing a serious hobby habit, but I couldn't begin to tell you why.

I somehow managed to get through the rest of the week with almost no interaction with Ex 13. Tuesday and Thursday he had late nights and I got sleepy early. Wednesday I claimed to be working a surveillance but went to the movies instead, and Friday I opted to use the Avoidance Method™ for a more professional matter.

A light shone in Vivien Blake's apartment, backlighting her silhouette in the window. She had the hunched posture of someone studying. There was no legal parking with a visual so I edged my car perpendicular to the palm-treed traffic island on Dolores Street. In a city with a dearth of legal parking, some reasonable rule-breaking has been quietly indulged. You could say that about San Francisco in general. We've had a naked guy roaming downtown for years.

I sat in my car, listening to a music-appreciation podcast that Henry had loaded into my iPod. It was as dull as I expected, but I promised to give it a chance. I wondered if five minutes qualified. But then Vivien extinguished her desk lamp, sparing me any more unnecessary educating. Five minutes after her apartment went dark, Vivien was walking east on Twentieth Street and I had to decide whether to follow her in the car (in case she hopped a cab) or hoof it. Since the Mission is rife with young people and booze-soaked establishments, I assumed she would stay in the vicinity. I left my car in the not-so-legal spot and followed subject on foot.

Vivien flashed an ID at the door to [redacted][1] and worked her way through the sloppy maze of inebriated hipsters. Her eyes darted around the room. She was looking for someone, but in the dim light she squinted to distinguish between patrons who seemed oddly homogenized considering how hard they were trying to brand themselves as unique.

Then she stood on her toes, waved, and pushed her way through the crowd to the back of the bar, where two pool tables divided the room. She worked her way to a corner booth and sat down. A young male in many layers of clothes, the top one adorned with a band's name, slid a pint of beer across the table. She took a gulp and turned to the young woman sitting next to her. Vivien said something and the young woman laughed. I saw no introduction take place between the two, and within minutes they were

---

[1] No, I'm not going to tell you which San Francisco bars have a bad eye for fake IDs.

whispering to each other behind the young men's backs. These details are important for one particular reason: The woman sitting with Vivien Blake was none other than Rae Spellman.

I snapped a few photos with my camera, but I couldn't be sure that they would turn out in the dim lighting. This was not the time to confront my sister. While there were two offenses I was witnessing, underage drinking and consorting with a client, it was the second that I took issue with. My parents could handle the first.

As I was walking back to my car in the uncomfortably crisp air, watching my breath blow plumes of smoke into the night, my cell phone buzzed in my pocket.

"My apartment has flooded."

"Okay, I'll be there in about twenty minutes to check on it."

"No," he said. "I mean this time, it really is flooded."

Thirty minutes later, I was helping Walter sop up the bathroom floor with old towels. We'd wring them out and start again. The bathtub had overflowed and spilled onto the bathroom floor. Walter arrived home just in time to stop the flood from bleeding into his bedroom carpet.

"The neighbor called from downstairs," Walter said. "I was on a date. I wasn't even thinking about the bathtub or the toaster. I'm sorry to call you so late. I don't know how this happened. How did this happen?"

"I don't know, Walter. But we'll figure it out." I twisted a heavy towel into the bathtub, dumping at least half a gallon of water. "There's something I should tell you . . ."

And then I told Walter about the previous leak, and the coffeemaker and the toaster that were plugged in when I knew that Walter always unplugged them. And then I mentioned the footprint. Walter reacted with an appropriate shade of concern, but something about his response was off. As if he expected this news. But still, he had to ask the obvious question.

"Why didn't you tell me?" he asked.

"Because, at first I thought you had just slipped up once or twice and I knew that if I told you things would only get worse. But then it occurred to me that something else was going on; someone else was responsible."

"Who would do this to me?" Walter asked.

"I don't know," I replied. "But I'll find out."

I stayed with Walter until there was only a pile of soaked towels as evidence of what had transpired. I dusted the front door for prints but figured I'd find only my own and Walter's. I asked him if anyone knew about his date and he said only his date. I asked where they'd met. Online. She had no idea where he lived. I asked if he would see her again. He told me that he'd asked her out again on the date, but now he wasn't so sure. She bit her nails, and maybe the flood was a sign. I made Walter promise me that if I found out who did this, he would go out with her again. I wouldn't leave until he promised, and he did, because by midnight he really wanted me to leave.

I was exhausted after fighting Walter's deluge, but my brain kept ticking and I knew I wouldn't be able to sleep, so I drove to the Philosopher's Club, hoping that the oafish, uncomplicated company of Bernie would serve as a kind of temporary brainwashing of the day's events. In the morning I could fret about conflicts of interest, investigator misconduct, a client with an unusual form of stalking, and the conversation I'd been dodging at home for the last two months.

But at that moment all I needed was a drink and Bernie's idle chatter. As tiresome as I often find him, you can rely on him for consistency, for making the world seem simple and easy. For Bernie, a beer, some potato chips, a regular poker game, and your life was full.

Unlike most San Francisco bars on a Friday night, there was space to navigate your way through the room with minimal physical contact. A new guy was pulling pints. A student, maybe. Bernie probably figured he could bring in a younger crowd to supplement the senior barfly crowd that closed up shop by eight. That night there was a refreshing mix of young-and-hip and old-and-weathered, each group sectioned apart like lunch bench cliques on a school playground. I couldn't spot Bernie, which means he wasn't spottable—his shiny pate, sheer berth, and booming laugh make it hard for him to blend. He always laughs, even when nothing funny is going on. Once I brought that fact to his attention; he laughed some more.

The jukebox silenced itself after Sinatra crooned his final line and then Nirvana replied. In that brief moment between songs I could hear Bernie chuckling from his office. I strode to the back and knocked on the door.

"Come back later!" he shouted through the splintered wood.

"Police. Open up," I said. I said it because I knew that it would make him open up.

If I could go back in time, things would have gone down differently. I wouldn't have gone to the bar that night; I wouldn't have knocked; I wouldn't have impersonated the fuzz; and Bernie wouldn't have opened the door, revealing him and Gerty, partially clothed, in a decidedly compromising position.

It was not unlike watching the aftermath of a car crash, just with less blood and smoke. But I could not avert my gaze, even as Bernie was buttoning up his shirt and Gerty adjusting her undergarments. Bernie, the most shameless man I know, was shamed enough to kick the door shut in my face. I was grateful to be spared the real-time tableau, but even as I stared back at the splintered wood, I could not erase the image from my mind.

SHELTER FROM THE STORM

I t was late, but I thought that my father might still be awake and desperate for company. It was past twelve thirty when I arrived at the house, so I entered quietly, to avoid disturbing my mother. Work and the sudden glut in extracurricular activities took their toll on Mom and whatever empty hours she had left were spent in bed.

I padded through the dark hallway to the illuminated kitchen, where quiet stirrings of life could be overheard. Literal stirrings, as D was mixing up a batch of awesomeness at the counter.

"What are you making?" I asked upon entering the kitchen.

D dropped the mixing bowl on the floor. It clanked twice then tipped over, spilling half of the chocolaty batter onto the linoleum floor. D started and tripped back against the wall, holding the metal whisk as a weapon. When he saw me, he doubled over and took a few deep breaths. Then he righted himself and attempted a smile.

"You scared me," he said, still catching his breath.

"I'm sorry," I replied. "I forgot."

I got on my knees and began to clean up the oozing matter on the floor. D crouched down to help, but I pushed him away.

"Sit down. I got it," I said.

D sat at the table. I could hear his breathing begin to slow.

"What did I ruin?" I asked, even though I was pretty sure I knew.

"Red velvet cupcakes."

"Damn," I replied. They were out of D's regular circulation since he hadn't yet figured out a healthy version to slip to my father.

"I can make another batch," D replied. "I'll be awake for a while now."

After I cleaned the batter spill, I made D some warm milk and suggested he take something stronger.

"Just a bit," D said. Apparently there were a few drunks in his family and he liked to be careful. I didn't quite follow the logic. We had some excellent drunks in my family too. I poured a splash of whiskey into the milk and sat with D as he drank.

When D was in prison, he lived in a culture of fear. It was no surprise that he required an adjustment period when he was finally released. During the first few months he was out, even basic luxuries stirred discomfort. He couldn't sleep on a regular mattress and ended up using the camping-style cot in the basement. When he finally was away from the endless clatter of prison noise—the screaming, banging, singing—the silence terrified him. I knew of his troubles at the beginning, but since I wasn't living under the same roof, it hadn't occurred to me that D was still coping with the profound changes brought about by his new life. D told me that he survived prison by adhering to strict schedules marking out every hour with a designated activity, whether they were enforced by the warden or by himself. But now there were more free hours than he knew what to do with.

"I take it you're not sleeping any better," I said.

"Better," D said. "Still have nightmares."

"Maybe you need a holiday. Get out of the city. Go camping. Or fishing. I hear fishing is very relaxing. Do you want me to arrange a fishing trip?"

"That's not a good idea," D said.

"Why not?"

"I've seen *Deliverance.* Uh-huh. I'm not ever going fishing. Ever."

D quickly got to his feet and started in on a new task. He measured the flour and baking soda and started all over again on his red velvet cupcake distraction. I got the feeling he wanted to be alone. Being surrounded by Spellmans all day long can take its toll; perhaps these late-night baking sessions were the only times he could truly relax.

"Save me at least three," I said.

"You have my word," D replied.

Then I left through the front door as quietly as I entered. I knew that I too wouldn't be able to sleep, so I drove to my brother's house because it was the most direct route to the best liquor cabinet.

It was late, so I knocked quietly instead of ringing the bell. For the record, if you ring the doorbell in the middle of the night at a house containing small children, sometimes the children start crying and the parents turn on you in the meanest way. There was no answer, so I decided to try the window by the laundry room; Maggie sometimes leaves it unlocked. I circled the house, shoved it open, and snaked my way through, landing with a hard thud on the linoleum. There's nothing like a sloppy window entry to make you feel your age.

The house was quiet and so I thought it best to leave them undisturbed and quietly help myself to enough booze to clear my head once and for all—or at least until the next morning.

The next morning . . .

I was in a house of doors, looking for an escape. I opened the first door only to find Bernie and Gerty in various states of dress or undress. I closed the door and apologized. I opened the next door to find Rae, sitting behind a massive steel desk, crunching numbers with an old-fashioned calculator. She was laughing malevolently, like a villain from an animated feature. I turned to another door. Behind it was Demetrius behind a glass divider; he was back in prison. The glass had holes in it, so I slipped him cigarettes and licorice. I wanted to sit down and talk, but visiting hours were over. Then I opened another door. My mother was seated behind a pottery wheel, reading a book. The rest of her class had their hands dirty on the assignment, but my mother did nothing at all. "What are you up to?" I asked. "Expanding my horizons," my dream mother said with a wicked wink. I slammed that door. Then I opened another one, thinking this had to be the way out. I found a child in the center of the room. She looked like my niece.

She said, "Banana.

"Banana.

"Banana."

I opened my eyes. Everything looked familiar but unfamiliar.

There was a child up close, right in front of my face. She said, "Banana." I sat up on the couch.

My head throbbed; my throat was dry.

"Banana."

I was in David's house. On the couch in the living room.

Sydney's bedroom is on the first floor. She must have woken up before her parents, broken out of the crib, and navigated into the living room. I thought they had a dog gate or something. I made a mental note not to call it a dog gate in front of my brother.

"You want a banana?" I asked.

Sydney nodded her head.

I got to my feet and stretched. My head throbbed more assertively. I put what was left of the bottle of bourbon back in the cabinet and took the glass into the kitchen. Sydney followed me. I found a banana in a bowl above the sink. I yanked one off the bunch and started to peel it. I'm not clear on whether 1.5-year-olds need help with such matters, but I was fairly certain she wouldn't be offended. I handed her the banana.

"No apple!" she screamed, and then she started crying. Loudly.

My head throbbed some more. "Please don't cry," I said. "Aunt Izzy has a terrible hangover." I poured myself a glass of water, downed it in a single sloppy gulp.

"Banana," Sydney said between teary hiccups.

"Got it. Banana. I'm on it," I said. I opened the refrigerator and pulled out a carton of milk. "Banana?" I asked.

"Banana!"

"Right," I said. "This is called milk."

"Banana."

I poured a glass of milk and Sydney said, "More banana."

"You can have more *milk* when you finish this."

It then occurred to me that I'd never seen Sydney drink out of a glass before and the consequences might be severe.

"Where are the sippy cups, Sydney?"

Then it occurred to me that I'd never used that phrase before and I started laughing. Sydney raised the volume on her crying jag and David entered the room with an expression that mingled exhaustion with horror, which probably matched my expression, catching sight of early-morning David. Truth be told, I've never seen early-morning New David before. I'm not saying that Old David woke up with perfect hair and brushed teeth and scrubbed skin, but he was always the first in the shower and never neglected his grooming. In fact, until the Age of Sydney there had been only a handful of days where I'd seen him with stubble or a razor cut or matted hair or an unpleasant body odor. This morning, he was a particular eyesore. His flannel pajamas were frayed at the bottom, paired with a well-worn JUSTICE 4 MERRI-WEATHER T-shirt.[1] And he wore two different socks; the one on the right had a hole allowing his big toe to peek through. His face bore creases from sleep and I'd rather not even mention the state of his hair. Not that I was daisy fresh myself, but I could fetch the newspaper without scaring the neighbor.

"Isabel, what are you doing here?" David asked.

"I'm looking for a sippy cup," I replied, and then I doubled over be-

---

[1] FREE SCHMIDT is also in his regular circulation. Rae and I are both peeved that during the time of these T-shirts' relevance, David refused to wear them outside where they might do some good.

cause it was even funnier saying it to an adult. Then it occurred to me that I might still be a tiny bit drunk.

"I mean," David replied, "what are you doing in my house?"

"I slept here."

"Did Maggie let you in late last night?"

"No. I crawled through the window of your laundry room. You should probably close the latch at night."

"I probably should. Why didn't you sleep in your own home?"

"I couldn't face him after what I saw." The image of Gerty and Bernie was burned in my mind.

"What did you do?" David asked.

"Banana," Sydney said. Although you probably figured out that it wasn't me or David saying it.

"I didn't do anything!" I shouted.

Sydney cried some more and asked for a banana.

"What does she want?" I asked.

David grabbed a box of Cheerios from the top cabinet and a bowl and showed them to his daughter.

"Do you want cereal?"

"Yes, banana!" Sydney sniffled.

"This is called cereal," David said.

He took the milk from the glass and poured it in the bowl.

"Milk," he said as he poured. "What do you say?" he asked.

"Tank you."

"I bet you're glad she didn't say 'banana.'"

David rolled his eyes and took a deep breath. "I keep thinking one day I'll wake up and have a normal family."

"I have that same dream," I replied. "Will you please make me some coffee?" I asked, taking a seat at the table. "Or do you call that 'banana' too?"

David made coffee (I suspect not just for me). He inquired about last night's events but my head was hurting too much to speak. Instead, I was trying to make linguistic sense of the whole banana mystery.

"What does 'banana' mean?"

"It means she's hungry. That's all," David replied.

"When you show her a banana, she calls it an apple."

"I am aware of that," David replied.

Sydney sat in her high chair across from me and ate Cheerios and milk. At least 40 percent of her meal ended up on that plastic platter thing that locks her in place. She was staring at me a lot, like I had an extra nose or something.

Then again, I was gawking at her horrendous table manners.

"She really doesn't have that spoon business down yet, does she?"

David kindly put a steaming mug of black coffee in front of me. I took a few sips, which seemed to clear some of the cobwebs from my brain. Before Sydney was born, David and Maggie placed her on several waiting lists for highly competitive preschools. My brother's goal is to have her reading by age three. There was not a moment of father-daughter quality time in which he didn't sneak in some educational activity. And yet the kid said "banana" when she was hungry and thought an apple was called "banana." But she sure as hell knew who Elmo is and what a sippy cup looks like, and she'd cry if you said "broccoli." Suddenly it all became clear to me. Well, not everything, just the whole banana mystery. "I believe I've cracked the case," I said.

"What case?" David replied, sitting down at the table with his own mug.

"It was Rae, wasn't it?"

David didn't reply.

"Rae did this. When she lived here, she used to babysit. Often. She had all the time in the world to mess with your daughter's early speech patterns. Oh. My. God."

David stared out the window. I could see the vein in his forehead throb the way it does when he's choking back anger.

"But why? Just as a joke? Even for her, that seems sick."

David combed his fingers through his matted hair. "She said it was a linguistics experiment. She was taking a class—"

"Rae was doing experiments on your daughter and there's no payback?"

"I kicked her out, didn't I?"

"Yes, but your response was not in proportion with your previous MO."

"Of course it is," David replied.

"When I was thirteen you took me to small-claims court after I borrowed your electric razor."

"Even now you won't admit you stole it?"

"I'm changing the subject. Don't you want some blood?" I asked.

"It's not my style, Isabel."

"Maybe you should give it a try. You might find you have a taste for it."

THE MORNING AFTER

The night before, shortly after I tumbled through David's window, I'd left a message on Henry's cell phone telling him that I was working an all-night surveillance and would see him in the morning. He never phoned back. When I arrived home, I immediately hopped into the shower and then bed, trying unsuccessfully not to wake Henry.

"Your hair is still wet," Henry said.

"You cops never miss a thing," I mumbled.

"Is there something you want to tell me?" he asked.

"I love you?"

"You're going to have to do better than that," he said.

"But that's my best material," I replied.

"Isabel, you obviously have something you want to say to me, otherwise you wouldn't be so desperate to avoid me."

There was some truth in his observation, but I was in no condition to be having a serious conversation, so I did some deflecting instead. And, frankly, I'm better at that anyway. "I'm sure there are many things I have to say to you, but now I'd just like to go to sleep."

"Where were you last night?"

"Where were *you* last night?"

"I was at home."

"Do you have an alibi?" I asked. I probably shouldn't have.

"No, but neither do you," Henry said. "I phoned your mother. There was no job."

"It was off the books," I replied. "And I don't appreciate you checking up on me."

"We need to talk."

"Not that again."

"We need to have a serious conversation."

"Well, since it's serious, I'll need to prepare. How about the first Tuesday in December, seven P.M.?"

"You need two months to prepare?"

"Sounds about right."

"I'm not waiting two months."

"There will be a PowerPoint presentation. And, currently, I don't know how to use PowerPoint. So I'll have to take a class."

"I'm not finding any of this funny."

"I'll also be working on some better material."

"One of these days, you're going to have to be honest with me."

"I'll need a clear head for that which requires sleep," I said, resting my head on the pillow.

Henry kissed me on the forehead and said, "I love you too," but he didn't look happy about it. When Henry's sad, his face loses all expression. His eyes go dead. It doesn't happen often. I prefer every other version of Henry over this one—even grumpy Henry, angry Henry, and making-me-clean-the-house Henry. In fact, all three of those rolled up into one, I prefer to sad Henry.

"I'm sorry," I said.

"That's not enough," he said, closing the bedroom door as he departed.

Six hours later . . .

I woke again, checked the clock: 2:24 P.M. If I got out of bed and Henry was home, I couldn't continue with my Avoidance Method™. I phoned

Demetrius from my cell phone to do a reconnaissance mission. "I need you to do me a favor and call Henry's cell phone."

"I see," D replied. "And after I call Henry, what do I say to him?"

"Find out where he is," I whispered.

"And why would I do that?"

"Because I asked nicely," I said, nicely, to compensate for the previous absence of niceness.

"There's some faulty logic in your plan," D said.

"Is there?"

"Why would I call Henry and ask for his coordinates?"

"I don't know. Can't you come up with something?"

"Maybe. But I don't see why I should."

"Scratch Plan A. Just call his cell and ask if I'm home."

"Why would I call Henry's cell phone if I wanted to talk to you?" D wisely asked.

"Good point. Call the home line. If he doesn't pick up, call his cell phone. Then say you're looking for me, but my phone is turned off."

"The plan is improving. But you could just ask him where he is yourself."

"Why can't you just do what I ask without asking all these questions?" I whispered, but as loudly as one can whisper.

"Why are you whispering?"

"So Henry can't hear me."

"Then you know where he is."

"I don't know for sure that he's home. He can be very quiet sometimes."

"I see."

"He reads books."

"Good-bye, Isabel," Demetrius said.

It was hard to tell whether he was hanging up on me to go about his day or if he was going to enact my plan.

One minute later, the home phone rang and no one picked up.

Five minutes later, D called me back.

"Henry is at the store. He will be back in approximately twenty minutes. Any more ridiculous phone calls you want me to make?" D asked.

"No, thank you," I replied, hoping he was merely fishing for some gratitude.

I hung up the phone and quickly got dressed. I had the sense that I was on the run. My heart raced as I grabbed all my essentials—car keys, identification, a warm coat, and pepper spray. I got into my car, started the engine, and, without even thinking about it, drove to Bernie's place. I rang the doorbell twice and knocked until my knuckles were red. Bernie opened the door while I was in midknock. My fist almost made contact with his face.

"Izzeee," he said with a sheepish grin. He didn't try to pull me into a bear hug. I was pretty sure my expression warned against all physical contact.

"Are you alone?" I asked.

"Aren't we all?" Bernie replied, trying to sound philosophical. It didn't suit him.

"Bernie, is the apartment empty other than you and your spent beer cans?"

"I'm here all by my lonesome."

"Invite me in," I said. I never thought I'd say that to Bernie.

"Where are my manners?" Bernie said. "Please come in. Can I get you anything?"

I opened the fridge, took out a beer, and sat down on his couch.

"How long has it been going on?" I asked.

Bernie got himself a drink, shuffled over to his threadbare La-Z-Boy, sat down, and shifted its gears into hospital-bed mode. He rested his beer on his belly. "Not very long."

"She's been in town five weeks. I want a number."

"We just celebrated our three-week anniversary."

"Jesus," I said.

"At my age finding love ain't so easy."

"Love?" I drank half the beer.

"You're always so judgmental," Bernie said.

"End it," I said.

"What if I don't want to?"

"She's married, Bernie. End it."

"They're separated," Bernie replied. "And you can't make me do anything."

"Watch me," I said.

AFTER THE FLOOD

I t had been five days since the flood and I hadn't heard a peep out of Walter. I called to check on him. "Are you home?" I asked.

"It's my day off. Where else would I be?" Walter asked.

"Out," I replied. "I could give you a list of places that are out, but that seems unnecessary."

"It's better if I stay home and keep an eye on things," Walter said.

"Like what?"

"My apartment."

"I really think you should go out, Walter."

"No, thank you. I don't like it there."

I imagined Walter roaming his apartment in an endless loop like a night watchman, securing faucets, tapping light fixtures, raking carpets. I decided to pay my favorite client a visit.

I found Walter in a matching pajama set and robe. He looked like an actor from a 1950s comedy. Rock Hudson's sidekick, maybe. He offered me a cappuccino, which he made with impeccable precision. It was on par with that Blue Bottle place the whole damn city won't shut up about. He even made some kind of frothy design on top.

"How are you doing?" I asked.

"How does it look like I'm doing?" he said. "I'm a complete mess."

"You actually just look like a normal person having a leisurely Sunday afternoon."

"Only it's Thursday evening."

"I know, Walter."

Walter and I went over a list of his known associates who had a key at one time or another to his apartment. His wife, his brother, the building super, and four previous housekeepers (all quit of their own free will). I asked him whether he'd changed the locks after their employment ceased and he responded in the negative. I inquired why and he said he didn't like change and that everyone who left him wanted to leave; they had no interest in coming back. I suggested that we hook up a video camera to a bookshelf in the foyer. Walter refused, saying he couldn't have equipment plugged in while he was gone. I reminded him that he keeps his refrigerator plugged in, but that did little to sway him. Plus, the equipment would look all wrong and he didn't want to be staring at a camera every time he walked through his own front door.

I argued for a good twenty minutes on this topic, until I realized it was a hopeless cause. "When's the last time you went out?" I asked.

"I don't know," Walter replied.

"Get dressed," I said. "We're getting out of here."

Walter resisted but eventually caved, though he dragged his feet getting out of the house. He changed his shirt twice, his shoes three times. Something was wrong with his left sock, and even though all his socks are exactly the same, he had to find a new pair that was just right. His shaving took a half hour; he cleaned his glasses twice.

"Jesus, Walter, you're like a debutante going to the ball," I shouted from the living room.

When Walter surfaced for the fifth time that afternoon, he looked exactly the same as the other four times, besides the shirt change, which was so subtle I wouldn't have noticed if he hadn't told me. I unplugged all the appliances and raked the carpet behind Walter's steps so he would resist the urge to return to his bedroom and make some other sartorial adjustment.

"Walter," I said with as threatening a tone as I could muster, "open the door. We're leaving *now*."

I used the carpet rake as a kind of blockade, backing Walter toward the door. I finished swiping clean lines on the carpet, erasing my final footprint, and left the rake leaning against the foyer wall. We locked the door and left.

Outside, we had to come up with a plan for how to kill time.

I asked Walter what he did for fun and he couldn't answer the question. When I suggested a movie, Walter described the myriad layers of filth one finds in a place where people eat with their hands and drink and spill syrupy beverages and laugh and cry and cough and blow their noses and use restrooms without washing their hands. So, a movie was out. I'm not known as a museum-goer, but I figured since people aren't allowed to touch the artwork, it might be a safe haven. Walter told me art gave him a headache, because he always wanted to change it. Then I mentioned a café, since it looked like it was going to rain, and Walter reminded me that in cafés people touch things too.

It was dusk by the time Walter and I left his apartment and made a plan for the evening. Since Walter had no hobbies beyond cleaning and chatting with fellow math geeks about impossible equations, I persuaded him to accompany me on a surveillance, which I considered at the time an incredible step toward recovery for Walter. The only glitch in the plan was my car. I opened the passenger door for Walter; he took one look and said, "No."

I grabbed a garbage bag from the trunk and cleaned out old newspapers, receipts, coffee cups, water bottles, junk mail, and any other unidentifiable item that didn't blend with my car's brown leather seats, and tossed it in the trash. Walter returned to his apartment to fetch a Dustbuster, which he used to vacuum every surface of the interior. Then Walter asked me to pop the trunk.

"Why?" I asked.

"So we can clean it," he replied.

"But you won't be sitting in the trunk," I reminded him.

"It would make me feel better," Walter said.

I acquiesced but insisted on taking over Dustbuster responsibilities to move along the evening. Walter hovered as I cleaned, making helpful remarks like "You missed a spot," "Over there," "Do the corner again," and such until I told Walter that I was done. The way I said it suggested that any resistance would be met with the emptying of the Dustbuster over his head. Well, it's likely I verbalized that scenario after I said more severely, "I'm done."

Clean car, surveillance waiting, once again, I opened the passenger-side door and said, "Shall we?"

To which Walter replied, "No."

"Walter, please. It's not dirty anymore."

"You just can't see it."

"Walter, this is no way to live."

"I thought I could, but I can't. Much has happened in that car," Walter said.[1]

"What are we going to do?" I asked.

"We could take my car," Walter replied.

"You might have mentioned that before I spent thirty minutes delousing my entire vehicle for you."

"You'll thank me later," Walter replied.

"No! I won't."

Twenty minutes later, I was in the passenger seat of Walter's Volvo as he drove down Market Street at exactly the speed limit of thirty-five miles per hour.

"You should have let me drive."

"I'm the only person who has ever driven this car. And it's going to stay that way."

---

[1] You have no idea.

"Not true."

"It is. I bought it brand-new."

"You don't think anyone test-drove the car first?" I asked.

"I don't like to think about that," Walter replied.

The notion that Walter hadn't been the only driver of his vehicle stirred some tension in the recycled air.[2] I distracted him by providing directions to our destination. He followed my instructions and every traffic law. When we arrived at the apartment on lower Haight, I had Walter double-park a few doors down. Then I made the phone call.

"What?" she said.

"You're on the clock tonight. The Blakes want Vivien surveilled this evening."

"On a Thursday night?" Rae asked.

"Thursday's the new Friday, haven't you heard?"

"Fine. What time should I start?"

"As soon as you can."

"Got it," she said, and disconnected the call without even a good-bye.

"Who are we surveilling?" Walter asked.

"My sister," I replied.

Even if my sister did follow my instructions, I knew it might take her some time to get ready. I decided to grill Walter about his potential enemies in the interim.

"I'm a nice person," Walter said. "I don't make enemies."

"But sometimes you get them without even trying," I replied. "For instance, how many students do you have at any given time?"

"I have fifty-three right now. Last semester forty-eight, the semester before that—"

"Do they all get A's?"

---

[2] Walter couldn't drive unless the windows were sealed shut.

"Hardly any of them get A's."

"Well, then any one of those students is a suspect."

"But I teach calculus, Isabel; there's no subjectivity in the grading. Most of the tests are done with a Scantron. No student comes to me asking to change their score. It's their score."

"You're telling me you've never had a run-in with a student before?"

"I'm telling you that I help my students to the best of my ability and that I cannot think of any one of them who would be capable of this."

"How about colleagues?" I asked.

"Unlikely," he replied, but I could tell it got him thinking.

"Impossible?"

"Tenure is a messy business," he said.

"Bingo. We've got motive."

"This is giving me a headache," Walter replied; then he did a subject U-turn. "You should really get your car detailed," he said. "But don't just take it to a regular car wash. I have a guy." Walter picked some lint off my jacket.

"Knock it off, Walter, we're on a job."

After a half hour passed, I pulled a pair of binoculars from my bag, wiped them down with the antibacterial wipes that Walter keeps in abundance in his car, and passed them to my driver. "Keep an eye on that building, second from the corner. Let me know if someone comes to the front door—specifically, someone small and blond. Any questions?"

"I'm on it," he said, already gazing through the magnified lens.

I buzzed Rae's door and then slipped around the corner. The gate release buzzed back, but no one came to the door. I waited a minute and buzzed again and slipped back into my hiding place. The gate release buzzed again[3] and I slipped away. This time I could hear footsteps descending the stairs, the gate clinking open and shut, and then footsteps

---

[3] This is common practice in San Francisco—you buzz someone into your building sight unseen and hope for the best. Don't get any ideas.

ascending the stairs. I threw the hood of my sweatshirt over my head and hightailed it back to the car.

"What did you see?" I asked Walter.

"Exactly what you described. A petite blond woman, looked like a teenager, came to the door, looked out, and then returned."

"That was my sister."

"So, she's home safe. That's a good thing, right?" Walter said.

"No," I replied. "It's not."

I sent Rae a text.

On the clock yet?

duh.[4]

GR8.

I clicked my phone shut, satisfied that I'd officially caught my sister in the act. Only now I had to figure out why.

"Do me a favor, Walter: Remember tonight, in case I need confirmation."

"I'll never forget it," Walter replied, almost beaming.

"Are you enjoying yourself, Walter?"

"I don't know," he said. "I think maybe a little."

"Most people like the idea of a stakeout but hate it in reality."

"I've never done anything like this before," Walter said.

"I'm glad to hear it," I replied, "because it's kind of like stalking."

"I was thinking it was more like being in a cop show and we're partners. Detectives Perkins and Spellman."

"I should get top billing."

"Spellman and Perkins."

"That sounds better," I said.

"I never break routine," Walter said, almost wistfully.

"It doesn't have to be like that."

"Easy for you to say," he replied. "All you do is break routine."

"Sometimes it certainly seems that way."

---

[4] While it wouldn't hold up in a court of law, it can be assumed this means yes.

Two hours later, when I was certain that Rae was going nowhere on her Vivien Blake surveillance, I took Walter home. His power was completely out. After checking with the neighbors, it became clear that only Walter was affected by this mysterious outage. We checked the circuit breaker and then called PG&E. Apparently Walter, with all of his identifying information, had informed the power company that he would be moving out of his residence and wanted the electricity and gas shut off immediately. Walter promptly informed them that the call was a fake and in a few hours the power was restored.

All his clocks had to be reset immediately, which required Walter to call the number for the exact time and reset them one by one. And then call the number again to double-check. Walter's mental state had clearly taken a turn for the worse.

"Maybe you should stay in a hotel tonight," I suggested.

"Do you have any idea what goes on in those places?"

"Walter, think about the list. E-mail it to me in the morning."

"Okay," Walter said, scanning the room for signs of intruders.

"If it makes you feel any better," I said, "no one came in."

"How can you be sure?" he asked.

"Because I put a piece of Scotch tape on the door, just in case. It was still there when we came back."

"I didn't see you do that."

"I didn't want you to see it."

"Thank you, Isabel."

"Good night, Walter."

If you're wondering about the tape business, I'll come clean. It was a lie. But I needed Walter to get some rest that night. Someone was playing games with his head, but I knew they weren't playing games with his life.

As I walked to my car, upon leaving Walter's apartment, my cell phone rang. The caller ID said the number was private, but I picked up anyway.

"Hello?"

"Is this Sandra?" a female voice asked.

"No, you have the wrong number."

"Lorraine?"

"No," I replied. "Maybe you have the wrong number and the wrong name."

"Can I ask who I'm speaking to?"

"It's you again, isn't it?"

"I'm sorry?"

"Where did you get my phone number?" I asked.

"You are up to some very unusual business," the woman said, and disconnected the call.

The first call had been a nuisance. The second one left me with a slightly queasy feeling in my gut. I was being watched. As you can imagine, it's not my favorite condition to be in.

HOME

I returned to what appeared to be an empty house. All the lights were out except for a single lamp in Henry's study. He was sitting at his desk, tilted back in a chair. A recently cracked bottle of bourbon on the desk, not from any rain boot I know of. A full glass sat next to it. But I could tell from the rings on the blotter that this was not his first drink.

"I'm sorry I'm late," I said.

He nodded his head and took a sip. Then he handed the glass to me. I took a gulp because it had really been a long day . . . well, more than a day. It seemed like a week since I'd had a moment to just sit and think. I sat down on the couch. Despite what he'd said in our previous conversation, Henry did not want to talk. I waited just to be sure. And even though I didn't want to talk, I knew that something was terribly wrong and so I had to talk because sometimes you have to do things you don't want to do. Which seems obvious to most people, but it's just another item in a laundry list of things I figured out later in life than I should have.

"Are you all right?" I asked.

"I don't know," he replied.

"Maybe you've had too much to drink," I said.

Henry's not a drinker; in fact, I can't recall ever seeing him sloshed. Miraculously, he was on the verge.

"Maybe I haven't had enough to drink."

"I shouldn't have left," I said, assuming the silence was my doing.

"It wouldn't have made a difference."

"Do I know what we're talking about?"

"No."

"Will you tell me?"

Henry poured another finger and then another. "My parents are getting a divorce," he said.

"Maybe it's just a trial separation," I said as I plotted diabolical plans against Bernie.

"No. They've been separated for a while, it seems. My father just filed."

"Where's your mother?"

"She's staying with a friend."

"What friend?" I asked.

"That woman from college."

"Have you met her?" I asked.

"Not yet."

"Can I get you anything?"

"No."

He looked like he needed to be alone and I needed some sleep, so I got up to leave.

"Isabel."

"Yes?"

"Things change. People don't stay in one place for the rest of their lives."

You might assume that Henry was speaking of his parents, but he wasn't. The message was for me.

"I know," I replied.

Henry left early the next morning. I phoned Gerty, but the call went to voice mail and I wasn't sure what kind of message to leave. "Break up with that fat slob" seemed like the kind of thing you should say face-to-face.

I went into the office and found my mother and Demetrius in the living room lounging by the fireplace. Mom was studying for a Russian quiz while Demetrius read her book club selection for the month.

"Ready for your quiz?" I asked.

"Vyshe golovy ne prygnesh," Mom said.

"Gesundheit."

"It means 'You can't jump higher than your head,'" Mom said.

"Your point is?" I asked.

"One can't do more than what is humanly possible," D said, clarifying. I had a feeling he'd been quizzing Mom on her Russian. *"Dosvedanya,"* I said, heading into the office.

"Surprise family dinner tonight. Everyone will be there," said Mom.

"Like the Pope?"

"No, I mean, like, the whole family."

"David agreed to be in the same room as Rae?"

"Opposite ends of the table, but not facing each other, so no eye contact is required. One of these days he's going to tell me what happened. This whole thing is ridiculous. We're making coq au vin."

"When you say 'we,' I do hope you mean Demetrius."

"I'm his sous chef," Mom said.

Then she turned to D, who was still "engrossed" in the book, which means he was staring at the pages with wide eyes and a baffled crinkle in his forehead.

"How is it?" I asked.

"Poignant," D dryly replied.

"I *hate* poignant," Mom said.

"Mom, why join a book club if you're never going to read the books and you don't like the company?"

"One of those women is bound to have a cheating husband and will want to put a detective on the case."

"I see. So it's purely a business decision. Still doesn't explain the crocheting and the Russian lessons and the cooking classes."

"Sweetie, some of us think that one should have extracurricular activities besides shooting pool and drinking beer."

"At least I enjoy my extracurricular activities. Is Dad in?"

"Nope. He's out."

"Where? On a job?" I asked.

"Chinese wall," my mom replied.

I entered the office, shut the door, and turned on my father's computer. It was password-protected but I'd figured his out four years ago and he still hadn't changed it. "ThreePete." The name of his bachelor-days dog. A three-legged mutt who came from the pound named Pete. Hence, ThreePete.[1] He had the dog for seven years until he met his future wife with the debilitating dog allergies and had to choose. I typed the password as I'd done many times before. An alarm sounded on the computer and the screen went black. Then red bricks surfaced against the black background, slowly building a wall.

Only one computer geek could have been behind this. The number was in the speed dial.

"Speak," Robbie Gruber, our abusive computer consultant, said.

"You and my sister should hang out. You have similar phone manners."

"I take it you tried to sign into your father's computer," Robbie said.

"Nice job with the wall. Would have been cooler if it looked like the Great Wall of China and not a Pink Floyd album cover."

"There wasn't time to get fancy."

"What'll it cost for you to give me his password?"

"Too steep for you. But now it'll cost you fifty to keep the bribe from your dad."

"Right," I said, not quite believing.

---

[1] Dad used to boast of the fact that he had a three-legged dog before three-legged dogs became fashionable.

"I'll call him as soon as we hang up."

"Will you take a check?"

"Cash. Today."

"Seventy-five if you tell me how to make the wall disappear so my dad doesn't know I tried to log on to his computer."

Robbie negotiated me up to a hundred and remotely reset Dad's computer. He told me that if I tried to infiltrate again, the hush money would enter the four-digit range. Robbie's threats were always real. I learned that lesson the hard way. After my failed security breach, I needed some non-Spellman air.

"Where are you going, sweetie?" my mom asked.

"Out," I replied.

"I hear it's nice this time of year. Make sure you're back inside by dinnertime. Oh, and invite Henry and Gerty."

"I think I'll spare them, if you don't mind."

The rest of us, however, could not be saved.

GUESS WHO'S COMING TO DINNER?

Some events in your life you wish you remembered perfectly so you could revisit them again and again. This was not one of them, yet I recorded it anyway. In my family's history, there may have been no better example of domestic misfortune. This night needed to be archived, if only to be used as evidence at a later date.

Mom and Demetrius prepared dinner as if they were cooking an innocent man's final meal. The kitchen bubbled with delectable sauces and a blend of mouth-watering aromas that my mother is incapable of creating on her own. It seemed like this meal could very well have turned out to be D's masterpiece. Too bad there was this inexplicable sense of doom hovering in the atmosphere.

I noticed something was amiss when Mom set the table. I've got simple math down and there was one extra place setting that didn't add up.

"Mom, Sydney still uses a high chair."

"I know that," my mother replied.

"Then who is the special guest?"

"It's a surprise."

"A good surprise or the kind of surprise you're keeping secret so no one can make a getaway plan?"

"What on earth are you talking about, Isabel?"

The doorbell rang. I answered it. No surprise: David, Maggie, Sydney. The usual family-like hellos were made.

"Sorry I missed you yesterday morning," Maggie said. "I hope the couch was to your liking."

"Sorry about that," I said. "Next time, I'll call."

"Or you could sleep in your own home," David suggested.

My mother grabbed Sydney from David and started making some very strange noises and asked ridiculous questions, like "Where's your nose?" "Do you have a toe?" "Who's my little banana?"

"Don't say that word!" David said, pulling Sydney away from her grandma.

Speaking of bananas, the doorbell rang again. It was Rae. David gave her a wide berth when she entered the house and refused to make eye contact. Maggie, more forgiving, gave her a kiss and asked her how she was doing.

Rae was about to reply but was interrupted by Sydney shouting her name from across the room, her arms outstretched as she tried to wriggle out of David's grasp.

"Rae Rae. Rae Rae. Rae Rae."

David mumbled, "*Mengele*."

"What did you say?" my mother asked.

"Nothing," David replied.

"Hi, Sydney," Rae said in an extremely high-pitched voice.

Sydney continued her escape attempts only to have David spin her around to keep Rae out of her line of sight.

"David, let her walk or she'll forget how," Maggie said, not for the first time.

The moment David put Sydney on her feet, she rushed to her younger and apparently far more appealing aunt and gave her leg a warm embrace. Rae bent down and kissed Sydney on the cheek.

"Did you miss me?"

Sydney repeated Rae's name several more times.

"Why don't you say hello to your aunt Izzy?" David said, trying to maneuver his daughter in my direction.

"Hey, how's it going?" I said.

David scowled.

Sydney clocked me and turned back to Rae.

"Why do you talk to her like that?" David asked.

"Like what?"

"Like she's your mechanic or something."

"We could use a mechanic in the family."

"Leave her alone," Maggie said. "If you're always snapping at her, Sydney will pick up on it."

"You need to babysit," David said, "and bond with your niece."

Before a date could be set, my dad arrived home with our "surprise" guest. Silence washed over the crowd the moment she passed the threshold. It was as if we were all frozen in place. No one could summon the appropriate words. Of course it was David, the one Spellman who aspires to normalcy, who spoke first. He even tried to toss some enthusiasm into his voice, but it merely added volume.

"Grammy Spellman, so good to see you."

I learned at an early age to avoid eye contact with Grammy, so I spent an awful lot of time staring at her feet. What I first noticed is that she was wearing the same black orthotic shoes as always, paired with opaque pantyhose in a flesh tone that made her legs appear like those of a mannequin. Since she's always wearing polyester pants, the pantyhose seem unnecessary. When I was twelve I made the mistake of asking her if she knew about these new things called *socks*. She insisted that I go to bed without supper. My mother, not in the mood to get tangled into another disagreement with her mother-in-law, simply sent me to my room and, when Grammy was out of sight, snuck up half the contents of the pantry into my bedroom, since she had a feeling I would be there for a while. Even when you slice away the emotional debris and just take in her physical appearance, Grammy still cuts a severe impression. Her short gray hair sits on her head like a helmet, and her frown lines have burrowed so deeply into her flesh that you can't imagine her muscles can fight the gravity to form a smile. And yet she still possesses an odd streak of vanity, which manifests itself primarily in her physique. I've heard at least one hundred and ten times that Grammy still weighs one hundred and ten pounds. When I was fifteen, Grammy repeated her announcement, after becoming alarmed to learn that I weighed one hundred and twenty-five pounds; I responded with "Who gives a fuck?" That was another night I was sent to bed without dinner—at least not that Grammy knew about.

When Rae was a little girl and I was reading her the Brothers Grimm, she once told me that every time there was a mean old woman in the story, she pictured Grammy. David was more diplomatic and said, "Not everyone can be like Nana Montgomery" (my mom's mom who died when I was six, a loopy old lady who always had candy and comic books stuffed in her massive handbag). My dad offered no excuses for his mother and simply apologized whenever she arrived and thanked us for our patience when she departed. Mom always acted as the guard, doing her best to shield her children from a very mean, bitter old woman. And while it is clear that no one in my family liked Grammy Spellman, I was her enemy number one.

David approached the Spellman matriarch and gave her a quick peck on the cheek. Other reserved greetings were made. Grammy looked Maggie up and down with generalized disappointment and said, unconvincingly, "Welcome to the family." One can assume that Grammy was still holding a grudge for not being invited to the wedding. In fact, I think David and Maggie kept the group under thirty for that very reason. Grammy turned to Sydney and asked if she had been a good girl. Sydney did not reply. My mother managed a Stepford-wife smile and gave

Grammy a stiff embrace, which was not returned. Then Grammy was introduced to D. I think she thought he was the butler or something, because she handed him her coat.

"This is Demetrius. He works for us, but not as a valet," my mother said as she took the coat from D and hung it up.

People started grabbing drinks immediately. Not Grammy Spellman, a teetotaler who doesn't even drink tea. When I was seventeen, I slipped some brandy in her apple cider, hoping she wouldn't notice, but she smelled it immediately and demanded that I be grounded for a week. My parents thoroughly embraced grounding during my teenage years, but this was one act of defiance that I got away with. In fact, my mom slipped me a twenty just for trying.

Once all the guests were seated at the dinner table, I turned on my tape recorder. A visit from Grammy Spellman is a rare enough event, but this visit, which started off as, say, a Category One hurricane, turned into a Category Four once the news was broken.

But first the silence at the dinner table needed breaking:

DAVID: The food looks amazing, Demetrius.

D: I'm testing a new recipe, so feel free to be honest.

[MAGGIE takes a bite of the coq au vin.]

MAGGIE: Incredible, D. You've outdone yourself.

DAVID: I feel like all I ever eat these days are fish sticks and grilled cheese sandwiches.

GRAMMY: You *have* put on weight, haven't you?

DAD: Mom, that's a little rude, don't you think?

GRAMMY: One side of our family tends to get heavy, so you have to be extra careful. You might have caught some of that gene, David.

DAVID: Or, I'm busy raising a child and don't have as much time to go to the gym.

ME: Maggie, will you pass the wine?

GRAMMY: Empty calories, Isabel.

159

ME: "Empty" is an appropriate word, since that's how I feel inside.

DAD: [warning] Isabel.

GRAMMY: I never understood this one.

RAE: You and me both.

ME: Shut up, *Mengele*.

GRAMMY: Watch your language,[1] Isabel.

RAE: I'm shocked you even know who that is.

ME: I know a lot more than you think. And a lot of it you're going to want me to keep to myself.

RAE: Do you have anything besides idle threats up your sleeve?

DAVID: [glaring viciously] I do.

GRAMMY: [to my mother] You should have sent this one[2] to finishing school, like I asked.

MOM: [ignoring her] Would somebody please tell me what is going on with you three? David, I've never seen you hold a grudge this long.

DAVID: I don't want to talk about it.

MOM: This can't go on forever.

SYDNEY: Banana.

DAVID: [to Maggie] She wants potatoes.

GRAMMY: Then why did she say "banana"?

ME: Don't go there.

GRAMMY: Don't go where?

D: [trying to cut the tension] Coq au vin is such a rich meal, I had to complement it with salad and sunchokes. However, I had an incredible recipe for fingerling potatoes; I couldn't resist.

GRAMMY: Does the cook usually eat with the family?

MOM: Ruth,[3] I thought Albert explained this to you. Demetrius is our employee at Spellman Investigations and he lives in the attic apart-

---

[1] Heh. She thinks *that's* language.

[2] "This one" or "that one" is always me.

[3] That's Grammy Spellman's first name, by the way. Nobody calls her that but Mom. And her friends. Have yet to meet one, but I'm told they exist.

ment. He enjoys cooking and so he was kind enough to make this meal for us, but he is *not* our personal chef.

[I pour some wine, scan the table for takers, until the bottle is empty.]

GRAMMY: I see. I apologize for the misunderstanding, Mr. Demetrius.

D: No apology necessary.

DAD: The fingerling potatoes are amazing.

MOM: So is the salad. Hint, hint.

DAD: This is a French meal, so the salad comes last.

GRAMMY: I think Morgan Freeman is an excellent actor.

[Complete silence.]

ME: Pass the potatoes.

D: Why don't you finish the ones on your plate first?

ME: Pass the salad then.

MOM: Save some for your father.

ME: Okay, I'll have more wine.

[While the conversation continues, I get up and search for another bottle in the kitchen. It's white and room temperature, but that's what ice cubes are for.]

GRAMMY: I really liked that movie *Driving Miss Daisy*.

RAE: Oh my God.

MAGGIE: Really, the food is simply amazing.

SYDNEY: Banana.

DAVID: Potatoes, Sydney. They're called po-ta-toes.

MOM: This banana obsession is a complete mystery.

ME: Not really.

GRAMMY: I also like Sidney Poitier.

DAD: More wine, please.

ME: Grammy, everyone likes Sidney Poitier. It's kind of like saying you like Mother Teresa or something.

GRAMMY: That doesn't make any sense. They're nothing alike.

ME: My point was that you don't need to mention that you like someone that everyone likes.

GRAMMY: I'm just making polite conversation.

DAVID: Maybe Grammy thinks we named Sydney after him.

GRAMMY: No. That thought never occurred to me. He really is a wonderful actor.

RAE: Oh my God. This is torturous.

DAVID: [mumbling] Sorry, D.

D: Relax.

ME: So, Grammy, how long are you planning on staying?

GRAMMY: [facing Dad] Didn't you tell them?

ME: Tell us what?

MOM: Ruth is moving in.

RAE: Oh my God.

MOM: That's enough, Rae.

ME: Seriously?

GRAMMY: It was either that or move into one of those awful homes. They're filthy and run by criminals.

ME: This place isn't so tidy and, well—

DAD: Isabel—

RAE: Where will she stay?

MOM: In David's old room.

ME: It's weird how you didn't mention this before.

MOM: We wanted to surprise you.

DAVID: You did.

RAE: [to Grammy] So you're going to be here all the time?

GRAMMY: I will be living here, so I suppose that I will often be around, should you wish to visit.

RAE: I live kind of far away.

ME: Two miles isn't considered far unless, say, there's a blinding snowstorm and you have to hoof it.

RAE: Was I talking to you?

GRAMMY: So, Mr. Demetrius, when did you start working at my son's agency?

MOM: Technically it's the family firm. It's not just Albert's.

ME: You can call him D.

GRAMMY: I don't think so. What were you saying, Mr. Demetrius?

D: About six months ago, ma'am.[4]

GRAMMY: What did you do before then?

D: I was in prison for fifteen years.

DAD: More wine, please.

MOM: We might need to run out for another bottle or two.

ME: There's whiskey in Dad's rain boot in the front closet.

GRAMMY: What were you in for?

D: Murder, ma'am.

Once we fortified with more cheap wine from the corner shop, the dinner continued on the same perilous path. We explained to Grammy that D was in prison for a crime he did not commit. She said, "Oh, I'm sorry to hear that. But mistakes do happen, don't they?" Rae just shouted, "Oh my God!" over and over again. Maggie tried to explain to Grammy that those kinds of mistakes shouldn't happen, but Grammy had lost interest.

D then served this amazing cherry dessert called a clafouti. The sound of people chewing has never been more beautiful. The chewing was followed by exhaustive compliments on D's cooking and clamoring for more wine. Then an intense awkwardness set in as Grammy Spellman began to interrogate each dinner guest, in lieu, I suppose, of a digestif.

---

[4] Grammy actually likes being called "ma'am."

GRAMMY: So, David, I hear you are unemployed.

DAVID: I am not working by choice. There is a difference, Grammy.

GRAMMY: Maggie, dear, don't you think a mother should be at home with her child? And the man in the workplace, providing for his family?

You get the picture. Now let me get to the good part: The next thing I knew, Mom had slipped into her coat, picked up her book bag, and called to us from the foyer. "You'll all have to excuse me," she said. "We're having a pop quiz in the last hour of Russian class. Simply can't miss it. *Dosvedanya.*" She was gone before anyone could protest. I looked at D, having solved my second familial mystery of the week.

"That explains some things," I said.

I had to give my mother credit. For years she had tried to school me against my impulsiveness, had shared the knowledge that a well-laid plan reaps the greatest reward. Mom had indeed laid the groundwork well in advance and now had the perfect excuse to evade Grammy's company as much as possible. Throughout the years, I've had moments of great admiration for my mother, but this moment left the rest in the dust.

However, I still had to question how my parents would survive with this intruder in their lives. In one evening, the Mussolini of grandmas had invaded the Spellman household. It was impossible to imagine that there wouldn't be a few casualties in her wake.

MEG COOPER/
MARGARET SLAYTER

The following Monday, I found Dad and Rae alone in the office.
"The Gopher is in the building," Rae said.

"What's the Weasel doing here?" I asked.

"I'm out of here in five," Rae replied.

"I never see you anymore," I said.

"I know. Isn't it nice?"

"Yes. I've been meaning to write you a thank-you note." I turned to my father. "Where are Mom and D?"

"Your mother is running errands and D has the morning off."

"I have a feeling 'running errands' will soon become a euphemism. So, Grammy drove D out of the house already?"

"No, he has a coffee date with a nurse who works the night shift."

"Let me be the first to compliment you on your secret-keeping skills. They've improved light years since the Just for Men incident of last year."[1]

"We promised not to talk about it anymore."

"So where is You Know Who?" I whispered.

"We're calling her the Goby," Rae said.

"No we're not, Rae," Dad said.

---

[1] Dad tried to gradually dye his gray hair, thinking that if it was a slow process no one would notice. I don't know what he was thinking.

Rae then turned to me and in an odious instructor tone said, "Gobies are fish that eat their young.[2] You know what a fish is, right?"

"Do you know what a fist is?"

"Girls, that's enough."

"Where is You Know Who?" I asked.

"She's trying out a new hairdresser down the street."

"I forgot. She doesn't wash her own hair. I hope that works out for her."

"It's a generational thing, Izzy."

"And they complain about the youth of today. Imagine only washing your hair once a week."

"Perhaps you can put your imagination to more pressing matters," Dad suggested.

"She can't," Rae mumbled, but loudly enough.

To fend off the volley of four-letter words that would eventually ensue, my father turned to Rae and said, "Don't you need to be in class? Or not here?"

"Excellent idea," Rae said. Before she left, she opened her desk drawer and tossed her candy stash into her backpack. My sister has always learned her lessons quickly and adapted accordingly. I've always admired her for that. After the Weasel departed, I turned to my father and tried to talk some sense into him.

"It's going to end badly, Dad."

"What is?"

"Come to think of it," I said, "all sorts of things come to mind. But mostly, I was thinking about having Grammy Spellman under this roof. She'll likely drive D away, cause Mom to file for divorce, and turn you into a babbling lunatic. I still remember her last extended visit. One night you spent four hours in the bathtub."

"That's how I relax."

"No. It's the only place she couldn't get to you. Though I do recall her chatting with you from outside the door."

---

[2] Male sand gobies are known to eat a third of their eggs. *Men.*

"It's not permanent, Isabel."

"True. She will die, eventually," I said.

"What I mean is, we felt that at her age it would be best if she lived in the same city. This was the only way we could convince her to make the move. However, it is our hope that after a few months of living with your mother (and with you underfoot) she might decide that a nice residential facility may be a better option."

"And having an ex-con in the house will certainly help matters."

"It can't hurt," Dad replied, quashing a grin.

I could tell that the Demetrius Effect was perhaps his favorite part.

"So, you invited your mother to live with you, just so you could smoke her out?"

"That's not how I would put it."

"But it's the gist, isn't it?"

"We believe there's an expiration date on her time here and, once again, I'm not referring to death. Is there anything else on your mind, Isabel?"

"Now that you mention it, yes. I would like to know why we have two intersecting surveillance jobs that are all highly suspicious."

"Unless we witness a client breaking the law, we simply do our job," Dad replied.

Ever since I discovered the connection two weeks earlier, I had on numerous occasions broached the subject with Dad and questioned where the harm was in sharing just a bit of intelligence. Each time I mentioned it, my father took another step in securing his client's information, even going so far as to lock his case files in his desk drawer and keep the key in an undisclosed location. If I pushed harder, my father would respond with yet another stern lecture on investigative ethics.

"Where is this code written?" I asked.

"We're just like lawyers or psychiatrists," he replied.

"No we're not," I said. "For one thing, we don't get paid as well. Also, PIs have a history of skirting the law. Half of our contacts are breach-ing protocol or civil codes when they give us information. Phone records should only be accessed by state or governmental employees, but if you really need them, you can get them. I've seen you break laws, Dad. I've seen it. This Chinese wall you've constructed to protect our clients is really to protect your business. You're worried that if a client learns that we investigated the merits of his or her case, we'll earn a bad reputation and get a nasty comment on some online review site. This isn't about ethics; it's about money."

"That seems reasonable to me," my dad replied. "I should remind you, Isabel, this business is your future. Who knows what's on the horizon for Rae? She has other interests and she really likes money; I'm not sure this is the job for her. She'll survive without it—in fact, I think she could survive a nuclear attack. But I have no idea what you'd do with your life if you ran this business into the ground."

"I appreciate your vote of confidence," I lightly replied.

I couldn't let him know how deeply his comment stung.

"I'm doing what's best for you," my father said with a note of finality.

The conversation was over. However, the conflict was not.

I believed a client was using our services to deceive her husband. The fact that her brother had her under surveillance only confirmed my suspicion. My father thought his firewalls would warn me away from pursuing the matter any further, but we had a tangled web of morally ambiguous clients on our hands. By providing information to one, we might have been playing into the hands of someone who had plans far more dangerous than a breach of trust. My problem was that I didn't know what Edward Slayter, Adam Cooper, and Meg/Margaret were capable of.

I couldn't be sure any of them could be trusted.

I have a burner cell phone that I use on rare occasions when I need to make an anonymous call. I slipped my hand into my desk drawer and dialed the number of my cell phone. I picked up on the second ring.

"Hello?" I said. "Yes. I think I can make it," I said. "I'll be there in twenty," I said to a dead line.

I grabbed my coat and bag and said good-bye to my dad.

"Where are you headed?" he asked.

"Chinese wall," I replied.

I drove home and worked off of Henry's computer. I still needed access to a public records database, so I used Maggie's account since I still had her user name and password from our work on Demetrius's case. This was a necessary precaution since my parents would be able to view my search history on the database bill.

Since Mrs. Slayter was on my side of the Chinese wall, I could have gone to her directly and asked if she was using our services to hide an affair, but it's always best to have answers to questions before you ask them. First, I got a glimpse into the Slayters' virtual lives.

Edward Slayter was clearly a wealthy man; he was also a man without any known heirs besides his wife. As I researched his finances, I found property records that estimated his worth to be at least fourteen million. There was bound to be a prenup with an adultery clause, but if Slayter died, it was quite possible that his wife would inherit it all.

That's a motive for all sorts of things.

Since Margaret and Edward had wed only ten years ago, I guessed that Mr. Slayter had at least one previous marriage, since he was fifty-five years old. Marriage and divorce records are extremely difficult to access because a couple can get married anywhere and the records only exist in the city where they were married. First, I pulled up Mr. Slayter's credit report and verified the cities in which he had lived. I searched marriage and divorce records in those cities and came up empty. Slayter worked at a law firm in New York City from 1977 to 1982. I phoned one of the partners—the oldest one on the company's website—and explained that I was doing a very sensitive background check on Mr. Slayter for a company that was about to embark on an extremely important business deal.

Pretext calls used to be a staple of our business, but in the days of complete disclosure on public networking sites with status reports on one's every move, there can be a counterbalance of extra paranoia among the older generations. Then again, Bernie recently reported what he ate for breakfast on Facebook,[3] so the dividing line is aging considerably.

I placed the call to Clayton Burroughs, prepared for defeat. Burroughs, a senior partner at an old-school law firm, would be loath to provide personal information on a previous employee. Unless, of course, that employee screwed his wife and then screwed him over.

Turns out, Edward Slayter's first wife, Claudia, was also Clayton Burroughs's first wife, which made Edward Claudia Burroughs's second husband. The illicit couple met at a company Christmas party; the affair began a few months later. Burroughs said as delicately as he could that he caught his wife and Mr. Slayter in bed together. He filed for divorce the next day. Clayton (at some point during a conversation where a man tells you about his tragic romantic past, you get to be on a first-name basis) and Claudia did not have a prenup. In those days, he explained, it wasn't as common. Claudia got half the estate. She then married Edward Slayter, and ten years later, when she caught him cheating with Meg Cooper, she filed for divorce. At that point they were living in California and, once again, the assets were split. Edward Slayter was able to use the money from the divorce settlement to invest in a series of extremely lucrative real estate deals, becoming a remarkably wealthy man in the past fifteen years.

"Do you ever speak to Edward?" I asked.

"I ran into him and Margaret—is that her name?"

"Something like that," I replied.

"We crossed paths at a fund-raiser a few years ago and spoke briefly. There's a remarkable symmetry to the whole affair."

"You have no idea," I replied. "Let me ask you a question: Do you think Edward had his new wife sign a prenup?"

---

[3] "Bernie Peterson just ate two eggs, two slices of bacon, and two hotcakes with a side of hash browns. Yum."

"I'd bet my vacation home on it."

"Thank you, Clayton. You've been very helpful."

"Isabel?"

"Yes."

"You're not who you say you are, are you?"

"Not exactly."

"Do you want to tell me what this is all about? I have to admit that my curiosity is getting the better of me."

"Let's just say," I replied, "that the pattern continues."

UNKNOWN CALLER

While I'm on the subject of pretext calls, I should mention that just a few days later I discovered that my repeat wrong number was just a low-rent pretext call.

"May I speak with Emily Proctor?" the voice on the line said.

The voice was different, but the pattern remained the same. I'd decided to try a different tack to throw the caller off her game.

"No, Emily is not here. Can I take a message?" I replied.

"Oh . . . when do you expect her?"

"She's vacationing in the South of France. I don't think she'll be back for another two weeks."

"I thought I was dialing her cell phone."

"You are. But she left it with me in her absence. She doesn't have an international plan, so there was no point in wasting the minutes."

"I see. How long has Emily been gone?"

"I don't keep track of that kind of information."

"Can you ballpark it?"

"Where did that phrase originate from?"

"I have no idea," the caller replied. "Thank you for your time."

"Wait, you never told me your name," I said.

"Jane."

"Jane what?"

"Jane Anderson."

"Very good," I replied. "Well, Jane, unless you plan on providing me with any more personal data—a phone number would be fantastic—I think I'm going to say good-bye."

"Are you the only person who has been using Emily's cell phone in her absence?"

"Good-bye, Jane."

When I disconnected the phone call with "Jane," all previous calls began to form into a plausible scenario that I could work with. My best guess was that someone had reviewed cell phone records and noted phone calls placed either to or from my number and wanted to know who their employee, relative, or, most likely, spouse was calling. I considered all the current clients who were likely to have my cell number on speed dial. Since Walter was my most frequent caller, I decided to drop by his house.

"Walter, how long have you and your wife been separated?"

"Six months. Why do you ask?"

"Are you still on the same cell phone plan?"

"Yes. The cancellation fee was too high."

"So who gets your phone bills?"

"I pay all of the bills."

"But she would have access to the phone records online, correct?"

"I suppose so," Walter replied.

"Who wanted the divorce?"

"Who do you think?" Walter asked.

I could tell this line of conversation wasn't good for Walter's mental health. He began raking his rug, removing my sock prints that led from the front door to the couch.

"Did you divorce on good terms?"

"It was amicable," he said. "Why all the questions, Isabel?"

"Maybe she has some regrets and is looking for a way to get you back."

"That's not it."

"Are you sure?" I asked. "I think I'd like to interview her."

"No. No. That's not a good idea," Walter said.

"I don't see the harm in having a little chat."

"No," Walter said. "It's someone else. I know it. Sasha has moved on."

"You're sure about that?"

"I'm positive."

I wasn't totally buying it, but I had to consider a few more leads before I made any further accusations.

"Can I make you a cup of coffee?" Walter asked.

"I have to go. What are you doing this weekend?" I asked.

"Oh, this and that."

"Are you going to leave your house?"

"It's possible."

"We can't catch your intruder unless you're gone."

"You make a good point."

"Promise me you'll go out, Walter."

"I promise."

"Okay. I'll be in touch."

I like to believe in my clients' instincts, but generally they hire us because they're unsure of those instincts. So when Walter batted aside the idea that his wife had any involvement in the mysterious happenings in his apartment or the unusual interruptions on my cell phone, I decided to trust my own instincts, not his.

It took all of five minutes to track down the phone number and address of the former Mrs. Perkins. I phoned Sasha from my burner cell phone to see whether I recognized her voice. The phone rang five times and went directly to an automated voice mail. Fifteen minutes later I was standing outside her door. I phoned her cell again from my regular number—still no answer. Then I buzzed her door. I could see a curtain twitch two floors up. I phoned again and buzzed simultaneously.

Finally she picked up.

"Sasha, come downstairs. We need to talk."

Sasha was younger and more attractive than I expected. She was also far less buttoned-up than I pictured. Her shirt possessed a few wrinkles (the overall look would have appeared starched and ironed on me, but for Walter's sensibilities, it bordered on disheveled); a strand of wavy hair hung loose from her bun and her shoes were scuffed the way shoes often are. "Hello," was all Sasha said as I took her inventory.

"Hello," I replied, trying to sound friendly and unthreatening. I don't often go for that angle, and I can't say that it worked. I held up the phone and said, "How did you get my number?"

Sasha looked down at her scuffed shoes.

"How about I answer for you?" I suggested. "You were looking through your ex-husband's phone bills and came across a number you didn't recognize. You wondered how a man with so many significant challenges could have met someone so quickly. And so you called to see whether your ex was in a new relationship. Only the woman answering the phone—that would be me—wouldn't give you any information. Have I got that part correct?"

Sasha nodded her head.

"Before I continue, let me put your mind at ease. I am not involved with Walter romantically. I work for him. At first, all I did was check on the apartment and make sure toasters were unplugged, faucets turned off, blinds closed or open—however they're supposed to be—and that no electrical fires or biblical floods had hit his apartment. It was an easy job. At least it used to be."

Sasha stared down at her feet.

"I'm sorry," she said. "I just wanted to know who you were."

"Do you want him back? Is that why you did it?"

"I thought I did. But then we met for coffee last week and I realized that I didn't."

"I'm going to have him change the locks."

"I don't think that's necessary," Sasha replied. "But if it gives him closure."

"Will you tell him?"

"If you think that's necessary."

"I do."

THE GRAMMY SPELLMAN
EFFECT

G rammy Spellman had been in the house less than a week, but I could already see my mother start to unravel. No matter how many tactics she used to evade her in-law, she still had a day job and Grammy was always no more than one room away, clutching her handbag around the clock, not unlike the way Sydney accessorizes with her blanket in a choke hold. At first when Grammy roamed the house with her stressed leather bag attached to her chest, my father was merely confused.

"Are you going somewhere?" he would ask.

To cover, Grammy would pretend that she needed a mint or lipstick at a moment's notice and reach into her bag for one or the other. She always showed extra teeth[1] and Emily Post manners when D was in the room, but no one was buying it. When D ran out to the grocery store, my mother tried to subtly intervene. "Ruth, why don't you keep your handbag in your room? I promise it's safe there."

"You never know when you might need something," Grammy replied.

I went for the less subtle approach.

---

[1] Her attempt at a smile, but it really comes off as if she's displaying her bridge work to a dentist.

"Grammy, Demetrius used to steal televisions, not handbags. We could get you one of those radio-sized TVs if you want to carry that around with you."

Grammy gave me a sharp, unpleasant stare.

"Mom, D's part of the family. You need to relax around him," Dad said, more sternly this time.

"I'm sure he's perfectly rehabilitated," Grammy replied. "But you never know."

My mother has this muscle in her neck that twitches when she's stanching anger.

"Ruth," Mom said, "put the freakin' handbag in your room and leave it there, or so help me God, I will steal it from you and use your checkbook to make outrageous donations to the NAACP."[2]

"Albert, are you going to let her talk to me that way?"

Dad casually shrugged his shoulders. "She does what she wants, Mom. That's how it works these days. Now, put your purse in your room and keep it there."

Grammy managed to follow Dad's orders while maintaining her own stand. She and her purse stayed in her room for the rest of the day.

It was a Wednesday afternoon when I called for an emergency company meeting, conveniently excluding Rae. I asked for my sister's latest surveillance report on Vivien Blake and then gave a ten-minute presentation, including photographs and diagrams (visual aids really do energize a personal takedown) illustrating the discrepancies, the outright lies, and, finally, the indisputable evidence of direct communication between investigator and subject.

---

[2] Actually, they kind of did that already. Grammy left a signed blank check for groceries and Mom donated $250 in Morgan Freeman's name.

"What on earth is she up to?" Mom asked.

"If you don't mind, I'd like to handle it," I said. "Take her off the case and I'll get to the bottom of this."

Dad had to think about it for a second. Our caseload had never been so rife with conflicts of interest. "Fine," Dad said. "But you need to find out immediately what she's up to."

"Excuse me," Demetrius said, "but wouldn't it be faster to sit her down and ask her?"

"We don't do that in this house," I said.

"If we ask her," Dad replied, "then she might tip off Vivien and then Vivien might confront her parents and it could look bad. We need to figure out what's going on first."

"I have one more request," I said. "I need you to punish Rae. I can't watch her get away with this anymore."

"What do you have in mind?" my mother asked.

"Use your imagination," I replied.

Mom paced back and forth in the living room for the next half hour and then returned to the office, tossed a set of car keys at me, and said, "Repo man, get to work."

You don't drive much in San Francisco unless you have to. Once you find a parking space you keep your car there until circumstances warrant driving. Rae didn't notice her car was missing until two days later, when she had to move it for street cleaning. She called the house in a panic.

"My car was stolen," she said.

"Your car is just fine," Dad replied.

"What?" Rae asked.

By the way, she was on speaker because we all needed an afternoon pick-me-up.

"I'm borrowing it for a while," Dad said.

179

LISA LUTZ

"But you have a car," Rae said.

"I feel like having two cars for a while," said Dad.

"This doesn't make any sense," Rae replied. "Why do you need two cars?"

"I don't *need* two," my father replied. "I just want two."

"Are you having another REAFO?"[3] Rae asked.

---

[3] "Retirement-age freak-out." I'd tell you where to learn more, but some of you get angry when I do that.

180

THE SCARLET B

Friday night, when I returned home, I found Gerty sitting on the couch watching the news. She had a glass of bourbon in front of her and refused to make eye contact. She picked up the bottle and poured me four fingers in silence. I sat down next to her.

We both pretended to be engrossed in the latest developments of the saga of the tree sitters. Hundred-year-old oak trees would be razed to build an athletic center on the Berkeley campus. One of the sitters had managed to stay up for a full week. He had a pulley and a bucket to transport nourishment and the by-product thereof. I'm assuming different buckets. I like trees as much as anyone, maybe more than a few, but it's hard to imagine caring for a small patch of high-rise vegetation with this level of vigor. Then again, on Arbor Day fifteen years ago Petra, my partner in crime for many years, and I spent eight hours overnight turning Mrs. Chandler's front bush into a topiary that looked not unlike a hand giving you the finger. So who am I to judge? I figured Gerty was too ashamed to speak, so I muted the sound and spoke first. "I didn't tell him about . . . you know." I couldn't even say his name.

"Thank you," she replied. "I'll do it."

"He doesn't have to know."

"He'll find out eventually."

"Not necessarily. You'd be surprised how many secrets can remain buried."

"I'm moving in with him," Gerty said.

"With who?" I asked. It still seemed impossible.

"With Bernie."

"No."

"Yes."

"You can't," I said.

"I can," she replied.

"It will never work. It's *Bernie*. This is just a rebound relationship. It'll be over in no time flat. Might as well flatten it right now and save yourself the heartache."

"He's a good man, Isabel."

Sigh. Was this the time to tell her otherwise?

"I was thinking about moving out here anyway to be closer to Henry. If it doesn't work out with Bernie, I'll find an apartment," she said.

I cradled my head in my hands, grasping for any strategy to derail this insane turn of events.

"There's no saving your marriage?" I asked.

"Alan and I have been separated for months. We've been living different lives for years."

"And Henry never knew?"

"We were in a bit of a standoff. Neither of us wanted to be the messenger."

"I see."

"Now, that's my story," Gerty said. "What's yours?"

"Huh?"

"You and Henry have to have an honest conversation one of these days."

"I know," I replied.

"What are you waiting for?"

"I know how it's going to end."

Just then Henry walked through the front door. It wasn't clear to me what my role in all this should be. Was I supposed to stay and help make peace or give them their privacy? I've always been better at leaving, so I did.

"I'll let you two be alone," I said, collecting my coat and bag.

Henry nodded, barely making eye contact.

I sat in my car for ten minutes, still clinging to the idea that this situation could be resolved. Then it got cold and I realized I had no place to go. If Grammy Spellman were out of the picture I would have dropped by my parents' house, but I was going to avoid contact as much as possible. Once Grammy got her claws in you, it was kind of hard to get them out.

And so I made one final, futile, and frankly pathetic attempt to solve the problem.

I knocked on his door. He opened it just a crack and looked me up and down as if I were a genuine physical threat. I did enjoy the unease I saw in his eyes.

"I don't want any trouble," Bernie said, raising his hands, as if this were a holdup.

"Just let me in."

Bernie backed away from the door and silently invited me in. He grabbed a beer from the fridge, uncapped the bottle, and passed it to me.

"I got some potato chips and some Cheez Doodles," he said.

"Not hungry," I replied.

"You don't have to be hungry for Cheez Doodles," Bernie replied.

"What does she see in you?" I asked.

"I'm a nice guy," Bernie said with an edge in his voice I don't think I'd ever heard. "And I know how to treat a lady. I know what they need."

"Okay. Change. Of. Subject," I said.

I reached into my bag and pulled out my checkbook. I had two thousand four hundred and twenty-five dollars in savings. I clicked my ballpoint pen a few times to get his attention.

"What'll it take?" I asked.

"You can't be serious," he said.

"Deadly," I replied.

"Put your checkbook away," Bernie said, taking a slug of his beer.

"Everybody has a price," I replied.

"You might be right, Iz. But unless you've just won the lottery, you're not going to be able to cover this bribe."

"But you could be bought, right?"

"Forgive me for getting psychological on you, but it seems to me that you're using me and Gerty as way of avoiding your own relationship issues."

"What are you talking about?" I asked.

"I heard Henry asked you to marry him and you said you'd get back to him on it. If we both played our cards right, you could be my stepdaughter once removed or something."

It was time to remove myself from the conversation. "This isn't over," I said, and then I let myself out.

It was only eight P.M. when I arrived at David and Maggie's, so I rang their front doorbell.

"Isabel!" Maggie said when she opened the door. She said my name more like it was an idea than a name.

She let me in and then shouted, "Hey, David, guess who's here?"

I'd like to think that a surprise visit from me is cause to celebrate, but Maggie was far too enthusiastic, which immediately put me on guard.

"I can come back at a better time," I said.

"No, this is great! Have a seat. Can I get you anything? Drink? Food? Water? Or seltzer water. We have one of those machines. Bubbles all the time."

"I'm fine," I said, trying to gauge the tenor of the room. Something was off; I sensed danger, of all things.

David descended the stairs, carrying Sydney.

"Isabel, what are you doing here?"

"I had to get out of my house and, well, the unit's place is kind of like Chernobyl right now."

"I hear you," he said.

"You know what I'm thinking?" Maggie said.

I had no idea.

"Nope," David replied. Apparently David didn't know either.

Maggie turned to me with pleading eyes. "Our babysitter has the flu."

"I'm sorry to hear that," I replied.

Dead silence.

I honestly had no idea what Maggie was getting at, so I misread the silence.

"It's not serious, I hope," I said sympathetically.

"What do you think?" Maggie said to David.

David shrugged his shoulders and said, "I dunno if that's such a good idea."

Maggie took her daughter from David's arms and said, "It's an excellent idea," then she passed Sydney to me and said, "We need to get out of the house *now*. Please, please, please babysit. She'll be asleep in no time flat. She's been fed and changed. You know where the crib is. If we leave in five minutes, we can still make the movie. We'll be gone three hours tops."

I'm sure that some protest emitted from my lips. I know words were coming out of my mouth, but they were in competition with other words not said by me, like "Hurry," "Where's my sneaker?" "Wear your loafers," "I hate being late for movies," and "Banana."

The next thing I knew, Sydney and I were gazing into each other's eyes with absolutely nothing to say.

She appeared bored at first and then panicked. She began to cry. I asked her not to cry. She continued to cry. I asked her again, more politely, meaning I used the word *please*. She still cried. Then I used that strange voice that people often use with children and still she cried. I said "banana," which I knew I was not supposed to say, and she stopped crying and said "banana." Then it took me exactly forty-two minutes to figure out which banana she wanted. Some kind of puffed snack made out of vegetables with a pirate as its mascot.

I wasn't sure if tiny kids brushed their teeth or not, so I skipped it. I figured since baby teeth just end up under a pillow one day, why go crazy?[1]

I read *The Cat in the Hat* twice, *The Cat in the Hat Comes Back* three times, and *Green Eggs and Ham* twice. Sydney seemed to conk out halfway through the last book, but I kept reading just to be safe. I put her in her crib, brought the baby monitor into the living room, and poured myself a stiff drink.

I spent the rest of the evening cycling through a couple hundred cable channels on David and Maggie's fifty-two-inch plasma TV. It was a relic from David's bachelor days—I don't suspect he'd approve of such excess now. Still, it was the perfect salve to my brutal day of reality-facing. I've discovered that if you watch real people on television, you suddenly discover that you and every person around you are the picture of sanity and decency. Some of the people on TV made me think that Bernie wasn't such a bad option. There are worse things than a cigar-smoking, strip-club-going, poker-playing, beer-bellied slob, right? Besides, Bernie said he was cutting back on the strip clubs. He was looking for a more cerebral connection.

Once again, I fell asleep on their couch. Maggie gently shook me awake and suggested I sleep in the guest room. Since I wasn't sure what was happening back at my place, it seemed wise. Or cowardly, depending on how you look at it.

In the morning, the sound of an ill-played xylophone woke me. (It would have woken Rip Van Winkle.) Since I had actually caught more Zs than David or Maggie, I was surprised to see how chipper they were at such an early hour. "Morning," I said as I shuffled into the kitchen. I had no idea where my shoes were located.

This house was starting to seem a bit like a footwear Bermuda Triangle.

"Thanks again," Maggie said, pouring me a cup of coffee.

"How'd it go?" David asked.

"Fine," I replied, "once I figured out that 'banana' meant 'beer and beef

---

[1] I did later discover that first teeth still get brushing—maybe just for practice's sake.

jerky' and that her bedtime reading was Henry Miller's *Tropic of Cancer*."

"*Tropic of Capricorn*," Maggie said, correcting me.

"Very funny," David said, not thinking it was funny at all. "We're not saying 'banana' anymore."

"I'll try to respect that rule in this house, but in the real world, it might slip out on occasion."

"What did you feed her? Because she already had dinner."

"I gave her some of that stuff with the pirate on it."

"And then what did you do?"

"We read the complete Dr. Seuss collection. Happy?"

David's brow unfurled and he crouched on the floor with his daughter. "Did you have a fun time with your aunt Izzy?" he asked in a high squeaky voice.

Sydney stared at him blankly.

"Say good morning to Aunt Izzy."

Sydney stared at me blankly.

"Remember me from last night?" I asked.

"Did you have fun?" Maggie asked.

"I wouldn't go that far," I replied.

"I was actually talking to Sydney," Maggie said.

"Oh, well, she'd probably agree. We had an *okay* time, didn't we, Sydney?"

"Why can't you talk to her like a normal person?" asked David.

"I'm the only one talking to her like a normal person. You sound like a eunuch."

"Children respond to higher-pitched noises," David said. "I'm not sure you have a maternal bone in your body."

"Me neither," I replied, feeling his comment like a cattle prod.

"That's enough, David," Maggie said.

"Banana," Sydney said.

"See you later," I said.

THE BERNIE PROJECT AND OTHER MISCELLANEOUS ACTIVITIES

Gerty was gone when I got home. Her bags had presumably been packed, her bed had been made (probably not by her, judging from the military corners), and every sign of the disorder that naturally surrounded her had vanished. Besides, the perennial note, *I'm not here,* was no longer there, which struck me as being ironic. But Gerty did send me a succinct e-mail explaining that she broke the news to her son. While I would never thank Bernie for the grenade he threw into my life when he and Gerty began their baffling affair, there was an unforeseen benefit that I couldn't ignore.

Once Henry had choked down the news from his mother, his hunger for any form of interpersonal communication was sated. His previous desire *to talk* had been replaced by an unprecedented desire *to watch.* I found him in the living room, staring blankly at a reality television show about reformed Dungeons and Dragons addicts. A show, under specific desperate circumstances, I could imagine myself toggling back and forth to, but not Henry. I removed the remote from his hand and changed the channel to cable news, which is his standby version of escape entertainment. He explained to me once that if you watch the news on what seems like a loop, suddenly it presents itself as fiction and you stop worrying (and maybe learn to love the bomb).

* * *

In local news, the oak trees got a stay of execution while the campus authorities continued their negotiations with the tree sitters. On the national front, their fifteen minutes of fame were at least fourteen minutes shorter and clearly skewed in favor of the Man.

"You know?" I said, as a conversation starter. And, frankly, this was one of those occasions when "Some weather we've been having" would have been superior.

"I know."

"Can I get you anything?"

"Popcorn."

"You need something to wash it down with?"

"Beer."

I put on my coat and headed for the door. Then I figured I ought to say something.

"In my defense, there was no way to predict this would happen. I mean, Bernie?"

"I don't blame you."

"Thanks. But I promise it won't last. I have a few more tricks up my sleeve."[1]

"Leave it," Henry said. "There's nothing you can do."

"If you say so," I replied.

But I've discovered very few situations in which there's nothing you can do.

While Henry quietly wallowed in the image of his mother with Bernie, I took action by attempting to machete every obstacle that lay in my path to . . . well, the status quo. What I wanted, I suppose, was for things to stay the same, for the universe to be in the same order it was in a few months

---

[1] Actually, I didn't, but I figured something would come to mind.

ago (a simpler time) and for people to behave in the manner I had come to expect. I've got nothing against change, but sometimes it's totally unnecessary.

There was no dearth of projects for me to sink my teeth into. I began with the Bernie Project, making several phone calls and e-mail queries and even composing a few handwritten notes, revisiting my second-grade year, when Mrs. Averly had failed me on every English assignment simply because she found my penmanship abhorrent. As I waited for replies to my inquiries, I phoned Fred Finkel in the hopes of taking a more proactive approach.

"Fred," I said.

"Isabel," he said.

"Wouldn't you agree, after your flubbed surveillance work, that maybe you owe me?"

"I hadn't thought it over."

"I did pay you in full for shoddy work."

"So the scales are tipped slightly in your favor."

"I'm happy to hear that."

"Is that all?" he asked.

"Of course not," I replied. "I need you to do something for me."

"I figured as much."

"How old are you now, Fred?"

"Twenty."

"Excellent. Do you have other friends in your age range? And when I say 'age range,' I mean under twenty-one."

"Uh, yeah. Where are you going with this, Isabel?"

"I'd like you to go to a bar—the Philosopher's Club in particular—and order drinks. Alcoholic ones, preferably. I'll pick up the tab."

"Can I ask why?"

"Plus twenty an hour."

"It's illegal, you know," Fred said.

"I know. Are you in?"

"Why not? I've always found the drinking age kind of random."

"Do me a favor."

"What?" he asked.

"Don't invite Rae."

"Hadn't crossed my mind."

Two hours later, Fred sent me a text: In position.

Five minutes later, I received another text: No go. Carded and discarded. UR paying travel costs, right?

Then I got an actual phone call.

"Izzeee," Bernie said with the perky satisfaction of a winner. "Nice try."

"I have no idea what you're talking about," I replied.

Clearly the Bernie Project was going to be more time-consuming than I'd planned. I patiently waited to set stage two in motion.

The next morning I moved on to the Chinese wall. I amassed a list of computer-repair establishments in the city, focusing on sole proprietors since I had a feeling I was most likely to find a hacker that way. I figured these people had some kind of code word for doing illegal activities, but I couldn't call Robbie, so most of my inquiries fell flatter than a French crepe. Our conversations, if you can call them that,[2] went something like this:

ME: Let's just say, hypothetically, that my father forgot the password on his computer. Would you be able to access it?

ROBBIE #2: Uh, probably. What system is he using?

ME: He's got a special password. Like, someone installed a serious firewall and he doesn't remember the password.

---

[2] While I'm sure there are many charming computer geeks across the globe, I repeatedly ran into the Robbies of this world. And if your name is Robbie, please don't take offense. I'm sure a few of you are all right.

ROBBIE #2: Do you even know what a firewall is or did you hear it in a movie once?

ME: Whatever you call it, there's something that's keeping me—I mean my father—from accessing his computer.

ROBBIE #2: Why isn't your father calling me?

ME: Because he's not good with computers.

ROBBIE #2: Oh, so you're the computer genius in the family.

ME Can you help me or not?

ROBBIE #2: This sounds like the kind of annoyance suited for the person who set up your quote-unquote firewall. He's probably waiting at home right now for your phone call.

ME: He's on vacation.

ROBBIE #2: Wait until he gets back. You'll survive.

ME: I have no idea when he's coming back.

ROBBIE #2: What does he say when you e-mail him?

ME: He doesn't respond.

ROBBIE #2: Amateur hour. He can't check his e-mail on vacation? Hilarious. Okay, since I'm an actual professional, maybe you can hire me to fix this. I have a few openings in my schedule.

ME: Do you work late? One A.M. would be awesome.

ROBBIE #2: I don't make house calls at that hour.

ME: I'll pay double.

ROBBIE #2: Is this your boyfriend's computer?

ME: No. Of course not.

ROBBIE #2: You think he's watching porn, right? Let me tell you something. It's perfectly normal.

ME: Okay, good-bye.

I suppose I could have gone with the truth, revealing Robbie as the wizard behind the wall and hoping that Robbie #2's hubris would cause him to try to hack another guy's system. I don't know much about his world, but I do know that those kinds stick together. They're like a cyberspace knitting circle. Five more failed attempts to get midnight tech support and I finally accepted that my father's computer and the surveillance reports on Meg Cooper were off-limits. But I had enough personal data to take a hammer and chisel to the wall in my own private way.

Most background checks involve criminal records, civil proceedings, property searches, and occasionally personal interviews. But finding the basic data on a person can take some time. I was trying to establish whether Margaret Slayter had any marriages prior to the one with Edward. She was thirty-five at the time of their wedding, so it was a distinct possibility. Margaret Slayter's credit report went back only ten years. She possessed only one credit card under her maiden name, Cooper. She'd spent several years in San Jose, but there was no birth record for a Meg (or Margaret) Cooper in California and I wasn't sure how to ask the client about her place of birth without raising suspicion.

I pulled the notes from my preliminary meeting with Adam Cooper.

We don't ask clients for birth records or Social Security numbers, but a home address can tell you whether the client owns or rents. And from there, more information can be gleaned. Adam Cooper owned an apartment in the Inner Richmond. From that information I could access a DOB and a credit report.

Cooper had a second mortgage out on his apartment and credit card debt hovering just over fifty thousand dollars. I reviewed the report a number of times because there was something familiar in the data that I couldn't put my finger on. Until I did: an address ten years ago in Fremont, California.

I pulled Meg Cooper's saved credit report from my computer and found the same address in her file. While it wouldn't be unheard of for siblings to live under the same roof well into their twenties, this revelation struck me as a bit odd. It also occurred to me that Meg and Adam bore no physical resemblance to each other.

Of course, it's easy to chalk that up to the disguise of the modern woman. If you bleach, freeze, or paint every major feature, even a detective would have difficulty discerning your natural appearance. I hadn't been looking for discrepancies in that part of the Slayter story. But once I started looking, they sprouted like weeds.

A quick marriage record search in Fresno verified my assumption: Meg Cooper was Margaret's name when she was married to Adam Cooper, the man now claiming to be her brother. That pattern I was speaking about earlier was losing its symmetry. So, the milquetoast, sweater-vested Adam Cooper hired us to follow his "sister" because it was less suspicious and ethically dubious than hiring us to follow his ex-wife. A job we would have at the very least questioned, and probably turned down. It's one thing if a client is interested in a current spouse's activities, but once the divorce proceedings are complete, surveillance begins to look an awful lot like professional stalking.

I was now presented with my own ethical dilemma: tell the unit and deal with the consequences of both the breach and the cleanup, or take matters into my own hands. To be honest, the debate didn't last very long.

Before risking a surveillance on a client, I performed a full background check on Adam Cooper. His credit report provided the address where he and Meg had lived as husband and wife. I did a property search and found a Louise Meyers who had owned a home next to their apartment building going on thirty years. I took an educated guess that she was familiar with the goings-on in her neighborhood; homeowners and the elderly tend to be more invested in their neighborhoods. I phoned Mrs. Meyers and left a message, explaining that I was a potential employer looking for information on Mr. Cooper. I couldn't provide any other information, since the job required some sensitive security matters. She phoned me back in an hour, eager to help.

Mrs. Meyers said she made a habit of getting to know the people who

194

lived in her vicinity (brownies were her icebreaker) and keeping up with the goings-on about town. As far as she could tell, Meg and Adam were a normal couple with their share of problems. When I inquired as to the type of problems they might have, Mrs. Meyers switched into generalizations, for fear of losing Adam a job, I suspect.

"We are already aware of Mr. Cooper's credit issues," I explained.

"I see," Mrs. Meyers replied.

"I understand your wish to be discreet, Mrs. Meyers, but this position could put Mr. Cooper's past under a microscope. It is better if we have all the information from the start so that we can protect him from any undesirable elements."

My generalized "we" was starting to sound like a preposterous fringe spy organization. I was hoping that Meyers watched too much television. Pretext calls are not my area of expertise (Mom, on the other hand, could probably get a Social Security number off an attorney). Fortunately, Meyers took the bait.

"The Coopers lived above their means," Meyers replied.

"How do you mean?"

"Always leased new cars; Adam used to park in my driveway every weekend and wash and wax it. He loved that BMW. They always wore expensive clothes; at least that's what Gloria told me."

"And who is Gloria?"

"She lived next door to them, in the apartment complex. Unit 4C, I think."

"Is she still there?"

"No, but I have her number."

"I'm going to need that."

Gloria took a bit longer to convince. I could discern from her voice that she was younger, so I skipped the spy act and asked when she'd last had contact with Mrs. Cooper. Since five years had passed, I gathered they weren't close and I explained that I was a private investigator working for her current husband and hoping to glean some information on Meg's past.

Gloria was more than happy to help, which led me to believe that Meg and she weren't neighborly neighbors. Friends can be virtually useless in a background investigation, but a five-minute conversation with an enemy can reveal more information than hours behind the glare of a computer screen.

The walls were thin in the Palms Caribbean apartment complex. Also, there was only one palm tree, which really got under Gloria's skin (she worked as a proofreader at a law firm). Meg and Adam had a happy marriage for the most part. They were often inseparable and their public displays of affection bordered on pornography (according to Gloria). But like any couple, they did fight. They fought over money. Meg wanted more and Adam couldn't provide it. But not for lack of trying.

Eventually Meg and Adam moved to San Francisco, where they hoped to find better job opportunities. I asked Gloria if she thought the couple was headed for divorce.

"Aren't they all?" she dryly replied.

Our call ended on that note.

I looked up the Coopers' divorce records (the ubiquitous "irreconcilable differences" were the cause) and learned that only four months after they moved to the city, they got divorced. However, according to Meg's credit report, she and Adam lived under the same roof for a full year after that. I phoned the landlord to verify.

He got back to me two days later.

I asked him how long the couple had lived in his building and he responded by clearing his throat.

"Excuse me?" he said.

"I'm curious how long Mr. and Mrs. Cooper lived in your building."

"*Miss* Cooper," the landlord said, clarifying. "Adam is Meg's older brother. It was a two-bedroom apartment. They lived there for a year and a half until Meg got married."

"I see," I replied. "Thank you for your time."

While there may have been other explanations for the ruse, I couldn't help wondering whether Meg and Adam had been working on a long con for years. And if that was the case, were they still in it together, or had Meg jumped ship?

BACK ON
PLANET SPELLMAN . . .

Monday morning, I arrived at the Spellman compound at noon. D and Grammy had recently discovered that they shared a guilty pleasure—D's soap opera, *Gossamer Heights*. However, this common ground did little to soften the tension between them. Grammy still held her purse to her chest, pretending she needed to access her medicine during commercial breaks. She sat on the farthest end of the couch, twisting her neck at an uncomfortable angle to see the TV screen.

Although she couldn't resist snacking on D's homemade Chex Mix.[1]

During commercial breaks she would attempt awkward conversation, continuing her habit of referencing any positive role model in the African-American community. She liked to talk about the president quite a bit. Although, in whatever etiquette class Grammy had taken, politics were apparently off the table, so she basically mentioned his excellent posture and choice of ties.

To stoke the fire of the conflicts that abounded, Rae paid us all a surprise visit. First on her agenda was repossessing her car. She planted herself in front of my father's desk and waited for him to look up.

---

[1] Generally called Crack Mix—it's that good. Mom keeps the real stuff in a safe in the pantry so Dad can't get his paws on it. Dad has access to a "healthy" version, which is basically cereal and raw almonds.

"Good afternoon, Rae. Is there something I can do for you?"

"Yes, as a matter of fact. I'd really like to have my car back."

"I'd like to have my hair back," Dad replied.

"Dad, if I had your hair, I would give it back."

"Actually you'd probably hold it for ransom."

"Maybe," Rae replied. "But eventually it would be returned, because I have my own hair."

"Thank you," Dad said. "I'm really glad to hear that. But this is all hypothetical. You don't have my hair to auction off."

"Are you going to give me my car back?"

"No. Not just yet. I need it."

"But that doesn't make any sense," Rae said, too baffled by the turn of events to summon much indignation.

"Many things in life don't make sense," Dad said. "If you'll excuse me, I have a phone call to make."

My father picked up the receiver and may have dialed a legitimate number, maybe not. Rae turned to my mother for an explanation.

"What's going on?"

"Nothing, dear. Remember, the car is in your father's name and he needs it for now. San Francisco has an excellent public transportation system. Many people in this city have never owned a vehicle."

"Some of those people even have a car and choose public transportation instead," I said.

Rae ignored me and continued her dialogue with Mom. "Something is going on that you're not telling me."

"I'm sure that's always true," my mother enigmatically replied.

Rae gave up on the unit and shot dagger eyes at me.

"You're behind this. I know it and when I find out how, you'll be sorry."

"My friend Lydia's children never threaten each other," Mom said.

"Lydia's not your friend," Rae replied. "She's just part of your knitting group cover operation."

"Crochet," Mom replied. "You know, her children have lunch once a week just to catch up."

"I'd rather kill myself," Rae said.

"How does Thursday work for you?" I asked.

Rae stormed out of the office and prowled the living room for a new victim. I followed her, to make sure she gave D some peace, since *Gossamer* hour seemed to be his one true escape. Rae plopped down on the couch between Grammy and D, waited for the commercial break, and then said, "Guess what, Grammy? I gained five pounds. Isn't that awesome?"

Grammy straightened her posture to appear as if her attention was too wrapped up in the television to hear a word spoken in the real world. But sometimes enemies unite against another enemy.

"I gained ten pounds since your last visit," I chimed in.

"Show-off," Rae said.

My mother then entered the room, overhearing the conversation, and added, "I got you both beat," she said. "Fifteen."

"Bullshit," I said, although Mom had indeed gained weight since D's arrival.

D muted the television and looked at three of the four Spellman women as if they'd gone insane. Although he knew better than to ask any questions. Though you might have some of your own. Grammy's weight obsession is perhaps her most insidious characteristic, and that's saying something. She could be downright cruel to my father, commenting on every pound he gained, every bite he put in his mouth. Some time ago, during a Grammy visit, Rae (age twelve) watched with discomfort as Grammy commented on my father's weight gain and suggested he didn't need a second helping of something. My sister noticed Dad's acute embarrassment and discomfort, and, I suppose, in an attempt to distract Grammy, she boldly announced that she had gained ten pounds since her previous visit to the doctor. I then jumped in with some weight-increase statistics of my own and Rae and I gave each other a congratulatory high five. This became a running gag for years whenever Grammy came to town.

"You people," D said, shaking his head.

"You people?" I asked.

"You know what I mean."

Grammy sighed at the old joke and clutched her purse more tightly to her chest, like a security blanket. Rae couldn't hold her tongue any longer.

"Grammy, you can leave your purse in your bedroom. D doesn't need your money. He could be a millionaire if he wanted to be."

My grandmother and Rae have dollar signs in common. That's it, but at least it's something. The comment got Grammy's attention.

"How do you mean?" Grammy replied.

"Demetrius has a lucrative lawsuit he'd win if he filed. In fact, it probably wouldn't even have to go to court. The police department and the DA wouldn't want the bad press—they'd make him an offer he couldn't refuse. For reasons that escape me, D refuses to litigate."

D no longer responded to Rae when she went on her diatribes. He unmuted the TV sound and blasted the volume.

The jingle for an anti-itch cream shook the room.

Mom spoke from the kitchen, where she was withdrawing more Crack Mix from the safe.[2] "Rae, are you bothering D again?"

"I'm watching TV," Rae said.

"Is she bothering you, D?"

"Everything is under control," D replied.

My mother cleared her throat. On cue, Rae got to her feet and returned to the office, where she was assigned one hour of filing as punishment for interrupting D's soap time. Demetrius returned the television volume to Grammy Spellman's preferred decibel level, and *Gossamer Heights* came back from break. I noted that Grammy Spellman clutched her purse with just a bit less vigor. I sat down in the kitchen, mindlessly chowing down

---

[2] The combo is my father's birthday, which seems cruel, if you ask me.

on this coma-inducing cereal concoction, and observed the odd tableau in the living room. When the show ended, D entered the kitchen and took the bowl of Crack Mix away from me.

"Thank you," I said, since I wasn't going to be able to stop eating it on my own.

"You're welcome," D replied.

"She's annoying," I said. "I'm referring to the young one, in case it wasn't clear."

"She's got big ideas," D replied forgivingly.

"I don't agree with her approach, but she's right," I said. "Fifteen years. I think you've got something coming to you. I don't understand why you won't even consider it."

"I have my reasons, Isabel," D replied. "I hope you can respect that."

Unfortunately for D, I really couldn't.

Since Rae was already in the house, my father decided to have the Weekly Summit four days early. The Chinese wall had pretty much short-sheeted all work-related communication, making these formal meetings super-fluous but blissfully brief. This meeting lasted five minutes. My mother suggested we all do a better job of emptying our trash bins and then my parents told Rae that the Vivien Blake case was currently on hold and she'd be notified if it resumed. This was the simplest way to cut her off from any intelligence on the case. In fact, no more intelligence on any case was shared. I wasn't provided info on Adam Cooper and Dad wasn't allowed to view any of my surveillance reports on Mr. Slayter. The wall was so thick, in fact, that when I inquired whether Cooper was paying his bills on time, my father slid his finger across his throat.

"Don't you think you're taking this too far, Dad?"

"We're in the business of investigating, not meddling, Isabel."

"Are you sure? Because you and Mom are kind of awesome at it, and I'm speaking purely of the meddling part."

Mom then began meddling—recreationally, of course. She asked D about his plans for the evening and he tersely explained that he was going to a jazz club in Oakland. My mother asked if he was going alone. My father said that of course he was not going alone. D concurred. My mother asked for the general statistics of his date and received what sounded like a rehearsed answer.

"Forty-one, divorcée, librarian. Hobbies include dancing, reading biographies, and vacationing anyplace warm."

"First date?" my mother asked.

"Yes," D replied.

"You've been going on quite a few first dates," Mom said.

This fact was disconcertingly true.

According to my latest count: thirteen. And, based on the intelligence that Mom and I had amassed, he had not gone on a single second date. What Mom was afraid to ask and therefore could not be established was whether D was hugely picky or totally off his game, which would be a reasonable assumption for a man who'd spent fifteen years in prison. That said, I've seen D in social settings, and there would be nothing to indicate that he couldn't hold his own in a conversation. Plus, he does that whole opening-doors-and-pulling-out-chairs thing, which some women totally go for.[3] My point is: Like everyone in my universe, D was hiding something.

"Meeting adjourned," Dad said, smacking a plastic-covered chocolate gavel on his desk.[4] D left for his date and Rae devoured another bowl of the Crack Mix, ignoring the strict rationing that D had implemented a few weeks ago (he simply couldn't keep up with the demand).

"I could eat that stuff for breakfast, lunch, and dinner," Rae said. "And dessert, of course."

My father took a few nibbles of his blander version and shook his head in confusion.

---

[3] I'm not in love with that ritual. I've been injured more than once when caught unawares.

[4] I think the greatest act of discipline my father has ever shown is not eating the gavel.

"Maybe there's something wrong with my taste buds. Olivia, do you think I should see the doctor?"

"No," my mother quickly replied. "Don't be a hypochondriac."

"I just don't understand why you all love it so much. Same for his baked goods. Granted, he's cooked some excellent meals, but I think he's hit and miss."

"Dear, you should keep that to yourself," Mom said.

Rae snacked and did some high-speed texting for the next five minutes, then abruptly got to her feet and said, "I'm out of here. Dad, I'd really like my car back one of these days. I'm willing to negotiate. Call me."

"Bye, sweetie," Mom said, furrowing her brow as she watched Rae depart. "What is wrong with her?" Mom said as soon as the door closed.

"She has been distracted lately," Dad replied.

"Maybe she's lost interest in the job. That's why she faked the report. She couldn't be bothered to go on a surveillance," Mom said.

"And isn't it out of character that she hasn't figured out that the car repossession was a punishment?" I said.

"Maybe she's depressed," Dad said.

"She's not depressed," I replied.

"And when is this feud with David going to end? I'm surprised you haven't figured it all out by now, Isabel."

"No one's talking," I answered. Rather than spoil my blackmail riches, I kept my knowledge under my hat. Also, there was another layer to my motivation. Something about David's refusal to retaliate seemed off. I wanted more information before I made another move.

The telephone rang, tabling the Rae conversation for the day.

"Spellman Investigations," I answered.

"Izzy, it's David."

"I know."

"I need a babysitter tonight," David said.

"You're a grown man. Take care of yourself."

BLAME IT ON PUCCINI

David, of course, was asking me whether I could babysit his child. Apparently, the fourteen-year-old neighbor was grounded for getting a D on her algebra test and the opera wasn't going to reschedule itself. I did point out to David and then Maggie that this was a perfect excuse for getting out of going to the opera, but both claimed to have been looking forward to it for weeks. I Googled *La bohème* while I was on the phone with David and asked him to summarize the opera for me, as a quiz of sorts, to ensure that he was as invested in the outing as he claimed.

"It's not about the story," he said. "It's the music."

"Good answer," I replied, trying to get the gist off the brief paragraph on my computer. "As far as I can tell people sing and someone dies. Wouldn't you rather have a cozy night in, watching reruns of *Taxi*?"

"Isabel, I need to have a night out with my wife; more specifically, my wife has demanded a night out with me. No, she's threatened me. She wants a proper evening out: dinner, opera, and me in a tuxedo. If she doesn't get that, she has threatened to call one of those makeover shows. I think she's joking, but I can't be sure."

"She's probably not joking. You might rethink this new look you're rocking. You're clearly the *before* picture."

"It's not a look, Isabel. I'm busy. I have a child that needs my full attention and there's no time for vanity."

"*Who are you?*" I asked.

"Help a brother out. Besides, you need to spend more time with Sydney so that she understands you're a relative. As it is, she shows more enthusiasm for the UPS guy than for you."

"Everybody loves their UPS guy. That's a no-brainer. He brings you stuff. And it's not like I haven't tried with your kid. The last time I bought her a gift, you got angry at me."

"A bag of Bavarian pretzels is hardly an appropriate gift for an eighteen-month-old child."

"Why not? Everything you give her she sticks in her mouth anyway. It might as well be edible."

"Leave the pretzels at home. Your presence will be gift enough."

"I think it's time to find a new babysitter. Do you really want a dropout with a compromised immune system watching your child?"

"Isabel, I will see you at five o'clock tonight," David replied.

"Why so early? Word on the street[1] is that the opera doesn't start until eight."

"We have dinner reservations beforehand, at six fifteen."

"And how long will it take you to get to the restaurant?"

"Fifteen minutes. But it will be at least forty-five to give you babysitting instructions."

Yes, I did point out that I had already babysat with marginal success, but David felt the need to provide a full debriefing on Sydney protocol should this sort of thing happen regularly. I pointed out that I had no intention of this thing happening regularly, but David disregarded my comment.

I arrived at five o' five on the dot to find my brother striking a remark-

---

[1] A.k.a. the SF Opera website.

able resemblance to Old David. His tux was pressed and creased and fit him like a glove. A little more like a glove than it used to, but the elegant cut concealed the baby weight he was still carrying. His hair was neatly combed back with one of those products Old David used religiously and he was clean-shaven and cologned.

"Where's David?" I asked.

"Hilarious," David replied.

"Doesn't he look wonderful," Maggie said, descending the stairs.

She didn't look so shabby herself in a simple black cocktail gown. Although I could tell she was having some trouble with the four-inch heels.

"You two make a striking pair. Are you sure about those shoes, Maggie?"

"Nope. But I've committed."

"Down to business," David said, interrupting the niceties.

The instructions took only forty minutes, if I'm looking on the bright side. The diaper-change discourse was the most time-consuming—not because of the basic instructions (which I probably could have figured out on my own with a good Internet connection) but because of my insistence that the diaper change could wait until the fat lady sang.

David had apparently anticipated the ensuing debate and figured it into his timeline. The baby monitor explanation was thankfully brief. I'm a PI; listening devices are hardly new to me. We did, however, have to go over emergency protocol, which involved car seat instructions just in case I had to take her to the emergency room or she wouldn't stop crying.

The last part was an off-the-cuff remark by David, but I pressed for an explanation.

"What do you mean, 'won't stop crying'?"

"Kids like cars," Maggie explained, deflecting. "This one, more than most; if she won't go to sleep by eight or so, then you might want to take her for a drive."

"Where?"

"Doesn't matter. She'll sleep as long as you drive."

"Do environmentalists know about this?"

"Once she's sound asleep, you can usually transition her from the car to the bed without incident."

"I see. Anything else I should know?" I asked, suddenly feeling the full weight of the responsibility that lay ahead of me.

"No swearing," David said.

"She only knows like five words. Seems unlikely," I replied.

"*You*. No swearing."

"How about I cut back?" I replied.

David gave me his *Don't mess with me* look and I responded with my *That window looks mighty inviting* look.

"I'm doing you a favor," I said. "Let's get our facts straight."

Maggie passed Sydney to David and took me aside.

"I owe you," she said. "My only request is that you don't respond to 'banana.'"

"What do I do if she asks for one?"

"Distract her and five minutes later give her a bottle. She already had dinner, so she should be fine."

"If you have any questions, you can text us," David said.

"No, David. You will not be staring at your BlackBerry while we're in a theater. We're not that kind of people. Izzy can call your parents if she has any questions. They've raised three children on their own."

"And two out of three are still children," David replied. "How do you like those odds?" he said to his wife.

"Hey!" I said, because my head was too full of regret to come up with a better comeback. But then I had a brilliant idea. "Why don't you call the unit? They totally dig Sydney."

"Thought of that, but we're afraid Grammy Spellman will invite herself along," David said. "And we already have enough food issues in this house; we don't want to add an eating disorder to the mix."

"That is indeed a sound argument."

"Thank you, Isabel. You are the best," Maggie said, kissing me on the cheek.

David didn't echo her sentiment. Instead, he put his daughter into my arms and said, "Ten fingers and ten toes. I'll expect that same number when I return."

Maggie and David then departed. Sydney and I watched through the window as their car backed out of the driveway and disappeared down the street. Sydney then turned to me and stared into my eyes for a full five seconds, showing no recognition whatsoever. Then she began crying. Perhaps wailing is a more appropriate term. Whatever it was, the sound pierced my ears and made it quite difficult to carry on the various telephone conversations that eventually followed after I tried giving her a bottle and dangling her favorite stuffed animal in front of her.

"Henry, I need your help."

"What's that noise?"

"It's a child."

"What child?"

"My niece. Who else?"

"Why is she so close to the phone?"

"Because I'm holding her."

"Put her down. I can't hear you."

I put Sydney on the floor. She stumbled to the front door and scratched at the wood like a dog wanting to go out. Only she was also crying.

"I'm babysitting," I said. "Don't ask. But you have to come over here immediately and help me."

"I'm sorry. I can't," Henry replied. "Have you tried giving her a bottle or a toy?"

"Of course. Now get over here."

"I can't. I'm on a stakeout."

"You wouldn't just be saying that, would you?"

"Using surveillance to evade personal obligations is your thing, Isabel."

"So there's no way you can help babysit," I said. "Please stop crying, Sydney."

"That's not going to do you any good," Henry brilliantly commented.

I figured that out on my own since Sydney was still crying.

"I have some phone calls I need to make," I said. "I'll talk to you later."

"Stay calm," Henry said.

"Easy for you to say."

I disconnected the call.

"Sydney, I beg of you. Please stop crying."

I picked her up again, but she squirmed in my arms, reaching for the door, crying, "Dada." I texted David: Sydney would like you to return home. Me too.

A few minutes later, Maggie texted me from her phone with the following words:

- Pacifier
- Bottle
- Dangling keys
- Television

I was given no specific TV instructions, so I gathered up their DVD collection (obviously the ones that appeared to be for children) and inserted the discs, one at a time, hoping to lure my niece away from the front door and in front of the TV. I tried a wide variety of entertainment options, beginning with what I was certain was a winner: SpongeBob SquarePants.[2]

This was the episode "Sailor Mouth," in which SpongeBob can't stop swearing.[3] His sidekick Patrick refers to profanity as "sentence enhancers." If there was ever a better description, I have not heard it. Then he later calls it a "spicy sentence sandwich." A beautifully apt description,

---

[2] Turns out this was Maggie's DVD, not Sydney's.
[3] Sure, a bit ironic.

void of all judgment. And, yeah, I've watched my share of *SpongeBob* in my life. Completely sober.

Next came *Bob the Builder, Zoboomafoo,*[4] and *The Wiggles.*[5]

Then I phoned my mother for some advice, but the call went to voice mail and I realized she was in the midst of expanding her horizons (a.k.a. evading Grammy Spellman). I grabbed Sydney's bottle, blanket, and stuffed elephant, picked her up, and put her in the car.

Then we hit the road.

The crying subsided as soon as we backed out of the driveway. I headed south on Van Ness and, after a mile or so, looked through the rearview mirror and saw my niece out cold. Since this whole driving-as-a-cure-for-crying was new to me, I was wary of red lights and stop signs. I avoided them as much as possible until it became obvious that Sydney was not going to wake up any time soon. Although the unnerving jingle on my new phone did cause her to stir.

I picked up immediately and whispered, "Shhhh."

The person on the other end of the line whispered back, "Is this a bad time?"

"I'm not sure," I whispered. "Who is this?"

"Walter."

"Hello, Walter."

"Are you in a movie theater?" he asked.

"I wouldn't answer my phone in a movie theater," I said. "Only complete assholes do that."

"I agree—in theory. I don't go to movies."

"I know, Walter."

"Where are you?"

---

[4] Whatever the sentence-enhancer that is.
[5] I have to admit that I was pleased this didn't work. Because that show almost made me cry.

"In a car," I replied.

This didn't answer Walter's primary questions, so I elaborated. "I've got a sleeping toddler in back. I'd like her to stay that way."

"You have kids?"

"No! It's my niece." All this still said in a whisper.

"Maybe this is a bad time. I'll call back later."

"What is it, Walter?"

"I have to go out tonight. Just for an hour or so. I offered a study session on campus for my students. The final is tomorrow."

"That's good, Walter. You need to get out."

I had stopped whispering. Sydney wasn't stirring.

"Will you be around later? I don't know what I might come home to."

"I'm sure everything will be fine, but call me if you have any problems."

"Thanks, Isabel. You're a saint."

"That's a first," I replied.

Since I was already in the car and only a mile or so from Walter's apartment building, I drove straight there, double-parking down the street. Within a minute of my arrival, I watched Walter exit his building and drive off in his immaculate Volvo.

Sydney remained asleep. Unprepared for a stakeout, I played several horrendous games of chess on my cell phone. Since I was competing against the easiest level (which they had the nerve to call "Silly"), losing put me in a sour mood and my already limited desire to study was diminished even more. To kill time, I followed up on that Bernie project I mentioned to you earlier with a few phone calls.

"Hi, Natasha. Have you had a chance to do that thing I asked you to do? . . . Remember the conversation we had the other day? I understand that it's hard to find a fax . . . If it would facilitate matters—Oh, I'm sorry. If it would make it easier, I could call you and we could record your affidavit and then I could type it up and just have you sign it. Will tomorrow work? Okay. I'll call tomorrow."

"Hi, Shelly. I got your report. Thank you. I just have one question. You mentioned that he'd leave his socks in the refrigerator in the summer. Were those socks clean or dirty? Really? That is unbelievably disgusting. That too? Yuck. Could you add that to the report and then I will need it signed and have the appropriate legalese—Excuse me? I just mean it needs to sound lawyerly. No, I didn't make up that word. I promise you. Oh, you did date a lawyer once. How'd that work out for you? I once used Litidate.com.[6] You'd be surprised who's out there. So, if you could send me the revised report, I'll type it up and then you can sign it and fax it back to me. You don't have a fax? Okay. Well, do you have an envelope and a stamp? Great. That will work just as well. Thanks, Shelly."

I checked my e-mails and tried, yet again, to hack into Rae's instant-message account, whilst keeping one eye on the front door to Walter's building. I should note that in his absence, I saw only one known neighbor depart and one known neighbor (Mrs. Averly—too old to be stopping up bathtubs for sport) enter the building. With all the driving and the plotting and the surveilling going on, I had lost track of time. When I looked at the clock on my dashboard it read eleven fifteen P.M.

The next phone call did not come as a surprise.

"Where are you?" my brother's shaken voice shouted into my ear.

"On a surveillance," I replied.

"Excuse me?" he said, even louder.

"You said take her for a drive if she wouldn't settle down. Well, let me tell you something, she wouldn't settle down. But the driving trick worked like a charm. Thanks for that."

"You took my daughter on a surveillance?"

"I took her for a drive that included surveillance."

"Bring her home immediately," David said.

---

[6] Still in business, as far as I know.

If he were talking on a landline, I can guarantee he would have slammed the phone into the receiver.

I drove directly to David and Maggie's place. David met me in the driveway, still in his opera suit, sporting a brutal scowl. The second I pulled the car to a halt, he opened the back door, gently removed his daughter from the car seat, and said, "That's the last time I ask you to babysit."

"Okay," I replied, wondering if he was planning to tack on a legitimate threat.

Maggie approached David, looked at her daughter, and said, "She fine; she's asleep. We told her to go for a drive if she wouldn't settle."

"She took her on a surveillance," David whispered loudly to his wife.

"What difference does it make?" I also whispered.

"It doesn't," Maggie said to me and David.

"It does," David replied.

I briefly stepped out of the car, counted Sydney's fingers and toes, and mentioned that not once in the entire evening did I say "banana." Maggie removed the car seat, whispered another "thank you," and followed David into the house.

When I returned to my car, I saw that the message light was blinking on my phone. Walter. I listened to his message on my voice mail.

"It happened again," Walter said.

Only this time, I knew it couldn't have.

INSIDE JOB

Someone had used Walter's toaster. Two cold, burned slices perched in its stainless steel pockets.

"Anything else amiss?" I asked.

"That's it," Walter said. "What do you think it means?"

"It means someone was wasting toast, if you ask me."

"I don't understand," Walter said.

"Me neither," I replied. "Is this your toast? Or did they bring it?"

"It's mine. Two slices are missing from the loaf," Walter replied.

"How much do you like toast?" I asked.

"I like it. But I only have it on weekends."

"Why is that?"

"Because of the crumbs. It's so messy. I need the time to clean it up."

"I see," I said, pacing through the apartment in my socks. I felt like a nursery school Columbo. "So, your intruder entered your home, made toast, burned it, and left. Is that the gist?" I asked.

"I believe so," Walter replied, sinking into his sofa, defeated.

"How friendly are you with your neighbors?"

"We say hello in the hallways and such."

"Have you ever angered a neighbor by, I don't know, suggesting they replace their doormat or organize their junk mail?"

"I've left a few anonymous notes."

"I'll need a list," I said as I sat down on the couch. I struggled to comprehend what would possess Sasha to repeat her trespass when she'd already been confronted. "Have you spoken to your ex-wife recently?" I asked.

"No," Walter replied. "Why do you ask?"

"No reason," I said. "Call me the next time someone makes toast," I said.

"Even if it's just Sunday and I'm making it?"

"No, Walter. Just call me if toast appears without your knowledge or anything in the same vein."

"Thank you, Isabel."

"Good-bye, Walter."

It was past midnight, but I phoned the ex-Mrs. Perkins anyway, looking for an explanation—one that involved her having the skills of a cat burglar. "Are you the toast bandit?" I asked.

"Excuse me?" she groggily replied.

"It's Isabel, by the way. The private investigator."

"It's late," she said.

"My apologies," I replied. "Are you the toast bandit?"

"I truly don't know what you're talking about."

"Have you talked to him?" Long silence. "I take that as a no."

"Not yet."

"Why not?"

"It's too . . . embarrassing."

"So you didn't break into his apartment this evening and make toast?"

"I wouldn't have made toast when we were married. The crumbs drove him mad."

"When was the last time you stepped foot into Walter's apartment?"

"Three months ago."

216

"Three months?"

"Yes."

"What did you do?"

"I rearranged his shoe tree. He likes all the slip-ons on the left and the laces on the right. I swapped sides. It was immature, I know. I just had to do it, after all those years of living under so many rules."

"Let me get this straight: You've only broken into his apartment once since the separation?"

"I used a key. I'm not sure it qualifies as breaking and entering."

"Do me a favor, Sasha. Wait a bit before you call Walter."

"Why?" she asked.

Because Walter never told me about the shoes. However, I didn't reply to her question.

"I'll be in touch," I said, disconnecting the call.

THE CONVERSATION

I arrived home to the kind of silence that's usually pierced by crickets. Henry sat on the couch reading a book. No, I don't know what book. I've learned not to ask, in case Henry suggests I read the same book so we have something to talk about over dinner. The problem with the books Henry reads is *nothing* happens in them. How hard is it to insert a freaking plot into a book? It's not like I need anyone murdered or anything. Although that does keep things interesting. But I digress.

Henry was on the couch. A single light lit the living room, and other than the quiet hum of street traffic, the only sounds were of pages turning and my footsteps crossing the room.

I'd had a bad feeling the moment I walked through the door.

"Sit down," Henry said.

"I was thinking of doing the dishes," I said, I think for the first time in my life.

"They're done."

"Do the floors need cleaning? Because I'd be happy to take care of that. Just point me in the direction of the mop. We have a mop, right?"

"We need to talk," Henry said.

One of my least-favorite phrases. Nobody ever says it when they want to talk about something good. "You sure about that?"

"Please sit down."

"Whenever somebody tells you to sit down, it's always bad. I'm surprised people enjoy sitting considering all the negative connotations."

"Isabel," Henry said in a tone that suggested it was time to be quiet.

I sat down and remained mute.

"I'm almost forty-eight years old," he said.

"I hear forty-eight is the new thirty-nine," I replied.

"I want a family."

"Okay."

"I want children."

"Are you sure?" I said. "I mean, have you met any? They're not all they're cracked up to be."

"What are you saying, Isabel?"

"I'm not saying anything."

"You have to start saying something."

I knew how this was going to go down. I suppose it's why I'd tried to avoid it for so long. In the past eighteen months, there were many things I learned to do in the interest of a peaceful cohabitation. Vacuum, speak in complete sentences, pay compliments, "learn" chess, make beds, not leave dirty towels on the bathroom floor. And those things I could continue to do, and I'm sure there are other compromises I could have made, but that was the easy stuff. I still wasn't sure exactly what I wanted, but I had a feeling I knew what I didn't want and it was time to come clean. "I want to say that I need more time."

"How much more time?" Henry asked.

"The problem is that I'm not sure that time will change how I feel. I know it's not normal, but I don't think I want the things you want. I know they're the things most people want but, I can't picture it. I'm not saying that I'll always feel this way. But I do now, and I don't see it changing in the foreseeable future. I might never change. Well, I hope at least a little bit, and you have to admit I've come a long way. But you know what I mean."

"I do."

"If all you wanted to do was get married, I would have said yes."

"Small consolation."

"There's no fixing this, is there?"

"I want children," Henry said. "And you don't."

"I suppose that's true."

"I don't think we can negotiate our way out of this one."

That was the end of the conversation but not the end of the relationship. When lives are tangled together for years, untangling takes some time. But living under the same roof became unbearable and we untangled that part as quickly as possible.

I took a few days off to pack up my belongings. I should clarify: I packed, and then Henry unpacked and repacked for me with a cohesive organizational system including labels on the boxes. This was the last chance he would have to create order out of my chaos, and he made the most of it. In fact, as "we" (eventually I just watched) packed, Henry tried one last time to educate me on the benefits of putting things in their rightful place. He tried to estimate how many hours of my life had been erased searching for objects because I didn't put them where they were supposed to be. While most of Henry's lessons had fallen on deaf ears, I hadn't misplaced my keys or wallet in months. Although my rain boots have been missing for weeks.[1] Once all my worldly possessions were packed, I had to transport them to their new home.

Maggie suggested I move (temporarily) into the now-vacated in-law unit. David agreed purely out of sympathy (he was still holding the whole taking-Sydney-on-a-surveillance grudge). Just four days after "the conversation," David helped me move all the boxes into my new pad. We stacked them against the wall and took a beer break.

---

[1] Later discovered that they were in the trunk of my father's car. Do not have any idea how they got there. And one had an excellent bottle of bourbon inside.

"Déjà vu?" he asked.

"Totally," I replied. "I hope I sleep better this time around."[2]

"A clear conscience and paying rent should help. Are you going to unpack?"

"I think I better keep my stuff in the boxes," I replied. "This might be the last time that all my worldly possessions are in order."

"Do you want to tell me what happened?"

"No."

"Do you want to talk about it?"

"No."

"Didn't think so. But, you know, if you do—"

"Probably won't."

Later that night, Maggie came downstairs in her pajamas, with a bottle of some of the upstairs booze. "I know you don't want to talk," she said, and poured me a drink. Then she turned on the television and cycled through the remote until SpongeBob showed up. "He always makes me feel better," Maggie said, folding her legs onto the sofa.

"Me too."

I tried to keep the news from breaking for as long as possible. Maggie and David remained mum, but Mom can sniff out a secret from just a few careless words, and when I came into work the next day, she wanted to talk.

"Sit down," she said when I entered the office.

My dad and D were nowhere in sight.

"I'll stand, if you don't mind," I said. You know how I feel about sitting.

"Are you sure, Isabel?"

"Yes, it's more comfortable this way."

"I mean about you and Henry. Are you sure?"

---

[2] A few years ago I squatted in David's in-law unit without his knowledge. I was so afraid of getting caught, I barely got a wink of sleep.

"No, Mom. I'm not sure about anything."

"This could be a mistake."

"Wouldn't be the first one."

"Sweetie, men like that don't fall out of trees."

"What kind of men do?"

"You're not as young as you used to be."

"Did you just purchase a cliché dictionary? If so, I already know the one about how it's just as easy to marry a rich man as a poor man and that's bullshit."

"At the rate you're going, Izzy, you won't be marrying anyone."

"Mom, hate to break it to you, but that's never been my life's mission."

"I understand that, dear. But if you spend your whole life pushing people away, eventually they'll stop coming back."

"You're not making me feel any better, Mom."

"Sometimes making you feel better isn't my priority."

Just then my cell phone buzzed and I got a text from Mrs. Slayter requesting a last-minute surveillance. I had never been more pleased to hear from that awful woman.

"I got to go," I said, grabbing my coat.

"I'm always here if you need me," Mom said.

"I know," I replied.

LOST IN TRANSLATION

I commenced surveillance on Edward Slayter at two fifteen in the afternoon. There was a chill in the air and an unpredictable breeze. I tucked my scarf into my jacket and shoved my hands in my pockets, but it was impossible to get warm—a common phenomenon in San Francisco. Unless you carry luggage with you at all times, you'll never be appropriately attired. I prayed that Slayter would be on the move so I could warm up. I paced back and forth, clocking Slayter's building on the return.

"Fancy meeting you here," a familiar voice said to my back.

I turned around to face Charlie Black. He was carrying his chess set and brown bag, which I assumed contained his lunch. "Hi, Charlie. How are you?"

"I'm very good, Jane. How are you?"

"Cold."

"You'll feel better when the wind dies down."

"When will that happen?"

"In forty-five minutes."

"How do you know this?"

"I took an online meteorology class."

"Really?"

"Yes," Charlie said. Then he took out his chessboard and began setting the pieces. "Can I interest you in a game?"

Just then my phone buzzed with a text from Margaret Slayter: Cancel surveillance. Ed will be in office all day.

OK, I replied.

Here's the thing: The point of surveillance is that you don't believe the person is where he says he will be. Once again, Margaret was confirming all of my suspicions.

"I think I'll be heading home, Charlie."

"You're not seeing your friend today?"

"I don't think so."

Charlie was setting up the chessboard in a particular pattern. "Since you've got the free time, sure you don't want to play?"

"No, thanks. I better go."

"You need to be taught young. It helps. I was five when I first learned to play," Charlie said.

"Five? Wow. That is young. I bet the five-year-old you could beat the thirty-four-year-old me."

"Probably," Charlie replied. "But it was in our blood. My father was a Russian grand master. He used to tutor people when he came to this country."

"Hang on," I said. "Your father's Russian?"

"So is my mother."

"Do you speak?"

"I'm a little rusty these days. I can only practice with my sister."

I shuffled through my bag, searching for my digital recorder with my mother's Russian quiz. While I now believed she was taking the class, what I really wanted to know was how seriously she was taking it. "Would you mind translating a few things for me?" I asked, pulling out the recorder.

"Okay," Charlie replied.

I played the digital file for Charlie; Final score: Russian 3, Mom 1.[1]

"Russian is extremely difficult for Americans to learn," Charlie said in her defense.

"She's supposedly taking a class twice a week. What are the odds of that?" I asked.

"Her pronunciation is pretty good. It just sounds like she might be sleeping through the lessons and picking up random phrases and remembering them phonetically."

"That's an excellent deduction, Charlie. I like the way you think."

"Thanks," Charlie replied. Then he pointed in the distance behind me. "I see your friend."

I turned around and saw Mr. Slayter walking toward the corner of Market and First. While I was officially off the job, it seemed wise to resume the surveillance since Edward wasn't at the office as he claimed to be.

I followed him south down Market Street to Post, where he took a right, walked a few blocks, and entered a medical building. I waited in a coffee shop across the street for forty-five minutes until he left and returned to his office. Honestly, I had no idea what the interrupted surveillance and Slayter's secret doctor's appointment meant. But I figured at some point the pieces would fit together.

I returned to an empty office and found a package of Twinkies and Ho Hos on my desk, along with a condolence card:

Sorry for your loss. Love, Rae.

I ate the Twinkies with a glass of milk and wallowed while I had a moment of privacy. Then I busied myself organizing a series of background reports for Zylor Corp., one of our major paperwork clients. This involved collating and stapling, a blissfully mind-numbing task. Until, of course, your sta-

[1] See pg. 117.

pler runs out and you can't find any staples in your desk. Dad's usually the office-supply hoarder, but his entire workspace was under lock and key these days. Mom's drawers were so packed with her hobby debris, it was like finding a staple in a haystack. So I turned to D's desk.

I opened the top right-hand drawer and lo and behold, there was a box of staples. And Scotch tape. And paper clips. And thumbtacks. And scissors. And Post-it notes. And drugs. Well, pill bottles. But drugs were inside of them. Perhaps at this point you think I should have grabbed a train of staples and closed the drawer. But I didn't. I gathered the pill bottles and read the prescription labels. All in the name of D. Merriweather. Of course, just as I was jotting down the names of the specific medications, D entered the office.

"I was looking for staples," I said.

"Did you find them?" D asked.

"Yes. Thank you," I replied, returning the bottles to his desk and shoving the drawer shut with my hip.

I took a seat behind my desk and began moving stacks of papers around, trying to look occupied.

"Did you find anything else?" D asked.

"I found some drugs. Not the good kind. I wasn't snooping. Look, my stapler is all out." I opened the mouth of the stapler to provide an alibi.

"I believe you," D replied.

I waited a moment to see whether D was going to offer an explanation. I didn't see one coming, and like most things, I couldn't just let it slide.

"Those pills are mostly . . . are you depressed?" I asked.

"I was in prison for fifteen years."

"But now you're out."

"Isabel, don't get me wrong, being out is . . . great. I thank the Lord every day.

"He had nothing to do with it."

"We will agree to disagree."

"Whatever," I replied. "Go on."

"Did you think when I got sprung I was going to be as good as new?"

"I figured you'd have a few convict habits to break, like guarding your food and eating super fast—you don't really do that, do you . . . but . . . yeah. I guess that's what I thought."

"Even freedom takes some getting used to."

D woke his computer and returned to work. I waited an awkward moment before I spoke.

"Um, D—"

"Isabel, I really don't want to talk about it anymore."

"I understand. But, um, I'm still out of staples."

BERNIEGATE

I had labored for hours amassing evidence against Bernie. And, if I do say so myself, my work on this case was well above par. As I painted the finishing touches of what I came to call Berniegate, I began to think of it as a parting gift to Henry.

Unfortunately it was a gift he would never see.

The next afternoon I waited until Bernie was at the bar and then phoned Gerty to see if she would meet me for lunch.

After we were seated at a corner table, we had to dispense with the elephant in the restaurant.

"Henry told me," she said.

"I figured," I replied.

"You were good for him. I worry sometimes. He's so much like his father. Everything has to be just so."

"It was my fault," I said. "I'm sorry I couldn't—I don't know why."

"That's not the kind of thing you apologize for. Only you know what's going on in that head of yours. No one else can tell you what to want."

"It goes against nature, doesn't it? Not wanting to procreate?"

"The unfortunate tattoo I have on my ass goes against nature," Gerty

228

said. "Modern medicine, electricity, cars, cell phones, four-inch heels, fake tits, Botox, hair color, all go against nature. And there are a lot of natural things that I wouldn't abide. Like an overgrowth of nose hairs or foot fungus. We have an infinite number of choices in front of us. All you can do is make the choice that's right for you. Of course, I wouldn't give this same speech to a serial killer, but I think you get my drift."

I did. I got her drift. And midspeech, I realized she wasn't just talking about me and Henry. She was also explaining—not justifying—her relationship with Bernie. That inch-thick file folder I had been carrying around with me for a week? I shoved it back in my bag and decided then and there that Gerty would never see it. Only she could know what was going on in that head of hers.

We finished lunch and stepped out into your typical foggy San Francisco day. She gave me a warm embrace and said, "You would have been a great daughter-in-law." Gerty caught a cab and told me that she was spending the afternoon at MOMA. I took my file and drove to the Philosopher's Club. While Gerty would never see my investigative masterpiece, I couldn't let all that hard work go to waste.

When Bernie saw me enter the bar, he turned to his collection of clean pint glasses and started shining them again as if they were champagne flutes in a swanky hotel. He refused to make eye contact, but when I sat down at the bar and ordered a beer, he obliged.

He served me a pint in the cleanest glass. I tried to pay him, but Bernie slid my money away.

"On the house."

"Why?"

"We used to be friends," Bernie said. "Remember those days?"

"I don't remember them the same way you do."

That statement could not have been truer.

"What happened to us?" Bernie asked.

"You know what happened," I replied.

"Let it be, Izzy. Gerty and I are just two old ships who collided in the night. It's romantic, if you think about it," he said.

"Your phrasing isn't," I replied.

"How long are you going to hold this grudge against me?"

"I'm done. You can stop looking over your shoulder."

"You're giving us your blessing?"

"I wouldn't go that far. But be good to her, Bernie. I know that woman very well. You get up to any of your old tricks and she'll leave you in a flash."

"She makes me want to be a better man," Bernie said.

"Lame movie quotes won't get you anywhere with her," I said.

"Already did," Bernie replied with a lewd wink.

"My business is done here. I just wanted to leave you with this," I said as I tossed the file folder on top of the bar.

"Oh yeah? What is it?" Bernie asked.

"Evidence," I replied. "Think of it as a reminder of the kind of man you can be."

I left Bernie and his background report behind. I thought a paper trail of Bernie's misspent middle age might convince Gerty that their relationship was doomed. But it was my plan that was doomed. Gerty chose Bernie because of his flaws—I suspect in part because he was so different from the man she had married. By highlighting them, I doubt I could have persuaded her to make a run for it. Although I'm fairly certain I could have planted a few doubts in her mind. The report contained photographic evidence of his previous homes and the state of debauchery into which he could sink; it included compromising photos from strip clubs and poker parlors that I found in my uncle Ray's old photo albums and affidavits[1] from every Bernie paramour I could track down in the

---

[1] If you're interested in a sampling, see appendix. I highly recommend it.

California/Nevada region, documenting years of dishonesty and vulgarity. Of the seven deadly sins, Bernie was a regular with six. As hard as I tried, I couldn't pin wrath on him. To his credit, he never had much of a temper.

After lunch I returned to the house and found only my father in the office.

"Where is everyone?" I asked.

"I ask myself that all the time," Dad replied.

"And you still didn't answer my question."

"Your mother's at the library, picking up her latest book club tome. She's hosting tonight. Then she's off to the store to buy frozen appetizers and white wine."

"Sounds like a fun evening. I'm surprised D didn't offer to cook. Where is he, by the way?"

"He offered to take your grandmother to a matinee."

"What?"

"A movie. In the afternoon."

"I'm aware of the term. But what are *they* doing going to a movie together?"

"A Morgan Freeman film is playing."

"Whose idea?"

"I don't know. He just asked for the afternoon off because my mother won't go to films after six P.M."

"Why not?"

"She thinks that's when the more unsavory types show up."

"Who cares? Isn't it weird that they're hanging out?"

"Yes, Isabel. But so many things in my world are that I'm starting to pay less attention."

With the cat away, my father then foraged in the kitchen for something to eat. Rae or my mother must have inadvertently left a stash of the Crack

Mix outside of the safe. Dad picked it up and brought it into the office. Since he thought it was his regular Chex Mix, he didn't indulge immediately. He opened a diet soda, leaned back in his chair, and gave me one of those sympathetic glances. "You okay, Izzy?"

"Yep."

"You want to talk about anything?"

"I'd love to talk about the Slayter case."

"I think we should talk about your feelings instead."

"I feel sad that you don't trust me with work-related information."

"I meant we should talk about Henry."

"I'd rather not."

"You sure? Because I think you should be talking to somebody."

"I'm positive."

"If you change your mind—"

"I won't."

"But, if you do . . ."

Dad kept staring at me, as if he were attempting to mind-read. Not that I thought he was capable of it, but I found it unnerving nonetheless. Besides, I knew that he'd pick up the topic again in five minutes or so, hoping to wear me down. So I found an opportunity and took it.

I approached his desk and scooped out a handful of Crack Mix. I left the lion's share behind.

"Be careful with this stuff," I said. "There's no turning back."

Dad reached into the bag and took his first bite of the manna from heaven. "What is this?" he said.

"It's the Crack Mix we've been talking about all the time."

Dad held the bag up to the light, gobsmacked, and said, "It's the best snack food in the history of snack food."

"Yeah, it's pretty great," I said.

"What the hell have I been eating all this time?" Dad asked.

I think he might have actually been tearing up.

"Just plain cereal with some unsalted nuts."

* * *

My mother would kill me if she knew I'd opened the door of this finger-food Pandora's box, but I'm the master of deflection. And I succeeded in steering my father away from having a heart-to-heart conversation with me. No good can come of that.

EDWARD SLAYTER
VS. CHARLIE BLACK

Sunday evenings were Edward Slayter's poker night.

    In the past five years, he'd skipped it only once, when he had the flu. So when Margaret overheard a phone call with one of his poker buddies in which he begged off for the night, she promptly phoned me and asked if I was available for last-minute surveillance. My schedule was wide open and since that Sunday was Halloween I was happy to have something to occupy my time. While I've never minded the glut of leftover candy, All Hallows' Eve has always gotten under my skin. For one thing, it always catches me unawares. I'm walking to the bus or work or a job and suddenly a skeleton appears or Charlie Chaplin or a weak imitation of Britney Spears.[1] But what gets to me most is the sheer volume of women who use the holiday as an excuse to dress up like a hooker or a sexy cat.[2] Ladies, what's wrong with Fidel Castro? Get some military fatigues, a green cap, a mustache, a lit cigar, and you're out the door.

    Mr. Slayter left his home at six P.M. and had his driver take him to the Mechanics' Institute on Post Street, where there's a chess club with open play. I had been surveilling Slayter for two months at this point. This was the first time I ever saw him attend a chess club.

---

[1] That said, a male impersonator of virtually any female celebrity perks me up.
[2] Whatever the sentence-enhancer that is.

He immediately found a partner for a match. Considering my recent breakup, this arena seemed cosmically brutal, but I figured I could blend. Well, not exactly. Many of the patrons were in subtle costume, Bobby Fischer suits, maybe, and I gathered a few other sartorial homages were going on, but not being an expert on chess, I can only comment that there were a few unusual ensembles in the mix, but that's always the case in San Francisco. But no hookers or sexy cats, thank you very much. There were a number of officious individuals who wished to make me feel welcome. I asked if I could just watch, and then I lurked in a corner. One of those officious individuals questioned whether I could see anything from the corner and I pulled my binoculars from my bag.

"We offer lessons," the officious man said.

"I'll think about it," I replied.

I watched Slayter through my binoculars. He had changed into a cardigan and corduroy trousers after his day in a suit. It made him look more regular, as if he'd made an effort to appear unassuming. He ran his fingers through his hair and squinted, staring intently at the chessboard, as if there was something there that was just out of his vision.

"Jane?" a male voice said. Then he said it again. I didn't respond because my name isn't Jane. Then I could sense a male presence standing next to me.

"Jane, is that you?" the voice said louder, as if maybe I had earplugs in. I turned around to find Charlie Black.

I'm not sure why I was surprised—chess is his game—but it's always disconcerting seeing someone out of context. Once I saw my ex-shrink at a hardware store and I had to leave immediately.

"Hello?" I said.

It had only been a few days since we last met, but something was different about Charlie.

"You look nice," I said.

"My sister visited. She made me get a haircut and a new sweater."

"I like both."

"Thank you," Charlie said. "I thought maybe you swore off chess after our game."

"No, I swore off it later."

"Then what are you doing here, Jane?"

"I have a confession to make."

"It's good to confess."

"My name isn't Jane."

"Do you feel better now?"

"I do."

"What's your real name?"

"Isabel."

"I like it. Why did you lie?"

"I don't tell strangers my name," I said.

"I can understand that policy," Charlie replied. "So does that mean we're not strangers anymore?"

"I guess not."

"So what are you doing here, if you're not playing chess?"

"I'm just hanging out, watching a few games. I have binoculars."

"I don't believe you, Isabel," Charlie said, but he said it in a friendly way, so I didn't mind.

"I'm not being a hundred percent honest."

"That's okay. We don't know each other very well."

As if to punctuate this point, we spent the next few minutes in complete silence.

"You come here often, Charlie?" I asked.

I thought Charlie might think my question was funny, but he didn't.

"Once or twice a week," he said.

"You see the man at the third table to the right?"

"With the gray hair?" Charlie asked.

"Yes."

"That's your friend, isn't it? The one who doesn't wave."

"You have a good memory."

"So I've been told."

"Have you seen him here before?" I asked.

"No."

"Do you need money, Charlie?"

"I'm not interested in breaking the law."

"I wouldn't ask you to."

I took sixty dollars from my wallet and gave Charlie my burner phone, with my number on speed dial. Charlie wasn't familiar with cell phones, which I found shocking but worthy of respect. I took a few minutes to explain the basics to him. Then I made a very simple request. "See if you can play a game of chess with Mr. Slayter. Learn what you can about him. Call me when he leaves."

I sat for the next few hours at Specialty's Café near the Montgomery BART station. I texted Margaret Slayter and informed her that her husband was, as she suspected, not at his poker game, but at the Mechanics' Institute playing chess. She seemed completely uninterested in his deception but made it clear that I should inform her when he left. I then phoned the house to see if the Tortoise was around. D said he was out and offered no further information.

Then I phoned my father on his cell. "Hi, Dad."

"Happy Halloween," he replied. "Are you going as yourself again?"

"Yes. You'd never recognize me. Where are you?"

"At an undisclosed location," he replied.

"Me too," I said, ending the call.

I think it was safe to assume that my dad was on his own surveillance of Margaret Slayter.

Three hours later (people who like chess will play it for a very long period of time), I got a call on my cell phone from my burner.

Charlie said "hello" three times and disconnected the call.

I watched Mr. Slayter's driver pull up in front of the Post Street building and Mr. Slayter enter the vehicle. I was hoofing it, so I merely warned Mrs. Slayter that Mr. Slayter was likely on his way home. Her text reply was Thx. Still more polite than Rae, but equally suspicious.

I phoned Charlie to see whether he had more success answering calls than making them. He picked up on the fourth ring.

"Hellò. Hello. Hello."

"Charlie, it's Isabel, formerly known as Jane. Would you like a cup of coffee?"

"I don't drink coffee."

"I'm down the block at Specialty's Café. Can you meet me here and I'll buy you a warm beverage and as many cookies as you can eat?"[3]

"Okay."

Charlie showed up five minutes later, at which point I showed him how to answer and end phone calls. I made him order something and so he got a hot chocolate and a pumpkin cookie.

"Good luck sleeping tonight," I said.

"Oh, I don't sleep," Charlie casually replied.

We sat down at the table and after Charlie took a few sips and a few bites, I began my inquiry. "How'd it go?"

Charlie then pulled out a notebook with algebraic notation and began to provide a truly mind-numbing narrative of the first game he played with Mr. Slayter.

I interrupted: "Charlie, I'm not all that interested in the game. Did you learn anything about Mr. Slayter while you were playing chess?"

"He favors his queen, seriously. She won't come out until the endgame. He couldn't care less about his knights. He treats them like pawns. But he has some good technique. He just seems rusty or something."

"Did he tell you anything personal about himself?"

"He said he hadn't played for years."

"Anything else?"

---

[3] Their cookies are huge (and awesome), so you can't really eat that many.

238

"He told me his name. Ed."

"That's a start. And?"

"He said he needed to stay sharp."

"And?"

"That's about it. He was a good sport. He congratulated me when I won."

"Congratulations," I said.

A CHINK IN THE ARMOR

I had to give my dad props for his ambitious Chinese wall. I couldn't help but feel a sense of pride in old Albert's stringent efforts to derail my various lines of attack. He knew me well, he considered me a viable threat, and he took unforeseen measures to lord over his cases. Dad never slipped and he kept close watch on my extracurricular activities. On one point I had to concede defeat. Dad's computer couldn't be cracked, but Robbie could.

As far as I knew, Robbie never left his house.

However, he did own a 1992 Toyota, which would lead me to believe that sometimes he went somewhere. I put a tracking device on his car. One evening at seven P.M., it alerted me that Robbie was on the move.

A few days later, when I had some time to kill, I tracked his car to an apartment building in Daly City. His Toyota was parked in front of a three-unit stucco building with a trio of carports. I checked the mailboxes—first initials and last names only. I took a chance and called his cell. He didn't pick up. I called again and firmly suggested he call me back. I phoned the office and had Demetrius run a reverse address check on the building.

Sally Shore, the only female under the age of sixty who resided in the building, lived in apartment #3 and she had a landline. I formulated a plan

240

on the spot. I've known Robbie almost eight years. He doesn't make house calls—he manages virtually all of his technical support and verbal abuse remotely. His relationship with Sally was personal. And Robbie wasn't the kind of guy who had a way with the ladies. He had an un-way. It was cruel, but this was my only opportunity to get what I needed from Gruber.

I phoned Sally's number.

She picked up.

"I'm sorry to bother you," I said. "Is Robbie there?"

"Um . . . yes," she said.

"Can I speak to him?"

"May I ask who is calling?"

"He'll know," I said.

In the background I heard whispering until Robbie took the phone. There was a nervous edge in his voice. "Hello?"

"Guess who?" I said.

"Oh, right. Um . . . I forgot I gave you this number in case of emergency," Robbie said, trying to cover.

"That was pretty good," I said. "You must like this girl."

"What can I do for you?" Robbie asked.

"I think you know," I said.

"The password?"

"Yes."

"And if I don't?"

"I'm right outside. I have a cheap wedding ring I leave in my glove compartment. I also have this mousy brown wig that makes me look extremely unattractive, which means potentially gettable for you. Sally probably isn't into dating married men, is she?"

"You've crossed a line," Robbie said.

"It's kind of my thing."

"Isabel," Robbie said.

"What?"

"'Isabel.' That's the password."

* * *

My mother phoned while I was heading back to the office.

"We have a problem," she said.

"I know," I replied.

I was speaking generally. My mother was speaking specifically.

"You know what I'm talking about?" she asked.

"No."

Sigh.

"What's up, Mom?"

"Guess where Demetrius and Ruth are at this moment?"

"I don't know, Mom."

"They're at the movies."

"Again?"

"Again."

"Together," Mom said emphatically.

"I assumed as much."

"This can't go on," she said.

"I wouldn't worry about it," I said. "I mean, how many Morgan Freeman films can be playing at one time?"

"He's doing the voice-over for some nature flick."

"What's it called? Maybe I'll see it."

"This is not a laughing matter," she said.

"I understand where you're coming from. But isn't it nice to have her out of the house?"

"You're missing the point."

"It happens sometimes," I replied.

"I used to like him, you know."

"Who?"

"Morgan Freeman."

"Everybody likes Morgan Freeman."

"I don't. Not anymore."

"Don't blame Morgan Freeman. You're going to have to figure out another way to smoke her out of the house. The old living-with-an-ex-con trick didn't work."

"This was entirely unexpected," my mother said dramatically.

"I'm sure it was. What are you going to do now?"

"Cook dinner."

"I like the way you think," I said. "If you start cooking all the time, she might decide she's had enough."

"It wasn't part of a plan, Isabel. I was just telling you that I was cooking dinner."

"Oh . . . sorry."

"One more thing, Isabel. I got a message from the Blakes. They want the Sparrow surveilled tonight. She mentioned something in an e-mail about Vivien saying she was going to a party."

"Who throws a party on a Wednesday night?" I asked.

"College students who don't have to wake up until noon. You really should have gone, dear," Mom said as she hung up the phone.

I dropped by the Spellman offices to pick up the surveillance equipment, check on my mother's mental status, and see whether the coast was clear to hack into my dad's computer. I found my mother in the kitchen, devouring the last of D's Crack Mix (the bit that was left in the safe).

"How are you doing, Mom?" I gently asked.

"I've got some ideas."

"Where's the Tortoise?" I asked.

"Out," my mother replied.

"Grammy and D?"

"Still at the movies."

"The Weasel?"

"I have no idea."

"Why don't you take a bath, Mom? You need to relax," I said.

My mother looked at the roast and the open cookbook on the kitchen counter.

"I can put the roast in," I said.

"Four hundred and twenty-five degrees," Mom said. "Ignore the recipe."

"Got it," I replied.

Mom climbed the stairs and I entered the office. The Weasel could be anywhere, and I couldn't risk having her walk in on me, so I sent her a text to get her coordinates. Five minutes later, no response.

Then I texted Fred.

Is Rae with you?

I haven't seen her in months.

Huh. I'm impressed you're making it work with all that time apart.[1]

??

Define: ??

We broke up. Didn't she tell U?

As a matter of fact, she did not. This new development would require further investigation, but at that moment I had other matters to attend to. Without having a tracking device on every Spellman capable of entering the office, I had to take the risk. I locked the door,[2] sat down behind Dad's computer, typed my name, and the next thing I knew I was copying files onto a data storage device that fit on my key ring.

I put the roast in the oven and checked the recipe. It called for three hundred and eighty degrees. Mom said four twenty-five; I jacked up the temperature to four fifty. I figured my mother had plausible deniability. She could blame me.

Then I picked up the surveillance camera, drove to the Mission, and double-parked in front of Vivien Blake's residence.

---

[1] Too long a sentence for thumbs.
[2] Everybody has a key, so it's not exactly high security.

SURVEILLANCE REPORT:
VIVIEN BLAKE

November 2
2330 hrs

Female subject, 5'5", 125 lbs, dark brown hair, wearing blue jeans and a gray hooded sweatshirt over a dark green military jacket, exits a San Francisco apartment building at Twenty-sixth and Noe. She walks east down the street, scanning the parked cars. She presses a remote key and looks for a flash of taillights. A BMW winks in the distance. Female subject spins in a circle, checking her perimeter; approaches car; gets inside; and starts the engine. She drives east down to South Van Ness Avenue and makes a left turn, stopping on the corner of Seventeenth and South Van Ness at the establishment of Oscar's Auto. Subject drives vehicle into covered garage. Unable to establish a visual on subject for fifteen minutes.

2345 hrs

Subject and an unknown male (midforties, heavyset, wearing blue mechanic's jumpsuit with the Oscar's Auto logo embroidered on the breast pocket) exit the office of establishment. They approach a tow truck with the same logo painted on the side. Subject slips an unidentifiable object into her pocket and jumps into a truck with unknown male. Investigator follows subject vehicle to a liquor store. Unknown male enters the store and leaves three minutes later with a large brown bag (about the size of a six-pack of beer).

The tow truck returns subject to the residence on Twenty-sixth Street where she was previously seen exiting. Subject rings the buzzer. (Could not establish unit number.) Female subject then enters the building and all visual contact is lost.

Like I said before: My father called, we got into an argument about the family nicknames, Dad asked me what Vivien was up to, and I lied. I lied because I didn't know what she was up to, but I believe that sometimes young people should be allowed to get up to something without their parents finding out.

I also needed to get a handle on the situation before I disseminated any information. You could argue that what I was doing was as ethically dubious as my sister's doctored reports. But there was a difference. I wasn't swindling a client; I was protecting a subject. And I'm a firm believer that withholding information is not in the category of lying.

I think you know how the rest of this goes. I waited outside unknown male's apartment and watched female subject defenestrate herself through a second-story window and walk back to her apartment. Then I arrived at Spellman central, where the Eagle was on the tarmac.

The smell of cremated roast lingered in the air.

My mother asked me about the Sparrow and then we sat in silence watching television. Breaking news on the tree sitters. Negotiations stalled. The newscaster reported the latest developments and the camera panned up the tree. My mother picked up the telephone and dialed.

"Rae. This is your mother calling. Get the hell out of that tree right now!"

Part III

RUINS

(November/December)

THE TREE INCIDENT

All of the Spellmans, sans David, are notorious for getting up to no good, but Rae's treetop triumph was the finest "no good" achievement in Spellman history. And that's quite an achievement.

Within five minutes of the news broadcast, Mom and Dad had left for the scene of the high crime. With the television blaring in the background, I picked up the phone and said to my brother, "You will not believe this." I might have said that phrase before, but I think it was the first time I really meant it. David's television was also blaring in the background. A different program—one involving grown men singing to children.

I provided the brushstrokes, which David misunderstood. He asked me to repeat myself and when I did, he said, "Who cares if Rae is in a teahouse?"

I repeated "tree house," enunciating to the best of my ability. David said, "Yeah, and so?" I switched up descriptive terms and said, "Rae is one of the oak grove protesters!"

"Ogre protest?" he asked.

"What is an ogre protest?" I snapped.

"You tell me," he replied.

"Turn off the TV," I said. By some strange miracle, he understood that. Without the soundtrack of those sentence-enhancers playing in the background, I told David to turn the TV back on and to which station. In retrospect, I probably should have led with that. Once David absorbed the full impact of his little sister showing up on the evening news, he spoke. "Since when does she care about plant life, or any life besides her own? Remember when I gave her the Chia Pet?"

"I do," I replied. "But that was ten years ago."[1]

"Still," David said. "This doesn't make any sense."

It didn't. And though I had many mysteries occupying my brain, Rae's sudden interest in a two-hundred-year-old oak grove sat at the top of the puzzle pyramid.

When Demetrius came in from (apparently) another one of his first dates, he stared at the television in awe.

"That girl is crazier than a june bug in May."

"No argument from me. What do you think she's up to?"

"Only one reason I can reckon for that kind of crazy," D replied.

"Care to enlighten me?"

"Love," D replied.

I phoned Fred.

"Fred."

"Isabel."

"What are you doing, Fred?"

"I'm watching TV. Just like you."

"Do you know something about this?"

"Maybe," Fred said.

He sounded guilty when he said it, so I was sure he knew more than maybe.

"I think I better head over there," he said, disconnecting the call.

* * *

---

[1] David gave Rae a Chia Pet as a stocking stuffer. Rae tossed the seeds in the trash, scraped a one-inch slot into the terra-cotta figurine, and used it as a piggy bank.

Twenty minutes later, the Spellman home and office lines were ringing off the hook.

Every person who had ever known a Spellman was keen to gather more details of Rae's sudden rise to environmentalist infamy. Grammy Spellman, who had been watching one of her programs in the bedroom, finally surfaced and asked what all the ruckus was about. I was going to tell her when D interrupted. He said we had a break in a case and promised that the phones would quiet down shortly. Grammy, mildly appeased, returned to her room.

An hour after that, Fred arrived at the oak grove and, with the assistance of very serious threats from the unit, the police, and the dean's office, managed to talk my sister down. At which point she was arrested. She spent four hours in a holding cell until my parents could post bail.

The following morning a family meeting (plus Fred) was called at my brother's house.

My mother had insisted on a separate location to avoid Ruth's endless inquiries. Grammy was utterly baffled by Vietnam War protesters; she certainly wasn't going to understand squatting in a tree to keep it from being razed. As the meeting commenced, all parties appeared worn out from the sleepless night.

My father opened with a broad question: "What do you have to say for yourself?"

"Photosynthesis is vital for all living species. Those oak trees have been providing oxygen for years. You can't just toss them aside when you want to build an athletic center. And think about how much oxygen *that* place will use up," Rae replied.

Dad wasn't buying it. "Seriously, Rae, what's this all about?"

Most things in life have come easily to Rae and those things that haven't, like athletic or artistic talent, she isn't much interested in. I think she always felt invincible, as if there were no situation that she couldn't master. Negotiating with a stubborn child is one thing, but fighting against the brick wall of a grown-up is different; her immovable spirit had become somewhat terrifying to me. My mother had repeatedly argued that it was a phase, but it had ceased to feel like one long ago. The tree incident was oddly indicative of both her stubborn spirit itself and the softening of that spirit.

Fred Finkel, environmental activist, Sierra Club supporter, founding member of the *Earthvibe* newsletter, and public planning major, had broken up with Rae over her selfish indifference to the physical world: her habit of driving when public transportation was readily available; her use of plastic water bottles; her tendency to print out draft after draft of term papers for review; her "languid composting";[2] and her general environmental laissez-faire.

Fred claims he'd spoken to Rae on numerous occasions about his concerns over their civic differences, but Rae had made only superficial changes that didn't convey respect for his beliefs. Only after Fred broke up with her did she fully comprehend how important the environment was to her boyfriend.

Rae grew up in a household motored by threats followed by ultimatums. Had she known that Fred would not have given her fair warning, she might have taken his requests more seriously. But Fred wasn't an ultimatum kind of guy. Unlike Rae, he didn't believe in bullying. He saw her disregard for his wishes as a serious symptom in their relationship and respectfully ended it. Rae, blindsided, tried some cheap measures to win him back—gifts of plants, sudden purchases of hemp clothing and even hemp stock, and buying all organic produce,[3] along with a marked improvement in Rae's *languid composting*.

When all of these motions fell flat, a grand gesture was required. Like

---

[2] This apparently means that some biodegradable items still end up in the trash.
[3] Both parties, however, agreed that with Rae's limited ingestion of all vegetation, this switch made little to no difference.

most grand gestures, it took some time to bring about, since she first had to insinuate herself into the fringe protest group, which required learning far more about oak trees than she ever desired or thought possible.

While Rae regaled the family with her tale of infiltrating the tree minders, Fred sat in the background listening with bewildered intensity.

"You will definitely be getting at least community service for this, young lady," my father said.

"Sometimes you have to take a stand," Rae said.

"Oh please," my mother said.

Rae ignored my mother and turned to Fred. "Do you forgive me now?"

"Those trees are a lost cause," Fred replied. "I think it's better to use our energy on a fight that can be won. And all I really want is for individuals to make small changes in their daily habits. The milk carton doesn't go in the recycling bin. It's compostable. I lost track of how many times I had to tell you that."

"I spend eight hours in a tree for you and that's all you have to say?" Rae replied.

Fred didn't look like he had a good response, so I interrupted: "I just have one question, Rae. Did you use the bucket?"[4]

The unit escorted my sister into David's office and had a private conversation with her where I suspect a very severe verbal lashing took place. David, Fred, and I sat in the living room, mostly silent, hoping to catch any bubbles of elevated words from the other room, but mostly we just caught bubbles of indecipherable elevated words. David bit his nails, which he does when he's particularly agitated, a condition that the situation didn't call for. I, for one, was enjoying myself immensely and experienced no elevated sibling concern.

---

[4] Rae once asked me the very same question, after locking me in a closet overnight. I couldn't help but return the favor. (Document #4, if you're curious.)

At one point Fred turned to me and asked, "Is this my fault?"

David answered, "No, I think it's mine."

When all the parties had departed, I asked David what he meant.

"Nothing," he replied.

But I knew that wasn't true. I pressed him for details, but he wouldn't answer.

Not then, anyway. But don't worry; I eventually beat them out of him.

MORE EVIDENCE

I should remind you that I still had the key chain with my father's entire file on "Meg Cooper" in my possession. With all the tree-hugging shenanigans going on, I hadn't had time to even take a peek at the file. After I got a full night's rest, I finally got back to the job. Well, my off-the-books job. I inserted the storage device into my laptop and downloaded two months' worth of surveillance photos and reports.

Most of the surveillance information that my father had gathered on "Meg" involved photos of her with a particular gentleman. They were compromising, indeed, and sufficient proof of infidelity. Certainly, it was all the evidence that Mr. Slayter would be required to show in divorce proceedings, or enough evidence to blackmail Meg so the photos wouldn't be revealed to her husband. Even more incriminating, perhaps, was that when I cross-checked the dates of Margaret's liaisons, they matched up exactly with her requested surveillance dates on Mr. Slayter.

My hunch was dead-on. Not that I ever doubted myself.

There was, however, an oddity in my dad's report. He never identified subject #2. It would have been procedure to run a license plate check or surveil subject #2 to his residence and perform a reverse address check. But Dad was holding out on the client. And the information wasn't in the file.

My father always taught us that domestic cases require caution because of the volatility of emotions. It's possible that he looked into the matter himself and discovered the true relationship between Meg and Adam. If he did, then he might have been reluctant to provide full disclosure to a client who represented himself under false pretenses. Unfortunately, the report couldn't tell me what my father had discovered or what he was thinking.

All I knew was that Dad was treading carefully.

Aside from documentation of an affair, my father's report covered a wide range of subject's daily activities, which included legitimate treks to the gym, lunch with girlfriends, shopping expeditions, and a visit to a few office buildings in downtown San Francisco, one of which included a law firm.

The latest report had not been delivered to the client for lack of payment. In fact, Adam Cooper had paid the retainer, a partial on his first bill, and nothing since then. And yet my father continued surveilling Meg/Margaret. This got me thinking that he could pretend all he wanted that he was merely an omniscient narrator to the client, but I had his number.

I also had Demetrius's number.

Or I got it the following Monday when I ran into him at Starbucks. A long time ago when D was in prison, I told him the price of coffee these days (or at least the price of a complicated coffee beverage). D swore to me that he would never waste money like that. Well, there he was spending four dollars on a caffeinated brew that took at least six words to order.

"You owe me twenty bucks," I said.

Once again, I forgot that it's unwise to approach D from behind and make demands right in his ear. D turned sharply in my direction and drew his hands into fists. For a second there it appeared that he didn't know who I was.

"Oops. Sorry. I forgot," I said.

D took a deep breath.

"I thought you hated these places," I said.

Wearily, D replied, "What can I say, you got me." Then he started getting all shifty-eyed, like he was casing the joint.

"Everything all right, D? You need me to drive the getaway car?"

"That was funny the first twenty times you said it," D replied. "Why don't you go ahead of me? I'm on a break anyway. Thought I'd read the paper."

"I'm on a break too. Although I was not planning on reading the paper."

"Don't you need to get back to the office?" D said in a way that seemed like he *really* wanted me to get back to the office.

"Why are you trying to get rid of me?"

Just then, a lovely woman approached, patted D on the arm, and said, "Honey, I changed my mind. I will have whipped cream on the mocha."

"Excellent choice," I said.

"Hello," she said, eyeing me suspiciously.

"I'm Isabel," I said.

"Izzy!" she said. "What a pleasure to meet you. I've heard all about you."

D then quickly made introductions. "Izzy, this is Mabel."

"Mabel," I said. "It's so great to meet you. D will not stop talking about you. Seriously, I feel like I could write your bio by now."

D then stepped on my foot. It didn't hurt, but I stopped talking.

"Do you want to join us?" Mabel asked.

"I'd love to," I said.

"But she has a meeting in ten minutes," D said, consulting his watch.

"Ah, forgot about that," I said. "Well, it's been a pleasure. You should come over for dinner sometime."

"Next," the barista said politely.

"Next," D said, not so politely.

"See you soon," I said, waving good-bye (to Mabel).

Mabel returned to their table. I ordered my coffee, followed by D. While we waited for our respective five-adjectives-and-a-nouns to arrive, I slipped next to Demetrius and said, "That must be one hell of a first date."

SMOKE FUMES

When I arrived at work, the house was empty except for Grammy Spellman. I found her at the kitchen table, playing a game of solitaire. Grammy has a special talent for driving people away, for never letting anyone past her harsh, judgmental exterior. If there was someone else beneath the surface, I'd never met her. However, watching her play cards by herself, I couldn't help but feel some regret for not trying a little harder, especially now, in her declining years. Perhaps she was lonely and her misanthropy was merely a mask.

My grandfather was a force of nature—the kind of man who could charm a drug dealer or a debutante; the kind of man who was always on your side even when he wasn't on your side. Grammy had always been eclipsed by his massive personality. In fact, I have no recollection of her before he died.

Later, she would visit once a year—always under a cloud of dread. We'd phone her on her birthday and Christmas, and pass the receiver from one person to the next, each engaging in a stilted yet mercifully brief discussion.

While Grammy was never my biggest fan,[1] she turned against me dur-

---

[1] I would certainly like to know who that is.

ing my mad adolescence. One night I forgot she was visiting and climbed through the guest room window after curfew, waking her out of a deep sleep. My black silhouette, topped off with a ski cap, resembled that of a home intruder. She screamed and threw her travel alarm clock at me. I turned on the light and identified myself, which didn't quiet her as much as you'd expect.

She asked me what I was doing and I explained as succinctly as I could, despite being incredibly stoned, that I had lost my house keys and didn't want to wake anyone. Then she started shouting my dad's name. Sleepy Mom and Dad quickly entered the room, were apprised of the situation, and groggily grounded me for two months, knowing that the result would simply be that I would be climbing in and out of even more windows over the next two months. During breakfast the following morning, Grammy refused to speak to or make eye contact with me despite the fact that I was the primary topic of conversation. She suggested a military academy and when that idea was shot down, she offered to pay for finishing school.

After much debate, I was given an Emily Post etiquette book and forced to write a ten-page report on what I had learned. I don't recall much from Post's seminal work, but the business about writing thank-you notes stuck. In fact, I developed an irksome habit of writing them for wholly inappropriate occasions. My father found them amusing and collected them in a shoe box.

Not too long ago, I came across a six-inch stack wrapped in twine in the garage.

Here's a brief sampling, circa 1995/1996:

Dear David,

  Thank you so much for that zit on your forehead. It's awesome.

Love,

Isabel

Dear Mom,

Thank you for not cooking tonight and ordering pizza.

Love,

Isabel

Dear Dad,

Thanks for shaving your mustache. I hated it. You look almost normal now.

Your daughter,

Isabel

Dear Rae,

Thank you for letting me eat some of your Halloween candy. I admire your generous spirit.[2]

Love,

Isabel

Dear Mr. Benjamin,

I am sorry to hear that you were ill yesterday but very grateful to not have the "surprise" quiz, which we seem to have on every Monday. You might want to look up "surprise" in the dictionary. I wish you a speedy recovery but think it would be best if you took a few more days off. Maybe a week.

Thank you for looking after yourself.

Best,

Isabel[3]

---

[2] I'm fairly certain I stole some candy off of her.

[3] You might wonder why my father had a thank-you card in his possession that was given to a non-Spellman. Mr. Benjamin used it as evidence of my character a few months later when he was trying to get me expelled for cheating on a history test.

Suffice it to say, there were several dozen of those by the end of the summer, and Grammy Spellman was certainly not excluded from the outpouring of gratitude. If I remember correctly, I thanked her profusely for the panty hose in a plastic egg that she gave me for my eighteenth birthday. I told her how I wore the sliced-up nylon as a mask in a liquor store heist and turned her two-dollar investment into three-hundred-and-seventy-two bucks. Of course, Grammy phoned my father in a panic immediately after receiving the missive to which he explained it was all a silly joke. It was indeed a joke. The panty hose were delivered straight into the trash bin, but I did store my stash of weed for years in that plastic eggshell.[4] My point is, on that first night that Grammy came to dinner, when she said, "I never understood this one," I couldn't blame her. I never understood that one. But watching her play cards by herself in a home where she clearly was not welcome, I felt something for Grammy. To be honest, I'm not sure what, because I was spending most of my waking hours trying to not feel anything at all. But there I was, maybe for the first time in my existence, seeing a lonely old woman, not my geriatric nemesis.

"Would you like some hot water with lemon?" I asked Grammy. "I'm making some for myself."[5]

"Thank you, Isabel. That would be lovely."

I started the kettle and waited for Grammy to finish her game.

"Do you want to play gin?" I asked.

I've watched Grammy and Dad play for hours on end, so I knew this activity was in her comfort zone.

"If you like," Grammy said, shuffling the deck like a card shark.

As Grammy dealt, I debated whether to throw the game or not and decided I was in favor of it.

We played in silence until Grammy broke it in her famous style.

---

[4] L'eggs, I know I'm not the only woman who has done this.
[5] Of course I wasn't making some for myself!

"Dear, you're not getting any younger, you know."

"You and me both," I said.

"I met your gentleman on my last visit. You were lucky to have him."

I couldn't argue with her. "Uh-huh."

"Women like you can't be choosy."

"I'll keep that in mind," I said as I choked back a tide of profanity. I could actually feel my body temperature rising.

"In my day you didn't move in with a man until you had a ring on your finger."

"In your day, you also thought you could lose weight by standing still with a vibrating band wrapped around your waist," I replied.

"You could lose a few pounds too."

"But then we'd have nothing to talk about."

"Men don't like women with a sharp tongue."

"Remind me again why are we talking?"

"Just giving you some grandmotherly advice. You don't want to spend the rest of your life alone, do you, dear?"

"Gin," I said.

"Already?" Grammy replied.

"No. I meant I'm going to drink it. As for the game, I forfeit."

"You never did have any follow-through, did you?" Grammy asked.

Oh, I have follow-through all right. But compared to Mom, I'm an amateur. An hour later, I heard the front door unlock and Mom's voice shout, "Heel."

The next thing I knew, a giant mutt with a plethora of sheddable hair preceded my mother into the house. The enormous dog bounded down the hallway, launched up the stairs and then down the stairs, jumped onto the couch, jumped off the couch, raced into the kitchen, and then ran back down the hall, throwing its full weight against my mother, who was approximately the same size. As Mom wrangled the animal with the leash, I approached cautiously. The dog didn't scare me, but my mother did.

"Hey, Mom. What's this?"

"Izzy, meet the newest member of the Spellman family. I think we'll call her FourPete. Get it? Named after your father's bachelor-days dog. Only this Pete is a girl and has four legs. But it's a dog, so who cares?"

"I'm speechless," I replied.

"She's cute, isn't she?" she said, and then she sneezed three times in a row.

"Gesundheit. You have some explaining to do. For years, David and I begged for a dog. Why now?"

"I had enough animals in the house when you were growing up."

"But you are severely allergic," I reminded my mother. Although I doubt she needed any reminding, since she was wheezing and had to take a hit on her inhaler.

"I am," Mom replied. "I'll just get some shots. I hear they work, and I'll try not to pet FourPete."

"Oh, now I get it," I said. My mother's game was suddenly obvious. An ex-con couldn't do the job, but a dirt-tracking, drooling, untrained eighty-pound mutt just might be the thing to snuff out the old bitch. And I'm not talking about the dog.

Grammy walked into the foyer, where my mother performed formal introductions. "Ruth, please meet FourPete, the newest member of the Spellman family."

Grammy's eyes began to water. She looked at FourPete as if she were seeing a ghost. Then she turned to my mother and smiled. "She's the spitting image of my childhood dog, Perdita,"[6] said Grammy. Then she did the oddest thing: She got down on her knees and wrapped her arms around FourPete. "Do you mind if I take her for a walk?"

My mother was too stunned to respond.

---

[6] In Latin it means "Lost one." Grammy found the stray dog by a creek or in an old barn or something. Perdita is also the name of the mother of the puppies in *101 Dalmatians*, but I doubt Grammy ever saw the movie. I don't think Morgan Freeman was in it.

She simply passed the leash to Grammy, who clucked a few times and asked FourPete if she wanted to go for a walk, in the same tone that people use on Sydney.

Once Grammy was out the door, Mom dialed Dad on her cell phone. "Al, didn't you tell me that your mother [*sneeze*] refused to let you get a dog when you were a child? . . . It doesn't matter why I'm asking . . . If you could [*sneeze*] answer the question . . . I see. I see. Thank you. I do have some news. But it can wait." My mother snapped shut her cell phone and entered the kitchen, defeated. I followed Mom and watched her make a cocktail.

"Your father always told this tragic story about [*sneeze*] having a golden retriever puppy as a child and his mother forcing [*sneeze*] them to give it away. I assumed Ruth hated dogs. Turns out, his father had the allergies like me."

"Just say 'allergies,' not 'the allergies,'" I said.

"For weeks your grandpa tried to live with it for the sake of the children, but it was simply too much for him."

"You're usually pretty good at this diabolical stuff. Are you getting soft on me?"

"Nope. I just have to step up my game [*sneeze*]," Mom said.

HOW TO NEGOTIATE
EVERYTHING

My mother wasn't the only person who had to step up her game. While I had two domestic mysteries solved and filed away—Rae's linguistic experiments and Mom's sudden hobby habit (which for the record did not abate), there remained a litany of unanswered questions that needed answering. I made a list to be sure that none slipped through the cracks.

- Why doesn't David want revenge?
- Has D been dating the same woman all along? And is it possible that D and Grammy Spellman have forged a friendship?
- Who made toast in Walter's house and performed the other acts of sabotage?
- What is Meg Cooper planning against Mr. Slayter, and is Adam Cooper in on it?
- Vivien Blake, who are you? And what is your connection to Rae?
- How much longer will Grammy remain in the Spellman household?

Over the next week, I made limited progress on all of the above. I gathered a few shreds of new information, but I only managed to close one "case."

As you might imagine, living under David's roof while he was unemployed (I realize that raising a child is a full-time job; I merely mean that he didn't go into an office for work) afforded me complete access to my brother in unguarded moments. I waited for the perfect time to strike. Sydney had been up all night crying and by morning had still not slept. My brother, showing signs of extreme sleep deprivation—lack of coordination, memory loss (where is the sippy cup? Where'd I put the dishrag?) irritability, etc.—was serving Sydney breakfast when she pulled a diva and demanded "banana," not oatmeal.

Sydney pushed the oatmeal away and David pushed it back and said, firmly, "Today you are having oatmeal." Sydney then tossed the oatmeal across the room.

Fortunately the bowl was plastic, but the off-white mud blasted against the wall and splattered like a faded crime scene. David appeared on the verge of tears. I grabbed several dish towels and sponges and gently pushed my brother out of the way. "I got it," I said. "Go back to bed."

Sydney started screaming "banana."

David approached with paper towels and said, "You can't handle this."

I grabbed David square in the shoulders and looked deep into his sleep-deprived eyes.

"Actually, I can. Go. To. Bed. I got it."

While my brother is in general skeptical of my coping skills, my instructions were too inviting to resist. He merely turned around, walked upstairs, and presumably went straight to bed.

I pulled out a bag of that weird pirate-themed snack and tossed it on Sydney's tray table. She too appeared on the verge of tears.

"You don't scare me," I said.

Then I proceeded to clean up the oatmeal, which actually took almost a half hour. Even my eyes glistened by the end. To ensure that David didn't get it into his head to serve this meal again in the near future, I hid the box in the coat closet.

Four hours later, after Sydney and I had watched eight episodes straight of *SpongeBob*,[1] I put her down for a nap. Conveniently around the time that David woke up from his. He even managed to bathe himself.

"You look like a new man," I said as he came down the stairs.

"I owe you," he said.

"Then pay up."

"What's your price?"

"It's a good deal. I suggest you take it."

"What?"

"I want to know—I need to know. Why have you been so forgiving of the Banana Offensive? While *I* might find it amusing, I certainly can't see why you do."

David poured us both a cup of coffee and then disappeared in the pantry for five minutes looking for something. He used to hide junk food from himself and so I could only conclude he was hunting for a particular item. He returned to the kitchen table with an unopened but battered box of something he called Arnott's Tim Tams, "mint crisp" flavor.

"Where'd these come from?" I asked. Having Rae as a sibling, I've become a kind of expert on sugared delicacies, and this was certainly unfamiliar packaging.

"My friend brought them back from Australia." David cracked the seal and dunked half his cookie in his coffee.

"How long ago?"

"A few years."

"You must have some serious guilt to spill."

"I have a bad feeling in my gut."

"It will only get worse after you eat these. Have you checked the expiration date?"

"Try one and then you'll shut up," he said.

---

[1] I'm not interested in your opinion about children and television. Also, *SpongeBob* can be very educational. At least I've learned a thing or two. Though I'm not sure it's factual. Still, I think it encourages an interest in sea life.

I did and was certainly quiet during the consumption of the exquisite biscuit.[2] "I'd keep these away from Rae, if I were you."

"Not a problem anymore," David replied.

"Speaking of Rae," I said.

"Nice transition."

"Your conscience will feel better if you just come clean."

"What makes you think my conscience is involved?"

"Sugar consumption and refusal to retaliate against the Banana Offensive. Oh, and that throwaway comment you made the other day when Rae was up a tree. Or had just come down from a tree—"

David swallowed a Tim Tam whole and removed himself from the table as I was still speaking.

"Hello?" I said. Then I snagged another cookie.

A few minutes later, David returned to the kitchen with a plastic binder containing professional (i.e., not by David) black-and-white illustrations. It was a mock-up of a children's book. I could describe it for you, but it's better if you see it for yourself.

---

[2] Why oh why don't we have these in every major U.S. supermarket? It's madness. Australia, I love you.

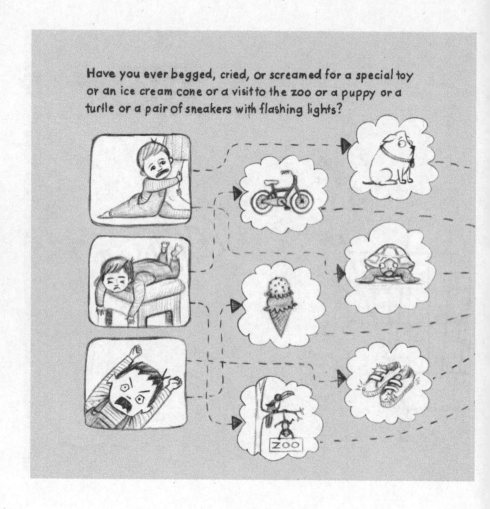

There are very few things in life that you can't get if you ask for them in a rational manner and offer something in return.

That's called "negotiating."
Let's see how Sammy
negotiates with his mother...

That wasn't the end, I'm afraid to admit.[3] Suffice it to say that the book does more than suggest that *everything* can be negotiated.

"You wrote this?" I said to David.

"I'm afraid so," he replied.

"When?"

"Sophomore year in college."

"What kind of crazy class were you taking?"

"I had to take a creative writing class—"

"You got away with turning this in? Damn, your looks have gotten you even further than I thought. The illustrations are good. Who is Jaime [I pronounced it "Hymie"]?"

"Jaime [pronounced "Jamie"]," David replied. "My girlfriend for a few weeks."

"The exact amount of time it might take to illustrate a book?" I asked.

"It was a side project. I was reading about publishing and it seemed like all the money was in children's books and this was a niche that hadn't been filled."

"What niche?" I asked. "Business books for toddlers?"

"*Why not teach them how to remain calm under pressure,* was what I was thinking at the time," David said, clearly not thinking that anymore.

"You weren't teaching them how to *use their words,* you were providing a play-by-play for deep manipulation."

"I know that now."

"I take it you read this book to Rae."

"That's an understatement."

"Excuse me?"

"No. She was my . . . I don't know what the word for it is . . ."

And then it all became clear to me.

"Rae was your guinea pig," I said.

---

[3] If you'd like to read more, *How to Negotiate Everything* will be available from S&S Children, Winter 2013.

"Yes," David replied.

"Wow."

"You see my problem."

"What she did was worse," I said. "You know that, right?"

"But I made her what she is," said David.

"Dr. Frankenstein, I think you're giving yourself a little too much credit."

OLD HABITS

I needed a drink after my morning with Sydney and my afternoon with David and my life with myself. I figured Bernie still owed me something and I could drink for cheap at the Philosopher's Club.

I found Gerty serving booze behind the bar.

"I missed that pretty face," she said.

"He's put you to work already?" I asked.

"I always wanted to be a bartender."

"Really?" I skeptically replied, even though I had my turn as a bartender and I can't deny that it had its perks.

"People tell me their troubles," she said. "So spill it, sweetie, because you've got trouble written all over your face."

I asked for a drink first. Then for another. I told her about my creepy siblings and their reciprocal experiments. I told her about my mother trying to smoke Grammy out of the house and Grammy telling me that I'd spend my life alone. I told her about the Chinese wall, even mentioning that I blackmailed our computer geek to breach it. Then I told her about Walter and his mysterious intruder and how even he found someone who could live with his grand flaws, and yet he couldn't live with hers. I mentioned the way he raked his carpet after I'd made footprints. And then I told her about Vivien and her awful parents who insisted on surveilling their own daughter. Although I also had to admit that her behavior was highly suspicious. Then I told her about Adam, Edward, and Meg and all the rejected lovers left in their wake. I contemplated whether happy unions were possible anymore. Or ever had been. Gerty wisely mentioned my parents, but I batted that idea aside. There are always exceptions to the rule.

Then Bernie showed his face. He kissed Gerty on the lips right in front of me.

I felt a little queasy.

"Do you have to do that?" I asked.

"My bar," Bernie replied.

"It used to be my bar."

"I'm willing to share," Bernie said.

I swallowed the rest of my drink and asked to use the phone. I dialed the number by memory.

"I'm drunk," I said. "I need a ride." Then I hung up the phone.

Twenty minutes later, Henry showed up. I noticed that the hand Bernie seemed to have permanently attached to Gerty's waist magically detached in Henry's presence. I wished he could show me the same courtesy. Bernie's manners also shifted in front of Henry. He suddenly stood up straighter, enunciated better, and kept an appropriate distance from Henry's mom. The two men shook hands and said their hellos. Henry kissed his mother, asked her how she was doing, and she suggested they have lunch the next day.

"What are you doing here?" I said to Henry.

"I heard you needed a ride."

"I called my brother."

"He called me."

"He shouldn't have done that."

"Let's go."

"I don't feel like going now," I said. "Bartender, I'll have another."

Bernie turned to Henry for guidance.

"Don't look at him. I'm the paying customer."

Then some silent exchange must have taken place because Bernie pointed to the sign that says that he has the right to refuse service.

"Do you really want to mess with me again?" I asked.

"You've been drinking free all night," Bernie said. "One of these days we're gonna be even. Now take the ride and get outta here."

Henry picked up my coat (which conveniently contained my wallet and keys) off the bar stool and headed out the door.

"I'll be back," I said, as a threat.

"Looking forward to it," Bernie happily replied.

"How've you been?" Henry asked as we shot down Portola Drive.

"Great. You know, enjoying my freedom."

"Is that how you're going to play it?" Henry asked.

"You don't actually want me to be honest, do you?" I said.

"Um, yeah. I do."

"Well, I must admit, the dishes don't wash themselves. I hope you're enjoying your clean kitchen."

"It's not all it's cracked up to be."

"So now you admit it."

"We didn't break up over dishes."

"Speak for yourself."

"We can still be—"

"Don't say it."

He didn't. In fact, nothing else was said until Henry pulled his car in front of David's house.

"Would you like some tea?" I asked. I don't usually ask questions like that.

"You have some on you?" Henry asked.

"No. I meant do you want to come in for some tea? Or another beverage? I relocated[1] some of David's booze to my apartment. They shouldn't keep it around a toddler anyway."

"You're inviting me inside?"

"I suppose I could grab the bottle and come back out to the car. Unless you want tea. Then that might take a while."

"What will happen in there?"

"I'm not exactly sure. I suppose you'll drink something, then feel the urge to straighten things up; I'll ask you to stop. Maybe you will, maybe you won't. I have no idea. I can't see into the future. Actually, that's kind of a lie. I can see into the immediate future. In two seconds, I'm going to get out of the car."

In two seconds (I counted), I said, "Thanks for the ride," and got out of the vehicle.

I circled David's house and entered the in-law unit alone. I didn't look back. I closed the door behind me, found that fancy booze that I had taken from Sydney, and poured myself a drink.

Five minutes later, there was a knock at the door. Some things can be predicted—a beverage was served, a few clothes were hung on hangers, a comment was made about the sink full of dishes, and another comment was made about switching in energy-saving lightbulbs for the forty-watts that remained. I told Henry to take it up with David.

What I suppose could not have been predicted was that my shirt was off as soon as we drained the above-mentioned beverages and topics. Then we were on the bed. And shoes and socks and other things were being tossed around the room. Oddly, Henry loses his ordered personality when disrobing in intimate situations. Of course, in the morning he then straightens everything up. But I'm getting ahead of myself.

"We shouldn't be doing this," he said as he was unbuttoning my pants.

"Agreed," I replied as I unbuttoned his shirt.

---

[1] Not stealing!

As he tangled with my bra clasp, he said, "I hate this thing. You need to be a rocket scientist to figure it out."

He fumbled with it while I waited patiently.

"Would you like my help or shall I call in a rocket scientist?"

"I got it," Henry said. He didn't.

"Just let me do it," I said, smacking his hands away.

It's one of those front-clasping things that require a twisting motion.

"No," Henry stubbornly replied.

"I bet there's a Learning Annex class you can take."

Henry kissed me. I'm sure he wanted to kiss me, but he probably also wanted me to shut up. He wrestled with the bra clasp for another minute or so until he had tried so many different variables that one worked. It was certainly one of the most inept unclaspings since some backseat wrestling match in high school.

At some point, both of us stopped saying that it was a bad idea. My whole life I've done things that were bad ideas. Climbing into bed with Ex-boyfriend #13 wasn't very high on the list of bad ideas that came to fruition. It seemed perfectly normal to crawl into bed with someone I had been crawling into bed with for two years.

Later, we fell asleep, as if nothing had changed, other than the location.

It was only when the light cracked through the curtain that we bothered with reality. Henry wrapped his arms around me and kissed my neck. "We probably shouldn't do this again," he said.

"Probably not," I replied. While I'm not one for rule-following or discipline or anything in those schools of behavior, this one directive we managed to keep. Nothing had changed that night. The truth was, in thirty years, I didn't know if I would be waking up next to anyone. I only knew that it wouldn't be Henry.

Before he left, we agreed to be friends. But then we decided that we should be the kind of friends who didn't see each other for a while. Then I started to worry about losing my police contact and Henry said that I could e-mail him if I needed information. I suggested I e-mail under an assumed name, to maintain some distance, but he didn't think that was necessary.

He made one final request, which I reluctantly agreed to.

"In the future, if you ever speak of me, please use my name, not my number."

"Deal," I replied.

I walked him to the door, where he kissed me good-bye. And that was the end. I closed the door, waited until I heard his footsteps quiet down the driveway. Then I cried.

But that was the last time I cried over him.

GENETICS 101

The Spellman compound was empty when I arrived the next morning. I found a manila folder on my desk. Inside it were several photocopies from a high school science textbook on the subject of genetics. Highlighted were explanations of dominant and recessive genes relating to eye color, hair color, cleft chins, and detached earlobes. Also included were family photos of Vivien Blake and her parents. Because the documents were photocopied into a large print with condescending notes in the margins, defining words like *dominant* and *recessive*—and because those margin notes were written in a familiar scrawl—I gathered that the material had come from my sister. However, she'd left no other message behind. It was simply a layman's genetic report on the Blakes for my review.

Vivien Blake had dark brown hair and brown eyes. Her mother was blond and blue eyed; her father had brown hair and blue eyes. It's rare for two blue-eyed people to have a brown-eyed child, but not impossible. Even Rae's literature suggested that. However, in the photo of Vivien, her cleft chin was circled and yet neither parent possessed that trait. This, according to Rae's textbook and my further research, would mean that she was at the very least not the biological child of both parents. Then I looked more closely at Vivien and it suddenly seemed startlingly obvious that she was

286

adopted. This had not come up in conversation with the parents as far as I knew, but I wasn't sure what it should mean, if anything, to the investigation.

I phoned my sister to gather the motive behind this latest development.

"Are you alone?" she asked.

"Yes," I replied.

"Did you get my material?"

"I did."

"Did you understand it?"

"You keep this shit up, Rae, and you'll lose more than your car."

"I knew you were behind that all along."

"Listen, I'm not enjoying this conversation and neither are you. Why don't you tell me why you sent me this information?"

"I thought you should know," Rae said.

"That she's adopted?"

"Yes."

"Does she know?"

"She got hair samples and ran the test a few years ago, although she'd been suspicious long before that, after taking a junior-high science class."

"You could have just told me about the DNA test," I said.

"Too easy."

"What do you want me to do with this information?"

"I want you to keep it in mind as you continue to investigate Vivien and feed information to her parents."

"Thank you. But let me give you a quick reminder. I never wanted to take this case. You did."

"I had my reasons," Rae said, ending the call.

When my mother arrived, I stuffed the folder in my desk and shuffled papers as I tried to clear the debris that had settled in my head.

"Guess who I just ran into at [none of your business]?"[1] my mother asked.

I wasn't in a guessing mood. "That little French guy who climbs sky-scrapers?"

"I'll just tell you since you're clearly in a foul mood. Demetrius."

"He likes that place. Why is it news?"

"He was with a lady friend and he didn't come home last night."

"Really? Did you say hello or did you just peek at them through the window?"

"Of course I said hello. She was lovely. Said that she'd heard all about me. It couldn't possibly be their first date."

"What was her name?"

"Mabel. I definitely think D has gotten over his first-date curse."

"Yeah, me too," I replied.

Twenty minutes later, D entered the office.

"Nice breakfast?" my mom asked.

"Yes," D quickly replied, and then switched subjects as soon as hu-manly possible.

"Should I get started on the Pierson report or the Zylor background check?"

"Actually you could tell me a little bit more about your lady friend," my mom said.

"Maybe D would like to keep his personal life personal," I said.

While my mother did not take kindly to my interrupting her interroga-tion, she was often more sensitive to D's privacy than to pretty much any-one else's on the planet. Mom glared at me, but her expression softened when she turned back to D. "Of course. Sorry, D. It was lovely meeting her, though, and any time you'd like to invite her over—"

"Thank you, Olivia."

"I guess the Pierson case takes priority," Mom said, catching the hint.

---

[1] It's a French bakery/café that already has an unruly line at all hours of the day. Sorry, I'm not going to tell you what it is and make the line longer.

* * *

We worked in silence for the next hour or so. I watched my mother out of the corner of my eye. I was itching for her to take a break. While I may have championed D's privacy, that was all for show. This Mabel situation had more going on than met the eye. Finally, Mom left to pick Grammy Spellman up from a dog obedience class at Crissy Field. Grammy's idea. Which was great because FourPete had been running amok since her arrival, but bad news for Mom because her allergies were on overdrive. Now she was stuck not only with Grammy but also with a dog. I could tell that the situation would eventually unhinge her.

"I'll be back in a bit," Mom said, taking a hit off her inhaler.

Once Mom was out the door, I shoved my paperwork aside, cradled my head in my hands, and stared at D until he noticed.

"Something on your mind, Isabel?"

"Now that you mention it, I'm starting to think that you and Mabel are maybe not so recent. Like all those first dates you went on with nurses and librarians and social workers—I don't think they happened."

"Is that so?" D said, giving away nothing. Although he refused to make eye contact, so he was giving away something, I just didn't know what.

"I think you've been dating Mabel for a while. I'm guessing two months. Am I in the ballpark?"

"Maybe," D replied.

"Three?" I asked.

D refused to reply.

"Why keep it a secret?"

"In this house? Are you really asking me that question?" D said with an unusual accusatory tone.

It's true we don't respect one another's privacy, but we've all made an effort with D.

"Fair enough," I replied. "I'm just glad you met someone."

"Thank you," D replied.

In the interest of respecting D's privacy, I didn't ask any more questions. But after a few minutes had passed and I'd contemplated the various elements involved in D's recent behavior, I deduced what should have been obvious from the start. "Oh, I get it!" I almost shouted.

"What do you get?" D patiently replied.

"You're ashamed of us. That's why we haven't met her!"

D straightened papers on his desk that were already straight. I had it on the nose.

"Don't worry," I said. "I won't tell. I'm ashamed of us too."

I got a 911 from Walter a few minutes later. He was convinced that he'd left the toaster plugged in. It was a Wednesday, and since Walter only made toast on Sunday, that seemed unlikely. But at least this was an old-school Walter emergency. On the way over, I dropped by a hardware store and picked up a new deadbolt. It was time to take further precautions whether Walter liked it or not.

I arrived at an empty apartment and slipped off my shoes. I padded into the kitchen to find the toaster unplugged as predicted but the blender plugged into the outlet. This was a first. I investigated the rest of Walter's place and saw nothing amiss. I raked the carpet in my footprint wake and continued into the living room, where I sat down on the couch, with one final rake.

I sent Walter a text message: We need to talk.

Walter doesn't text; he phoned.

"Everything all right?"

"Do you like to blend things?" I asked Walter.

"I'm not sure I understand what you're implying. Is everything all right?"

"Your apartment is just fine."

"And the toaster?"

"Unplugged. But the blender was plugged in."

"That's odd," Walter said, sounding concerned, but not that concerned.

"Why do you have a blender?"

"Excuse me?"

"They're messy and hard to clean."

"I agree completely."

"Maybe you should get rid of it."

"Maybe I should."

"I mean, you or some unknown entity can't plug in an appliance if you don't have that appliance. Correct?"

"I can't find fault in your logic."

"When will you be home, Walter?"

"In approximately twenty-five minutes."

"Great. In the meantime, I'm going to change the locks on your door. I think it's time we put a few more security measures in place. Do I have your permission?" I didn't wait for Walter to reply. "Great," I said, and ended the call.

Walter phoned me back, but I didn't pick up. I took an old towel from my car and placed it on the rug while I changed the deadbolt. Walter returned home just as I was testing the new keys.

"Thank you. We probably should have done this ages ago," Walter said with a decided lack of enthusiasm.

"Probably," I replied.

"You okay, Isabel?" Walter asked. He asked it in a way that implied he knew I was not okay.

"Why are you asking?"

"Your shirt is wrinkled. It's normally not so wrinkled."

"I suppose you're right," I said. Henry used to iron my shirts.

"You look sad. Are you sad, Isabel?"

"I suppose I am."

"Do you want to talk about it?"

"Here's your key. Don't give a copy to anyone."

"What if I get locked out?"

"I can't imagine you losing a key, Walter. But if you do, you can call me. I have the spare."

"Thank you, Isabel. I don't know what I'd do without you."

"Lose the blender."

I returned to 1799 Clay Street during the *Gossamer Heights* hour. D, Grammy, and FourPete all sat on the couch watching the television together. During commercials, Grammy and D would consult each other about prospective story lines.

"I wish Nicole and Joey would get back together."

"They were a good couple," D agreed. "But I think Nicole has her eye on Jameson."

"I don't trust that one," Grammy said.

"He's up to something," D replied.

My mother watched the scene from the hallway, sniffling (allergies, not tears), her enemy and her confidant sharing a common interest. My father approached, wrapped his arm around Mom, and kissed the top of her head. I had to admit, something about this scenario was disturbing. Sure, they had *Gossamer Heights* and Morgan Freeman in common, but it couldn't be possible that You Know Who and Demetrius were becoming friends.

"How did this happen?" Mom asked, taking another drag on her inhaler.

"Even the best-laid plans of mice and men go oft awry," Dad said.

DRIVING MRS. SPELLMAN

My mother called me first thing in the morning on a blackout day. Mom and I have an official understanding that we do not speak on Saturdays, unless there's an emergency.

"This better be an emergency," I said when I answered the phone.

Sneeze.

"Allergies don't count."

Sneeze.

"Did you forget what day it was?"

"They're making plans," Mom whispered.

"Who?" I whispered back.

"Ruth [*sneeze*] and D. They're spending the day together."

"That is unusual, and I can understand how it would be distressing. But it's not grounds for breaking the blackout-day rule," I firmly replied.

"I think they're going to a movie," Mom said.

"Wouldn't be the first time," I replied. "Though it does beg the question: Is Morgan Freeman getting enough rest?"

"Two weeks ago," Mom said, "I asked D to go with me to a matinee and he said he had too much work to do."

"Was there work to do?"

"Yes, but that's not the point."

293

"Mom, is this conversation going anywhere? Because I have a long day of doing nothing ahead of me."

"Something about this isn't right."

"I agree."

"You need to follow them," Mom said.

"Why don't you do it?" I said.

"Because Saturday is the one day a week I can get your father to do any physical activity. We have yoga in twenty minutes, and I think we'll go for a hike in the Marin Headlands a little later."

"Are you trying to kill him?"

"Isabel, do this for me."

"I'm going to need some incentive."

"Overtime and I'll give you two blackout days to use at your discretion."

"How about four?"

"Three."

"Deal."

"If my intelligence is correct," Mom said, "they leave in an hour."

We disconnected the call and I turned off the TV and quickly dressed. D knows what my car looks like, and while he wouldn't be expecting a tail, a beat-up Buick stickered on your rearview mirror might not go unnoticed. I considered the available options and David's Prius was the best bet.

I knocked. Maggie answered and let me in. David and Sydney were seated on the living room floor, listening to some classical music station and finger-painting. I should note that David was working on his own art piece and not simply assisting Sydney with hers.

"Are you out of coffee again?" Maggie pleasantly asked. "I just started a fresh pot."

"No, thanks," I said. "I'm good."

Maggie invited me inside, nodded in the direction of David and Sydney, and said, "Arts hour. Although it usually lasts at least two."

"Remember to use your complete color palette, Sydney. Not just blue," David said.

Sydney then planted another blue thumbprint on the construction paper.

"David, can I borrow your car?"

"Something wrong with yours?"

"No. I need to surveil D and he knows what my car looks like. I'll bring it back with a full tank."

"Why are you following D?" Maggie asked. David was clearly uninterested.

"Mom wants to know why he's spending so much time with Grammy. It's driving her crazy. Hello, Sydney," I said.

Sydney took one look at me, her eyes welled up with tears, and she said, "No Izzy. No no Izzy. No Izzy."[1]

"She thinks you're babysitting again," Maggie said apologetically.

I backed toward the door and stepped out into the foyer. "Relax," I shouted. "I'm leaving. See?" I said, leaving.

Maggie passed me the car keys. "Sorry," she said.

"No problem. Thanks, David. *Good-bye,* Sydney." I emphasized the last part to hammer home the point.

I opened the garage door, unlocked the Prius, phoned my mother for a status report, and backed out of the driveway onto the street. As I put the car into drive, Maggie raced out of the house with one arm in her coat and approached the passenger-side door. I rolled down the window.

"Take me with you," she said desperately. She jumped into the car and we were off.

An hour later, Maggie and I had followed Grammy, with D chauffeuring, on what can only be described as a carefully edited tour of the city. He covered the more family-friendly tourist destinations—Fisherman's Wharf, the Marina, Twin Peaks. Then he traversed the hills: Nob, Russian, and

---

[1] It doesn't matter who says it, it always stings.

Noe (somehow bypassing the Mission). He skipped Chinatown, Japantown, midtown, and even downtown. Eventually he took a leisurely route through Golden Gate Park and ended up at a restaurant overlooking Ocean Beach. While the odd couple took a lunch break, Maggie and I waited in the parking lot, taking in the view.

"Hungry?" she asked, pulling an oatmeal cookie wrapped in a napkin out of her pocket. For years David had been trying to break her of this habit but had apparently failed. She split the cookie in half and generously offered me the larger piece. I took the other one. Once we finished our snack, I decided it was time to get to the bottom of her jailbreak.

"Don't families like to spend their weekends together?"

"I suppose that would be normal," she replied, clearly nonplussed by the turn in the conversation.

"You want to talk about it?"

"You want to talk about your troubles?" Maggie replied.

"No, thank you. But your troubles are for more interesting. And, since I think they involve my brother, I might actually be able to provide some insight."

Maggie leaned her head against the window and closed her eyes. "He's just so, so obsessive with her," she said. "I don't understand why."

"You don't?" I asked. I figured it would be obvious.

"No. I don't."

"He's convinced she'll turn out like me or Rae, if he doesn't take action. So he's taking action."

Maggie opened her eyes and drew her hand to her forehead. "Oh my God. I never even thought of that."

"Maybe you could cut him slack," I said.

Before Maggie could reply, I had the car in reverse, peeled out of the parking space, and raced to the end of the driveway, making a sharp right onto the Great Highway. I hit the gas, trying to make the green light on Fulton Street, but slammed on the breaks when the light turned red. Maggie lurched forward.

"What just happened?"

"We were made. D and Grammy just gave us the slip."

I phoned my mother. She was in between activities and picked up her phone.

"What are they doing?"

"They *were* having lunch."

"Lunch?" Mom jealously repeated.

"Does D have a GPS on his car?"

"No, it's not a company vehicle. Where are they now?"

"I'm sorry, Mom. We lost him."

THE BLAKE FAKE

The Blakes' requests for surveillance on their daughter had waned after I turned in the last doctored report. Without being clear on the nature of Vivien's extracurricular activities, I didn't feel confident relaying their suspicious nature to her suspicious parents. Let's just say it was dull reading even for a layman. However, I received an e-mail from Mrs. Blake shortly after my derailed surveillance on Grammy and D. She insisted on a surveillance that evening, claiming to have received an unusual e-mail from her daughter. When pressed for details, Mrs. Blake didn't respond, she merely repeated her surveillance request and, for the first time, asked for visual documentation, specifically video.

While it was unusual for me to hear directly from Mrs. Blake, I thought nothing of it at the time.

At nine P.M., I commenced surveillance on subject Vivien Blake.

At nine fifteen the coed left her apartment on Dolores Street and walked to a bar on Folsom. She sat down at the bar; spoke briefly with a white male, approximately twenty-five; passed him what appeared to be a roll of bills; and the male slipped something into the palm of her hand, which she quickly pocketed. She then left the bar and walked to an apartment building three blocks away. She pressed the buzzer and waited until the gate was released. I circled the building and found a light on in the first-floor apartment where subject had entered.

Inside were approximately four greasy-haired coeds, smoking cigarettes and weed. I had a clear visual of the unusually well-lit apartment from the back of the building. Using a small digital camera I captured the image inside the unit. Vivien pulled a baggie out of her pocket, presumably the item procured at the bar. She knelt down beside the coffee table, where a small mirror and razor blade were splayed next to overflowing ashtrays and pipes. Vivien tipped some of the contents of the baggie onto the small mirror and edged it into a line with the razor blade. She then took a straw and snorted it, licked her finger, and swept up the rest of the powder, rubbing it into her gums. She offered the pixie dust to a few of the hipsters in the room, but they all waved it away.

Did they really expect me to buy this charade? From experience I can say with certainty that, had it really been cocaine, there would have been a few takers. But snorting powdered sugar isn't the most pleasant sensation.[1]

I pressed three on my speed dial.

"I appreciate the homage," I said to my sister.

If the reference is lost on you, let me briefly explain: Not too many years ago, when I found myself under close parental scrutiny, I retaliated with a little performance piece I called "Isabel Snorts Cocaine,"[2] which I managed to convince my sister to both watch and film. I figured if my parents wanted to catch me in some kind of criminal act, I might as well go all-out. However, Rae (at the time fourteen) intervened and held an unloaded gun pointed at my actor friends Len and Christopher, who were playing the stereotypical dealers. While I let Rae in on the ruse, I still forced her to show the footage to my parents. And now it became clear to me that all of Vivien's unusual activities were pure theater. This was just another

---

[1] And, yes, I am familiar with this activity. The powdered sugar part.
[2] See Document #1.

show for her parents' benefit. Vivien, aided by Rae, wanted revenge and was using me as a pawn in my own game.

"You don't expect me to show this video to her parents, do you?" I asked.

"Of all people, I thought you'd understand," Rae said.

"I take it that it wasn't Mrs. Blake who requested the surveillance this evening?"

"No. Viv hacked into her mother's account."

"I see. Call Vivien," I said. "Tell her to meet me out front."

Five minutes later, Vivien surfaced from the apartment. She grinned sheepishly.

"What tipped you off?" she asked.

"All sorts of things," I replied. "But mostly it was just too easy. The lighting was perfect."

"I wanted to use a crack pipe," Vivien said, "but I wasn't sure what baking ingredient was safe to inhale."

"I'm glad you played it safe," I replied.

"So you have the footage?" she asked.

"I have it."

"What are you going to do with it?"

Fifteen minutes later, Vivien and I were in a café on Mission Street. She was spooning the whipped cream off the top of a double mocha I had just bought her and she suddenly seemed years younger than the woman I had been tailing for the last few months.

"Nice performance the other night, by the way. Taking the BMW to a chop shop. That was impressive. I had you pegged for a degenerate."

"Thank you," Vivien replied.

"What do you want, Vivien?"

"I want different parents."

"Too late. What do you really want?"

"Payback, I guess."

"And what good will that do you?"

"I don't know. It'll even the score."

"I'm not showing them the video; I'm not giving them a report of activities that were just for show. I'm telling them that they have a normal, law-abiding daughter whom they should cease investigating. They'll leave you alone if I tell them to. No more phony degeneracy, okay?"

"Just the real deal from now on," Vivien said.

"You're free now, Vivien; try to stay that way. Are you going to behave yourself?" I couldn't believe these words were coming out of my mouth. I felt so old.

"On one condition," Vivien said.

"What?"

"I want you to find my real parents," Vivien said.

TAXI DRIVER

Outside Edward Slayter's office, Charlie Black found me again. He was wearing the same new sweater, but it wasn't as new anymore. "Hi, Isabel."

"Hi, Charlie."

"Mind if I sit down?"

"Of course not."

"Can I interest you in a game of chess?"

"I think my chess days are over."

"That makes me sad."

"It makes me sad too, in a way."

"Are you watching your friend again? The one that you don't wave at or speak to?"

"Yes."

"You worry about him, don't you?"

"I do."

"I saw him the other day."

"That's his office," I said, pointing to the building. "And this is your office," I said, pointing to the cement steps where we were loitering. "You were bound to cross paths at some point."

"We crossed paths," Charlie said. "He even waved at me."

"Did you speak to him?"

"Don't worry. Not about you."

"What did you talk about?"

"He walked over to me and asked for directions."

"Directions to where?"

"That was the strange part. He wanted to know where Montgomery Street was."

"But it's right over there."

Montgomery Street is a major road that runs perpendicular to Market, just a few short blocks from Slayter's office. Any resident of San Francisco should know Montgomery Street, let alone someone who works downtown.

"That's what I said," said Charlie. " 'It's right over there.' Then he thanked me and said he was confused."

"Did he ask you any other questions?"

"No. He said he might see me again at the Mechanics' Institute."

"Is that all?" I asked.

"Did he do something wrong, Isabel?"

"I don't think so."

"Then why are you watching him?"

I never answered Charlie's question.

Mr. Slayter exited his office building and walked up to Market Street, where his driver waited for him.

"Excuse me, Charlie."

"See you later, Isabel."

I hailed a cab and pointed out Slayter's black Town Car.

"Follow that car," I said to the cab driver.

"Why?" the cab driver replied.

"I don't think that's any of your concern," I replied.

The cab driver pulled into traffic and proceeded to casually tail the sedan; his interrogation continued. "It's my cab. I can ask questions if I want to."

"And I can refuse to answer them if I want to."

"Who are we following?"

"You're following that black Town Car up there. That's all you need to know."

"Is your husband in that car?"

"No."

"Boyfriend?"

The cab was now going well below the speed limit.

"You need to drive faster."

"Boyfriend?"

"No. If you miss this light, we lose him."

"Answer the question."

"Yes. He's my boyfriend."

The cab driver floored the gas and raced through the yellow light, weaving through traffic, shortening the distance lost during his slowdown threat.

"Do you think he's cheating on you?" the cab driver asked.

I checked the license on the dashboard.

"I don't know, Phil Vitus. They should name a disease after you."

Phil took his foot off the gas and repeated his question.

"Maybe," I said, and we accelerated again. "He's called the same number on his cell phone three days in a row."

"You shouldn't be snooping," Phil said.

"I wasn't," I replied. "I needed a number and I looked on his phone."

"Did you dial the number?"

"No," I replied.

Phil Vitus clearly thought I was holding out on him, because he slowed down again.

"What kind of crazy game are you playing?" I asked.

"Tell me the truth. Did you dial the number?"

"Yes," I replied.

"What happened?" Phil asked.

I could feel the car slowing again, so I spoke quickly. As long as I talked and answered questions, my taxi driver had a lead foot. "I dialed the number from his phone. A woman answered and said, 'Hey, baby.' Then I hung up. She dialed back, but I let the call go to Jack's voice mail."

"Jack's your boyfriend?"

"Yes."

"How long have you and Jack been together?"

"Two years."

"How did you meet?"

"He picked me up in a bar."

"What was his line?"

"Excuse me?"

"What was his pickup line?"

"'What's a nice girl like you doing in a place like this?'"

"You're lying."

"How do you know?" I found it intriguing that he singled out one particular lie in a library of them.

"You don't look like such a nice girl."

"I'm not."

"So, what did he say?"

"'Can I buy you a drink?'"

"You're that easy?"

"Yep."

"Did you sleep with him on the first date?"

"You're crossing a line here, buddy. I got your license number. Do you want me to report you?"

"Let's skip ahead two years."

The Town Car headed west on Fell Street and moved into the center lane.

"I think he's going into the park," I said. "Hang back."

The taxi driver let a few more vehicles cut in the lane and then the queries continued.

"Cut to two years later and you find a suspicious number on his cell. Do you know who this woman is?"

"I'm almost positive she's his dental hygienist."

"What does she look like?"

"Blond, big boobs. The standard package. I think he's going to the museum," I said. "Follow them into the turnaround."

The Town Car pulled to a stop in front of the de Young.

"Is Jack an art lover?"

"Why not?" I replied.

Mr. Slayter, all fifty-eight years of his well-groomed, moneyed self, stepped out of his Town Car. My taxi driver took one brief glance at him and then one good, long look at the thirty-four-year-old woman in a wrinkled shirt, blue jeans, and a sweater that had an obvious hole in the front. I won't even mention how my hair looked that day. "That's not your boyfriend," Phil Vitus said, finally realizing that he had lost the game.

"What tipped you off?" I asked.

"Men like that don't date women like you."

The meter read $11.80. I gave him twelve.

"Keep the change," I said as I got out of the taxi.

THE PORTRAIT
OF DORA MAAR

Museums are expensive. You probably know that already. I toyed with the idea of waiting until Edward Slayter had soaked up all the culture he could get and needed a coffee in the café or something. But I was ready to talk to him and thought that a museum approach was more practical than accosting him in the park.

Even in the middle of a workday, the de Young was swarming with sweaty tourists. A Picasso exhibit on loan from France was drawing in record crowds. Slayter, I assumed, was there for the same reason. Mr. Slayter, in many ways, was a perfect surveillance subject. He was over six feet, with a full head of salt-and-pepper hair—easy to spot in a crowd. He was also the only suit in a sea of cotton-wear and baseball caps.

He stood in front of a painting of a woman. I clocked him. Five minutes, staring at one piece. A woman with two eyes and two noses. I stood watch behind him as he stared intently. Then I approached the placard on the wall and read that it was a portrait of Picasso's lover. I'm no art expert, but it looked to me like he couldn't figure her out. I wondered if Edward felt that way about his wife. Was she an enigma or a threat or neither? I wondered if he still loved her. Did she stray because she was being neglected, or did she never have any intention of being faithful? Did she marry Slayter just for his money, or was it merely a perk?

I had followed the man for months but couldn't tell you what kind of man he was. Until I knew that, I could only plan one step at a time. I found some open space next to Mr. Slayter and held my gaze on the Picasso painting. Once I was sure he noticed my presence, I spoke.

"I don't get it," I said.

"What don't you get?"

"All of it, to be honest," I whispered.

"Then what are you doing here?" Slayter whispered back.

"My boyfriend thinks I need more culture."[1]

"How does it make you feel?"

"I think he should keep some opinions to himself."

"I meant how does the painting make you feel?"

"I'm not very in touch with my emotions. How do you feel?"

"Unnerved."

"Do you think that's what Picasso was going for?"

"I wasn't talking about the painting. I meant you."

"I wasn't going for that either."

"Why are you here?" he asked.

"For the art."

"No, really, why are you here?"

"I think we need to talk."

Slayter wouldn't talk until after he had his fill of the exhibit, so I remained in his company and got a bit of an education. After we'd traveled through the entire exhibit, Slayter looked at the program and insisted on circling back to the portrait of Dora Maar. "This is what I came here to see," he said.

"I know," I replied. "And you already saw it."

"In France, twenty years ago."

[1] In truth, I got plenty of culture in the two years I dated Henry Stone and have been to my share of art museums. I like Picasso just fine, for the record. But that's kind of like saying you like Morgan Freeman.

"And here, an hour ago," I said.

Slayter returned his gaze to the painting and took a deep breath. "I think I need a cup of coffee," he said.

I bought Mr. Slayter a coffee from the café and at his insistence, we took it to the botanical gardens. It felt odd meeting with the subject of the investigation where I first met the client. Although the two days couldn't have been more distinct. I met Margaret under the glare of an unusually bright sun. The day with Slayter was so thick with fog that you could see a dusting of mist covering all the leaves.

"Are you warm enough?" Mr. Slayter asked. "I could give you my coat."

"I'm fine," I replied.

"Do we know each other?"

"That's an odd question," I replied.

"It is, isn't it? But I don't know if we do or not."

"You have Alzheimer's," I said.

"I do."

"How long have you known?"

"I was diagnosed just over a month or so ago, if memory serves me, and, well, it doesn't."

"Have you told your wife?"

"No. *That* I am sure of. How do you know I have a wife?"

"You're wearing a ring."

"Ah, yes."

"But that's not how I know."

"I think I would remember you if we had met," Slayter said.

"I'm a private investigator."

"I would certainly remember that."

"Your wife hired me to follow you."

Slayter turned to me and smiled. "You've been following me?"

"Yes," I replied.

"For how long?"

"Two months."

"I hadn't noticed."

"I'm good."

"Or I'm not terribly observant."

"I prefer the way I'm looking at it," I said.

"Tell me, why did my wife hire you? Does she suspect me of adultery?"

"I'm not sure she suspects you of anything."

"I take it you never caught me in an illicit act?"

"I think you know the answer to that," I replied.

"These days, I'm not so sure."

"My job was to keep tabs on you. Nothing else."

"Why?"

"Do you have a prenup?"

"Of course," Mr. Slayter replied.

"Is there an infidelity clause?"

"Yes."

"I believe your wife is having an affair and hired me to surveil you on days she was with her lover so that she wouldn't be caught in a lie. She never wanted to know anything more than your current location and when you would be heading home."

"I see. Do you have evidence of her affair?"

"Here's where the story gets a little more complicated."

"And I was thinking it was complicated enough," Edward replied.

"Does your wife have a brother?"

"You mean Adam?"

"Yes, Adam."

"What about him?"

"There's no good way to tell you this, but Adam Cooper is Margaret's ex-husband, not her brother."

Like a true businessman, Mr. Slayter contained his emotions. I saw only a flicker of surprise and maybe sadness cross his face. "This coffee isn't doing it for me anymore," he said. "I think I'd like to get a drink. Do you know a place around here?"

* * *

I know a place around anywhere. Mr. Slayter and I retired to a nearby Irish watering hole. I assumed it was a bit low-rent for him, but he didn't seem to mind. He removed his tie, stuck it in his pocket, and ordered a Guinness. I was certain by then that Mr. Slayter was merely an innocent, but wealthy, bystander. I explained to him that it appeared to be mere chance that we were separately hired by Margaret and Adam, to fulfill each of their wanton agendas. I wasn't clear on his wife's plan, but I was fairly certain that Adam wanted documentation of an affair to blackmail Margaret. I asked Mr. Slayter if they had given money to Adam in the past.

Mr. Slayter had indeed invested in a number of failed businesses until last year, when he decided to cease entering into any monetary deals with his "in-law." I asked how much he invested over the years and Slayter estimated over a hundred thousand dollars. He said that when he decided to cut Adam off, Margaret was in complete agreement and had thanked him for all the help he had provided for her brother in the past.

After we drained our first beers, I was about to order another round when my cell phone buzzed.

It was a text from Mrs. Slayter.

"She'd like to know where you are," I said. "Where are you?"

"Tell her I'm in a bar with a young woman."

"Are you sure you want me to do that?"

"I insist," he said.

I texted the line. She promptly texted back.

"She wants me to describe her."

"Tall, brunette, late twenties,[2] a little rough around the edges, but attractive."

I texted the "tall, brunette" part and substituted a more accurate age.

Take pictures, she texted back.

Can't. Lighting is impossible. Will try when they surface.

---

[2] Mr. Slayter was certainly growing on me.

I closed my phone and returned my attention to Mr. Slayter.

"I've given you the facts. Now the question is: What do you want to do?"

"I suppose I should get divorced."

"You're sure that's what you want?" I asked.

"Ah, you're thinking that an unfaithful spouse might be better than no spouse as I drift into oblivion. Is that it?"

"No, that's not what I was thinking. But I have just given you quite a bit of information. You might want to think it over for a day or two and see how you want to proceed."

"Perhaps you're right. But before I proceed, I need to know one thing: Do you have documentation of the affair?"

"I do. But there is a matter we need to discuss."

"How much?"

"Huh?"

"How much money do you want?"

"I don't want your money. "

"What do you want?"

"Mostly, I don't want my father to disown me."

THE LAST SUPPER[1]

As Thanksgiving Day approached most work-related communications died down. Vivien reluctantly returned to the suburbs; Walter took two Valiums and got on a plane to St. Louis, where his elderly parents still resided; Edward Slayter endured one final, brutally uncomfortable feast day with several coworkers and the woman who will eventually be the former Mrs. Slayter. And I have no idea how Adam Cooper passed the time. Perhaps he was selling rubber turkeys in a makeshift storefront.

As for the rest of us, all I can say is that we survived. Demetrius and my mother slaved over the stove for two days straight, with Grammy Spellman keeping a close vigil and an almost sportscaster-like commentary. The only difference being that her comments would end with the upturned tone of a question.

You're putting the pie crust in now?

Do you need an entire stick of butter for the mashed potatoes?

Are you sure you want to cook the turkey at one hundred and sixty degrees?

Oh, so you're making pecan pie?[2]

---

[1] I wish.
[2] Apparently the most fattening of all T-day desserts.

313

What's in the bottle?

D's gift to Mom that day was politely answering all of Grammy's questions, while Mom remained serene and mute, like a Buddhist monk.

I like to make the crusts the day before. You don't sacrifice taste and it saves time.

One day a year, you can splurge.

Any higher and you risk a dry turkey.[3]

Yes. That's what the pecans are for.

Aspirin.

Dad, as usual, sat on his ass and watched one football game after another, carrying on interactively with the TV; Maggie did the same, determined to set a proper example for her daughter. Between the two of them, they went through a six-pack of beer by two o'clock, at which point they started making not-so-friendly wagers on the game. Four beers after that, Dad and Maggie had actually started putting up their cars as collateral until I confiscated the beer and took them for a sobering-up stroll.

David, usually one to sit on the fence of gender roles—one eye on the kitchen, two on the game—this year had all three eyes on Sydney. He killed all of Thursday morning regaling my distracted niece with stories of the early settlers and lies about their friendly cohabitation with the Native Americans.

"Don't forget to tell her about the blankets with the smallpox," I said.

"She's too young for that, Izzy," David said, annoyed.

"She's too young for American History 101," I replied. "And yet you continue. What happened to counting and simple nouns? For instance, a yellow fruit that you peel from the top?"

"It's three o'clock, Izzy," David replied. "Aren't you usually drunk and passed out on the couch by now?"

"I'm evolving," I replied.

---

[3] Still better than death.

"I wish you wouldn't," David replied.

Previous holiday dinners—all of them, really—would eventually devolve into a series of one-on-one bouts, words flung like fists until one individual became the unspoken victor. Tonight, however, began peacefully enough—this being the first T-day with D playing dual roles as guest of honor and chef. The turkey was moist, the stuffing impeccable, the mashed potatoes every bit as good as Crack Mix, and, well, you get my drift. Food-wise it was one for the record books. So we ate ravenously and indulgently and when people are chewing, even the low-mannered Spellman variety, they don't talk that much, which is a blessing. But at some point you need a breather and conversations begin. And that's when the trouble started.

Grammy seemed to be taking notes on everyone's food consumption during the meal and commented accordingly. That's when most of the family began announcing their weight gain during the meal. The only individuals who refused to play were D, Maggie, and Grammy.

My father could feel the temperature dropping at the table, like a typical San Francisco afternoon. He tried to navigate the conversation into the holiday spirit by suggesting that we go around the table and mention something that we were grateful for that year. He tries this every year and always bombs.

DAD: I am grateful to be alive and have all of the most important people in my life at this table. Mom?

GRAMMY: I am grateful for good health and this food we are about to eat and my new companion, Perdita.

DAD: FourPete.

GRAMMY: That's no name for a dog.

DEMETRIUS: [interrupting to fend off argument] I am grateful for this fine food and the health of my new friends and family, and I am mostly grateful for being a free man.

ME: No one can follow that.

MOM: It's not a competition, Isabel.

ME: I'm just saying, maybe we should leave it at that.

Then Sydney pointed at the mashed potatoes and said "banana." Maggie suddenly caught Rae's eye and gave her a look as sharp as a blade.

"I *know*," Maggie said. "I know what you did."

Black Friday was an aptly named day for Rae, who was required to pay not only her debt to society but also her debt to Sydney or Maggie and David. Once my sister-in-law got the lowdown on her sister-in-law's vile experiments, she wanted her own payback. She also wanted a garden, which was now Rae's domain. Maggie's food hangover was spent in front of the computer with my sister as they worked on an interactive landscape design program. If there's anything Rae hates more than vegetables, it's vegetation. But the punishment did indeed fit the crime.

GOOD—BYE, WALTER

Soon after Walter's return from Saint Louis, he called again. "I think I left the water running in the bathtub."

"Do you take baths, Walter?"

"No. They're disgusting. Swimming around in your own filth."

"I didn't think so. So how could you have left the water running?"

"I don't know. I just have a bad feeling. Maybe somebody else did it."

"But we changed the locks."

"There are windows, and there are locksmiths and people who know how to pick locks. And I did have to give a key to my super."

What originally motivated Walter to hire Spellman Investigations had morphed into something else. I was stalling, hoping to figure it out on my own and deal with it accordingly, but I had far too many other unsettled matters on my plate. It was time to stick this one in the dishwasher. I was certain Walter was sabotaging himself; what I didn't know was why.

And I didn't have time to waste waiting for Walter to slip up and explain himself. Direct confrontation isn't always the most thrilling option, but it's reliably the most expedient. "I can be at your apartment in a half hour. When can you be there?"

"My class is over at five. Five thirty?"

I looked at my watch. Only an hour to kill before my reckoning with

Walter. "I'll see you then," I replied. I drove to Walter's apartment and found his bathtub on a slow drip. But there was no stopper in the tub and therefore no flood. The lock on the door had not been tampered with, and no footprints could be found on the pristine shag rug. In fact, I had developed a keen sense of Walter's carpet-raking pattern (as opposed to mine) and could easily determine that no one had entered his home since he left that morning.

I raked myself a path to Walter's couch and picked up an art book on the coffee table. I cracked the spine, realized it hadn't been opened before, and put it back in its place. I phoned Mr. Slayter to be sure he remembered the events of the previous afternoon and the instructions I had given him. He reminded me that his disease had not progressed very far. Although, when we hung up, he said, "Good-bye, Bella." I didn't bother correcting him.

Then I telephoned Vivien Blake and called in a favor. With all the hassle she had caused me and the lost hours I couldn't bill on doctored reports, I figured she owed me one.

"Do you have a decent digital camera?" I asked.

"It takes video, too," Vivien replied.

"You need a disguise," I said.

"Oh, I have that," she confidently replied. "You want a blonde or a redhead?"

"A blonde. Definitely.[1]

"I don't know the time yet, but it usually happens on Wednesdays."

"No problem," Vivien replied.

Then I heard the key in the door.

"I'll be in touch," I said.

Walter entered and smiled hesitantly. "Isabel, so nice to see you in the flesh."

---

[1] Listen, gingers are no good for surveillance, and I've always found them highly suspicious individuals.

"That's usually how you see a person."

"Right."

"Do you want to sit down?"

"Can I make you a cappuccino first?" he asked.

I thought this might be my last perfect cup of Walter cappuccino, so I agreed. Then I waited for twenty minutes while he brewed the flawless beverage. He even made a little four-leaf-clover design in the froth. I almost regretted what I was about to do. Almost.

Walter took a seat next to mine and managed to ignore the sock treads he'd left behind. "Drink it while it's hot," he said.

I took a sip.

"How is it?"

"Excellent, as always," I replied.

"You look like you have something on your mind, although I'm not sure what you'd look like if you had nothing on your mind."

I took another sip of coffee and put it on the coffee table. Walter picked up the coffee and slid a coaster underneath. It was a glass table. They don't need coasters, I hear, but I didn't say anything.

"Why have you been lying to me, Walter?"

"Excuse me?"

"When I first started working for you, I was checking on nothing. You thought something was on fire, but it wasn't; you thought you'd left a faucet dripping, but you hadn't; maybe an electrical cord was plugged in, but it was unplugged, or the window was ajar, but you only open your windows twice a week to clear the air—and you only do that in the morning when the air is freshest. For two months I entered your home to check if anything was amiss, and nothing was ever amiss. Then, suddenly, things start to go wrong. Bathtubs overflow, footprints are left on the carpet, electrical appliances are mysteriously plugged in, and toast is made. Around that time I got a series of phone calls from your ex-wife."

"Sasha called you?"

"Yes. She gets your phone bill and saw you dialing this number repeatedly. She called it and heard a female voice and assumed that you had moved on."

"I see," said Walter. "She never told me."

"Your wife had a key, as you admitted, so I came to the logical conclusion. That is, until I confronted your wife."

"You spoke to Sasha?"

"I did."

"You should have mentioned that."

"Maybe, but I needed to understand what was going on."

"And what's going on?" Walter nervously asked.

"Honestly, Walter, I don't know. All I know is that your ex-wife isn't doing this to you, and no stranger is, either. I surveilled your house one night when you didn't know it and nobody came or left—except one elderly neighbor—and when you returned home, you called me because something else was amiss. So there is only one conclusion I can draw: You're doing this to yourself. The next logical question is, why?"

"Let me explain," Walter said, inching closer to me on the couch.

"Please do."

"I worry all the time. Never a day goes by that I don't think something has gone wrong and I needed your help."

"And I did what you asked. But then you started sabotaging yourself." Walter remained silent.

"You flooded your own bathroom, didn't you?" I asked.

"Yes," Walter replied, staring at the raked carpet.

"You made toast?"

"I did."

"How did you manage the power outage?"

"I phoned PG&E while you were vacuuming your trunk."

"But why?"

"I started to worry that if nothing ever happened, if nothing was ever out of place, perhaps you'd quit or suggest I hire a student or pass me along to someone else or tell me to get help again."

320

"Eventually, I might have suggested you hire a student. They work for cheap and there are probably a few who have a serious case of OCD."

"But I didn't want that," Walter said. "I wanted your help and so I figured I had to keep you engaged in the problem. And then sometimes you would come over when I was here, not at the campus, and I liked that. And I wanted to see you more. And I really liked that date we went on when we followed your sister."

"It wasn't a date, Walter."

"We could go on a date, maybe. Couldn't we? I know about your boyfriend."

"How do you know about that?" I said.

"It's obvious. You're all wrinkled and buttons are missing and you're sad and you weren't like that before." Walter inched closer to me on the couch. His hand hovered above my knee. "Anyway, that doesn't matter."

"No, it doesn't matter, Walter," I curtly replied. His hand shifted back to his own leg. "I'm sorry. But I need to be firm here. Our relationship is professional and will remain that way. Unfortunately, I don't think I should be your primary contact anymore."

"I think you'd be good for me."

"You can't even get in my car, Walter."

"You could get a new car."

"I'm sorry. I don't feel the same way."

"I see. Well, that's different. I'm sorry to hear that," Walter calmly replied. He remained seated on the couch but seemed a bit stunned.

"I understand what it's like to be lonely," I said. "And I know that you have challenges that perhaps some other people don't have. I still believe that you should seek professional help, but in the meantime my mother can check on things while you're at work. She is a very small, clean woman who will leave things just so. It's been a pleasure knowing you, Walter."

I held out my hand. Walter shook it limply.

"I guess this is good-bye," he said.

"Good-bye, Walter."

$$ JUSTICE 4
MERRI-WEATHER $$
AND A FEW OTHERS

Shortly before Thanksgiving, David finally broke the news to Maggie about what Rae had done. He also explained his reluctance to retaliate based on his own youthful exploitation of his baby sister. Since Maggie didn't have any comparable guilt, she relished the chance to enact punitive measures against Rae and followed her instincts. But still, adjusting to my family had taken its toll at times. Something about the sheer insanity of the banana debacle left Maggie with a slightly queasy feeling in her gut. What other Spellman skeletons would one day come out to haunt her? One evening when David was trying to undo the damage done, giving Sydney a thorough lesson on all the common fruits, Maggie knocked on the door to the in-law unit and said, "Let's get out of here."

Over drinks at a nearby watering hole—one with some sort of logging theme, which seemed incongruous in their tony neighborhood—we drank beer and traded intelligence on all of the current Spellman matters.

Maggie, despite everything, was representing Rae in the tree-hugging case—though one did have to wonder how ardently she was fighting for her, since Rae got forty-five hours of community service. And not the country club kind. My sister would be wearing an orange reflective vest and cleaning up debris on the side of the highway. I asked Maggie if the punishment fit the crime and Maggie shrugged her shoulders ambivalently. We briefly touched on the subject of Fred and Rae and whether he had taken her back; Maggie said that as far as she knew they were still negotiating.

We then began to brainstorm about D's afternoon excursion with Grammy.

"It's not possible that they're becoming friends, right?" I asked.

"I don't know," Maggie said. "We were talking the other day about his case and I asked him about his excursion with Ruth and he immediately changed the subject."

"You were talking about his case?" I asked. Suddenly the Grammy Spellman element was far less intriguing. Maggie and I had been instrumental in D's release from prison and we were the first to suggest he file a lawsuit against the DA for malicious prosecution. The money could never compensate for the years he was incarcerated, but it could certainly improve the time he had left. But after tangling with the legal system for so many years to garner his release, D couldn't bear the idea of setting foot in a courtroom as a free man. But later on, there were other factors influencing his decision. Maggie suggested that Mabel was one of them.

Questions then flooded my mind. "What does Mabel have to do with it?"

"He felt that a lawsuit would be time-consuming and interfere with their relationship."

"But he's only been seeing her a little while."

"Six months."

"That long? Wow. He's better than I thought," I said, genuinely impressed.

"He's learned from the best," Maggie replied.

"I assume Mabel knows D was in prison?"

"He told her on their first date."

"It doesn't make sense that D wouldn't want justice. I understand it could be time-consuming . . ."

"I think he wanted to see if Mabel was able to like a rehabilitated ex-con. Not a man who spent years wrongly incarcerated and could potentially receive a windfall for his ordeal."

"Has he come to a conclusion yet?"

"Yes," Maggie said. "He dropped by my office last week and we're currently drafting a complaint."

"Have you met her?" I asked. "Mabel."

"Briefly. We've tried to invite them over for dinner, but he has always politely declined."

"He's hiding us because we embarrass him," I said.

"Can't say I blame him," Maggie replied. "You're all nuts." She knocked back the rest of her drink.

"You want another?" I asked.

"Definitely," Maggie replied.

I approached the bar and ordered another round of two beers and two shots of whiskey.

We both downed our shots and then silence set in. The kind of silence that precedes nonsilence. Well, I suppose all silences are like that. But this was one of those deliberate pauses intended as a conversational palate-cleanser to move on to another subject.

"I saw Henry's car parked out front the other night," Maggie said.

"He brought it by for an oil change. You know he doesn't like to get his hands dirty."

"Still don't want to talk. Got it," Maggie said.

"There is something I would like to talk about."

"What?"

"It's a legal thing."

"Not what I had in mind, but go ahead."

"Based on the Spellman company structure at this point, can I be fired?"

The following day, Demetrius broke the news to the family about his pending lawsuit. We celebrated with Crack Mix and champagne. Then D and I decided to take a drive. We felt it was important that Rae hear the news, but we wanted to provide it to her in the right context, at a place where she couldn't gloat or celebrate.

Mom found out where the orange chain gang would be picking up litter that afternoon, and D and I got on the 101 South. When we found my sister and her probation cohorts, we pulled the car onto the shoulder and snapped several photos. At first Rae tried to hide her face, but eventually she approached the car, tripping on the hem of her orange jumpsuit. They don't make those things for Rae-size people, so she looked more like a child playing dress-up in a hazmat suit. It was a glorious sight.

"Is there something I can do for you?" she asked.

"We have some good news we wanted to share," I said.

"What?" Rae impatiently replied.

"I've decided to file a civil suit for my wrongful incarceration," D said.

"I knew you'd come around eventually," Rae said. "I'd like to think I had a little something to do with your decision."

"You didn't," D replied. "But we thought you should know."

Just then the foreman, or whatever the orange-wrangler is called, told Rae to get back to work.

Rae sighed deeply and headed back to the group, dragging her trash bag in her wake.

"See," I said. "You can't be smug in an orange reflective vest."

D took one more photo, just to make sure we had an album's worth, and then we took the scenic route home. I asked D what he hoped for in the future; his plan was startlingly clear: a wife, kids, and maybe one day he'd open his own restaurant or bakery. Then he returned the question.

"I don't know," I said.

GOOD-BYE, GRAMMY

The next morning, when I arrived at the office, Demetrius and Grammy were out again.

I looked at my watch.

"What Morgan Freeman[1] film is playing at nine thirty in the morning?" I asked.

"They took FourPete to the dog groomer," Mom replied as she scurried around the office, tidying up. "Empty the wastebaskets, please."

"Is a VIP coming in?"

"Just the Blakes," Mom said. "I didn't like the way she was studying our debris the last time she was here."

Dad showed up a few minutes later, gathered all the paperwork on his desk into one messy pile, put it in a box, and shoved it under his desk. The doorbell rang and my mother led the Blakes into the office and pulled out two chairs beside her desk. I sat back and watched as my mother guided the outtake meeting and my father provided backup with carefully timed head-nods.

They offered the Blakes a complete set of the Vivien Blake surveillance reports[2] (falsified, yes, but the subject's activities were also falsified, so I

---

[1] I promise that is the last time I will mention his name.
[2] Which my parents still believed were accurate.

considered it a wash) and provided sound parental and professional advice to the couple:

"Your daughter is behaving like a typical coed. She has friends. She goes to a few parties. Sometimes she stays out too late, and sometimes she's at home on a Saturday night, studying. Her GPA is 3.7; she doesn't have any warrants for her arrest; she has not been seen participating in any illegal activities; she doesn't own a vehicle, so there are no traffic violations to consider; and she appears to the naked eye to be happy and well adjusted. We believe that there is no reason to continue this investigation and hope that you feel confident in letting your daughter go about her life on her own now. Our professional opinion is that it is in everyone's best interest to refrain from any further investigation of Vivien. We hope that we've been helpful."

The Blakes appeared relieved by the information that they received, and as far as my parents could tell, they were cautiously optimistic about their daughter's future. They seemed willing to forgo any further invasion of privacy.

That didn't mean our invasion of privacy was over. My mother gave Mrs. Blake the genetics file compiled by Rae and explained that one of her most observant investigators noticed that certain genetic markers were inconsistent.

Mrs. Blake's first response was incomprehension, so alarmed was she by the sudden change of topic. But then she looked at the file, passed it to her husband, and asked my mother what the meaning of all this was.

"Our investigator noticed that your daughter is most likely adopted," Mom said. "Vivien is an extremely intelligent young woman. She probably figured it out on her own. It might be time to come clean."

The Blakes sat frozen for a few moments, taking in the information. Mr. Blake cleared his throat several times, as if he'd lost his voice; Mrs. Blake visibly paled and her hands trembled a bit as she placed the file into her handbag. The couple slowly got to their feet, thanked my parents for their work, paid the final bill, but never responded to my mother's last sugges-

tion. I phoned Vivien out of courtesy to let her know her shadow was officially over.

"It was fun while it lasted," she said.

"How's that other thing going?" I asked.

"I should have something for you very soon," she said. "And do you have
anything for me?"

"Still working on it," I replied.

A few days later, when I returned to the Spellman compound, several suitcases were clustered by the front door. My mother was using her inhaler
like a scuba diver with an oxygen mask, but there was a calm glow on her
face that I hadn't seen in, well, exactly six weeks and four days. Demetrius
and my father were lugging one of those old, boxy twenty-seven-inch televisions out to a pickup truck parked in the driveway.

"This brings back memories," D said.[3]

"Be careful of your back," Grammy said to my dad as she watched nervously. "You're not a young man anymore."

"Yes, Mom, I'm aware of that. It would be nice if you didn't tell me that
every single day."

After D and my dad headed down the front steps, I turned to my mother
for an explanation.

"Grammy's moving out?"

"Yes," Mom replied, nodding her head effusively.

"How'd you make that happen?"

"I didn't," Mom replied. "It was all D. He saw how miserable we all were
and he convinced Ruth that she should hang on to her dignity and indepen-
dence as long as she could and he took her on a tour of the city and helped
her find an apartment. He said it didn't take much persuading. She thinks

---

[3] Back in his lawbreaking days, Demetrius's primary income source was stealing and
reselling television sets. He purchased a flat-screen with his first Spellman paycheck.

we're a bunch of animals anyway. Ruth signed a yearlong lease last Friday," Mom said. She was so happy, she was almost crying.

"So *that's* what they've been up to," I said.

"I think he might be my favorite person in the whole world," said Mom.

"Shouldn't that be Dad? Or maybe even me?"

"No, it's D," Mom replied.

"I guess he's kind of tops on my list too," I replied.

Mom, desperate to move the move along as quickly as possible, picked up one of Grammy's daisy-print suitcases.

"That's too heavy for you, dear," Grammy said to Mom as she entered the foyer. "Let the men handle it. Or Isabel."

My mother ignored Grammy and comfortably lugged the suitcase to the truck.

"So, you're moving out," I said to Grammy.

"I found a lovely garden apartment just two miles away. We can see each other as much as we'd like. I should be very comfortable there. It's quite clean, and they take pets. A rare combination."

"Pets?" I asked.

"I'll be taking Perdita with me."

"Who is Perdita?"

"You people know her as FourPete. Such an undignified name for a dog. Don't you think?"

"Actually I think dogs are supposed to have undignified names."

"We'll have to agree to disagree."

Yeah, on everything, I thought. But I kept that to myself. I picked up two more suitcases and loaded them into the truck, while Dad and D removed the dresser from the guest bedroom, which was Grammy Spellman's dresser from years ago.

A few more odds and ends were extracted from the house and then FourPete[4] hopped into the back of the truck and Grammy, Dad, and D

---

[4] She can call the dog whatever she wants. She'll always be FourPete to me.

filed into the cab. Mom and I waved from the driveway as they departed.

As soon as the truck turned the corner, Mom pumped her fist in the air, shouted with glee, and gave me a high five.

"How does it feel?" I asked.

"Like I just lost one hundred and ten pounds."

Mom strode back into the house and over to her desk. On top lay the latest book club tome, which she dropped in the trash. Then she picked up her crochet bag and emptied the yarn into the steel bin. She tossed her Russian workbooks in there as well and then picked up the trash and carried it into the backyard. She grabbed the lighter fluid next to the barbecue and sprayed a good stream inside the can. Then she lit a match and set the whole thing aflame.

"*Dosvedanya*," she said.

"Congratulations," I said as we watched Mom's hobbies burn to ash.

THE SPARROW FLEES
THE NEST

I met with Vivien at a café in the Mission. She was spooning her way through a pyramid of whipped cream atop a bowl-sized serving of mocha. A manila envelope rested on the table. I ordered a regular coffee and took a seat. "Was it difficult?" I asked.

"Not at all," she replied, sliding the photos in my direction.

I perused the new and improved evidence: expertly shot images of Margaret Slayter and subject #2—later identified as Boris Gavrilenko, Margaret's Ukrainian trainer—in most compromising positions. One image showed them kissing in her Mercedes, and another had them embracing at the back entrance to her gym. The pictures satisfied my prerequisites: They provided sound evidence of an affair and did not in any way resemble my father's work.

"Good job," I said. "You're a natural."

"So, like, how does somebody get into your line of work?" Vivien asked.

"If any side jobs come up, I'll keep you in mind."

"Do you have something for me?" Vivien asked.

"I do," I replied, placing a sealed envelope in the middle of the table.

Vivien didn't reach for it right away. She let it sit there.

"What's inside?"

"I have the names and current addresses of your biological parents and some basic background information, photos, occupations, and so on."

She took another sip of her mocha. "Hmmm," she said. "You know, when I figured out I was adopted, I had a lot of ideas about who my bio-parents were. Sometimes I'd picture them as Ivy League intellectuals. Sometimes criminals. For a while I was really keen on the idea that my father was a cat burglar and my mother a fence. Of course, a baby couldn't fit into that picture. I'm sure that they're perfectly ordinary, but I never thought of them that way. They could be anything I want them to be."

"If you open that envelope," I said, "that will no longer be the case."

"I just figured that out," Vivien said. She picked it up and looked it over.

I had this overwhelming urge to grab the envelope from her and rip it to shreds. "Before you do something that you can't undo," I said, "think about this: The way you see your birth parents is kind of the way you see yourself. You can be anything. Sometimes when you know where you come from, it limits you. Sometimes you feel stuck. Think about that before you make any decision."

Vivien put the envelope back on the table.

"Why don't you just hang on to that for a while," she said.

After my meeting with Vivien, I took a cab to Mr. Slayter's office. A man who was not Phil Vitus drove me straight there, no questions asked. Slayter holds a corner office on the fifteenth floor. It was about the size of Bernie's entire one-bedroom apartment. A gray-haired man was seated on his couch, going over stacks of paperwork.

Mr. Slayter greeted me with a warm handshake and a masculine pat on the shoulder.

"Isabel," he said deliberately to make sure he got it right. "Meet my attorney, Ritz Naygrow."

"Nice to meet you, Mr. Naygrow."

"Call me Ritz," he replied.

"Really? Thanks, Ritz. I've actually never known anyone named Ritz, Ritz."

"She'll grow on you," Mr. Slayter said, as if it were an order.

"Are the plans in motion?" I asked.

"We've transferred all the money from my wife's bank account and closed all but one of her credit cards."

"Has she noticed yet?"

"Not yet."

I passed the envelope with Vivien's photos to Slayter. I could have easily given him the pictures I'd found on my father's computer, but I wanted my dad to have plausible deniability. I didn't care if *I* did. And if everything went correctly, the plan was for Slayter to tell his wife he'd hired his own investigator and no one named Spellman would ever be mentioned.

"This is all you should need for the infidelity clause. Plus, you're likely to get Adam Cooper to testify against her if he knows there isn't any money coming in. When you tell her . . ."

Edward had stopped paying attention to me as he looked at photographs of his wife with another man. For as long as I'd known her, Margaret Slayter had been a sketchy, two-dimensional figure, a woman that I couldn't imagine a man being heartbroken over. But Edward must have married her for some reason.

"I'm sorry, Mr. Slayter. This must be very difficult for you."

Edward slid the photos back in the envelope and gave them to his attorney, who had the decency not to take a peek at that time.

"I filed for divorce this morning," Mr. Slayter said. "I plan on telling Margaret this evening."

"She'll stay in the house," I told him. "Once she realizes all her resources are gone, she'll hang on to what she can."

"I plan on moving into the Fairmont for the time being. Once the divorce is settled, she will receive a lump sum that should keep her for some time, if she's careful. And then she'll have to move out."

"Is anyone else living in the house?"

"Just our housekeeper, Marta."

"How do they get along?"

"They loathe each other."

"Tell Marta to slack off for the next few weeks. Tell her to catch up on her daytime television and to ignore any threats that the soon-to-be-ex-Mrs. Slayter makes. Does Margaret have any allergies?"

"No," Slayter replied.

"That's unfortunate. I was going to suggest Marta get a dog."

"Have you thought about what we discussed?" Slayter asked.

"I have. But I think I need to see the fallout first."

"As you wish," Mr. Slayter replied.

"Mr. Slayter, I think Margaret and Adam are harmless, but that was quite an unusual scam they pulled. Please err on the side of caution. I don't know what they would become if they got desperate enough," I said as I took my leave.

Edward gave me a quick peck on the cheek before I left. "You're an angel," he said.

"That's a first," I replied. "See you around, Ritz."

I phoned Adam Cooper as soon as I left Mr. Slayter's office. I told him that I had some pressing news that needed to be relayed immediately. He suggested I come to his apartment, but I thought it best to meet in a public place. We agreed on the library.

An hour before our scheduled meeting, I waited outside Cooper's apartment in the Richmond. It was a modest twelve-unit building, from circa 1970, that needed a paint job. The units couldn't have been more than six hundred square feet each. I was curious what kind of car he drove, since he was no longer financially solvent. I wasn't surprised when Cooper winked the lights of a brand-new BMW, with a top-of-the-line security system. He would be that asshole whose car alarm goes off in the middle of the night, keeping the entire neighborhood awake.

The first time I met Cooper, he seemed so ordinary—in a good kind of way. The clothes so deliberately uncool. I recalled my interview with Meg and Adam's neighbor, who described his expensive tastes and vain affectations. I realized the sweater vest was as much of a disguise as the car. When he met me, he wanted to come off as a simple, harmless man concerned about his sister's well-being.

Since I knew where Cooper was heading, I beat him to the library with ten minutes to spare.

I returned to the government section of the main library and pulled the California Code of Civil Procedure and sat down in one of those glass booths. There was a particular section that I wanted to share. As I paged through the substantial book, I felt a shadow over my shoulder and heard a familiar voice.

"Are you the Gopher?" Cooper asked. The sense of déjà vu was disturbing.

Up close, he looked considerably changed this time around, as if he were no longer trying to hide his smarmy ways. His shirt was purple and had a sheen to it. In fact, everything he wore seemed mildly reflective, including the sunglasses that he'd left on. He sat down across from me.

There was a homeless man or an unkempt older student studying nearby; we spoke in hushed tones for privacy.

"I was glad to hear from you. Your father is not the best communicator in the world."

"I'm sorry to hear that," I replied.

"I've been waiting on photographs for the last two weeks. And his surveillance reports so far have illuminated nothing."

I was unaware that my father was not feeding information to Cooper. I needed to see what little information he did offer.

"I'm afraid my father hasn't been the best communicator with me, either. He's quite overworked these days. What has he given you?"

"A few surveillance reports and some photographic evidence that Meg is going to the gym. But I already knew that. She's been a gym rat her whole life."

"Have you seen her recently? How did she seem?" I asked.

"We haven't spoken in weeks. Ever since I questioned the state of her marriage. That's what this whole thing was about. I was concerned for my sister's well-being."

"I see."

"Mr. Spellman suggested that she was perhaps having an affair. I thought that he'd provide more information, but I don't even have the name of the individual."

"I do," I said. "I even have pictures."

Cooper couldn't contain his excitement. "You do?" he asked, and then he coughed, trying to cover his eagerness with a more benign expression.

"I do," I repeated. Then I found the page in the California Code of Civil Procedure. I spun the book around and slid it across the table. "Are you familiar with California Penal Code Section 518?"

"No. Should I be?"

"You definitely need to check out this code. I'll just explain it to you because it might take you a while to read all the legalese. Basically, it defines extortion as trying to obtain property—in your case, cash—through force or fear. Now, fear can simply mean the threat of exposing the individual to shame. The sentence for extortion can be up to four years in prison and a fine of ten thousand dollars. Based on your latest credit report, there's no way you can get that kind of money unless you extort someone."

"Why are you telling me all this?" Adam asked, although he already knew.

"You, sir, are not Meg's brother. You're her ex-husband and you're seeking information so that you can blackmail her and siphon as much money as possible off of her extremely wealthy spouse."

"I've done nothing illegal."

"Maybe, maybe not. I don't know your entire biography, but you were *planning* to blackmail your ex-wife."

"What do you want?"

"Two things: I want to reimburse you for services not rendered. I believe you paid a twenty-five-hundred-dollar retainer. Then you stopped paying your bills, which might explain the lack of investigative product. But I also suspect Dad grew suspicious and was reluctant to provide evidence when he wasn't sure how it would be used."

Cooper stared at the check, folded it in quarters, and put it into his shiny pocket.

"I know what you're thinking," I said.

"Doubtful," he replied.

"You're thinking you'll just hire another investigator to get evidence against Meg. Do you call her 'Meg' or 'Margaret' or 'sis'? That is really creepy, you know."

"Get to the point."

"The jig is up," I said. "Mr. Slayter has proof of Mrs. Slayter's affair and has just filed for divorce. Your ex-wife will receive an extremely modest stipend to live off of for the next two years and that is all. So, you're going to have to find someone else to shake down, but when you do, make sure that you can handle four years in prison. Because I think I'm going to keep an eye on you. Any questions?"

"You wouldn't by chance know how Edward Slayter acquired proof of his wife's affair?"

"No idea," I replied.

Cooper flushed in anger. He got to his feet.

"Are you leaving?" I asked.

"I think we're done here."

"Have a nice day!" I said cheerily. I found that people who aren't having a nice day really loathe that phrase.

"You won't get away with this," Adam said as he walked away.

"I just did," I replied.

HIDING OUT

I drove straight to the Philosopher's Club to take the edge off before there was an edge to take off. Bernie, as always, approached me like a scuba diver in shark water, observing, moving slowly, but always with that uncertain feeling. I sat down at the bar. Bernie, without making eye contact, said, "What can I get you?"

"Bourbon," I said.

"Maybe you want to start with a beer," Bernie suggested.

It was sound advice, and coming from anyone else, I might have taken it.

"Maybe I don't want a beer."

"You usually do," Bernie said. True, but none of his business.

"What happened to 'the customer is always right'?"

Bernie shrugged his shoulders and poured a bourbon on the rocks. If I drink bourbon, I drink it on the rocks, but I didn't order it that way, so I decided to be difficult.

"Did I say 'on the rocks'?" I said, eyeing the drink as if it were peppermint schnapps.

"My apologies," Bernie replied.

He reached for the drink, but I beat him to it. "Forget it," I said. "I don't like to waste booze."

After a few moments of satisfying silence, Bernie spoke.

"How's life?"

"About to get very messy."

"Care to elaborate?" Bernie asked.

"Nope," I replied.

Another enjoyable break from conversation passed. Unfortunately, the only thing Bernie hates more than quiet is an empty refrigerator.

"Maybe I'll put some music on," Bernie said.

If it were up to Bernie, only Old Blue Eyes would be playing in this bar. In fact, he'd probably change its name to the Chairman's Club if the sign didn't cost so much.

"If you play 'I Get a Kick Out of You,' you'll get one," I said.

Bernie set the jukebox on random and took his chances. A stale Beatles song blanketed the silence; then Bernie started humming, adding another layer to the soundtrack; then my phone rang. I pulled it out of my pocket and laid it on the bar. It was the call I had been expecting.

"You going to pick up?" Bernie asked.

"Does it look like it?" I replied.

"Not really," Bernie said as the ringing cut off.

Then my phone rang again. Different number on the screen, but the same caller, I assumed. Bernie watched me.

"I'm not picking that up either."

"Then maybe you want to put it on mute."

"Milo used to have a no-cell policy, but I don't see any signs," I said.

"It's just basic courtesy," Bernie said.

"And you're an expert on that," I replied.

My phone rang again. This time, I muted the sound on the first ring. Ten minutes passed and the phone rang again. This call was from David, so I picked up.

"Hello."

"He's angry," David said.

"I expected that," I replied.

"He's making threats, serious threats," David said.

339

"He's bluffing," I said, unconvinced.

"I would be genuinely concerned, if I were you," David said. "I hope you have a plan."

"I do," I replied. "But I was hoping I wouldn't have to implement it."

"Care to enlighten me?"

"Not just yet."

I disconnected the call and ordered a beer. Bernie pulled the pint and handed me the sports section of the newspaper he was reading. This was his version of a peace offering, since that's the only part of the newspaper he even glances at. Then the bar phone rang. It had one of those regular rings and a cord that doesn't let you wander. I found something oddly comforting about the relic.

Bernie answered. "Hello . . . Yep. I see. I don't know about that. Okay. Okay. Uh-huh. Yes, sir. We serve beer here. Talk to you later."

"What was that about?" I asked.

"Guy wasn't sure if we were a bar or a think tank."

"Aren't you listed under 'bars' in the yellow pages?"

"Taverns," Bernie said, correcting me. "But I think he saw the sign and didn't have time to check."

"Huh," I replied. If my mind hadn't been otherwise occupied, I would have realized that Bernie was covering.

Twenty minutes later, my father entered the bar. It would have been easy if he were merely angry, but there was another expression that I couldn't put my finger on—one I hadn't seen before. In my father's eyes I hadn't just crossed an imaginary line, I was Fredo in *The Godfather*. My punishment, however, wouldn't be so steep. Unlike Fredo, I knew what my family was capable of.

Dad sat down next to me. He took several deep breaths to control his anger. I spoke first.

"I understand that you're angry. But I don't regret what I did."

"My company, my rules," Dad replied.

"My case, my decision."

"When I tell you to do something, I need to trust that you'll do it."

"Have you ever been able to do that?" I asked.

"You make an excellent point."

"Why don't you give me a week off without pay and we'll call it even," I suggested.

"No, that won't do it."

"Two?"

"You're fired, sweetie," Dad said. He kissed me on the forehead and left the bar.

I sat stunned for a few minutes. Then Bernie cautiously approached.

"You okay?" he asked.

"No," I replied. "The glass is empty."

PROPOSITIONS

I slept late since I was officially jobless. Or, as they say in England, made redundant, which always struck me as a particularly brutal way of putting it.

In the morning, I drank David's coffee and once again watched, slack jawed, his breakfast ritual with Sydney. He must have found the oatmeal I hid in the closet because there it was again, bubbling on the stove.

"Don't you learn from your mistakes?" I asked.

"It's good for her," David flatly replied.

My brother had the front page of the newspaper open while he read Sydney the headlines in the singsong voice he uses for children's books. He used that same voice to provide a summary of the news in plain English. Not plain enough for Sydney—she was entirely uninterested in the lesson plan; instead she made herself busy trying to put as many grapes as possible in her mouth without chewing them—but at least I was getting schooled on current events.

"Let's see," David said. "Oil prices are on the rise again. Sydney, it's very important that we reduce our dependency on foreign oil. Remember the war we were talking about last week? It's all about oil. What else? Once again, another congressman tweeted inappropriate photos of himself to a coed. Senator [redacted] was caught with a prostitute. I'll explain prostitutes to you in a few years."

"You know, maybe if you had some breaking news about Elmo she'd be more invested in this conversation," I said.

That was apparently a mistake.

"Elmo. Elmo. Elmo," Sydney shouted.

"Elmo later," David replied. "Thanks a lot, Izzy."

"Elmo. Elmo. Elmo."

"Is there any way to stop this?" I asked.

David, frustrated, tossed the newspaper on the kitchen table, turned on a small television in the corner of the kitchen, and tuned it in to *Sesame Street*. "*That* is the only way."

This program has been brought to you by the letter B.

"Sydney, what words begin with B?" David asked.

"Elmo," she said.

"No, that's E," said David. "What words begin with B?"

David held up a Dr. Seuss tome. I think he was hoping she'd say "book."

"Elmo," Sydney said again, with rapt attention on the TV.

"I know, I know," I said, raising my hand. Then I mouthed "banana."

"I will throw you out the window if you say that word," he said. So I didn't say "banana." But it was really, really hard.

David stirred the oatmeal on the stove and spooned it into a small bowl. He added milk and blueberries and stirred that up as well. Then he placed the bowl in front of Sydney.

"I'm not cleaning it up this time," I said.

The telephone rang.

David picked up. "Hello. Who is this? Yes, that name sounds familiar. Um, what can I do for you? One moment, please." David covered the receiver and turned to me. "Can you watch her? I need to take this."

David stepped into the other room. I watched Sydney grab fistfuls of oatmeal and shove the cholesterol-reducing whole grain into her mouth.

After ten minutes or so had passed, my brother finished his phone call and returned to the kitchen. He was about to say something to me. Something important, I suspect, but he became distracted by Sydney's eating method.

"Izzy, there's a spoon right in front of her."

"Tell her that. I was just glad that she was eating it and not throwing it. Besides, where does it say that you have to eat oatmeal with a spoon? She eats practically everything else with her hands."

David soaked a dish towel in water and wiped Sydney's hands clean. Then he placed the spoon in her tiny fingers and said, "Look at Mr. Spoon. He is your friend."

"Mr. Spoon, Twitter porn, and senatorial liaisons, all in the scope of one morning. This intellectual whiplash cannot be healthy."

Once the spoon was firmly set in Sydney's hand and she was using it (to bang on her food tray), David turned to me. "I just got a very interesting phone call from a man named Ritz Naygrow."

"Ritz and I go way back."

"So you know the nature of our conversation?" David said.

"I do," I replied.

"What's going on, Isabel?"

"The choice is yours. I don't want to influence it. I will only say this: You can argue about how I live my life and it would be fair to say that for a thirty-four-year-old, I may not be the most evolved human being. However, I like my job and I do it well and what I did on that case may not have been good business, but it was right."

"What do you want me to do?" David asked.

"I want you to do what you think is right. Thanks for the coffee," I said.

I kissed Sydney on the forehead, said a few encouraging words about Mr. Spoon, and left.

As I was unlocking the door to my temporary abode, I got a text message from Margaret Slayter.

We need to meet. Immediately.

Where?

My house.

I didn't have anything better to do, so I figured it was best to know what she was plotting.

I can be there in 20.

Margaret, with her hair pulled into a tight bun and her face scrubbed of its usual mask, led me into her house. While I had never been in the Slayter home before, I suspect that it was usually tidier. Clothes were strewn about, mail was piled up on the dining room table, empty cocktail glasses were littered across the living room, and coffee cups filled the kitchen sink.

"Marta is on strike," Margaret said as she watched me take in the scene.

"What can I do for you?" I asked as I sat down on a plush suede couch.

"I called your office and your father told me that you no longer work there."

"I'm taking a sabbatical," I replied.

"I asked if I could hire them to continue working on my husband's case. Your father said that there were not enough employees to meet the workload and turned me down." Margaret pulled on the collar of her shirt as if it was choking her. "So I contacted you directly. My husband has just filed for divorce. He apparently has evidence of an affair."

"He does?" I innocently asked.

"Yes. And with that evidence, I get virtually nothing in the divorce, unless I can prove that he was also having an affair. I need your help."

"What can I do?"

"You can help me prove that he was seeing someone."

"But he wasn't," I said.

"What about the woman in the bar?" Margaret asked.

"She was no one," I replied. "He sat with her for a bit and talked. That was it. There was nothing intimate in their encounter."

Margaret suddenly took in a few nervous breaths and began pacing. "There has to be something you can do."

"I don't see what," I said.

"He wouldn't actually have to be unfaithful. Certainly there are ways to make it appear so."

"I've heard of that sort of thing," I said.

"Can you make it happen? I don't care what the cost is."

I got to my feet.

"I'm afraid that's not really my area of expertise. Good luck with everything. And don't worry about paying your final bill. I understand money is tight right now." I let myself out, got into my car, and checked that my recording device had gotten everything. Then I went to the movies. Alas, not a single Morgan Freeman[1] film was playing.

That night I slept as soundly as I had in weeks. Until, of course, I was awakened by an intruder. There's a window over the kitchen sink that can be accessed along the side of the house. My intruder dislodged a mug from the dish rack, which dove to the floor and broke into three neat chunks. I was startled by the sharp noise and looked in the direction of my intruder, who was slithering through the window headfirst. Then I recognized the silhouette and watched it collapse on the kitchen floor.

"I have a door, Rae."

"I know," she replied. Then she held up a flashlight and shone it in my eyes. "I was going to wake you up with this."

I squinted and turned away. "I'm awake. What do you want?"

Rae approached the bed and sat down on my legs. I turned on the reading lamp and confiscated the flashlight. Then I looked at the clock.

---

[1] I lied.

One thirty A.M. "Couldn't this have waited until morning?" I asked.

"Most things can wait until morning, but I felt like talking now. I brought you a brownie in case you were hungry," Rae said, passing me a brown square in plastic wrap.

"Regular brownie?" I asked.

"That's your bag," Rae said. "I eat the straight stuff."

I was kind of hungry. So I took a bite.

Then Rae took the brownie from me and split it in half.

"I worked up an appetite on my way over."

"Is there something I can do for you?" I asked.

"I got a very interesting phone call this afternoon."

"Did you?"

"What game are you playing?"

"It's not a game, Rae. It's my life."

"It's a good offer. I don't know what to do."

"I think this is the question you need to ask yourself: What do you see yourself doing in five years?"

Rae thought about it for a moment and replied, "I really don't know."

"Will you be working for Spellman Investigations?"

This question she didn't have to think about. "No. That, I'm sure of."

I was startled by the certainty of the response. She had never mentioned this before, to me or my parents. I had definitely noticed my sister's general workplace apathy, but I chalked that up to the stresses of mingling school, work, and a thriving social life. It hadn't occurred to me that she had completely checked-out.

"I used to think that one day it would just be you and me running the business," I said.

"I used to think that too," Rae replied.

"What happened?"

"We're just watching people do things," Rae said. "I want to do my own things."

There was a time when my sister's ambition would have served only to remind me of my lack thereof. But she was right, my work is about sitting back and observing and, for me, that's enough.

"You should be clear with the unit, even though I think they've figured it out. All that yawning during Friday summits."

"I've been trying the subtle approach," Rae replied. She finished her half of the brownie and then took what was left of mine and ate it. "Now, what do I do about this other thing?" she asked.

"I want you to make the decision," I said. "Just know that the business will be in good hands, no matter what you choose. But if you take the deal, there will be some backlash. Be prepared."

Rae poured herself a glass of milk and downed it in a quick gulp.

"I'm going to need a ride home now. Remember, I don't have a car."

"How'd you get here?"

"I was at a party in the neighborhood. Got a ride."

"Sleep on the couch. I'm tired."

Rae removed her shoes and socks and got into bed with me. After an hour of being abused by a somnolent thrasher, I got out of bed and slept on the couch. By the time I woke the next morning, Rae was gone. She must have used the window, since the door was still locked.

She left me a note on my nightstand.

Let's do lunch.

THE COUP

Two days into my retirement, Mr. Slayter phoned. "I have the paper-work for you. Drop by my office anytime."

I took the California 1 bus downtown to Slayter's office. As I approached the building I caught a glimpse of Charlie and his newish yellow sweater on the cement steps. I waved. He waved back.

Then I had an idea; I walked over to him and took a seat. "How you doing, Charlie?"

"It's a beautiful day, isn't it?"

The air was thick with fog. Charlie was a true San Franciscan.

"Why don't you have a job, Charlie?"

"I used to work. For the city. In the recorder's office, for twenty years. Then they asked me to retire and I couldn't find another job. I don't need much to live on. My sister helps too."

"You know the city well, don't you?"

"Like the back of my hand. Though, that's just a saying. I don't look at the back of my hand all that much. I probably know the layout of San Francisco better than that."

"You don't get lost, do you?"

"Never."

I gave Charlie a fifty-dollar bill.

LISA LUTZ

"What's this for?" he asked.

"I'd like you to go to the shopping mall at Powell and buy a wool sweater in gray."

"Why?"

"I think you'd look good in gray. And I might have a job for you and I think that's a good color for a job interview."

"A job? What kind of job?"

"As a navigational consultant. I'll know more later. Take my phone," I said.

I gave Charlie my burner phone and reminded him how to answer calls and end them. Then I said good-bye and headed into 101 Market.

Mr. Slayter and Ritz were seated in his office. The paperwork had been drawn up and awaited my signature.

"I don't know how you managed it," I said.

"Your brother was easy," Slayter said. "Your sister, however—she might be the most brutal negotiator I've encountered. Let me know when she graduates college."

"I suppose I should have warned you about her," I said.

"That's all right," Edward said. "It keeps me sharp."

"I don't know how to thank you."

"A steep discount on all investigative services, until my days are over, will do."

"A deal is a deal."

I kept the pen poised upon the signature line for a long moment. This was the point of no return.

"What are you waiting for?" Slayter asked.

"I hope they'll forgive me," I said.

"From what you've told me, they're the forgiving sort, considering your previous exploits. I think they'll come to understand. I'm happy to speak to them anytime and put their minds at ease."

350

"Thank you, Mr. Slayter," I said. Then I signed the paperwork and slid it into the envelope.

Before I departed, I left behind the digital recorder with the audio file from my last meeting with the soon-to-be-ex–Mrs. Slayter.

"This might come in handy," I said.

"If there's anything else I can do to help you, say the word," Edward replied.

"I think I know someone who might be able to help you," I said.

"Excuse me?"

I wrote down the cell number on the back of my card along with Charlie Black's name.

"You've played chess with Charlie. He knows his way around the city. His days are free. He'd work for cheap and in his company you'd never get lost. And I know for a fact that he's trustworthy. He might be the most guileless person I've ever met."

"Are you suggesting I hire a babysitter?" Mr. Slayter said without too much offense.

"I told Charlie the job was called *navigational consultant*. I'd go with that if I were you."

"I see," Edward said.

"You'd have freedom with less risk. Think about it," I said.

"I will," Mr. Slayter replied, pocketing the card. "Now, what's your next step?"

"I think I'll go back to work," I replied.

A half hour later, I unlocked the door to 1799 Clay Street,[1] entered the office, and sat down behind my desk, which had already been partially cleared. Demetrius gave me a look of warning, and my mother and father simply stared in dismay.

---

[1] Pleased to discover that the locks had not been changed.

"Have you come to clean out your work space?" my dad asked.

"No," I replied. "And I want all of my pens back and my stapler. I bought that with my own money."

"Sweetie," Mom said, "what are you doing here?"

"I'm working," I replied, trying to find something on my desk that I could use as a prop.

Dad cleared his throat. "Did you go on a bender and forget that you were fired?"

"Funny. No," I said. "Any new cases I should know about?"

"Isabel, you don't work here anymore. I don't know how else I can phrase it to make you understand," Dad said.

"I thought maybe after a few days of cooling off, you might have changed your mind," I said.

"We haven't," Mom replied.

"Maybe you want to rethink this decision one more time and consult with Demetrius while you're at it, since he'll have to pick up the slack with me gone."

Dad stood over my desk and maintained the most severe expression he's capable of. His face doesn't morph into stern all that easily. It's a face meant for levity, not gravity, but he was doing a good job.

"I love you, Isabel. But you were fired, which means you don't work here anymore. You are welcome to come for dinner anytime. But your employment with Spellman Investigations has been terminated."

I played it the way I did because I thought it would be nice if I could change their minds without forcing their hand. But clearly my backup plan was the only option. I took the envelope out of my bag and passed it to my father.

"You can't fire me," I said. "Only the primary shareholder has the authority to hire and fire, and now that person is me."

Demetrius suddenly needed a cup of coffee and left the office. My father didn't even look in the envelope. He chuckled a bit and shook his head.

"Do you really think doctored paperwork will change the situation?"

"Dad, when you reorganized the business a few years ago, the split became forty percent you and Mom, thirty percent me, and fifteen percent each to David and Rae. I now own David and Rae's shares, which means I own sixty percent of the business. Only I can fire me. I can also fire you. But I won't do that. And, for the record, I have no immediate plans to abuse my power."

Dad finally disrobed the paperwork and sat down behind his desk to review the documents. He remained silent for close to an hour. My mother used her head-tic nod to motion for me to meet her in the other room. I found her in the kitchen pouring herself a stiff drink.

"What have you done?" she said.

"Can I have one too?" I said. She was drinking vodka, but I would have had peppermint schnapps at that point.

Mom slid the bottle in my direction and said, "Help yourself."

Demetrius eyed us warily. "I think I should go do that thing that I was going to do."

"You don't have a thing," I said.

"I have a thing," D said insistently.

"Please stay," I said. I figured my father could only get so angry in front of witnesses.

"I don't think so," D replied. "I did real time and you people *still* scare me."

He was out the door before any further protest was made.

My mother and I stood at the counter, drinking vodka and avoiding eye contact. Her cell phone rang, which was a welcome interruption to the tense silence.

"Hello, Walter," she said. "I seriously doubt that the upstairs apartment is leaking . . . has it happened before? Yes, there is a first time for everything. This isn't the best time, Walter . . . I see. I see. Okay. I'll be right over." Mom grabbed her keys and purse and headed for the front door.

"You can't leave me alone here with him," I said.

"Sweetie, you want to plan a corporate takeover, you deal with the fallout."

And she was out the door.

FALLOUT

I sat in the kitchen drinking vodka and grapefruit juice and eating Crack Mix for a full hour until my father surfaced from the office. I have no idea what was keeping Mom, but she managed to stay missing just like D. Dad sat down across from me and sighed deeply. He then grabbed a handful of D's delicacy.

"People seem to be making sport out of duping me," Dad said. "Any other food deceptions I should know about?"

"Most baked goods have been modified, and a few side dishes at meals."

"You sure pulled the wool over my eyes."

"I'm not taking the fall for everything. This was not my idea." I slid the rest of the bowl in my father's direction. "Eat up," I said. "I don't know when you'll get another opportunity."

My father snacked for a full five minutes before speaking. It was hard to tell if Dad was trying to get in as much Crack Mix time as possible or if he was genuinely contemplating how to speak to the daughter who had betrayed him. "I just got off the phone with my lawyers and your new benefactor, Mr. Slayter."

"He's just an investor."

"And it looks like all your paperwork is in order," he said. "You sure got me."

"That wasn't the point."

"There had to be another way," Dad said.

"Maybe. But I've been working for this business twenty years. When you and Mom retire, which is no longer in the distant future, I get to run it the way I want to. I'm thirty-four years old. I'm a grown-up now. Or I'm as grown-up as I'm likely to become. I can run Spellman Investigations on my own, but if this is going to be *my* business, I'm going to run it my way."

"It's the family business, Isabel."

"Except that one day, I'll be the only member of this family working here."

Of course, that was only the beginning of the conversation. Over the next few days a good chunk of the Spellman dirty laundry was aired. My mother went to visit Rae, still shocked by her decision to relinquish company power to me. The price was good, but Rae already had a decent nest egg. It was then that my mother truly understood that Rae had lost all interest in investigative work. The six-year-old girl who begged for days on end to join the family on a surveillance job was no more. It could easily be argued that she burned out early.

Then my mother visited David, looking for some explanation for why he made the choice he did. David reminded her that the only Spellman capable of running the business in the future was me. He didn't want to see Spellman Investigations retire when his parents did.

It was that simple.

Then my mother asked him about the rift between him and Rae, and David finally told her the truth. My mother's response was atypical as usual. With all the scientific experimenting going on, she couldn't help but lament the fact that out of her three children she couldn't get a single doctor.

And so, for the time being, all current secrets had been unearthed and we were free to begin interring a few more. The holidays passed without any noteworthy event, other than Grammy Spellman appearing at Christmas dinner with a gentleman friend she met at a polka class. When the holiday break was over, my mother and father decided that they needed a disappearance.[1] They figured a company restructuring was worthy of an extended weekend away at Big Sur.

Upon their return, they appeared both rested and accepting of all that had transpired. But, if I've learned anything in the course of my life, appearances can be and usually are deceiving. Mom and Dad both demanded raises and more vacation time and put in requests for new cell phones. As they settled into the simple fact that I was now their boss, our work relationship took a sharp U-turn. Instead of acting like bosses, they behaved like employees, and not very good ones at that. They began slacking off on the job and showing up later and later, despite the fact that they had no commute. This often forced me to come into their bedroom in the morning, pull the blinds, and bribe them with coffee. I even had to reprimand my mother a few times for extended phone calls with friends back east and tell my dad that a FREE SCHMIDT T-shirt was not appropriate attire for a client meeting. I suspect all this was for show, but the end result was the same. I was saddled with unprofessional employees who had limited respect for their superior. Which, I suppose, was a burden my parents had endured for years.

After the most recent Weekly Summit, my dad winked at me and said, "Be careful what you wish for."

---

[1] This means "vacation" in Spellman-speak.

TWENTY-ONE

The three months after the coup seemed to rush by like the landscape on a road trip. Occasionally I'd have a moment to sit back and reflect, and only then did I grasp how quickly this world was passing me by. Everywhere I looked, someone was hitting a milestone. David had a child; Demetrius was engaged; what was left of my father's hair had gone completely gray; my mother had to take prescription calcium supplements. I suppose those last few things aren't milestones. But Rae turning twenty-one most definitely was. I remembered when she was fourteen and would plant herself on a bar stool in the Philosopher's Club and demand ginger ale, only to be expelled . . . eventually. My family decided to throw her a surprise party at the Philosopher's Club. It seemed only fitting that we should celebrate her coming-of-drinking-age at what had been her unofficial watering hole for years.

The crowd was the typical Spellman mismatch of associates—David and Maggie (sans Sydney), Mom, Dad, Grammy Spellman, and an assortment of unknown coeds that Rae had apparently befriended. Vivien Blake, Robbie Gruber (I don't know who invited him), and a couple of guys from my dad's time on the SFPD even made a showing. Demetrius and Mabel arrived bearing gifts of edible items. (A few months before their engagement, D gave up his secret life with Mabel and invited her to dinner to meet his second family. Everyone was on excellent behavior, but that's probably because D made us do a run-through the night before, with written critiques and all.)

Of course Bernie was also at the bar; he owns the place and I'm learning to accept that. Gerty has yet to discover the man in the affidavits[1] and I'm hoping that maybe that man is gone for good. Although I suspect he's just in hibernation. Of course, Henry was present for the event. For years he had served our family, providing Rae extractions from this very establishment. Like all relationships, my sister's and Henry's morphed over time. But I remember the days when they were inseparable (mostly because Rae wouldn't leave Henry alone).

The surprise party ruse was that I wanted to buy my sister her first legal alcoholic beverage. I texted her after all the revelers had arrived. Some hid in the office, others behind the bar, and a few of the smaller coeds under the pool table.

ETA?

2 min.

"The Weasel is two minutes out," I said as silence washed over the joint. Even the jukebox was mercifully mute.

The reveal went the way most surprise parties do. People jumped out of their hiding places and shouted, *"Surprise!"* Rae tried really hard to appear alarmed and delighted, but I could spot that knowing look in her eye. Someone had inadvertently dropped a piece of intelligence and Rae had known all along. She faked it well, but I can read her like a book, although I should probably just read more books. As she scanned the room, searching through familiar faces, I knew that there was only one face she was looking for. But he was nowhere to be seen.

Gifts soon followed. Dad handed her the keys to the car he repossessed.

---

[1] If I haven't mentioned it before, see appendix.

She had the common sense to be gracious about it. But I could tell her thoughts were elsewhere. In between accepting wrapped offerings and greeting her fellow revelers, she clocked the front door repeatedly.

"Come on, where's your party spirit?" I asked. "You usually love birthdays, especially your own. Maybe only your own."

"It's hard to celebrate being the legal age to do anything but rent a car and be president when I'm wearing an orange jumpsuit twenty hours a week and cleaning garbage off the side of the highway."

"Try to forget about it for just one night," I said. Then I gave her my birthday gift. It was wrapped in a business envelope.

"What is this?" she asked.

"I have enjoyed visiting you at the work site and taking photographs as you fulfill your probation. And I'm not kidding, you look amazing in orange. But in honor of this momentous occasion, I decided to erase the images from my computer. I have a letter from Robbie Gruber confirming this fact. It's not legally binding, but you can take my word for it. However, I did put them on a storage device should you ever need them for any reason. I promise, these pictures will not come back to haunt you."

Rae took the envelope and stuffed it in her pocket.

"From you, that's a pretty decent gift."

"Happy birthday," I said. Then I spotted Fred at the entrance. "I think your real gift just arrived."

Rae stepped away from the bar and walked toward Fred, meeting him halfway, which seemed fitting considering that was all he had ever asked for.

I scanned the room and found Henry sitting alone at a table in the corner, nursing a drink.

"What's a nice guy like you doing in a place like this?"

"I have no idea," Henry replied. "What's your excuse?"

"I'm apparently not so nice."

"I beg to differ."

I looked over at the bar and caught a nauseating glimpse of Bernie and Gerty kissing. "If those two can make it work, you have to wonder," I said.

"Indeed," Henry replied.

And then silence fell over us.

But it was hard to notice with the hum of conversation in the room. Eventually someone would have to say something; it was Henry who spoke first.

"How have you been?" he asked.

"I've been better," I replied.

"It won't last," he said.

And that was true, because nothing lasts. And as many times as that idea causes pain, it can also erase it. I wanted that night to end and it did. But there would be other nights in the future that I would want to go on forever. And those nights wouldn't last either.

After Rae tore apart the rest of her presents with a little more enthusiasm, she sat down at the bar and reviewed her boozy options.

"What'll it be?" Bernie asked.

"I'll have the usual," Rae replied.

"Refresh my memory," said Bernie.

"Ginger ale."

It was comforting to know that in a world where you can't count on a single thing to be true from one moment to the next, there can be one small, insignificant thing that stays the same.

APPENDIX

Dossiers

Albert Spellman

Age: 67

Occupation: Private investigator

Physical characteristics: Six foot three; large (used to be larger, but doctor put him on a diet); oafish; mismatched features; thinning brown/gray hair; gives off the general air of a slob, but the kind that showers regularly.

History: Onetime SFPD forced into early retirement by a back injury. Went to work for another retired-cop-turned-private-investigator, Jimmy O'Malley. Met his future wife, Olivia Montgomery, while on the job. Bought the PI business from O'Malley and has kept it in the family for the last thirty-five years.

Bad habits: Has lengthy conversations with the television; snacking; thinks he's the boss of me.

Olivia Spellman

Age: 59

Occupation: Private investigator

Physical characteristics: Extremely petite; appears young for her age; quite attractive; shoulder-length auburn hair (from a bottle); well groomed.

History: Met her husband while performing an amateur surveillance on her future brother-in-law (who ended up not being her future brother-in-law). Started Spellman Investigations with her husband. Excels at pretext calls and other friendly forms of deceit.

Bad habits: Willing to break laws to meddle in children's lives; likes to record other peoples' conversations.

Old David Spellman (for New David, see this document)

Age: 36

Occupation: Lawyer

Physical characteristics: Tall, dark, and handsome.

History: Honor student, class valedictorian, Berkeley undergrad, Stanford law. You know the sort.

Bad habits: Makes his bed every morning, excessively fashionable, wears pricey cologne, drinks moderately, reads a lot, keeps up on current events, exercises.

Rae Spellman

Age: 20½

Occupation: Junior in college/part-time Spellman Investigations employee

Physical characteristics: Petite like her mother; appears a few years younger than her age; long, unkempt sandy blond hair; freckles; tends to wear sneakers so she can always make a run for it.

History: Blackmail, coercion, junk food obsession, bribery.

Bad habits: Too many to list.

Henry Stone
  Age: 47
  Occupation: San Francisco Police Inspector
  Physical characteristics: Average height, thin, short brown hair, serious brown eyes, extremely clean-cut.
  History: Was the detective on the Rae Spellman missing persons case over six years ago. Before that, I guess he went to the police academy, passed some test, married some annoying woman, and did a lot of tidying up. Was Ex-boyfriend #13 for a while, but now he's just Henry Stone.
  Bad habits: Doesn't eat candy; keeps a clean home; likes to iron.

Demetrius Merriweather
  Age: 43
  Occupation: Employee at Spellman Investigations
  Physical characteristics: Tall, athletic, a few prison scars.
  History: Wrongly incarcerated for murder; spent fifteen years in prison for a crime he did not commit. Was released, moved into the Spellman household, and currently works for Spellman Investigations.
  Bad habits: Must have back to wall at all times; jumpy; good at keeping secrets.
  To learn more about wrongful convictions, please visit *www.innocenceproject.org*. And if you're interested in a FREE SCHMIDT! T-shirt (mentioned in Document #4), they're still available at www.freeschmidt.com.

Maggie Mason
  Age: 36
  Occupation: Defense attorney
  Physical characteristics: Tall; slender; long, unkempt brown hair.

History: Dated Henry Stone; they broke up. Rae introduced her to David, and they began dating. Then they married.

Bad habits: Keeping baked goods in pockets; camping.

Bernie Peterson

Age: Old

Occupation: Drinking, gambling, smoking cigars, being there. And bar owner now, I guess.

Physical characteristics: A giant mass of human (sorry, I try not to look too closely).

History: Was a cop in San Francisco, retired, married an ex-showgirl, moved to Las Vegas, moved back to San Francisco when she cheated on him, reconciled with her, moved back to Las Vegas. See this document for the latest in the Peterson saga.

Bad habits: Imagine every bad habit you've ever recognized. Bernie probably has it.

And, for the hell of it, I'll do me.

Isabel Spellman

Age: 34

Occupation: Private investigator

Physical characteristics: Tall, not skinny, not fat, long brown hair, nose, lips, eyes, ears. All the usual features. Fingers, legs, that sort of thing. A few more wrinkles than last time I described myself.

History: Recovering delinquent, been working for Spellman Investigations since the age of twelve.

Bad Habits: None.

Other Organizations That Use the CIA Acronym

The Cleveland Institute of Art

The Certified Internal Auditor® program, the only globally accepted
    certification for internal auditors
The Chemical Industries Association
Cosmic Internet Academy
Cru' in Action!, a hip-hop group, which consisted of K-Dee, Sir Jinx,
    and Ice Cube
[There are more, way more]

AFFIDAVITS AGAINST BERNIE

GENERAL AFFIDAVIT

STATE OF: **Nevada**

COUNTY OF: **Clark**

PERSONALLY came and appeared before me, the under-signed Notary, the within-named **Shelly Sheen,** who is a resident of **Clark** County, State of **Nevada,** and makes this his/her statement and General Affidavit upon oath and affirmation of belief and personal knowledge that the fol-lowing matters, facts, and things set forth are true and correct to the best of his/her knowledge:

I, Shelly Sheen, being of sound mind and body,[1] dated Ber-nie Peterson on and off (mostly off) from the summer of 1998 through the winter of 2002. During that time, I never saw him wash one dish or pick up a single item of clothing off of the floor. The neighbors complained of his snoring and I was almost evicted. He never brought me flowers. There were always potato chip crumbs under the seat cushions and he would pour day-old beer into my plants. During summer he would store his dirty socks in the refrigerator, right next to the milk. I also think he was seeing at least three women on the side.

And he would never put the toilet seat down.

DATED this the 25 day of Oct , 20 11

Shelly Sheen

Signature of Affiant

SWORN to and subscribed before me, this 25 day of Oct., 20 11

Claudia Kim

NOTARY PUBLIC

---

[1] Shelly took the liberty of inserting this legalese herself.

GENERAL AFFIDAVIT

STATE OF: **California**

COUNTY OF: **Alameda**

PERSONALLY came and appeared before me, the undersigned Notary, the within-named **Natasha Slovenka**, who is a resident of **Alameda** County, State of **California,** and makes this his/her statement and General Affidavit upon oath and affirmation of belief and personal knowledge that the following matters, facts, and things set forth are true and correct to the best of his/her knowledge:

Bernie always leave toilet seat up. I ask him again and again to stop and he keep leave toilet seat up.

Bernie very friendly with my friends. I think he too friendly. I stop dating Bernie when he start dating my friend Ivanka. He leave toilet seat up for Ivanka. She break up with him too.

DATED this the _28_ day of _Oct_, 20 _11_

Natasha Slovenka
Signature of Affiant

SWORN to and subscribed before me, this _28_ day of _Oct._, 20 _11_

NOTARY PUBLIC

GENERAL AFFIDAVIT

STATE OF: **Nevada**

COUNTY OF: **Washoe**

PERSONALLY came and appeared before me, the under-
signed Notary, the within-named **Daisy Doolittle**, who is a
resident of **Washoe** County, State of **Nevada,** and makes
this his/her statement and General Affidavit upon oath
and affirmation of belief and personal knowledge that the
following matters, facts, and things set forth are true and
correct to the best of his/her knowledge:

I was married to that dog for three long years. Just because we met at a strip club didn't mean we had to spend
all our free time there. I think he took me to a movie
maybe five times total during our entire relationship. Not
once did he spring for popcorn. The man has some bad
habits. And never give him a cent of your hard-earned
cash because he'll gamble it away, stuff it in the G-string
of some other gal, or blow it on beer and potato chips. And
he could never, ever remember to put the toilet seat down.

DATED this the ___24___ day of October, 20_11_

Daisy Doolittle

Signature of Affiant

SWORN to and subscribed before me, this _24_ day of
Oct., 20_11_

Glen Lin

NOTARY PUBLIC

ACKNOWLEDGMENTS

A s you might imagine, sincerity isn't really my thing. Generally when I compliment or thank someone, I follow it up with an insult. Or I lead with the jab. However, sometimes it's good to break character and just say something nice and be done with it. Here I go.

I am ridiculously lucky to be a writer, and there are many people responsible for this state of affairs.

I must begin with my agent, Stephanie Kip Rostan. Without you, the line I'd speak most regularly would be "Do you want fries with that?" The rest of the Levine Greenberg Literary Agency team is positively fantastic, and I'm not just saying that because you give me cake when I visit: Jim Levine, Dan Greenberg, Monika Verma, Melissa Rowland,[1] Elizabeth Fisher, Miek Coccia, Julie Villar, Lindsay Edgecombe. Thank you; even I don't know all the things you do for me.

I am incredibly grateful for the outstanding people at Simon & Schuster. As always, I am indebted to Carolyn Reidy for her unwavering support for the Spellman series. And to Jonathan Karp: I'm really good at finding fault with people but I can't think of an unkind word to say about you. You've been amazing. Sammy Perlmutter and Amanda Ferber, your patient work

---

[1] I swear, every email from you is good news!

371

on my behalf has been saintly. I hope you've at least talked some trash behind my back because I'm sure I've been a pain in the ass at times. A huge thanks to Richard Rhorer, Michael Sellick, Jackie Seow, and Danielle Lynn. And thank you Kerri Kolen for all your hard work and for leaving the book in excellent hands.

Oh and a big whopping thanks to Jonathan Evans, my very cool production editor. You never make me feel stupid, unlike some people on this page.[2] Without you, these books would be a total mess and my characters would be aging in a really funky way.

I am ridiculously lucky to have met the brilliant illustrator Jaime Temairik. You're one of the funniest people I know and I'm proud to call you a friend. Thank you Jay Fienberg, my cousin, my website guru, and my Robbie Gruber consultant. Anastasia Fuller, thanks for all the thoughtful reads and the awesome website design. I must also mention Julie Ulmer and Steve Kim because I don't know what I'd do without them. And I'm thanking my cousin Dan Fienberg because he'll say something if I don't.

Dave Hayward, you're a great friend and editor. When I write a joke, I know it works if you get it. You could be a better chaperone, though. While I'm on the subject of Haywards, I'd like to thank Linda Hayward for being my Sacramento publicist.

And I'd also like to thank anyone else who might have read the book and offered careful and considered criticism. I'm not the kind of writer who can work alone. This book would have been far worse without you.

I'm sure I'm missing some people,[3] so thank you _____.[4]

Most importantly, I want to thank the booksellers who are still fighting the fight.

* * *

---

[2] See David Hayward.
[3] See previous documents.
[4] Please write your name in here.

Since I've got some extra space here, I want to at least touch on the changes in the book world. Call me naïve, but I don't see the end of days. I believe that eventually readers will smarten up and realize that a book isn't a bargain just because it's cheap. Agents, editors, and publishers exist so that the books you get in your hands are worth reading. I understand the desire for convenience, and if you saw some of the shortcuts I make in life, you'd know I've got nothing against e-books (I even read them myself). But I do ask readers to think of this: As bookstores are closing at alarming rates across the country, there's still something you can do about it. Even if you're a diehard e-reader, every once in a while walk, drive, or take a bus to a bookstore and buy a real book off of the shelf. Booksellers aren't just managing the register; they're people who love books and, ideally, know how to match the right book with the right person.

I don't have any kids, so I'm not as worried about my heirs as the rest of you, but still: I think the youth of tomorrow might be better off if they knew the physical sensation of cracking a spine and turning the page.

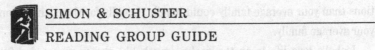

TRAIL OF THE
SPELLMANS

Introduction

In *Trail of the Spellmans*, the fifth installment of Lisa Lutz's bestselling series, the quirky Spellman PIs again find themselves with more questions than your average family could handle. Luckily for them, they aren't your average family.

Isabel's love life is on the rocks—much like the unexpected drinks she's sharing with her boyfriend's mother, Gerty. Rather than face the fact that she and Henry may want different things in life, she resorts to The Avoidance Method by burying herself in work.

And there's plenty of work to be buried in: objects are going amiss at math professor Walter Perkin's immaculate apartment; suspicious parents hire the firm to follow their daughter, though her only suspicious activities seem inexplicably tangled with Rae's; and two clients' surveillance requests present the Spellmans with a conflict of interest, causing Isabel's father to enact a "Chinese wall of privacy." But there isn't a wall big enough to keep Isabel out when she puts her mind to tearing it down, and she soon learns that she was right about one of her client's dishonest intentions.

Topics & Questions for Discussion

1. Of Albert and Olivia Spellman's three children, Isabel is the only one who wants to follow in her parents' footsteps and be a true part of the family business. Why do you think this is? What sets her apart from her brother and sister?

2. In the early chapters of the novel, Isabel spends time discussing her opinion of "Old David" versus her opinion of "New David." Ultimately, how do you think she feels about each of the two versions of her brother? If she had to choose between them, which do you think she would prefer to have around? Which would you prefer?

3. What did you think about Rae Spellman's manipulation of Sydney's vocabulary, using the "Banana Offensive"? Was it a retaliation against David for "training" her when she was a child, or was it just a genuine scientific inquiry?

4. Isabel is surprised to find how well she gets along with Gertrude "Gerty" Stone, her boyfriend, Henry's, mother. Why do you think the two are drawn to each other? What do they have in common?

5. According to Bernie, he and Gerty are "just two old ships who collided in the night." Isabel clearly takes issue with their relationship; did you? Did you support Isabel's decision not to tell Henry about Bernie and Gerty's courtship?

6. Of the unlikely friendships in the novel—Isabel and Gerty, Isabel and Charlie Black, Demetrius and Grammy Spellman—which were you most surprised by, and which do you think makes the most sense? Can you think of any other unlikely friendships that emerge during the course of the novel?

7. How did you react to Isabel's relationship with Henry? Did you suspect that their relationship was coming to an end? What characteristics do you think a man Isabel could be with permanently would need to have? What do you think she is looking for?

8. Do you think Albert's installment of the "Chinese wall" is helpful or hurtful to the family's work? Isabel makes clear how she feels about it; why do you think she so strongly opposes it?

9. Isabel is notoriously skeptical of and slow to trust people she doesn't know; however, she chooses to place her trust in Charlie Black. Why do you think this is? What does Isabel like about Charlie? Do you think the Slayter case would have ended differently without him?

10. How are each of the members of the Spellman family—including Demetrius—affected by the arrival of Grandma Ruth Spellman to their household? Similarly, how would you describe Grammy Spellman in just three words? How do you think Olivia would describe Grammy Spellman in three words?

11. "As much as one might like to believe that I've eased into adulthood without a fight, let there be no mistake. I'm still fighting." At what times in the novel do you think Isabel is fighting becoming an adult? At what times does she embrace the transition?

12. Did your opinion of Walter change from the beginning of the novel to the end? Were you surprised to find out who had been messing with his apartment?

13. By coming clean to Mr. Slayter and providing him with evidence of his wife's infidelity, Isabel gets personally involved in the case, thereby breaking one of her dad's most important rules of being a personal investigator. Do you think she did the right thing, or should she have remained neutral?

14. If you've read Lisa Lutz's previous four Spellman novels, discuss: Which one is your favorite? Why?

Enhance Your Book Club

1. Rae and Al enjoy creating code names for the members of the Spellman clan; for example, they dub Isabel "the Gopher" because she likes to dig through the dirt. Have the members of your reading group choose nicknames for one another, and don't forget to give explanations as to why you think the names are fitting.

2. From cranberry scones and cherry clafoutis to his famous "Crack Mix," Demetrius's homemade treats never go unappreciated by the members of the Spellman family. Choose one or more of your favorite dishes from the novel and make them for your reading group to eat during your discussion.

3. Even Isabel's father found her high-school self's snarky, "wholly inappropriate" thank you notes amusing. Is there anyone you'd like to "thank" in the Isabel way? Have the members of your discussion group write quirky thank you notes—but unlike Isabel, you might want to think twice about actually sending them!

4. Cast your ideal *Trail of the Spellmans* movie with your discussion group. Who would play Isabel? Rae? How about paranoid Walter, or conniving Margaret Slayter?

5. Lisa may be available to call in to your book club discussion. You can email your request for a call-in with the subject line, "Request to call my book group."

A Conversation with Lisa Lutz

Isabel tells her readers that they should "quit guessing and let the story unfold as it may," that even she doesn't "know how all the pieces will fall." Do you know how all the pieces will fall when you begin writing a novel? Or does the novel unfold while you write?

I have story threads and themes that I've noted ahead of time. I usually have a sense of where my characters are personally and ways in which they might transform throughout the novel. But I never know at the outset how the book will end, nor do I ever stick to my original plan.

Which Spellman do you relate to the most? Do you have a favorite? Why or why not?

The obvious answer and the most honest one is Isabel. However, I relate to all of them in different ways. I relate to Rae's indifference to social mores. I understand Olivia's desire to enforce her desires on her mini-universe. And I completely comprehend Albert's experience of having no control of those around him.

If you had a Spellman clan nickname, what do you think it would be and why?

The Aristocrats!

You've said in a previous interview that you did some surveillance work yourself. What was the most exciting thing to happen to you while you were on a job?

I followed a lunatic who had apparently shot a priest (this may have been a rumor) and believed he (the lunatic, not the priest) was the true inventor of "bifurcated jeans" (which are just plain old blue jeans, but he made a point of writing "bifurcated" in some documents we found—that's how I learned the word). During the surveillance, the subject dropped off in a cigar shop rather complicated drawings of an invention for a new kind of toilet that wouldn't require toilet paper. It would, however, require a seat belt (this is true; I saw the drawings). Anyway, when I was surveilling this unusual fellow, I tailed him into a bar and overheard the barmaid say, "Joey, are you talking about killing people again?"

Demetrious's "Crack Mix" sounds like, as Al says, "the best snack food in the history of snack food." Where did you get the idea for this heavenly snack? Is it based in reality? If so, can you divulge the recipe?

I imagine Crack Mix to be the Chex Mix of the gods. Do I know what secret ingredients would make it that? No. But I will admit that I really like Chex Mix. And if anyone does have the recipe for Chex Mix of the gods, call me.

SpongeBob SquarePants has made a few appearances throughout Trail of the Spellmans. *Is it a guilty pleasure of yours?*

Sometimes when I'm sick or depressed or both, I watch. And I don't feel a tiny bit guilty about it.

Which character do you think has changed the most since Document #1 in the series, The Spellman Files?

That question is tough. I think the youngest characters were likely to change the most, since that's the nature of growing up. But when I sit down and write each book, I want every character to change in the story. That's what happens. People transform in some ways and they remain exactly the same in others. Often the thing you'd like to change the most about yourself is where you will forever remain stuck.

How was the experience of writing the fifth book in this series different than the experience of writing the first?

Actually, Document #5 was rough. While I had no intention of ending the series after *The Spellmans Strike Again,* I did close many doors in that book and, with the fifth one, I was opening a lot of doors and not finding anything behind them and then opening another door and another until I found something. It was a while before I found my stride. I'm very pleased with it, but it took a long time to figure out where I was going.

Do you have any idea of what's in store for Isabel and the rest of the Spellman clan for the next book?

I have a few things up my sleeve. And I should probably transcribe them from my arm before my next shower.

Isabel has had her high points and her low points in each Spellman novel. If you could have a conversation with her face-to-face, what advice would you want to give her?

I've got no business giving advice to anyone. Even a fictional character.

From the (classified) files of the next Spellman caper,
Here is a sneak peek at

THE LAST WORD
by Lisa Lutz

Coming in July 2013, in hardcover and as an e-book,
from Simon & Schuster

Voice memo

12:38 A.M.

Can't sleep. Again. The final notice for the electricity bill came today. I shredded it, paid the bill out of pocket, and then shook down a delinquent client by reminding him that company policy is to tell a cheating spouse about an investigation when payment is past due three months. It's never been policy before, but I'm warming up to it.

A fed came to visit today. Bledsoe is his name. Agent Bledsoe. B-l-e-d-s-o-e. He knows about the money. If he has the evidence, I think we could lose the business. Thirty years down the drain because somebody wasn't paying attention. Embezzlement. Of all the stupid things that could take us down. It isn't even enough money to save us.

Some days I wish I weren't the only one doing the fixing. I feel like I'm playing a solo game of toy soldiers with just a few pieces out of my control. Some days I really believe there might be something left to salvage if we know when to call it quits.

Some days I think that this just might be the end.

Part 1

OPENING STATEMENTS SIX WEEKS EARLIER

"BOSS"

Three lazy knocks landed on the door.

"It's open!" I said as I'd been saying for the past three months. I leaned back in my new leather swivel chair. It was less comfortable than you'd expect, but I wasn't letting on.

My father entered the Spellman offices carrying a bowl of oatmeal, topped with a few raisins, walnuts, and honey. I don't have a problem with people eating at work, but I did take issue with his attire—boxer shorts, a wife-beater (the likes of which he hadn't owned until he started wearing his skivvies into the office), and a cardigan that had been feasted on by a hungry moth. I foolishly thought that lowering the thermostat would encourage my father to put on slacks. Live and learn.

The Spellman offices are located on the first floor of my parents' house at 1799 Clay Street in San Francisco, California, a three-story Victorian sitting on the outskirts of Nob Hill. A Realtor would tell you that the house has "good bones"—three floors, four bedrooms, three baths—but everything needs to be updated and the exterior demands a paint job so badly that some of the neighbors have taken to writing *paint me* on our dusty windows.

Even a few "anonymous" handwritten letters have arrived from a *concerned neighbor,* but since Dr. Alexander has sent other handwritten missives in the past, his anonymity was lost. Point is, my parents have a nice house in a nice neighborhood that looks like crap from the outside and is not so hot from the inside, and not enough money to do anything about it. I remember the blue trim on the window frames from when I was a child, but I'm not entirely certain that I'd know it was blue now since it's almost gone and the thirty-year-old lead-loaded green paint beneath it is what ultimately shines through. Those now-retired painters must have been really good.

The office itself is a fourteen-by-twenty-foot room with an ancient steel desk marking each of the four corners. The fifth desk is parked between the two desks with a window view. Perhaps "view" is an overstatement. We look out onto our neighbor's concrete wall and have a slight glimpse into Mr. Peabody's living room, where he sits most of the day, watching television. There's nothing to recommend the décor of the office. The white walls are covered with bulletin boards so tacked over with postcards, notes, memos, cartoons, they resemble the layering of a bird's feathers. The collage of paperwork hasn't been stripped in years. In fact, I wouldn't be surprised if an archeological dig produced data from as far back as 1986. It's not pretty, but you get used to it after a while. The only thing that begs for change is the beige shag carpet, which is so worn down you can slip on it in footwear without treads.

As for my father's extreme casual wear, it would have made sense that my parents might find the home/workspace divide difficult to navigate, but they'd been navigating it just fine for more than twenty years. These wardrobe shenanigans were purely for my benefit.

"What's on the agenda today?" Dad said through a mouthful of steel-cut oats. He shook his computer mouse, rousing his monitor from slumber, and commenced his workday with his new morning ritual: a two-hour game of Plants vs. Zombies.

"Mr. Slayter will be here in an hour, Dad."

"Should I have made extra oatmeal for him?" Dad asked as he planted a row of flowers and a peashooter. I would have used the spud bomb and taken the extra sunlight. But Dad seemed to be doing fine on his own.[1]

"I think Slayter would prefer pants over oatmeal."

"You can't eat pants," Dad said.

The pants conversation would have continued indefinitely if my mother hadn't dipped her head into the doorway and said, "Everybody decent?"

"No, Mom, everybody is not decent," I said.

Then Mom entered, indecently. While less skin was exposed, her sartorial choice was perhaps even more perplexing. Her hair, coiled in plastic curlers, was imprisoned in a net that she must have stolen from Grammy Spellman. She wore a housecoat pockmarked with daisies and pink fluffy slippers on her feet. I had not seen this outfit before, and were we at a Halloween party, I might have found it mildly amusing. My mother, at sixty, is one of those classic beauties, all neck and cheekbones, sharp lines that hide her wrinkles from a distance. She still gets whistles from construction workers from three stories up. With her long bottled auburn hair flowing behind her, a carnival guesser wouldn't come within a decade of her birth date. Although today, in curlers, she was looking more like her true age.

"Mom, those curlers must have taken you hours."

"You have no idea," she said, easing into her chair, spent from the chore. I would bet my entire share of the company that Mom hadn't used curlers since her senior prom.

We'd never had a dress code before all the trouble began[2] and it was foolish of me to think that a memo posted on bulletin boards scattered

---

1   I've probably clocked in a full workweek of Plants vs. Zombies hours, I'm ashamed to say. But Dad played as if he were an employee of PopCap Games.
2   I'll explain all that later.

throughout the house would have any impact. But I think it's important to note that the dress code was perhaps one of the least ambitious dress codes that ever existed in an office setting.

And to further illustrate my laissez-faire management protocol, I even instituted pajama Fridays (so long as a client meeting was not on the books). The next Friday Mom showed up in a muumuu and a turban, resembling Gloria Swanson in *Sunset Boulevard,* and Dad slipped on his swim trunks and a wool scarf (I was still keeping the thermostat low, stupidly certain of an auspicious result).

For more than three months I had been president and primary owner of Spellman Investigations, and I can say with complete certainty that I had more power in this office as an underling. My title, it seemed, was purely decorative. I was captain of an unfashionable and sinking ship.

Edward Slayter, the man responsible for my position at my family's firm—and for close to 20 percent of Spellman Investigations' income—was coming in for a ten o'clock meeting. I had to get my parents either out of the office or into suitable clothing in less than twenty minutes.

Just then Demetrius entered in a tweed coat and a bow tie. While I appreciated the effort he put into his attire, I had to wonder whether this was his own form of self-expression or an act of mild derision.

"Demetrius, you look great. I guess you saw the memo."

"It was hard to miss," D said.

"That was the point," I said, glaring at my parents. Twenty-five posters on the interior and exterior of the house. If they opened the refrigerator, used the restroom, opened their desk drawers, or took a nap,[3] they couldn't have missed it. "Why are you rocking the bow tie, D? This is new."

"I'm going to San Quentin this afternoon to interview an inmate for Maggie on a potential wrongful-conviction case."

Maggie is my sister-in-law, married to my brother David. She is a de-

---

3 Put one in large print on the ceiling of my parents' bedroom.

fense attorney who devotes 25 percent of her practice to pro bono wrong-ful-incarceration cases. Demetrius, having once benefited from Maggie's pro bono work, regularly assists her with those cases. Because we believe in the work that Maggie is doing, we help out when time allows, and even when time doesn't allow. I'd like to think that if I were in prison for a crime I didn't commit, someone would be trying to get me the hell out of there.

"That's great. Still doesn't explain the bow tie."

"I'm not wearing a slipknot in a maximum-security prison."

"Excellent point. Speaking of nooses," I said, turning to my parents. The clock was ticking. "What will it take to get you to change into real clothes and lose the hair accessories?"

"These curlers took *three* hours," Mom said.

I really couldn't have my first Slayter/unit meeting under these circumstances.

"I have an idea," I said. "Why don't you go back to bed?"

"I'm hungry," Dad said.

I turned to D, the de facto chef, for assistance.

"I'll make some pancakes and bring them up," he said.

Mom and Dad filed out of the office.

"See you tomorrow," Mom said.

I wish I could say that this was an unusual workday, but that was not the case. I wish I could say this sort of negotiation was uncommon; also not true. The worst part: I had to consider this a win.

Not-So-Hostile Takeover

It happens all the time. One company is struggling and another company buys that company, and it thrives. Or one company puts itself up for sale and accepts the best offer. Or in a smaller, family-run company, it can go like this: One member of the family-owned company buys (through a wealthy proxy) the shares of her two siblings and becomes the primary shareholder of the company, in essence the owner, blindsiding the pre-vious owners, who happen to be her parents. This isn't the first time in the history of family-owned businesses that there has been conflict among the filial ranks. Although one could argue that our conflict was strangely unique.

But I'm already getting ahead of myself, so please indulge me briefly for a quick refresher on all things Spellman.[4]

I'll start with a name. Mine. Isabel Spellman. I'm thirty-five, single, and I live in my brother's basement apartment. If I were a man, you'd as-sume there was something wrong with me, like a porn or video game ad-diction or some kind of maladaptive social disorder. But I'm a woman, and so automatically the response is pity. Let's remember something here: I am the president, CEO, and probably CFO[5] of Spellman Investigations Inc., a relatively successful private investigative firm in the great metropolis of San Francisco. I am the middle child of Albert and Olivia Spellman, the ill-dressed people you met three and four pages ago. There are other things that you'll need to know eventually, like I have an older brother, David (an occasional lawyer and full-time father to his daughter, Sydney); a sister-in-law, Maggie, the defense attorney I just mentioned; and a much younger sister, Rae, twenty-two, a recent graduate from UC Berkeley, which makes me the only Spellman spawn without a college degree. But, hey, who owns this sinking ship? As for Rae, it would be difficult to reduce her essence to a few sentences, so I'll save her for later and leave the essence-reducing to you. I also have a grandmother who lives within walking distance. You'll meet her soon enough. There's no point in rushing that introduction.

There are two other Spellman Investigations employees worth men-tioning. Foremost, Demetrius Merriweather, the bow-tied fellow you just

---

4 For brief dossiers on family members and a few other relevant parties, see appen-dix.
5 Why not?

met. D, as we call him, is a complex, multifaceted human being, but if you had to describe him in an elevator ride, this is what you'd say: 1) He spent fifteen years in prison for a crime he didn't commit. 2) He's a freaking unbelievably great chef and shares his gift with anyone in the vicinity. 3) He doesn't take sides. 4) He really doesn't like snitching, but he understands the value of the subtle dissemination of information under a specific set of circumstances. He's also been employee of the month for the past twelve months.

If you were to find yourself alone in a parking garage with him, you wouldn't automatically assume ex-con. He doesn't possess any identifying prison tattoos; he doesn't have the hardened look of a man who spent fifteen years behind bars, although he's not a small man—six-two, softer in the middle than when he first got out, because he has other pastimes besides going to the prison gym, and his favorite hobby is cooking, and there are more ingredients on the outside than the inside. He's black. Did I mention that? He has a few freckles, like Morgan Freeman, but the resemblance ends there. Unfortunately. He shaves his head, not because he's going bald, but because the look works on him. He can look intimidating sometimes, but when he smiles he has these ridiculous dimples. They're adorable. But you never want to call an ex-con "adorable" no matter how harmless he is. And the truth is, I doubt D is all that harmless. He was in prison for fifteen years. You're going to tell me he never got in a fight? I've asked (repeatedly); he just doesn't answer.

And, finally, our part-time employee, Vivien Blake. A college coed who used to be the subject of an investigation, but we've never been good with boundaries, so now she works for us. Something about Vivien reminds me of the old me: a recklessness, a history of inappropriate behavior, a penchant for vandalism. Some years back Vivien managed to steal an entire fleet of golf carts from Sharp Park Golf Course in Pacifica and relocate them to a cow pasture ten miles away. I've asked her at least twenty times how she managed to do it, and she refuses to reveal her professional secrets. The seventeen-year-old delinquent who still resides somewhere deep in my core has profound respect for that.

Vivien has only just returned from one month abroad in Ireland. She was supposedly taking a four-week intensive summer course on James Joyce's *Ulysses* at Trinity College, but I noticed that when my sister pressed her on the details Vivien only mentioned castles and pubs and a walking tour of Joycean Dublin, which Rae said was totally open to the public.

Viv has taken some time settling back into San Francisco life. The last time I saw her she was in the midst of a heated phone call that might have suggested she was working in the drug trade (and completely unconcerned with wiretaps): "Where is my stuff? The delivery was supposed to happen five days ago. I've called you every day since then and you say it will be the next day and every day I wait around like some patsy and it never shows. I should charge you for my time. My rate is twenty-five dollars an hour. I've now waited over twenty hours. So, let's see, you owe me at least a thousand dollars.[6] You will not get away with this. I know people. I know terrifying people, people who have done time,[7] the kind of people who make weapons out of soap. Why do they make weapons out of soap? Isn't it obvious? What are you, an idiot? Because if you murder someone with a sharpened blade of soap, then the rain and the blood will . . . change the form of the weapon and you lose fingerprints and the blade won't match. That's irrelevant. I really hope it doesn't come to that. Listen to me carefully. Every hour of my life that you destroy, I'm going to take an hour from your life. Hello? Hello?"

Vivien put her phone in her pocket.

---

6 Her math gets iffy when she's angry.

7 Demetrius, at that point, walked over to the chalkboard and wrote, *I will not get involved.*

D said, "Honey, not vinegar."

"I want to pour a vat of boiling vinegar on that bastard's head," Viv said.

"Assault with a deadly weapon. Two to four years. Or attempted murder, five to nine," D said as he strolled over to the pantry. He pulled out a bar of Ivory soap and then collected a paring knife from the kitchen and placed them in front of Vivien. "You might want to get a jump start on these soap weapons you've heard about. Or you can take a walk and chill out."

Vivien took the soap and paring knife and stepped outside.

"Is she okay?" I asked after Viv left.

"She'll be fine. Customer service just isn't what it used to be."

I would like to say I delved deeper into her hostile phone conversation, but I had more pressing matters to contend with. If any of the information I've provided thus far is confusing or you need a refresher, I suggest consulting previous documents.[8]

Now is probably as good a time as any to explain how I became boss and why my two most seasoned employees were wearing undergarments to work.

I began working for the family business when I was twelve. I won't pretend that I was a model employee, and I'll come straight out and say that I was an even worse teenager. Some might have called me a delinquent. A more generous sort would suggest I was finding myself. I would probably tell the generous sort where to stick their new-age bullshit and own the delinquent part. So, I admit I was trouble, but I grew out of that phase at least five, six years ago and now I'm a relatively upstanding citizen. As you know, your average citizen probably commits between one and five misdemeanors a day.[9]

---

8 All available in paperback!

9 "Crime and No Punishment: Misdemeanor Rates Skyrocket as Criminals Realize Prison Time Is Shorter for Nonfelonies" (2011). See appendix.

About nine months ago our firm took on a series of cases that turned out to be interconnected. A man hired us to follow his sister. His sister hired us to follow her husband. Two of the three people involved were not who they said they were. When I noticed their stories didn't match, I began investigating the client. Generally, a private investigator investigates the subject, not the client, but I believe that if the client is hiring us under false pretenses, it is our job to set things right. My father, however, believes we should serve the client, lest we develop a reputation for being the private investigators with a de-emphasis on the *private*. During our company standoff, my father enacted a Chinese wall and only allowed the assigned investigator to work on his or her respective case. I tried to climb the wall a few times, only to be met by an escalating series of warnings from my father, which culminated in a direct threat: If I continued to defy company policy, I would be fired. I disregarded his warning, took a sledgehammer to the Chinese wall, and uncovered our clients' true and malevolent motives. While I considered my investigation a success, my father considered it a breach of the basic tenets of our livelihood. My dad's threat to fire me was, in fact, not a bluff.

I politely and then impolitely asked for my job back. I even pretended that bygones were bygones and simply showed up for work day after day. If we were a major conglomerate, a security team would have promptly surfaced and escorted me out of the building with my one sad box of belongings. Instead, each day of each week, I was shown the door and then invited back for family dinner on Sunday.

After a great deal of soul-searching and scheming, I did the only thing I could do. I warned the person whom our clients were surveilling, one Edward Slayter, of the potential danger posed by his scheming wife (now ex). Mr. Slayter, a wealthy businessman, became my benefactor in a way. When he heard that I was fired because of my work on his behalf, he offered to intervene, in this case negotiating a buyout with my siblings, who, for the record, took my side.[10] At the time, the parental unit had a 40 percent share of the company, Rae had 15 percent, David had 15 percent, and I had 30 percent. After Slayter bought out my siblings' shares, I owned 60 percent, which, according to the company bylaws, gave me the authority to hire and fire employees and veto power over all major company decisions. My first order of business was giving me my old job back.

But power comes at a cost. The coup made me enemy number one to my father and rendered me permanently beholden to Edward Slayter. So, even though I'm technically the boss of Spellman Investigations, Edward Slayter is kind of the boss of me. Our deal is quite simple. I do jobs for him at a discounted rate and when he asks me to do something, I generally do it.

That's just so you understand why I'll be jogging in seven pages.

---

10   Or they really needed money. But I prefer my first theory.

Printed in the USA
CPSIA information can be obtained
at www.ICGtesting.com
JSHW030525240923
48810JS00002B/13